AN END TO SUMMER

AN END
TO SUMMER

Cynthia S Roberts

This first world edition published in Great Britain 1994 by
SEVERN HOUSE PUBLISHERS LTD of
9–15 High Street, Sutton, Surrey SM1 1DF.
First published in the USA 1995 by
SEVERN HOUSE PUBLISHERS INC., of
425 Park Avenue, New York, NY 10022.

British Library Cataloguing in Publication Data
Roberts, Cynthia S.
  End to Summer. – (Heritage Coast Series)
  I. Title II. Series
  823.914 [F]

  ISBN 0-7278-4667-1

Typeset by Hewer Text Composition Services, Edinburgh.
Printed and bound in Great Britain by
Hartnolls Ltd, Bodmin, Cornwall.

Further Titles by Cynthia S Roberts from Severn House

THE SAVAGE SHORE
THE STORMS OF FATE
THE HUNTER AND THE HUNTED

Chapter One

Rebecca Stradling, glancing from the casement of Thatched Cottage, knew a momentary sadness, fierce and swift as the movement of the child within her. An end, now, to summer. The swallows leaving. Shadows stretching long upon the grass as the days grew short. She watched the early morning mist seep from the earth, as coldly sulphurous as the fogs from the sea. In the pastures beyond, sheep, cattle, even the landscape itself, would be swathed in greyness; veiled, remote, a strange, uncharted land – as strange and uncharted as her own life and what lay ahead.

Her hands moved instinctively to the swollen flesh that sheltered her child, as if she would protect it from birth and death. The harsher pains of loving. Joshua, always sensitive to her mood, drew her to him, smiling, coaxing, lovingly teasing her from her introspection, complaining with absurd extravagance because he could no longer hold her close. Almost against her will she laughed with him, then stayed for a long moment with her cheek pressed hard against the roughness of his jacket, taking pleasure from the familiar male smell of his flesh, his touch and nearness. When she drew away it was reluctantly, and to remind with a rueful smile: 'You had best be away, Joshua. Robert Knight will not be best pleased if his parish constable fails to arrive at the courthouse.'

'Although the prisoner at Pyle gaolhouse most certainly would be!' he conceded good-humouredly, brushing aside the cluster of dark curls at her nape to settle a kiss. Then, straightening, he exclaimed in exasperation, 'Oh, damnation to the justice, the law, and all else, Rebecca! I will not pretend longer! My place is here with you. I shall have thought for no other. I shall scarce be able to think straight.' He reached absently for his helmet, complaining,

1

'The justice will judge me an imbecile, a candidate for Bedlam.'

'Then you must disabuse him, my dear,' Rebecca said equably, 'although I do not think he will relish your appearing in my best blue velvet bonnet, although, I'll own, it is vastly becoming.'

Joshua, who had been fingering it unthinkingly, replaced it with a muttered oath and a shamefaced grin, and took up the ornate helmet designed by the parish vestrymen, acknowledging sheepishly, 'For all his urbanity, Robert Knight might consider such modishness a little extreme for a parish constable. Do you not agree, Rebecca?'

'He might take it as proof of initiative and originality of mind.'

'More as contempt of court! I could well find myself in the cells with the prisoner, or on a treadmill in a house of correction! Would that not grieve you, Rebecca?'

'Not a whit! The exercise would undoubtedly benefit you,' she assured him blandly. 'It would test both your strength of leg and character.'

Joshua, unable to suppress a smile, protested, 'I fear the justice will always set less store upon my strength of character than upon the lure of your bright eyes, Rebecca. He is ludicrously susceptible.'

'Agreed. He is a gentleman of exquisite taste and refinement,' she stated comfortably. 'None can doubt his superiority.'

'Nor his parade of it!' Joshua exclaimed with feeling, adding,' And I shall bear the full brunt of it, and the rough edge of his tongue if I do not ride out directly.'

Rebecca, who knew that his clumsy teasing was no more than a ploy to hide his anxiety and postpone their parting, took firm hold upon his arm, saying, 'I shall fetch my cloak and walk with you to the stables. The fresh air will do me good. I have been closeted too long indoors.'

Joshua stood for a moment indecisively, wondering whether to forbid it, before blurting awkwardly, 'You will stay within the house afterwards, Rebecca . . . not venture abroad alone? You will take no foolish risks. Stay always within sight and sound of Ruth and Mrs Turner in the kitchen. You will send for Dr Burrell and the midwife the minute you have need? Promise!' he commanded urgently, 'else I shall know no peace of mind.'

Rebecca's pretty mouth twitched, but she said gravely, although her blue eyes were warm with affectionate amusement, 'You have my solemn word upon it, Joshua, I shall send word to Sophie Fleet, too, for she is calm and reliable and I would have her with me, as friend, above all other.'

'Yes, Sophie is dependable,' he approved. 'She will not throw you into panic, nor flurry nor harass you, as others might. She will not fuss nor grow hysterical . . . become a hindrance even.'

'No, Joshua,' she concurred meekly.

'It is essential, my love, that you remain calm, you understand? That you will not be unnerved by the anxieties of others.' Joshua's strong-boned face was tense under the thatch of corn-coloured hair, voice taut. Rebecca knew, with an absurd rush of tenderness, that it was she who was the comforter and he the comforted, and that he spoke without irony from loving fear for her. There would always be two human lives dependent upon her in future, she thought, with a mingling of love and exasperation, Joshua's and the babe's. For all his courage and dependability, his protection of others, Joshua was as much in need of reassurance, the certainty of unconditional loving. Impulsively she stretched high upon the toes of her silk slippers to plant a kiss upon his cheek, a movement so awkward and ungainly for a moment that Joshua was forced to steady her and hold her firm, helmet clattering to the floor.

To forestall his concern and recrimination, she confessed lightly, 'I would retrieve it, my dear, were I able . . . but I fear it would delay you longer. I would need the efforts of the entire household, and the militia besides, to right me again.' Her laughter was so cheerfully infectious that, against his will, Joshua found himself laughing with her, good-humour restored. He shook his head resignedly and fetched her warm cloak, settling it about her shoulders, fastening it at the neckline, delaying the moment of leaving.

'You will send word if I am needed, Rebecca? If, for any reason . . .?'

His fear lay unspoken between them.

'There will not be need. You will be away but a few hours, Joshua.' she sought to reassure him.

'The child is overdue . . .'

'A first birth is always unpredictable . . . a matter of days, weeks even, is of no great import. Dr Burrell has said that all is well.'

'But you will send word?'

'If that will ease your mind, my dear, I shall hire the town crier to summon you all from the courthouse and publish the good news throughout the three hamlets, the quarries, the brickyard and the port,' she assured him wickedly. 'Then, perhaps, a string of beacons along the coast? Fireworks. A trio of fiddlers, with dancing upon the village green . . .? She broke off, unable to stem the hilarity at such a prospect.

'Rebecca! You are incorrigible! I can expect neither sense nor reason from you,' Joshua remonstrated, but his smile was openly indulgent and belied his words as he escorted her without the house, then carefully across the uneven cobbles of the yard.

Stenner, their pauper-groom, emerged, blinking, from the darkness of the stable, lean face alert with pleasure, and with Joshua's powerful grey ready saddled. Stenner's smile and greeting for Rebecca were warmly respectful, his pride in both horse and master clear. Joshua was, without doubt, the most handsome and commanding figure in all the three hamlets and beyond, Rebecca thought with pardonable satisfaction. There was no other to rival him for height and presence or for handsome looks. She could claim so honestly and without undue prejudice, for none could dispute it. He was all of six feet three inches of well muscled height, finely proportioned, and as elegant in dress as manner. He was an imposing figure astride the grey, his magnificent helmet adding a good eight inches to his impressive height, his skin bronzed by outdoor life and weather. There was an easy, unselfconscious grace about him, an arrogance reflected in the pride of the fine grey, which nuzzled her shoulder now, seeking approval. She stroked its neck gently, but her eyes were upon Joshua.

'Take care,' it was the caution she always gave.

'And you, my love.'

She watched him ride out, alert, expectant, his mind already upon the task ahead as, with a word to Stenner, she slowly retraced her footsteps across the yard. It grew no easier with time, she thought bleakly, to accept that every time Joshua rode out it was to some scene of violence, some duty, or meeting, that set him fiercely at risk. Yet his work as constable gave force and meaning to his life. She could not selfishly deny him that, nor claim his total commitment, else he would not be the man she loved and admired, but only the shadow of it.

She walked now, out of sight of others, with slow, cumbersome steps, scarce able to drag herself comfortably for the awkwardness of pregnancy and the persistent ache in her back and muscles. She felt unbearably tired, clumsy, ungainly, and low in spirits. Already the birth was a week and more overdue, and although Dr Burrell insisted that such delay was normal and without hazard, she was not wholly convinced, although she had been at pains to reassure Joshua.

Once safely within the parlour of the cottage she eased herself with awkward effort into the depths of the comfortably wide sofa beside the fire, grateful to rest awhile. The pain, when it came, was so sharply unexpected that she involuntarily cried aloud, breath raw in her throat. She tried to calm herself, but the pain and agitation returned more fiercely as, panting and whimpering, she forced herself across the room to the bell-pull to summon aid.

Ruth, her serving maid, ran in at once, face as palely fearful as Rebecca's own, calling out sharply to the cook to lend assistance. Then, haltingly and with effort, they supported her to her bed.

'You had best send Stenner for Dr Burrell!' Betty Turner's voice was brisk. 'Quickly, Ruth. Now! At once, girl! Do not linger. Then summon the midwife and send word to Sophie Fleet that Mrs Stradling is in labour.'

Ruth hesitated, eyes wide with apprehension, before blurting, 'But . . . Mr Stradling? Would you have him recalled?'

'No!' Rebecca's denial was swift.

Betty Turner, freckled cheeks flushed red as her hair, echoed firmly, 'No! It is better not,' before peremptorily hustling Ruth without. Her humorous gaze met Rebecca's in complicity as she helped her into the voluminous cambric

5

nightgown, which lay ready within a chest, with the layette and all else that would be needed. Her deft fingers worked with reassuring gentleness as she affirmed good-humouredly, ''Tis my honest opinion the delivery room is no place for a gentleman. 'Tis enough to have care of *one* babe, and that not a whit more helpless nor contrary. No, men are infants all at heart, for all their blustering . . . well, saving Dr Burrell,' she amended fairly, 'and he does not rightly count, since he will be too busy to carp or harass, or demand attention.'

A spasm of pain raked through Rebecca making her cry out and immediately Betty Turner was all practical concern and efficiency, taking Rebecca's hands firmly in her own, bidding her grip hard, saying soothingly, ''Tis no more than a contraction, my dear . . . they will come more strongly now, but have no fear, it is but the child giving sign that it is well and strong, and anxious to be birthed. It will not come yet awhile, and I shall stay beside you for as long as ever there is need.'

Rebecca nodded, grateful for Betty's placid, unflurried presence, her calm capability. She surrendered herself willingly to the older woman's care. The anguish would all too soon be forgotten, Betty Turner assured her, for, miraculously, it always proved so with a birthing.

'Tis a shared loving, my dear, a tie as strong as the cord that binds you both. Though cut at birth, it is never really severed. A new life. A new beginning.'

'Rebecca, aware of Betty's love for her own child, Thomas, and the cruelty she had endured through pauperdom and the violence of her husband's neglect and abduction of his own child, said quietly, 'Yes. We have need of that, a sense of security, of belonging.'

'And we have found it here, Thomas and I.' Betty Turner's plump, homely face was aglow with honesty. 'I thank you for that, Mrs Stradling, yes, I thank you for that. But I will not speak of it more, for the past is ended. With the dead, it no longer has the power to hurt us, save in memory . . . and only if we will let it.'

Rebecca, with vivid memory of William Turner's death, lived again that violence of storm and sea, the horror of his self-destruction and the destruction he had so nearly brought to others. She felt a rage of grief and pity, a hurt deeper than any physical pain she bore. She wished that she might somehow comfort Betty Turner as she, in turn, was comforted by her. Yet there were no words. Should Joshua die, she knew that even with the child she carried, there would be no joy in living, no hope. Nothing but an empty using up of days. Surely even such hatred and despair as Betty Turner had endured could not altogether kill the warmth of loving, of closeness shared?

She glanced up to surprise a grief upon Betty's homely face that could not be hid, raw, yet so fleeting that she might have imagined it. She knew inexorably then that Betty Turner's scars would be slow to heal, flesh tender beneath the skin, excoriated always by a chance word or memory. The past, like the dead, forever retained the power to hurt, for they were as much a part of us as living flesh and bone. Savage or mourned, it made no matter. Without the past, and those who had made it, we were bereft.

Rebecca reached out and took Betty Turner's work-roughened hand into her own, trying by touch alone to convey her understanding, the shared wholeness of birth and loving which bound them close. And Betty Turner nodded, and smiled, but did not speak.

Joshua, riding out upon the grey, tried to set his mind to the duty that lay ahead at Pyle courthouse. It was no more than a run-of-the-mill exercise, the sentencing of a common thief and footpad who had had the temerity, or misfortune, to choose as victim one of the parish vestrymen. All are equal under the law, Joshua reflected wryly, as Robert Knight, as justice, squire and rector of the three hamlets, would be swift to testify. Yet the dignity of those who served the public must be upheld. Fortunately, the dignity of the rough hoi-polloi lay in their honest labour upon the land, and was less easily bruised. Indeed, had the footpad set upon one of the villagers it was likely that *he* would have been the one bruised, if not totally disabled, for his impertinence. It was rough old justice, swift and biblical, and Joshua was not totally convinced that the justice's considered and elegantly phrased judgements proved any the more effective.

Joshua's own evidence would be brief and non-contentious,

and required no great effort of intellect. His part in the affair was purely subsidiary. The assault had, after all, been witnessed by three of the victim's fellow vestrymen returning from a convivial meeting at the Lamb Inn at Nottage, and their integrity was absolute – even if joint memory was somewhat blurred by the landlord's generosity and the quality of his ale. Anyway, despite Robert Knight's strictures about the stern impartiality of the British legal system, and his proud claim that every man was adjudged innocent until proven guilty, Joshua was in little doubt as to the outcome. The poor, misguided wretch would certainly expiate his sins in a cell at a house of correction, with, as like as not, a spell in the stocks or upon the treadmill.

Joshua's thoughts returned to Rebecca and their unborn child, and her affectionate teasing, her determination to lift his spirits. But his spirits would not be lifted, not until he knew that she was safely delivered of the babe and that both were strong in flesh and mind . . . that naught was amiss. He hoped that Stenner would ride out at once to fetch John Burrell, Sophie Fleet and the midwife, as commanded, that he would not delay. But, of course, he would obey! Joshua castigated himself sharply. The man was utterly reliable, as conscientious as he was loyal. But if Rebecca herself delayed? What then? John Burrell might be called out upon some emergency, too far away to respond. A summons to a remote farmstead perhaps or some isolated cottage upon the shore . . . stranded . . . cut off by the tides. Joshua felt a sense of panic rise, a sickness of fear. He knew a coldness within, yet his hands were damp with sweat, and he felt the prickle of it at his nape, and beading his lip. He had felt such raw fear before, when sudden danger oppressed him, but always with a surge of excitement. Now there was nothing save fear itself, not for himself but for Rebecca and the child. Anguished. Irrational. Primitive as a curse. He all but turned the grey and rode back, so powerful was his sense of urgency. He felt the grey stiffen, then stumble upon a cart-rut, sensing his indecision and fear. Then, with a feeling of shame, and a reassuring word as the horse righted itself, he set it firmly upon its proper way.

Joshua was so preoccupied and ill at ease, despite his resolution to think only of his evidence at Pyle, that he was barely aware of the countryside about him. He had passed through the lush pasture lands of Nottage, with its small, fertile farms and holdings, with only the briefest acknowledgement to those who respectfully greeted him in passing. From the cluttered stone smithy, open to the weather, Ben Clatworthy, the blacksmith and farrier, had hailed him cheerfully, grateful to be back, after long absence, as ruler of his simple domain. Joshua had not even heard him, so deep in thought was he, and Clatworthy, who knew what ailed him, had paused in his labours to shake his head knowledgeably, smile indulgent. He had pushed back his springing black hair, face aglow with sweat and heat, to wipe a brawny fist across his mouth, chiding his apprentice, ''tis best always to keep your mind upon the work in hand, my lad, and not upon the ladies. Take telling, now, else you might well get your fingers burned. Aye, and much else besides! Best stick to horses. They give you little expense and no aggravation . . . being dumb!'

His lad, who was but twelve years of age, nodded hasty agreement. 'Aye,master, 'he ventured, breath labouring as fiercely as the bellows he wielded. His young face was more flushed from the heady pride of being addressed as an equal than from his exertions. There was no one on God's good earth with whom he would have changed places in that moment of rare companionship. No, not even with Mr Stradling, the constable himself, for all his fine uniform, his authority and the grey. The apprentice set down the bellows, his thin-muscled arms suddenly imbued with all his master's whipcord strength and purpose.

Ben Clatworthy was slyly amused to see the lad wipe his mouth, swagger, then rub the sweat from his palms upon the scuffed leather of his apron in uncanny imitation. He carefully hid a smile. How often, he thought, he had damned aloud the searing heat of the fire, the relentless clanging of iron, the acrid stench of burnt hoof and hair, claiming it a foretaste of hell. To his lad it was very heaven on earth. Ben Clatworthy began to whistle cheerfully, and the lad, pleased by his approbation, busied himself vigorously, then attempted a self-conscious whistling, too. Aye, he was a good enough lad, the blacksmith conceded, and shaping well enough. In time he would trim the rough corners from him as patiently and skilfully as he trimmed iron horseshoes to shape. It was best to learn from example and easier to like a lad who was willing and saw no fault in you. Even if it was hard to live up to.

Joshua riding now, upon the stony highway that traversed the acres of windswept dunes which bordered the rocky shore towards Maudlam, stayed deeply meshed in thought. He was as unaware of the cool morning mist upon his face and the rhythmic pounding of the surf beyond as of all else about him, his thoughts upon Rebecca and the babe. How strange, he thought, that it had no separate life of its own, no real identity, although its very existence dominated the whole of their future lives. A boy or girl child? Darkly arresting of the de Breos blood or as fair as that sturdy yeoman line from whence he had sprung? A fusion of all that was good in them both, if God willed it. A new life, a new being, with all of happiness and sorrow before it, a path untrod. Joshua had been scrupulous in not declaring a preference as to the gender of the child, maintaining, with honesty, that all that mattered to him was Rebecca's health and the babe's. Even now he would admit no more to himself than that. He would not reason beyond it nor speculate, lest, in making a choice, its denial might seem to be proof of rejection. He could not doubt that Sir Matthew, Rebecca's grandfather, would be pleased to see an heir to the de Breos line. With the estranged death of his only son Rebecca's father, and Edward's cruelty in keeping Rebecca's birth secret for so many years, the old gentleman had believed his line extinct. With his discovery that Rebecca lived, his growing love for her, he had found new energy and purpose in living, the future inheritance of his great estate and the care of the tenancy no longer a grief to him. Rebecca and Joshua himself had grown not only to respect but to love the austere, aristocratic old man for his fair-mindedness and selfless devotion to those dependent upon him. He, in turn, had found in Rebecca the courage and steadfastness of spirit which his son had lacked. It grieved him, but filled him with pride, too, that from early childhood she had earned her living as fishermaid upon the shore, braving the savagery of wind and weather, nursing her father through disillusionment and illness until his death. It was a sorrow to

Sir Matthew that his son had shown bitterness and rejection to the end and that there had been no reconciliation. He had felt deeper sorrow that through Edward's corroding bitterness he might have been denied all knowledge of Rebecca's birth. To carry such hatred beyond the grave, to corrupt the lives of others, seemed to him the final cruelty. He had found it hard to forgive. Joshua hoped that the birth of their child would bring the old gentleman some of the joy in living that his son's intractability and weakness had denied. He was deserving of that. And Jeremiah Fleet, the old fisherman who had been mentor and friend to Rebecca, and a more loving and generous father than her own, would welcome the child's coming, feeling as close to Rebecca as blood kin. It was his wife, Sophie, whom Rebecca had chosen to be with her as friend and companion at the birth.

Joshua, glancing up, saw that the early morning mist had risen from the hollows of the dunes, the marram grass rippling silver now in the stiffening breeze from the sea. Far beyond, the white-capped waves were a restless seething greyness, as bleak as the restlessness within him. Overhead a lone swan, elegant in flight, made graceful way to the great freshwater pool at Kenfig, as remote and ageless as the city buried deep beneath the shifting sand. Joshua heard the beating of the swan's wings, steady and rhythmic as a heartbeat, a pulsing of vigorous power and life. He thought of his child unborn, and those alien people entombed for ever beneath the encroaching sand. Those who had been flesh and blood, made love, sorrowed, known happiness and pain . . . He paused for a moment, filled with a sadness almost too raw to be borne, then he stirred the grey into movement, and rode on.

Stenner had ridden out with commendable speed to the Clevis Hill at Newton to summon the physician, Dr Burrell. Joshua's instructions to him had been firm and explicit and reiterated so forcefully in the past few days that the groom might have followed them in his sleep, had he been so minded. As it was, he grew so flurried and inarticulate in his nervousness that John Burrell thought, with wry humour, that the unfortunate wretch seemed more in need of his urgent ministrations than Rebecca, his patient.

With a terse explanation to his partner, Dr Mansel, John Burrell called for the gig to be brought and made to ride out to Thatched Cottage. Their housekeeper, discreetly efficient in her black bombazine and starched house-bonnet, watched surreptitiously from a window of the house, austere and sharply inquisitive as a magpie. The two physicians could scarcely have been more different, she thought with affectionate amusement; Dr Burrell, so lean and attenuated, and Obadiah Mansel, plumply cherubic, with his protuberant, boiled-gooseberry eyes and corolla of baby-fine hair. Yet, despite their physical differences, there was a harmony between them, an integrity and firmness of purpose that drew them close. She had no doubt that it was to attend Mrs Stradling that Dr Burrell went, for the call for her *accouchement* had been daily expected.

The past cast long shadows, she thought compassionately. It was hard to escape. Yet the violence and bloodiness of it had brought the two men close. How strangely their two lives had been interwoven: John Burrell, imprisoned, then cruelly hounded for a murder that Madeleine Mansel had committed and for which she had finally paid full price. Yet Dr Burrell, although innocent, had suffered even more fiercely than she, for, with her death, *her* penance was ended. Her victims had been the young woman whom John Burrell had so passionately loved and the child who died with her, life not even begun. It would be a harsh reminder to face, the birth of Mrs Stradling's child, the housekeeper thought with pity. His dedication and discipline could not soften the anguish of it, nor remembrance of what might have been.

She watched him drive off in the gig, thin hand raised in salute to Dr Mansel, a dark, saturnine man, face deeply scored. Obadiah Mansel turned back to the house with a sigh. It might have been better had he attended the confinement, for each new birth must excoriate John Burrell anew. Yet Rebecca had asked for John Burrell's presence, and he would not deny her that, for so much was owed to her.

It was she who had hidden and protected Burrell when all others were turned against him, thinking him a murderer. She had been sure of his innocence and would not be swayed. He had come seeking revenge and would have killed

12

Mansel, believing him culpable. So long ago, thought Mansel dispiritedly, and so much lost that could never be found again. Love. Innocence. Trust. And so many lives destroyed . . . Burrell might one day find love and contentment with Emily Randall who had so long loved and protected him. She was a fine, intelligent woman, compassionate and warm. There was joy and hope, too, for Rebecca and Joshua Stradling in the birth of their child. A new life, a new beginning. For him there was naught save memory, not even the remembrance of love past, nor a promise of hope. The agony lay in that Madeleine had scorned and despised him, betraying him from the first. If he could learn to hate her it might lessen the hurt. His work was a salve, but it was not enough to fill the emptiness within him. In time, perhaps, in time . . . What was the phrase that eluded him? 'Physician, heal thyself.'

Chapter Two

Jeremiah Fleet, the old fisherman, had returned to his small cottage at the edge of the Burrows in rare humour. His gaily painted fish-cart, with its placid Welsh cob, was piled high with lobster pots and willow frails, many with plump cargoes of lobsters and crabs, pouting and sea bass and succulent molluscs. It had proved a good day's fishing and the catch plentiful. His night lines had yielded an almost embarrassing abundance of fine saleable fish. Even the tedious work of raking the cockles, then riddling them clean in the sea water rock pools had seemed less of a back breaking penance, for the morning mist had lifted early with the promise of a fine day.

Jeremiah, a handsomely impressive figure, seemed to have grown in stature with age rather than been diminished by it. His large-boned frame remained muscular and spare of flesh. His blue-grey eyes shone keenly intelligent from a weathered face, its lines, although deeply-scored, etched more by experience and cheerful survival than ill humour. His grizzled beard and luxuriant grey-white hair, if seeming at first glance profligate, added to the impression of extraordinary vigour. He was, his wife Sophie thought, for all the world like some commanding Old Testament prophet; powerful, self-disciplined, exacting, yet filled with a zealous, almost crusading, generosity towards his fellow men. Indeed, she might have added, towards all his fellow creatures save those he was reluctantly forced to sell for very existence, and he indulged Charity, the dog, and that ancient pot-bellied cob most shamelessly.

Sophie, her plump face wreathed now in anxious concern, hurried out into the cobbled yard where Jeremiah was unloading the cart, to explain breathlessly, ''Tis Rebecca, Jeremiah.'

'Rebecca?' his voice was raw with fear. 'The little maid has taken no harm, Sophie? There is naught amiss?'

'No, no, my love,' she hastened to reassure him. ''Tis only Stenner come as promised to tell me her time is nigh for the birthing and all. I am needed at Thatched Cottage.'

Jeremiah set a basket of shellfish to the cobbles, exclaiming despairingly, 'And I shall serve only to hinder you, Sophie, unless you will ride upon the cart as it stands!'

Charity, the bull terrier, sensing his anxiety, lent urgent voice to the exchange, rushing and darting at Sophie with sharp Stacatto yelps of excitement until Jeremiah, driven to distraction, was forced to remonstrate sharply, 'Quiet, now! Take telling!' he rebuked, chiding pushing him aside so irritably that Sophie was moved to fondle the dog in consolation.

''Tis no use venting your spleen on that poor creature, Jeremiah. He is in no wise to blame.'

'No more he is,' Jeremiah admitted, shamefaced.' 'Tis anxiety drives me, Sophie. I will not deny it.'

Sophie, painfully aware of how all those long years ago Jeremiah's young wife, scarce more than a child herself, had died in childbirth, and his only son with her, said with gentleness, 'Rebecca will be in safe hands, Jeremiah. John Burrell is both doctor and friend. He will do all that is needed, have no fear.'

'Aye, Sophie. He is a good man, as he showed in his care of the cholera victims. He has proved himself so in letting the past go without bitterness, in forgiving those of us who . . . 'he broke off, flushing, to say quickly, 'Shall I take you, then, to Thatched Cottage?'

'No, no, my dear, rest easy.' Sophie knew as soon as she had uttered the words how useless they were, for she herself was in a state of the greatest agitation. 'You had best remain here and do what must be done, the boiling of the cockles, the unloading of the cart and the unharnessing and feeding of the cob and all. It will serve you better, occupy both hands and mind. Joshua has ordered Stenner to take me in the gig, for Dr Burrell and the midwife have already been summoned.' She hesitated, saying awkwardly, 'You will tell Illtyd when he returns from Stormy Downs from his duties at hayward? You

15

know how dearly he cares for Rebecca, and Joshua too. You will be company one for the other.'

'Aye, I will tell him. And you, my dear, you will send word the moment there is news?'

'The very instant,' Sophie promised earnestly, 'for Rebecca is like your own child.'

'As Illtyd is!' Jeremiah reminded, with fierce honesty, of her own son. He glanced with pride to where his own name and his stepson's were painted upon the side of the fish-cart. 'Jeremiah Fleet and Son,' he murmured. ''Tis a real mark of Illtyd's quality that he can read and write where we cannot, having no schooling and all. He is a fine figure of a man, Sophie. A son to be proud of. We are richly blessed, as I pray that Rebecca will be.'

Sophie, eyes uncomfortably blurred with tears, reached up and set a loving kiss to Jeremiah's roughened cheek, saying, 'You are the dearest of men, Jeremiah. The dearest and the best. You see all so clearly.'

Jeremiah, looking bewildered, smiled and shook his head in denial, but was unable to hide his pleasure. 'You will give my love to Rebecca, Sophie?'

'Yes, my dear. It will bear retelling, although she is already as assured of it as of breathing,' she said with a wide smile. 'I had best be gone, Jeremiah.'

'Aye.' He turned and began resolutely unloading the cart, then suddenly stooped low to fondle the dog's ears, an act of remorse and contrition. Sophie heard Charity's lean whip of a tail beating response upon the cobblestones as she hurried from the yard to take up her cloak and bonnet.

Once upon the gig her thought was all for Rebecca. Yet deep within her was a warmth of belonging. She would never grow accustomed to giving and receiving such love as she and Jeremiah now shared. A love all the more precious for coming to her so late, when she had thought such closeness ended. A sharing of flesh and spirit, a complete understanding, whatever the future might hold. She would be thanking God for the blessing of it all the days of her life and beyond.

The birth had been protracted and painful, despite the patient ministrations of Dr Burrell and the midwife, a stout, practical countrywoman, capable and cheerfully serene. Sophie had proved friend and comforter, her unobtrusive presence a boon. She came not only as Jeremiah's wife but as one who cared in her own right, her strength and gentle encouragement forging a closeness between them.

When all was finally ended, with Rebecca so savagely beaten by pain and exhaustion that she could scarce find strength enough to speak, John Burrell took the child into his arms and touched its cheek with gentleness. His smile was tender and his eyes preternaturally bright as he delivered the babe, swaddled and wrapped, into Sophie's eager hold.

'If you will give Rebecca's son into her keeping,' his voice was low, scarce audible, and Sophie, witness to the joy and anguish which bedevilled him, nodded, unspeaking.

Rebecca looked long at the child cradled within her arms, her face, still flushed and drawn from the birth, radiantly transfigured. She felt such a surge of atavistic love and tenderness as she laid her cheek to her son's that its fierceness all but crippled her. She traced the soft contours of his cheek, exclaiming in wonderment, 'He is perfect!'

'Yes, he is perfect. Thanks be to God!' Sophie's joy was as healing as her tears, her pride unbounded.

Rebecca knew that Sophie's thoughts, as her own, were upon Illtyd, whom they both loved. The little hayward, awkwardly mis-shapen, whose courage and gentle humour were an inspiration to all he knew, for he was without bitterness or self-pity, and bright with the joyousness of living.

'Illtyd will be pleased,' Sophie said.

There were many, John Burrell thought with an ache of pity, who would have been proud as Sophie to own to such a son. There are flaws which cripple us all, but those visible and overcome serve only to strengthen us. The griefs that fester within are slower to heal.

'Joshua will be proud,' he said, 'and rightly, for he has a fine son who will go far. And what fine name have you in mind for this hero? This adventurer, Rebecca?'

'John, Jeremiah, Matthew. He is named for those who have played part in my life and Joshua's. Those whose friendship we value most and would wish remembered . . . would wish to live on in another.'

17

John Burrell had paled and grown uncertain, his lean, cadaverous face unreadable.

'You will not refuse us, John?' Rebecca probed anxiously.

'No, I will not refuse you. It is the greatest honour I have known in all of my life, the greatest compliment.' His voice was warm with pleasure. 'I accept most willingly, my dear.'

'And Jeremiah, Sophie? You think he will be pleased?' Rebecca's hand crept involuntarily to the little heart-shaped brooch of seed pearls at her throat. It had been Jeremiah's most treasured possession, for he had given it to his young wife upon the birth of their son and then, as he declared, 'To Rebecca, my daughter, for that is how I think of you.' Rebecca, loving him, had vowed then that it would remind her always of his goodness, for Jeremiah had been father and friend to her, and protector when she had no one to speak for her. 'You think he will be pleased, Sophie?' she repeated.

'Yes,' said Sophie, smiling at John Burrell. 'He will be pleased. Jeremiah will be the proudest man in all the three hamlets, bar none.'

'Bar one, Mrs Fleet,' John Burrell corrected. 'I beg you will remember. Bar one.'

Joshua had found the delays and legal machinations at Pyle Courthouse more than usually frustrating. At any other time he might have been amused, for the justice's scholarly interventions and the prisoner's feigned innocence held all the makings of a first class farce. The result had, from the first, been a foregone conclusion. Joshua's evidence briskly given, he had hoped as devoutly as the prisoner for an early release. There was, however, to be no reprieve. Robert Knight was of a mood to linger. His summation, bolstered by a lacerating attack upon the accused's character, habits, appearance and antecedents was masterly. Yet to Joshua it seemed interminable. He tried to stem his rising irritation but could not. He thought, sourly, that if Robert Knight in his role as rector were ever to preach such a long-winded sermon, then his entire congregation would have a fit of the staggers. As it was, even the vestrymen who had been summoned to give evidence were in danger of narcolepsy. It might take at least a firkin of ale apiece at the Lamb Inn to restore them to consciousness.

The sentence delivered and the prisoner hurried, protesting, to the cells. Joshua made to leave and retrieve his grey from the courthouse stables.

'Stradling! A word . . .' The justice's sonorous, well-rounded voice halted him.

'Sir?' Joshua tried to keep the irritation from his own, although even to his own ears it seemed undeniably curt.

'I shall not delay you, for I know how time is pressing,' the justice's protuberant brown eyes were amused, smile kindly in the plump-jowled face. 'There is news of Rebecca? It would comfort me to hear it, for she has been much in my thoughts and prayers of late, as you, my boy, as have you.' There was no doubting his honest concern, and Joshua immediately felt guilt at his own churlishness.

'She is well, sir. I shall deliver her your kindest regards,' he promised warmly. 'It will comfort her to know of your care for her.'

The justice nodded, jowls forced high over his well starched collar, only to blink short-sightedly and confess, 'You have found a rare prize in Rebecca, my boy. A rare prize. She is a gentlewoman of character, intelligent and spirited yet always with a care for others.' Joshua was not inclined to disagree. 'You will be pleased when the child is safely delivered. It is a trying time. Yes, a trying time for all. My good friend, Sir Matthew, will be vastly relieved. Yes, and your tutor, Dr Handel Peate.'

Joshua murmured assent, anxious only to be away.

'Dr Peate thinks highly of you. He judges you the finest student he has been privileged to teach. A born academic, with an enquiring mind.'

'Then I fear I have disappointed him, sir,' Joshua said good-humouredly.

'No!' The justice's denial was emphatic. 'You have set your intelligence to good use, Stradling. The upholding of the law is paramount. It affects us all, every man, woman and child, from the richest to the poorest. No, you have not disappointed him, nor me, believe it.' He sniffed audibly and fidgetted with his high silk hat, conscious that in forgoing his customary abrasiveness he had made himself vulnerable.

Joshua, startled and confused by the justice's approval, did not know how best to answer. He was spared the necessity for Robert Knight said testily, 'You would serve best by riding home to Newton, Stradling, to be at your wife's disposal, not lingering idly.' Before Joshua could balk at the injustice of it, he continued more benignly, 'I have taken the precaution of having both my coach and my gig in attendance. A groom shall deliver your grey to your stables directly. My coachman will drive you, for you are plainly too nervous and abstracted to be trusted. I shall take the gig.'

As Joshua, bewildered, made to protest, the justice held up a plump hand to silence him, saying, 'I hold it as no criticism. Your concern for Rebecca is right and proper. Indeed, I go so far as to say it is to your credit, sir. It would offend me were it otherwise.' As the justice's coach drew alongside them on the cobblestones and the footman leapt down to open the carriage door. Robert Knight put a hand to Joshua's arm to declare gruffly, 'Such weakness upon my part is to be taken in no way as a precedent, Stradling. It is merely a device to make you work harder, to see that your time is utilised to advantage. You understand?'

'Perfectly, sir,' said Joshua, straightfaced. 'It would be impertinent to think otherwise, to attribute any other motive. It might be misconstrued as charity.'

'Precisely, Stradling.' The justice's dark-grained jowls began to tremble and his shoulders shook to his ponderous laughter. He looked, Joshua thought, not for the first time, like some benign frog, squat, plump and comically self-satisfied. Yet there was nothing absurd about him, for he was a man of the keenest intellect and integrity. A man to trust and respect and whose loyalty was absolute, as all in the three hamlets would testify, as they would testify to his countless small acts of pity and love so unobtrusively made.

Joshua, secure in the depths of Robert Knight's coach, felt ridiculously uplifted by the justice's approval. It had been ungrudgingly and honestly given; the more valued for its rarity. Robert Knight was not given to hyperbole. It pleased Joshua that such praise had not been on Rebecca's count alone, although the justice was devoted to her. Yet he had given clear warning that armed hostilities would resume. It was but a hiatus, a small truce in the continuing battle of wits and

20

words waged between them. As in any war, the final outcome was unpredictable and the more vigorously fought for being so. It scarcely mattered who won or lost a skirmish. The trick was to survive one's immediate wounds and redouble the attack. He did not doubt that Robert Knight was already planning his future strategy. Surprisingly, the thought did not depress him. He found that he relished the prospect almost as sharply as the justice's praise.

Robert Knight, delayed, to his disgust, by the court usher upon some triviality, was slow to make his way to the gig. His efforts to leave were further hampered by a group of vestrymen, anxious to discuss the court case. He had tried vainly to hide his chagrin, for they were all parishioners all and he felt that he owed them the courtesy of listening to them. For sheer inanity they were hard to beat, he thought, stumping his way testily to his carriage. He had heard more sense from the prisoner who at least had the virtue – or vice – of being an out and out villain. 'May God protect us from those profoundly incompetent and bent upon doing good!' he thought with asperity. 'They are a hard cross to bear.' He knew that as one in holy orders he was required to bear such crosses, if not gladly, then at least with equanimity and forbearance, and show forgiveness. But that was a counsel of perfection, designed for saints.

He entered the gig and took up the reins of the horse, driving off with such frenzied abandon that he all but dragged the luckless ostler under the wheels. Nor did he slow his pace, jolting and swaying so violently upon the rough track that once he all but hurled both horse and carriage bodily into a ditch. From the painful twinges in his foot he was certain that his gout was returning. Moreover, he felt distinctly queasy and choleric. After all, he had neither eaten nor drunk a morsel since leaving Tythegston Court. Such extreme self-denial was more than any man should be called upon to bear.

It was in a mood of sullen rebellion that boded ill for the servants that he drove through the griffon-topped pillars of the court before bringing the gig to a furious halt. He saw that his coach had already returned, and felt in no better humour.

His old manservant, Leyshon, came awkwardly from the

house to greet him, cruelly bent, but with a delighted smile revealing his ruined teeth. 'There is news, sir.'

'News, Leyshon? What news? Speak plainly, man!'

''Tis Mrs Stradling, sir. She is safely delivered of a child. A son. The coachman has this moment brought word.'

'They are both well, Leyshon?' he demanded, softening perceptibly.

'Indeed, sir. That is what I am led to believe. I have taken the opportunity of setting out your finest Madeira and cognac, sir, by way of celebration, and a meal awaits you.'

Robert Knight nodded curtly, unwilling to show unseemly pleasure or eagerness.

'It has been a successful morning, sir?' Leyshon enquired discreetly.

'Tolerable, Leyshon! Tolerable!'

Leyshon hid a smile as he followed his master within. It had not escaped his notice that the justice strode out purposefully, ill-humour dispelled and without the slightest suspicion of gout.

Abel George Stenner, attending to his duties within the stables of Thatched Cottage, felt a warmth of pleasure envelop him, a happiness so rare that he could have wept with the sharpness of it. For the first time in all of his life he had a place to call his own, a small cheerful room over the stables which was refuge and shelter both. A pauper child, he had been farmed out from earliest memory, working at every menial task, labouring from dawn to dusk, often for no more than his meagre keep. He had been the butt of every man's ill-humour, his very meekness a spur. He had suffered beatings and curses; known neither affection nor settled home. His patient diligence availed him nothing, and his lack of rancour served only to convince others of his weakness and to anger them the more. Here, at Constable Stradling's house, he had been assured of his worth. His work had become a joy rather than enforced drudgery, for the constable was swift to praise a task well done, and treated him always with civility and humour, and young Mrs Stradling was kindness itself. His growing friendship with Betty Turner was a rare and fragile thing, the first real companionship that he had ever known. More, he had gained the affection and trust of her young son, Thomas. It had been hard won and slow to come, for he still bore the scars of his father's physical and emotional violence.

Stenner was awkward at friendship, he knew, for none had ever sought him out for his own sake, held good opinion of him save, perhaps, the animals he had tended and grown to understand. If he were calm and patient, never rushing things nor expecting more than they were able to give in return, the future might yet be kinder than he had dared to hope. He would not expect nor dare to think of love, for that was too rich a blessing. Yet he had health and strength, and now the dignity of a home and a sense of belonging, and a man's need for the solace and flesh of another. Oh, but he was pleased to have been entrusted to ride out for the doctor and midwife, and to drive Mrs Fleet to Thatched Cottage in the gig. It was a rare privilege, an honour even. He had felt a real sense of worth – as if he were not just an ex-pauper, but a person of standing. More, as if he were part, not just of a household, but a family, and counted as such.

He paused in his painstaking grooming of the horse, its hide still damply lathered with sweat from its excursion with the gig. Stenner stiffened at the unexpected sound of footsteps scurrying urgently across the yard, and moved to the stable door, wary with curiosity. Betty Turner was hurrying towards him, freckled face alight with importance and scarce able to contain her excitement. To his bewilderment she flung her arms ecstatically around him, hugging him close, and even setting a kiss upon his cheek, then waltzing him upon the cobbles without a hint of restraint or self-consciousness.

"Tis Mrs Stradling!' she exclaimed delightedly. ''Tis a boy, Mr Stenner! A fine boy!' She hugged him again. 'Oh, 'tis a rare blessing and no mistake. Mr Stradling will be beside himself with joy and that is a certainty, for he has been all but demented with worry and uncertainty.' She shamefacedly released her hold, and face rawly began setting her apron to rights, awkwardly fidgeting with the mob cap upon her wayward red curls. There were smudges of tears upon her cheeks and Stenner saw her turn and surreptitiously wipe them away on her sleeve, then glance towards him. He pretended an absorption with his filth-spattered boots, shuffling in them

23

awkwardly, fearful lest she already be regretting the closeness between them. It would serve to further humiliate her were he to misconstrue her natural joyousness at the birth. Shyness made him painfully stilted.

'I am sure that the constable will be pleased, Mrs Turner, and I thank you for thinking to inform me,' he said stiffly. 'It was a kind act but I will detain you no longer, for I know you would sooner be about your business. You are as hard pressed as I . . .' He saw the pleasure fade from her face and cursed himself for his cold inadequacy. As she turned to go he blurted, impulsively, 'I am awkward with words. I meant no great harm. I beg you will believe me. I have been too long alone.'

Betty Turner put a comforting hand to his arm, smiling, and declaring with grave honesty, 'I have never placed overmuch value on words, Mr Stenner. They are easily spoken and as easily broken, as I have harsh reason to know. 'Tis those who claim the least who oftimes feel most deeply. 'Tis actions which count in the end.' He nodded. 'You are a kind man, George Stenner, an honest worker and a man on whom to rely. 'Tis a rare combination. Be proud of it.'

Stenner flushed, then said hesitantly, ''Tis a rare gift, the birth of a child. A joy and blessing, like Thomas.'

'Save to those who feel neither love nor responsibility,' she reminded without bitterness.

'Aye,' he said soberly. 'I have thought long and hard about those who left me to fend alone . . . vagrants, perhaps, or those fallen upon evil times, parted by death or sickness. 'Tis a family Constable Stradling will have and I do not grudge him that satisfaction, for he is deserving of it.'

'We do not always have the happiness we deserve.'

'No, it is a hard old life for many, but the only one we have so 'tis best to accept it first as last.'

She nodded and half turned to go, then walked slowly back, asking quietly, 'If Constable Stradling comes, will you keep silence? Not make mention of the babe, I mean? 'Tis fitting that Mrs Stradling be the first to give him news of it. It is her wish.'

'Aye,' he promised. 'I shall keep my silence. 'tis a moment to savour and share, and for no other to witness.'

24

She watched him walk away, a thin gaunt figure, sparing of flesh and words. She felt for him a sudden tenderness and compassion, deep as her protectiveness for Thomas. Yet there was something more, a stirring of love, primitive, disturbing, and not purely maternal. She walked with a lighter step, head held high, thinking with secret pleasure of how it would startle him to know.

Joshua, alighting from the justice's coach at Thatched Cottage, saw Stenner emerge swiftly from the stable yard to help steady the horses, and gave him an absent-minded greeting before hurrying within. The house seemed strangely quiet, with no sign of Ruth or Rebecca in the hall or parlour and no response to his tentative call. Surely Rebecca would not be wilful or foolish enough to drive abroad upon some shopping excursion or to visit a friend? He had warned her most vehemently against it. She would not be so perverse! No. She must be somewhere safely close by. In the garden, perhaps, or seated beside the kitchen fire with Betty Turner for company. She would not risk all with the birth so near.

Betty turned, hearing his increasingly anxious calls and their rising urgency, hurried from the kitchen. Her homely face was polished red from the heat of the fire, and beneath her rolled-up sleeves her freckled arms wore a thick dusting of flour. She wiped them hurriedly upon her apron.

'Mrs Stradling, sir? Why, I believe that she is quietly resting and I dare say that Ruth is with her, busy at some small task, or keeping her company.'

'Resting?' Joshua was all concern. 'There is naught amiss?' he asked sharply. 'She is not unwell?'

'No, sir. I believe that she is in the best of health and spirits. I have seldom known her happier or more relaxed.' Betty Turner's delighted smile was spontaneous, her amusement genuine.

Joshua nodded sheepishly and mounted the stairs, eager to regain composure before seeing Rebecca. He was in no doubt that his discomfiture had been noted by Betty Turner and viewed with that exasperated indulgence reserved for awkward puppies or petulant small boys. She had certainly been in fine humour.

He pushed wide the door of Rebecca's room, then halted, transfixed, his face a comical mixture of bewilderment and disbelief. Ruth, smiling broadly, had sidled out at the sight of him, and Sophie, unspeaking, had thrust a small swaddled bundle into his arms and made her escape.

'Mr Stradling, sir, I present your son.' Rebecca's voice was tender with affectionate laughter. 'Well, will you not welcome him?'

Joshua touched his child's face in wonderment, then glanced to where Rebecca lay against the pillows, eyes deeply shadowed, yet bright with happiness. 'With all my heart,' he said. 'With all my heart.'

Chapter Three

Joshua was besotted with his son. He scarce had willpower enough to wrench himself away to fulfil his parish duties, and returned each night fretting lest he had missed some landmark in the boy's development by his absence. Rebecca vowed that the rate of unsolved crime in the three hamlets had never been so high. Joshua's unquenchable good-humour was encouragement to every footpad and cutthroat for miles, she declared. Indeed, it would not surprise her if the justice descended irately upon his constable, swearing retribution. Joshua thought this highly unlikely as Robert Knight was to stand as godfather to the child and already thought him a paragon of all the virtues and marked for distinction. It seemed that everyone in the Stradling household, and even beyond it in the hamlets and Vale, was elated by the birth of John Jeremiah Matthew, and all who saw him fell victim to his enchantment. Had he not been blissfully unconscious of such adoration, Jeremiah maintained stoutly, it might well have turned the boy's head.

While Rebecca was still abed, recovering from the birthing, Joshua had sent immediate word by messenger to Sir Matthew at Southerndown Court, and begged him send news to Dr Peate and to Elizabeth Devereaux, Rebecca's dearest friend and former companion, now settled in the Dower House upon the estate. Elizabeth had, to her great joy, given birth to a daughter a few months earlier, her only regret that Roland, her husband, had not yet seen the child, since he had set sail upon a voyage to the Indies. Yet, with his return, she knew, would come full compensation for the lengthy partings his command of *The Pride of Glamorgan* demanded. Sir Matthew, upon receipt of the news of his great-grandchild's birth, had taken himself to the little family chapel in the grounds of Southerndown Court, and first given thanks for the safety of Rebecca and her son, then prayed most earnestly to God that he be spared to take some small part in the boy's growing.

His discovery that Rebecca lived had seemed miracle enough, for he was an old man and had believed himself alone and without blood kin. He knelt now, stiffly and with painful difficulty, for his bones grew awkward with age. Yet there was such fierce joy within him that it all but unmanned him and made him weep. He was a foolish old man, he thought, to dwell upon those who were lost to him and were no more: Emma, his dead wife, whom he had so dearly loved. Without her, despite the softening of the years, without her he still felt bereft, betrayed by time. And Edward, his only son. He would not dwell upon the foolish pride and acrimony that had riven them apart. It was too late for repentance, too useless to apportion blame or quell the hurt of it.

He pulled himself to his feet, swaying unsteadily, a tall austere man, spare in flesh and fine-boned features. There was sternness and dignity about him, a natural authority which set him apart from others, and he had often grieved it. But he had made his choice and must not regret it. In taking responsibility for a large estate, its tenants and labourers, its servants and cottagers, he was governed always by the needs and demands of others. Until Rebecca's coming and the birth of the child, it had been all of a family he knew. He prayed silently, and where he stood, that Rebecca and the boy would be strengthened always by love; that their decisions need not be made in loneliness. It had been a long, hard road to travel and too often of late he felt the lassitude and confusion of age oppress him. He had yearned so often to lay down the burden of the estate. Now he knew that there would be others to take it up, to ease the load upon him; others of his own flesh and blood on whom he could rely. He would send immediate word to his old friend, Dr Handel Peate, to Elizabeth Devereaux and her mother, Louisa Crandle, in the lodge, and others. They would share in his rejoicing. There would be gladness, too, at Joshua's father's farmhouse in the Vale of Glamorgan. The Stradlings were generous people, of good yeoman stock, intelligent and hard-working. They would give the boy firm, common sense values, as they had given such values to Joshua. Yes, the Southerndown estates would be well cared for and in safe hands.

Sir Matthew ignored the insistent ache in his bones and carefully drew himself straighter, a lean, upright gentleman at peace with himself and the world. He would see that there were beacons lighted and order a celebration, prepared for all, upon the estate. Some worthy mementoes, too, for the children of tenants and cottagers. His estate manager and Louisa Crandle would know what was fitting and help organise the affair. He would order the smaller de Breos coach to be made ready as soon as ever Joshua gave word that Rebecca was well enough to receive him. Hughes should take him and no other, for although the old coachman was retired he would feel hurt were he excluded from such a rare family reunion. Hughes had shared so many in times past, in both sadness and joy. This, save for Rebecca's coming, would be the most joyous of all. Yes, he thought with gentle satisfaction, the most joyous of all.

Rebecca, lying abed upon Dr Burrell's firm instructions, felt the time hang heavy, for she was not yet allowed the diversion of visitors. She was not of a disposition to long remain idle, but, despite her increasingly importunate pleas, neither John Burrell nor the midwife would relent. She, like Joshua, was besotted by their son, but Sophie, Ruth and the new nursery nurse, a model of devoted efficiency, made her feel all but superfluous. The babe, or John as she had to remind herself to call him, was a picture of relaxed contentment, as indeed who would not be, given such selfless adoration? He seemed, Rebecca thought, to sleep interminably, although his devoted acolytes assured her that this was merely further proof, if any were needed, of his absolute superiority. Sophie could see that Rebecca's inactivity was making her fret and did not know how best to counteract her boredom. Messages conveyed from Rebecca's friends, the villagers, and news of their daily alarms and excursions, were soon exhausted in the telling. Sophie would have read to her, had she been able, and Ruth, at Rebecca's insistence, was continuing to help with teaching the

29

youngest children at Emily Randall's schoolroom in Newton village.

It was Joshua, seeing Rebecca's increasing restlessness, who came up with a diversion to raise her spirits. The persistent clanging of the handbell beneath her window alerted her as the sonorous tones of the town crier carried the message, vibrant and clear: to Mrs Joshua Stradling he brought respectful greetings and congratulations and to every villager the glorious, nay, incomparable, news of the birth of her son, John Jeremiah Matthew Stradling. He was further commanded by the constable to the three hamlets, one Mr Joshua Stradling, to convey the brave news to every tavern, ale-house and inn in the hamlets that every man, aye, and woman, were she so minded, might drink the health of the aforementioned child at the said constable's expense. The crier's proclamation ended with an extravagant flourish of bell and verbiage and a rousing 'God Save The Queen!'

Rebecca, overcome by hilarity, yet absurdly touched, heard Sophie murmur that she did not doubt that the quarries, brickyards, the fields and Port were already deserted, and the landlords fit to expire from overwork. None but the dead, the deaf or the simple-minded could remain in ignorance! Yet she was pleased that Rebecca was so amused. An amusement which erupted into helpless laughter as the assembled fiddlers upon the lawn began to strike up a rousing, rollicking tune.

'Joshua is quite incorrigible!' she exclaimed to Sophie when she was able to control her laughter enough to speak. 'He must have taken leave of his senses!' Yet it was said with such a warmth of indulgent affection that Sophie was not deceived. Soon Sophie and the others were dancing and cavorting most shamelessly in time with the music and singing with equal vigour.

It was into this scene of disgraceful abandon that Dr John Burrell came unexpectedly. His dark, saturnine face registered first shock, incredulity, then reluctant approval. 'Pray, ladies, do not restrain yourselves on my account,' he declared expansively as the dancers faltered, then stumbled into embarrassed silence, standing awkwardly about. 'I am sure that Mrs Stradling is as entertained and uplifted by your efforts to divert her as I. Your sheer good spirits will prove a better tonic than my poor pills and potions may provide!' He chuckled delightedly and gave Rebecca first a wink then a broad conspiratorial smile, as he confessed, 'Were Mrs Stradling not temporarily indisposed, and I permanently handicapped by two left feet, then I'll own that I might well have invited her to join the revels.'

He strode briskly across to the wickerwork crib where his namesake lay peacefully sleeping, as blissfully unperturbed by the continuing clamour without as by the newfound quietness within. 'Well, young John,' he confided cheerfully, 'you are wise to take comfort while you may. With so many devoted admirers of the fairer sex, you do well to stay unimpressed,' adding, straightfaced, 'I'll wager that it will not always be so!'

'There is no merit in wagering on a certainty!' Rebecca said, smiling. 'It is to be hoped, sir, that you will set him good example.'

John Burrell's mouth twisted wryly, his dark eyes shadowed and unreadable, as Sophie and the others went quietly and unobtrusively about their tasks. 'No,' he said, so low that only Rebecca could hear. 'I am the last to set example. I pray God that he may never tread the same path that I have trod, in grief, or misunderstanding, that his future will lie clear.'

'Then I hope that he will at least show the same courage and the same compassion for his fellow men,' Rebecca said with grave honesty. 'It will hold him in good stead.'

John Burrell flushed under her scrutiny, saying, 'As I would hope for him that friendship and purpose in living that I have found here, in the three hamlets.'

'Then we are agreed,' Rebecca concluded, smiling.

'Yes, we are agreed.'

They regarded each other with the comfortable understanding of old friends, warm, affectionate, and totally at ease. John Burrell continued, 'In a few days, Rebecca, you may receive your first visitor, all being well, but you must promise neither to overtax yourself nor to attempt too much, you understand?' At her murmured compliance he continued with mock seriousness, 'I fear, though, that perhaps we had best postpone dancing to the fiddlers' band yet awhile.'

31

'Then I shall hold that pleasure in reserve, sir, to give me added incentive,' she promised.

He nodded good-humouredly. 'Perhaps, ma'am, by the time young John attains his majority, I might even have mastered the waltz.'

'Save that by then, sir, we might both be too incapacitated to attempt it,' she objected.

'Yes, that is an immutable fact of life, Rebecca,' he conceded. 'We can but live in hope.'

'And practise diligently, sir?'

'As if my very life depends upon it,' he promised, cheerfully taking his leave.

Joshua found no alarming increase in crime in the three hamlets, despite Rebecca's conviction that his total preoccupation with his son would encourage wrongdoing. He was, nonetheless, fully occupied in combating the usual misbehaviour and mayhem, the petty larceny, aggravation and violent dispute, too often occasioned by drunkenness. It was not to his credit, he reflected, that his generosity in providing free ale at the taverns served as encouragement to lawlessness. However, there had been no murder, attempted murder, or riotous assembly, for which blessing, at least, he had cause to be thankful. In addition to his day-to-day duties, his court work and paper work, his counselling and investigations, he was at the beck and call of the justice, whose gout had not noticeably improved his disposition. In additon the exciseman, his friend Peter Rawlings, had warned him of suspected smuggling from one of the many small creeks and inlets upon the coast. His involvement in this, plus a plea from the local farmers for protection from marauding sheep stealers, meant that he had little enough time to squander.

It was when he was actually riding out from Thatched Cottage to visit a smallholding upon Stormy Downs that he was halted by an urgent message from Tom Butler, landlord of the Crown Inn, requesting his immediate presence. The message had been garbled and incomprehensible, the sweeping boy who brought it sullenly confused. All Joshua could elicit from his patient questioning was that it was to do with, 'an infant . . . a newborn babe.'

'My son?' he demanded. 'Did Mr Butler speak of my son?'

The boy, pinched-faced and ragged, stared at him vacantly. ''Twas all he said, sir, to fetch you on account of the babe.'

Despite himself, Joshua felt his irritation rising, but the boy was so pathetically ill-nourished a creature and so obviously lacking in wits that he merely nodded, then offered the child a halfpenny, which was so rapturously received that it added guilt to his aggravation. He tried again stoically, 'Is there something amiss with the babe at the Crown, Tom Butler's grandson?'

The boy stared at him blank-faced, bare feet shuffling aimlessly, trying to show some glimmer of intelligence, then shook his head, shamefaced. ''Tis all I know,' he blurted, face tight with misery.

Filled with contrition, Joshua leaned down from the grey and touched the boy's shoulder, saying, 'You have delivered the message, think no more on it. I shall tell Tom Butler that you have done well to find me. He will be well pleased.'

The boy's face was aglow with incredulous delight as he reached out a tentative hand to stroke the grey's muzzle.

'Ossie, the ostler at the Crown, lets me help in the stables,' he confided, 'clearing the muck, and all.'

Joshua nodded. 'Then you may be sure that he values your help,' he ventured quietly. 'He employs only those he trusts, those who are honest and kind. It is a good recommendation.'

He saw the boy straighten his bony shoulders under the tattered, too-long coat, then speed, barefooted, across the cobbles. Joshua felt a surge of regret, a sadness, tinged with relief that his own son would never know the misery of pauperdom. There were so many deprived of food and shelter with neither family nor friend, deprived of all, even hope. He would have a word with Ossie, see if the boy might be judiciously helped in some way. At least given food and shelter. The boy was slow mentally, yet how much was owed to deprivation, the cruelty of neglect and abandonment, he could not be sure. Would it be harder to suffer, unknowing, or to feel the added keenness of pain at being aware? It was an enigma designed to confuse Solomon himself, much less a parish constable; a paradox that Robert Knight, as clergyman and justice, would find hard to resolve or even to explain. Strangely disturbed, Joshua set the grey firmly upon the highway to the Crown Inn.

To his disappointment, Ossie, the little bow-legged ostler to the inn, was nowhere to be seen in the stable yard, and he delivered the grey into the hands of a willing stable-lad, eager to have care of so fine a mount. Within the inn Joshua had to run the gauntlet of those anxious to thank him for their bounty of free ale, or eager to return the favour. Indeed, as he protested good-naturedly, were he to accept all such generous offers he would scarce be able to sit astride a horse and ensure his own safety, much less that of the three hamlets! Congratulations, mild ribbing and jocular forecasts had to be entertained and replied to, and it was only after individually greeting all those present that he was finally able to extricate himself, without offence, and go in search of Tom Butler, the landlord.

It was Phoebe Butler, the landlord's wife, who he first came across when in the small private parlour at the rear of the inn. Her plump, normally placid, face was creased in vexation, hair awry under her lace-trimmed house bonnet, and she seemed in the greatest agitation. 'Oh, Constable Stradling, sir!' she arose, flustered, 'you have come about the babe?' She twisted her hands nervously. ''Tis the greatest worry, I have scarce slept a wink! But you will already know the burden of it, and can best advise.'

Joshua, seeking only to calm her, gently took her arm and led her, still protesting, back to her chair at the fire, begging her to be seated and not to alarm herself further. 'I know nothing, ma'am,' he confessed when she was safely seated, 'save that Tom sent for me urgently.'

'Nothing? Nothing at all?' she demanded, muttering help-lessly. 'Where best to begin then?'

'If you will begin at the beginning,' he suggested practically. 'Give me the barest details.' As she once more became flushed and agitated, he continued calmly,' I beg that you will take your time, ma'am, and not distress yourself unfairly, for it will serve no purpose.'

''Tis the babe,' she blurted.

'Joseph? Your grandson?' he asked sharply.

'No . . . 'Twas left upon the cobbles of the yard, do you see? In darkness and with naught to warm or succour it. 'Twas a mercy that Ossie was not abed, but tending a sick horse, for he caught glimpse of it in the light of his lantern. It would surely have perished else.'

'Some foundling, then? A child abandoned to paupery?'

'No!' Phoebe's denial was emphatic. 'No foundling, Joshua, of that I am sure. But whether left from choice or misfortune.' She broke off, awkwardly wiping her mouth with the palm of her hand. 'I would keep the child gladly, but there is Joseph and the work of the inn and all.'

'The child,' he said gently. 'A boy child or a girl? And what age do you suppose? Newborn, or older?'

'A girl. Not newborn, but scarcely weaned. Six months or thereabouts . . . I can but guess.'

'Neglected? Ill-used?'

'No! Thank God. For that would have been past all bearing!' she exclaimed fervently. 'No, that is the strangeness of it, Joshua, the mystery.' Joshua waited in silence as she broke out impassionedly, 'I can make no sense of it! It has neither rhyme nor reason. I would have sent for a wet nurse, to the village, you understand?'

'A wet nurse?' Joshua echoed stupidly.

'Yes . . . but as I say, the child was already weaned, too soon, do you see? Much too soon. 'Tis not natural, not the right way of things, leastwise not with humble folk!'

Joshua was at a complete loss.

''Tis my opinion,' Phoebe continued, 'that such early weaning was deliberate, served some purpose. Yet I am at a loss to know what, or why. There is but one thing of which I am certain, sure' she maintained stoutly.

'And that?'

'That I have never seen a child so handsomely dressed. No, not in all my born days. 'Twould put a princess to shame and that is a fact that none could deny! Whoever the child may be, Joshua, she is not of common stock. She is high born. From some noble family, like as not.' Phoebe's gentle brown eyes filled with sudden tears and her wide mouth trembled as she confessed painfully, 'There will be some poor soul

35

bitterly grieving, you may depend upon it, as I have cause to know, losing our Bella in childbirth and all, and still raw with the hurt of it. With Joseph motherless,' she broke off expressively. 'He is both joy and comfort, Joshua, do not doubt it, and I would keep him by me for Reuben's sake, him being always at sea and not able to care for the child. But Tom and I are old, Joshua. We grow tired.' She pulled herself together with an effort to say briskly, 'But you will want to see the babe. And decide what is best to be done.' She scrambled up awkwardly, admitting, ''Twould break my heart to send her to a foundling home, for she is a pretty, gentle-natured thing, sweetly contented, despite all. If there is some other way? Tom and I are not lacking in pence. We would count it a Christian duty to help.'

'I will do what I can,' Joshua promised with honesty. 'The Poor Laws are strict and it will lie with the justice to decide.'

'Well, he is an honest man,' Phoebe conceded with fairness, 'but he is ruled by his head, not his heart, and children do not live by bread and discipline alone, they exist merely. 'Tis affection that makes them grow, Joshua, that and the knowledge that they are valued for themselves alone and not what pence their labour brings to the poorhouse.'

Joshua followed her up the rickety wooden staircase to a small room upon the upper landing where, supervised by a pinched, anxious-eyed little serving girl, Joseph sat upon a mat before the fire, building a wooden tower of blocks. The serving girl scrambled to her feet, all embarrassed clumsiness, scarce able to speak for shyness at seeing Joshua. Joseph, however, boldly ran to take his hand, knocking the blocks aside in his childish eagerness, and drew Joshua towards a small cradle in the corner of the room. Joseph's gait was unsteady, but his excitement plain. 'See!' he exclaimed triumphantly. 'See!'

The child within stared at Joshua solemnly, then reached out her arms to him trustingly, crowing with expectant delight. She was so exquisite a child, so gently appealing with her pale skin and eyes of clearest cornflower blue, with the soft thistledown fine hair escaping her lace-edged bonnet, that Joshua could only stare at her in astonishment. He kept firm hold of Joseph, but stretched out a tentative hand towards the cradle, and the infant's small fist closed over his finger, gently

36

possessive. Phoebe saw that Joshua could not bear to wrench himself free; that he was wholly captivated. She watched him study the tiny, starfish hands, enchanting in their perfection, and the pity and tenderness that rose within him could not be hidden.

'I will do what I can,' he repeated, voice low.' I will find out from whence she came and why she was brought here. You have my solemn oath upon it, Phoebe! She shall not be taken to the poorhouse, not while I still have voice to persuade the justice and strength to rebut all others.'

There was confused shouting from below, a harsh crying out and the urgent banging of doors, with tread of heavy-booted footsteps upon the wooden stairs.

'Joshua!' Tom Butler's florid face was ugly with shock. ''Tis Elwyn Morris come from the Port. There has been some tragedy at the breakwater. A drowning . . .'

'Dear Heaven!' Phoebe gathered Joseph protectively to her and crossed herself devoutly, demanding anxiously, 'a fisherman, Tom? One of our own?'

'No, a young maid by all accounts, one unknown. Elwyn Morris could not rightly fetch her, for she is wedged fast within the rocks. He has come seeking help.'

'Then I will come at once.' Joshua was already moving purposefully towards the staircase, all else forgotten. He paused. 'You will bring ropes and grappling irons, Tom, should they be needed?'

'Aye. It is all arranged. I will see that the cart is harnessed, and manned, Joshua. You had best ride ahead with Morris. Oh, but he is in a rare taking and no mistake, trembling, and all but sick with shock and distress. Yet I could not persuade him to rest awhile nor take a strong draught to stiffen him.'

They clattered down the stairs swiftly and with no word spoken until Joshua stood facing Tom Butler upon the stone-flagged floor. 'There is no possibility that the girl still lives, Tom? That Morris might be mistaken – ' He broke off clumsily, knowing how foolish he sounded.

'He would not be mistaken.' There was absolute conviction in Tom Butler's voice.

From the stairs Phoebe Butler listened unseen, a sickness of fear rising within her as they hurried away. Was the babe upstairs to know further tragedy, she wondered? The burden of suicide? What grief and despair had driven the poor creature to abandon the child? What torment? She knew, even without proof, that the dead woman and the child were inextricably bound. Tom, her husband, would call it womanly nonsense. A foolishness. How could she abandon so innocently vulnerable a child, whatever fears beset her? Phoebe could not even begin to guess what violence had driven her. She could only pray, now, for the repose of the poor creature's soul. It was the child who mattered.

Chapter Four

Joshua, uneasily reining the grey alongside Elwyn Morris's simple, flat-bottomed cart, could not relish the macabre task which lay before him. His work as constable demanded that he be firmly in command, a man of authority and purpose. Yet, try as he might, he could never become reconciled to the finality of death, whether through the violence of another or self-inflicted. The waste and futility of it grieved him. Whatever its value, a life was all we have. To rob oneself, or another, of it seemed to him the ultimate betrayal.

He glanced towards Elwyn Morris upon the cart and saw by the intensity with which he gripped the reins how the finding of the body had unnerved him. Morris's lean, intelligent face still bore its ingaining of coal-dust from his work as haulier upon the horse-drawn tramway. His workaday clothing was as dirt-grimed and from the frayed cuffs of his jacket his bony wrists protruded, thin and fragile as the wrists of a child. Yet, notwithstanding the filth of his labour, there was about him a natural dignity. When he looked up at Joshua it was to say regretfully, 'I did not like leaving her there, Mr Stradling, although I knew that she was dead and I could do naught to help her.'

'You did right to inform me,' Joshua reassured.

'It was my first thought, sir.' He paused before adding with rough honesty, 'Yet, to my shame, I feared to call upon any other at the Port lest they think me in some way to blame. I am not proud of it.' Under its smearing of coal-dust, only the whites of his eyes gleamed bright and the moist flesh of his lips and teeth.

Joshua said, to case his mind, 'None could suspect you of involvement. You are known for your honesty. There is not another man in all the hamlets who would have given evidence against the wreckers, knowing the risk to his own life and those of his family.'

'I thank you for that, sir,' Elwyn Morris said, and turned the cart towards the wild acres of dunes and rock-strewn common land that bordered the sea. Joshua saw the grey raise its head, nostrils flaring wide, as it sniffed the salt-laden wind. The smell of iodine, salt and wet sand were a sharpness upon the air and above the rocking of the cart he could hear the wild cries of the gulls and the subdued suck of the tide, its ceaseless ebb and flow.

'It is not much further, sir, but the tide is on the turn and we cannot easily reach the place from the bay, for the flow is too treacherous. The cart would be bogged down in the wet sand.' Joshua nodded agreement as Morris continued earnestly, 'It would set lives and horses at risk. The race is oftimes violent and the rocks and deep trench across the bay hidden from view. We shall have but ten or fifteen minutes at most before – ' He broke off, saying, shamefacedly, ''Tis you are in charge, sir, I beg you will forgive me my forwardness. It was sight of that young girl.' His face was ugly with the remembrance of what he had seen; a stiff mask of tragedy. Joshua could not repress the thought that it was not Morris's blackened face that he saw, but the dead girl's; bruised, agonised, made ugly by the tug of the sea.

He heard the steady pounding of the hooves of the horses and the rattle and creak of Tom Butler's cart not far behind, with the jangle of harness and the cries of the men. They had brought the cart to rest upon the salt-cropped turf of the common lands and swiftly, and in near silence, unloaded the ropes and tackle from the boards. Almost before they had halted, the harbour master, Captain Ayde-Buchan, well liked by Joshua from past dealings, was beside them, all keen energy and naval exactness. At Joshua's request he had firmly cleared from the breakwater all save those who would be of assistance; men well used to the securing of vessels at the quayside, sturdy and reliable and responsive to command. It was they who had secured the ropes to the bollards and who, with the more agile from among Tom Butler's crew, had descended the massive, rough hewn stones to the rocks beneath.

Joshua, precluded from taking active part on account of

40

his height and build, and with Tom Butler and Elwyn Morris standing awkwardly beside him, watched with increasing anxiety the feverish activity below. The race of the tide was fiercely unpredictable and so swift that, almost without warning, the men might have been dragged into the swirl of the current, held fast by the undertow, then swept out to sea. The south-westerly wind cut like a knife, coldly lacerating, so that exposed hands grew numbed and useless and clothing sodden and heavy. Buffeted by sea wind, lashed by spray, they set themselves against the greater violence of the sea, and Joshua and those upon the breakwater were fearful that the living might be sacrificed with the dead. They had neither escape nor shelter, exposed as they were upon the tempestuous seaward side of the breakwater, their efforts slowed by jagged rocks, made treacherous now by seaweed and slime. Over all lay the sickening urgency to free the dead girl, that she might be hauled ashore before the relentless rush of the tide claimed them and her.

It had been a hard and gruesome task, fraught with danger for those who toiled, and as charged with anxiety for those who watched and waited. When all was completed and the volunteers safely ashore, they could scarcely speak or stand for cold and exhaustion. Joshua, in thanking them and all others who had helped recover the body, urged that they go at once to the Ship Aground tavern at the Port, to warm and refresh themselves with ale at the parish's expense. He had no qualms about the justice being amenable, indeed Robert Knight would have insisted upon it, had he been witness. Even the local vestrymen, who were notoriously tight-fisted, could scarcely cavil at such well-deserved reward. Joshua, with reluctance, turned his attention to the corpse, the poor human remains of the girl. She had been in the water a day at most, he thought, yet the depredations of drowning, sea creatures and predatory birds had wrought savagery. He tried, in vain, to think of her as an anonymous, lifeless thing, a feelingless husk. Yet he was unable, for all he saw was the warm vitality of Rebecca, his wife, in vibrant joyousness in living and could have wept for the waste of it, the ugliness of a life cut short.

'One never grows used to it,' The quiet voice was Ayde-Buchan's. 'Death I mean. It is always shocking, a reminder of one's own brief mortality. The sea is always cruel.'

'Yet not so cruel as men, perhaps?' Tom Butler's bluff good-natured face was wry as he stamped his boots for warmth.

'No. The sea gives up its dead, its secrets. It does not keep them hid'. The harbour master's glance lingered upon the huddled shape beneath the covering of tarpaulin, then turned enquiringly upon Joshua. 'Was there some sign of violence, Constable Stradling? Other than that from the sea itself?' I ask not from idle curiosity but because, when the news gets abroad, as it must, it would be better to quell rumour with fact. There will be malice and speculation enough.'

Joshua nodded, saying with awkwardness, 'I asked those who helped to free the girl and bring her ashore to search for evidence, some clue, anything, however trivial, which might give some lead.'

'And there was nothing?'

'It seems not. Yet, I was not sanguine,' he confessed, 'expected little, or perhaps too much,' he admitted, shame-faced,' of them, I mean. They were set at risk enough, doing what had to be done.'

Ayde-Buchan looked at him keenly, intelligent eyes missing nothing of Joshua's turmoil and self-doubt. 'Their recovery of the body was an end to their labours,' he said briskly. 'Yours begin. Who is to say which will prove the harder task, Mr Stradling? Or the more gruelling?'

Tom Butler fidgetted in his boots before declaring stoutly, "Tis my opinion that Dr Mansel's will, for he is Home Office pathologist. I thank God devoutly that I am merely landlord of the Crown and need carve no more than pies and home-cured hams. Each man to his craft or trade, and be grateful for it!'

Joshua and Ayde-Buchan knew that it was not from callousness that he spoke, but to lighten the horror of the drowning and to set them at ease.

'Come, man!' Butler commanded Elwyn Morris brusquely. 'Let us help carry the poor creature to my cart, for it is all we may do for her now.' As Morris and those few who had remained made to assist him, he said gruffly, 'There will be room for you upon the haulier's cart, unless you would choose to return on mine. There will be ale and victuals for you at the Crown, for you are deserving of it. You may eat and drink your fill.' He turned to Joshua, demanding tersely, 'Would you have me deliver the body to Dr Mansel's house upon Clevis Hill?'

'If you please' Joshua said gratefully. 'And I shall ride ahead on the grey, give warning of your coming.'

As the grisly work of placing the cadaver upon Tom Butler's cart was being completed and the men took their places upon Morris's dusty cart, Ayde-Buchan said carefully, 'She seemed a . . . presentable young woman, Stradling, appealing in features and dress. Not a gentlewoman, nor yet a fishwife or whore upon the docks . . . a common trull. I'll own it puzzles me.'

From some ship, perhaps?'

'Unlikely. Else why should she disembark here, only to kill herself?'

'Or be murdered by someone? Someone lying in wait,' Joshua hazarded. 'Someone, perhaps, afraid of what her coming might bring.' He broke off, to say ruefully, 'I fear that it is the idlest speculation. We had best deliver her to Dr Mansel, await *his* verdict, for there might be no mystery at all.'

Ayde-Buchan murmured grudging assent, then exclaimed vehemently, 'No, dammit! That will not serve at all! Enquiries are best made when the trail is fresh, not grown cold. I shall make judicious enquiries, discreetly of course. Learn whatever I may from the sailors and labourers upon the docks. If there is some innocent reason for her death, a fall, or tragic accident, then it will be merely time wasted.' As Joshua thanked him, he added with quick abrasiveness, before he turned away, 'Better time wasted than a life, Constable. A life ended almost before it began.'

Joshua, riding the grey through the pillared gateway to Dr Mansel's imposing house upon the Clevis Hill, felt an unusual melancholy; a deep compassion for the dead girl. It derived in part from his love for Rebecca and his newborn son. As Ayde-Buchan had been at pains to point out, sudden, violent death is a salutary reminder of one's own fragile mortality. The dead girl had been much of an age with Rebecca, yet had lacked her vividness of colouring. In the drowned girl, Rebecca's sloe-black hair and arrestingly blue eyes had been muted and restrained, as if all colour had been drained out of them with the draining of life. Joshua thought that even in death, Rebecca's chiselled perfection of bone and voluptuousness of colouring would remain undiminished. He tried to throw off the mood of pessimism which engulfed him, but could not. With Phoebe Butler, he was convinced that the child at the Crown Inn and the finding of the unknown drowned girl were inexorably linked. As the grey's hooves skittered along the small stones of the carriageway, Joshua tried to compose himself to give an explanation to Mansel, to prepare him for the arrival of the corpse. All about him the manicured lawns, the incised and meticulously planted flower beds, the classical symmetry of statues and shrubs, spoke of the physician's precision of mind, his orderliness. Yet in the far rose garden the Bourbon, damask and moss roses, fading now but richly full blown, straddled grey stone walls and arches with determined waywardness. Exotic, richly perfumed. Profligate. Upon the earth their heaped petals and fragrance lingered and died.

'Constable Stradling? Joshua?' Obadiah Mansel had materialised beside him as if, in thinking about him, Joshua had unwittingly conjured him from the air. The physician's plumply rounded face was anxiously creased, opaque eyes concerned, as he demanded, 'It is not Rebecca or the child?'

'No. They are well. I come upon a matter of business, sir. A death.'

Mansel sighed, thrusting the pruning knife he held into the pocket of his coat, and saying reluctantly, 'I had best postpone my attack upon the roses,' adding with irony, 'I shall doubtless be expected to set my skills to a less fragrant purpose.' When Joshua did not reply, Mansel cleared his throat, asking sharply, 'It is not some villager? Someone known to me?'

'No, sir. A young girl, unknown, found drowned upon the seaward side of the breakwater.'

Mansel grunted, demanding sceptically, 'So that is your considered opinion, Constable? Your careful conclusion?' It

44

was a ritual that Joshua had grown to accept without acrimony or resentment, for it was the nearest that the physician ever came to humour, a humour as obtuse and heavy-handed as he. 'Well?' Mansel persisted abrasively, 'You say she was drowned?'

'A slip of the tongue,' Joshua conceded placidly.

'You are lucky, sir, that your occupation allows of such slips. As pathologist, my own is more precise and demanding!'

'But you have the advantage of me, sir, in that your . . . clients . . . are not in a position to make complaint!' Joshua reminded.

Mansel's face was wreathed in smiles, his laughter a sharp, dry bark. 'Yes,' he said. 'You do well to remind me. But I had best go within, make preparation.' His pale, boiled-gooseberry eyes twinkled with gentle malice as he asked with seeming negligence, 'Will you not accompany me within, Constable? Stay with me for the post mortem examination. It will be a valuable insight and experience. I would appreciate some objective advice.'

'I thank you, Dr Mansel, but I fear that I would be more hindrance than help since, as you so rightly point out, I have already come to a false and unsupported conclusion.' Joshua found himself guiltily repeating Tom Butler's words, 'Each man to his trade or craft.'

'Indeed,' Mansel approved in amusement. He paused to ask with an abrupt change of manner, 'But is there something I should know of the girl, Joshua? Something you would have me check upon? Something you might suspect?'

Joshua said carefully, 'There was a child abandoned at the Crown Inn last night, a babe, a girl child. Phoebe Butler puts the infant's age at some six months or so.'

'Abandoned, you say? By whom?'

'That I cannot say, sir.'

This child, would you have me see her? Make examination?' he asked gruffly. 'It were better done before she enters the foundling home. I will have just cause, then, to visit her, should the need arise.' He sniffed audibly, awaiting Joshua's reply, and pretending indifference.

'That would be a kindness, sir.'

'Kindness?' he repeated with acerbity, 'not kindness, merely an attempt to . . . what was the phrase . . . to follow "my trade or craft"!'

Joshua smiled, 'Then I had best be about mine, Dr Mansel, for I have urgent explanation to make to Robert Knight.'

'You will, perhaps, find him . . . a little discomposed. Abrasive, even,' Mansel goaded slyly. 'He declares himself a martyr to gout, although I would beg leave to query the description. I know, for I attended him at Tythegston Court but yesterday. Still, as you say, Constable, each to his trade or craft . . . or chosen vocation!' He turned and walked away, shoulders lifted, jaunty with self-satisfaction.

Joshua did not grudge him his small victory, much less the task ahead. He remounted the grey and rode back along the carriageway, still amused by the encounter. Immediately without the gates he heard the unmistakable sound of Tom Butler's old cart, its familiar creak and groan. Joshua's brief amusement vanished. As if fearful of the encounter, he turned his mount determinedly towards the open highway and the justice's house. Better the live justice, martyred or not, than the uneasy dead. It was only her silence that he would have wished upon Robert Knight. The ludicrousness of the thought made him smile again.

As he rode through the griffon-topped pillars of the court, Joshua was silently rehearsing what he would say to the justice. He had little enough to impart to him in all conscience! The body of an unknown girl, the cause of her death not yet established, as Mansel had reminded him. He delivered the grey into the hands of a deferential groom who had emerged from the stables and knocked upon the solidly imposing door; a door, he thought wryly, to reflect the justice's own unassailable position as squire, rector and justice to the three hamlets.

The door was opened by Leyshon, the justice's aged manservant, with whom Joshua was a particular favourite, serving as they did the same demanding and infuriatingly exacting master. Leyshon's seamed face lightened at sight of the visitor and he reverently took the constable's ornate helmet and set it upon a liveried servant's hall chair.

'The justice is well, Leyshon?'

Leyshon raised his eyes expressively heavenwards.

'Do not stand there wittering, Stradling!' the justice called out irritably. 'If you have come to enquire as to my health then have the common courtesy to ask *me*. Come to the fountain, not the vessel!'

Leyshon gave a dry smile, shaking his head indulgently, to murmur so low that only Joshua might hear, 'The justice has lost none of his vigour, sir, but is a mite lacking in patience.'

'Then you have virtue enough for two, Leyshon.'

Leyshon chuckled his appreciation as Robert Knight cried out petulantly, 'It seems, Stradling, that you have a rare gift for amusing my household servants. It is to be hoped that you may provide the same diversion for me.'

Joshua might have begged leave to doubt it.

'Well?' the justice demanded when Joshua entered the library where he was ensconced in a stout, wing-sided chair. 'Well?' he repeated ungraciously, 'what aberration or calamity brings you here? I am to take it that this is no mere social visit?'

'No, sir. A matter of business.' Joshua tried stoically not to let his gaze dwell upon the justice's engorged and mummified foot resting ostentatiously upon a footstool, but it was difficult to ignore.

'What business, Stradling?' he asked suspiciously. 'Something that you are unwilling to resolve for yourself?'

'A death, sir.'

'A death?' His air of long suffering languor died away to be replaced by a lively intelligence. 'A suspicious death?'

'Yes, sir. A drowning at the Port – the breakwater.'

'One of my parishioners?' he asked sharply.

'No, sir, a young woman unknown to me. A stranger to the three hamlets.'

'You have informed Mansel, as Home Office pathologist?'

'I have, sir, and had the body delivered to his house.'

'Good! Good!' he relapsed momentarily into moroseness, only to take off his gold-rimmed eye-glasses and tap them absent-mindedly upon the gadroon-topped wine table beside his chair. 'You fear that some crime has been committed, then?' His protuberant eyes were alert with intelligent interest.

'I think it possible, sir.' Joshua told him all that had

occurred, omitting not the slightest detail and including the discovery of the child at the Crown Inn.

The justice considered the facts for a few moments in silence before saying brusquely, 'You have contacted the relieving officer to the poor? Asked that the child be taken into the foundling home at Bridgend?'

'No, sir.'

No, sir?' he echoed querulously, 'and why not, may I ask. It is your statutory duty to do so.'

'Mrs Butler begged leave to keep the child awhile, to help to pay for its keep.'

'Fiddlesticks!' Robert Knight exclaimed so violently that he jerked his gouty foot, crying aloud at the pain of it, then subsiding shamefaced. 'There are channels, Stradling,' he chided impatiently. 'Regulations, officially approved and laid down. It ill behoves you as so called upholder of the law to blatantly defy them, to let sentiment cloud reasoned judgement. The child must be delivered at once to those whose responsibility is properly to care for it, to bring it up in Christian charity, with discipline . . .'

Joshua, notwithstanding the justice's heightened irritation, skilfully tried another tack, asking innocently, 'You would have me contact Mr Littlepage, sir? The workmaster at the poorhouse? To seek his advice?'

'Littlepage?' Robert Knight exclaimed scathingly. 'The man is a humbug, a charlatan! Advice, you say? What advice? The creature is a nincompoop! I would not allow him to care for my hounds, much less a child.' Agitation had caused him to start so violently that his face was drawn with pain, an agony so intense that, for a moment, it rendered him speechless. 'Very well, Stradling,' he conceded when he was finally in command of himself again. 'Against my principles and better judgement I will allow a brief interlude, a hiatus in which other arrangements may be made by Mrs Butler at the Crown Inn. This is not to be taken as a precedent, a sign that my heart is more tender than my head.'

His dark eyes twinkled as he erupted into irrepressible laughter, dark jowls shaking. 'Hell and damnation, Joshua! You know well enough what I meant. This confounded gout affects not only my foot, but my brain!' he exclaimed. 'What would you say to a glass of cognac?'

'I would say thank you, sir' Joshua answered straight-faced.

'And so, my boy, would I,' declared Robert Knight emphatically. 'Will you be so good, sir, as to tug the bell-pull to summon Leyshon. I am scarce in a position to do so.' But Leyshon was already at the door, bringing in both cognac and Madeira wine, glasses, and some of his master's finest cigars.

'I thought, sir,' he ventured hesitantly, 'that in view of Mr Stradling's good fortune . . . by way of celebration?'

'Quite so, Leyshon,' Robert Knight said expansively. 'I cannot but approve initiative.' He had replaced his eye-glasses and looked at Joshua speculatively over the rims of them.' Yet not too much of it,' he advised jocularly. 'Whether achieved by clever diversion, Constable, or guile, it makes no matter. It comes perilously close to insubordination. Do I make myself understood?'

'Perfectly, sir.'

The justice nodded. 'To my godson, John Jeremiah Matthew Stradling,' he continued benignly, raising his glass and adding slyly, 'to whom I willingly offer the devotion of both a tender heart and a wiser head.'

Leyshon raised his eyebrows expressively at Joshua and Joshua looked respectfully at the justice and solemnly drank.

Upon leaving Tythegston Court in a more mellow humour than upon his arrival, Joshua would have ridden first to the undertaker's at Newton village to make funeral arrangements for the dead girl with the rapacious little undertaker, Ezra the Box. It was not a prospect to relish for there was a long-running feud between them, as Ezra's extra-mural activities were never strictly within the law. He was infamous for his parsimony. Joshua thought him as ill-mannered and odious a little creature as it was possible to meet, as spiteful and mean-minded as he was insensitive. Since there was no option but to employ him, it was well that his clients were dead. No one living would willingly have delivered himself into Ezra's cantankerous hands. As it was, he was spared any immediate encounter, for as he rode past the track that led to Stormy Downs he was intercepted by one of the pauper labourers from a smallholding isolated and set high in the windswept hills beyond. There had been a dispute, it seemed, over boundaries and the ownership of sheep, and neighbours had erupted, first into argument, then savage blows. The pauper, terrified lest the violence turn to murder, had ridden out in agitation to seek Joshua's aid.

The settling of the dispute had been bitterly protracted, with the acrimony and resentment between the protagonists spilling upon Joshua himself. Finally, good sense and fear of being taken bodily before the justice had triumphed and a grudging truce declared. With order restored, Joshua had been cordially invited to take refreshment and was showered with congratulations upon the birth of his son. There had been small gifts of new-laid eggs and homemade cordials for Rebecca which it would have been churlish to refuse, for they were kindly meant. He had the greatest difficulty in extricating himself from the warmth of their hospitality, for each vied with the other in generosity. When he was finally seated upon the grey, saddlebags bulging with largesse, he took his leave. He could not resist a smile, for they waved him off in the most cheerful good humour, sated with ale, their swollen faces, closed eyes and split lips the only visible signs of discord.

When he reached Clevis Hill, Joshua rode not towards Newton village but through the pillars of Dr Mansel's house. The physician, his work upon the dead girl completed, greeted him with obvious pleasure. Mansel was restored to his usual high-starched neatness, fly-away hair tamed, the skin of his hands pinkly scrubbed. The intelligent, opaque green eyes regarded Joshua steadily.

'You have something of importance to tell me, sir? Something relating to the dead girl?'

'Facts, Stradling, I deal in facts.'

'And the facts, Dr Mansel?'

'First, she did not die of drowning. There was no water in the lungs.'

'Then she . . .?'

'She died from a stab wound. A single blow that pierced the heart.'

'Then it is a murderer I seek.' Joshua rose from his chair, unable to control his agitation.

'That is not all, 'Mansel continued firmly. 'You will need to search elsewhere for clues to the child.' As Joshua stared uncomprehendingly, he confirmed, 'The young woman has never given birth to a child.'

Chapter Five

Joshua had hoped to keep news of the unknown girl's death and the abandoned child from Rebecca for a while, knowing that it would distress her. With John's birth she seemed unusually vulnerable and occasionally tearful, and he had merely thought to spare her hurt. He had reckoned without the natural curiosity of the villagers and their close-knit intimacy. They were, as Sophie Fleet declared, like one great family, spread wider perhaps, yet close kin. What affected one affected all. The news of the tragedy at the breakwater and the plight of the babe left in the stable yard of the Crown Inn was confided to Rebecca even before he had left Dr Mansel's house upon the Clevis Hill.

Sophie, who had received news of the drowning from Jeremiah, and of the babe directly from Phoebe Butler, had wisely kept it from Rebecca, reasoning, as Joshua had, that it would serve no purpose save to distress her. It was a chance visitor, Rebecca's close friend, Rosa Doonan, who had unwittingly blurted it out having, Sophie declared forcefully, 'More use from her tongue than her head!'

Rosa, an affectionate, sweet-natured girl, had praised John Jeremiah so lavishly, and with such genuine delight and envy, that Rebecca felt quite light-headed at achieving such a miracle. Rosa, delicately pretty as her name, with her extraordinarily translucent skin and abundant pale hair, could scarce be persuaded upon to set the baby down in his cradle. She was totally enchanted with him, wishing always to touch him and hold him close, as if he were too fragile and precious to leave.

'Oh, Rebecca!' her pretty face was flushed with admiration. 'He is the dearest, sweetest babe . . . a darling! I'll own that I am vastly jealous. I would give all I own to have such a perfect treasure.' The words were lightly spoken, her smile bright, yet Rebecca sensed a painful yearning, a discontent.

'You and Doonan will soon enough have a house full of infants! You will scarce know what to do with your time.'

'Cavan is as eager and unhappy as I . . . for we have been wed all but two years and . . .' she faltered, biting hard at her lip.' 'Tis worse for Cavan,' she blurted, 'being a man and all, for he bears the sharp edge of the quarrymen's humour, their endless teasing. 'Tis his manhood they hold in question. He will not openly say so, but I know it grieves him raw.'

'Cavan? They make sport of Cavan? I can scarcely credit it, Rosa!' Rebecca was genuinely distressed, for the powerful, gentle-hearted Irishman was a great favourite with her and with Joshua.

Rosa's pale blue eyes were washed with vicarious tears as she exclaimed heatedly, 'Oh, but it is downright cruel to see him humiliated so, Rebecca. And he will not retaliate, for he knows that violence will serve only to show that their goading has struck its mark . . .'

'What will you do, Rosa?' Rebecca asked anxiously.

Rosa shook her head and fiercely tried to brush away the tears which had spilled onto her cheeks, 'I have told him 'tis best to ignore such jibes, for they are not worth the aggravation, not worth dwelling upon.' She hesitated, 'There is but one way, Rebecca, and for it I must beg your cooperation and Joshua's too . . . and have your solemn promise that whatever I ask you will never be told to Cavan.'

Rebecca, puzzled, agreed quickly, 'But, of course . . . I shall help in any way I can. You have my word upon it although I cannot see – ' She broke off in confusion.

'There is a young babe at the Crown Inn, Rebecca.'

'Joseph, you mean? Reuben Butler's son?'

'No, a babe of some six months or so, a girl child without known home or kin. It is thought that her mother abandoned her and may have taken her own life.'

'Dear heaven, Rosa!' Rebecca had paled with shock and pity. 'But where? How?'

'By throwing herself from the breakwater. Drowning herself, 'tis feared.'

'What would you have me do?' Rebecca was all solicitude.

'If you would ask Joshua to beg, as a favour, that Cavan and I take the child in. It will be sent as a pauper-babe to the poorhouse else, for Phoebe cannot raise both Joseph and another.' Rosa was actively pleading now, her desperation plain. 'Please, Rebecca, I beg of you, will you let Joshua plead with the justice? Will you ask him to speak out as to my character and such?'

'But the justice thinks highly of you, Rosa, and of Cavan, too. You are your own best advocates.'

'But that is the whole point of it, Rebecca, Cavan must not know that I have spoken. It would grieve him sore. We cannot plead with the justice for fear he might be refused. It would belittle him the more. Yet, if the justice or Joshua ask his help and mine, he will not refuse, although he will pretend it a burden. You understand?'

'I understand, my dear. Joshua will speak for you. You have my promise. Now, do not cry more for you will have me weeping with you.' She embraced Rosa and they clung together in understanding, laughing and crying shamefacedly both. Then, 'You will not . . . feel the anguish too keenly, Rosa,' Rebecca probed anxiously, 'should the child one day be claimed?'

'I have thought of it,' Rosa admitted gravely. 'Indeed, Rebecca, I have thought of little else since Phoebe first gave me news of the babe. It has been torment and vexation, for I could speak of it to none save you.'

'And your decision?' Rebecca's face was as strained as Rosa's own as she awaited answer.

Rosa hesitated only briefly, then said, 'It is better that I suffer than the child, if need arises, for I shall be stronger to bear the hurt. It is kinder that she has a loving home and those to care for her, whatever comes.'

Rebecca hugged her friend, saying with honesty, 'She will have that, my dear, with you and Cavan, and will be happy and well blessed.'

'As I, Rebecca, and Cavan, too,' Rosa reminded. 'It will be for our sakes as well as hers that I make offer. She will be needed and loved.'

Rebecca nodded, glancing with protective tenderness towards the crib where John Jeremiah lay, and wondered if she could feel such selfless, all-devouring love for another's child as she felt now for her son. She could find no answer within herself but hoped that, like Rosa, she would show faith and courage enough. 'Come, my dear,' she said briskly to hide her compassion. 'You must choose whatever is needed for your daughter from John's layette, for people have been so generous-hearted. Were he to wear fresh clothing every minute of the day and night until he outgrows them, he could never wear them all!' Then, sensitive to Rosa's fears, she added, 'I shall not send them to your cottage until the babe is yours. Cavan will know nothing of my involvement or Joshua's, I swear it, and think them the gift of a loving friend, and given as affectionately and wholeheartedly as they were offered to me. He will not deny them?' she asked anxiously.

'No, he will not deny them.'

'And he will not deny you the child?'

'No,' Rosa said with certainty. 'Cavan is a proud man. He would accept neither pity nor charity, for that is his way, nor would he lay his sadness raw. But he loves me and will take the child. More, he will never think of her as other than our own.' She kissed Rebecca with affection, and with one last gentle word and caress for the sleeping child in the crib was gone.

Rebecca, despite her promise to help her friend, was not easy in her mind. She was certain that Rosa and Cavan would care for the child devotedly and save it from the wretchedness of paupery, the aridness of life in the poorhouse. She could not altogether say why she was not wholly in favour, perhaps because she could not contemplate a future in which John did not share, a future in which she might be denied him. It was a cruelty that Rosa and Cavan might well have to face. Their love for the babe would be no protection. Rosa's confident words came back to Rebecca. 'He will never think of her as other than our own.' That might be blessing or disaster. Rebecca felt a chill of foreboding and moved instinctively towards the fire. Yet the coldness remained and not all the remembered warmth of Joshua's love or the birth of her son could ease it.

Joshua had left Dr Mansel's house in a turmoil of indecision and self-doubt. He had been foolish to suppose that the dead girl and the abandoned child at the Crown Inn were related.

He had, as Mansel rightly accused, leapt stupidly to that conclusion. Suspicion and circumstance were poor substitute for fact and he had been guilty of tailoring the little evidence available to suit his own theory. He felt shamed by his lack of professionalism and Mansel, seeing his real distress, had tried to ameliorate it by saying gruffly:

'My own work is, of necessity, exact, a scientific examination based upon certainties. Fixed. Immutable. The parameters set by others . . .'

'Then I should have based my own upon them,' Joshua admitted, shamefaced, unable to hide his dejection.

Mansel's wispy, fly-away eyebrows lifted over the pale eyes as he said wryly, 'As you once so pertinently reminded me, Joshua, I am able to bury my mistakes. It gives more comfort than agonising over them!' He smiled his rare disarming smile before admitting unexpectedly, 'I fear that dealing in absolutes has its disadvantages, it makes one inflexible, intolerant even, unwilling or unable to extend the scope of one's thinking. It would be a disaster were you to become so hidebound.' As Joshua looked at him keenly, Mansel continued, 'Your own explorations have a starting point but no more than that. It is not a predetermined journey with a single road. You do well to consider every probability, every possibility. There are twists and turnings upon the way.'

'And too many blind alleys!' Joshua interjected feelingly.

'Indeed,' agreed Mansel, smiling. 'But you at least have the satisfaction of making your own way, being responsible for all from start to finish. I see only the one small part of the landscape, Joshua.'

Joshua said with a rueful smile, 'And I had best ride out into it as far as Tythegston Court at least, to apprise the justice. I could wish him the same clarity of mind as you, sir! The same generosity of spirit!' The words were humorously spoken, but Mansel, seeing Joshua's tiredness and strain, said crisply:

'There is no need. I have written a report for the justice and will have it delivered at once. Would you have me send word to the undertaker, too? Ask him to keep the body until after the inquest? He is an odious, money-grubbing little reptile, but needs must when the devil drives!'

'I might appreciate even the devil himself to drive me,'

Joshua admitted wryly, 'so damnably lost and confused am I! But haggling with Ezra Evans is more punishment than I could safely bear.'

'Then I shall send word to him. Instruction.'

Joshua nodded his gratitude, saying with feeling, 'I could wish him as patiently uncomplaining as one of your corpses, Dr Mansel, and as amenable, too.'

'My dear Joshua!' Mansel exclaimed, mock-scandalised. 'Have I not clearly explained myself? I deal in realities. Facts, I lay no claim to divinity!' At Joshua's look of enquiry he said, 'I cannot work miracles!' With a rich chuckle and a reassuring touch to Joshua's arm he returned cheerfully within.

Joshua had been grateful to be relieved of both the necessity of returning to Tythegston Court and making arrangements with Ezra the Box for the disposition of the dead girl's body. He could only hope, for her sake and his own, that someone might come forward to claim her before the burial. The interment of a pauper or unknown was a meagre affair, and the local vestrymen both hard-headed and hard-hearted. They were loath to squander public funds upon outsiders and with so little to show for their expenditure. An earth-covered plot, unmarked and with the corpse buried uncoffined in a winding sheet was ostentation enough, without the added expense of hiring paupers to follow the coffin at a halfpenny a head. Those who wilfully took their own lives or were careless enough to be murdered were in no position to complain. It would have been better had they expired in their own parish and not become a charge upon the ratepayers.

Joshua was of a mind to return to Thatched Cottage to seek solace with Rebecca and John. The thought of his son still filled him with a warm glow of pride and achievement, a sense of wonderment. It was enough to set a man's paltry worries into proper perspective, to restore his faith in himself and humanity. It was in this spirit of optimism and Christian charity that he rode into Newton village.

'Constable, Constable Stradling, sir!'

In a moment Joshua's altruism was gone. 'Mr Evans?' his voice as he addressed the undertaker was coldly discouraging. 'A moment of your time, sir,' Ezra Evans's pinched, ferret face was ingratiating, his manner unctuous. ''Tis a matter

57

of some importance, sir.' He hovered indecisively upon the cobblestones as Joshua reluctantly dismounted. 'The shop, sir, into the shop.'

As Joshua hesitated, Dic Jenkins, Evans's pauper apprentice, hurried to take charge of the grey. He greeted Joshua deferentially, eyes downcast, and Joshua, to Ezra's impatience, stopped to have word with him. Joshua was fond of the ex-pauper, a conscientious, hard-working man, who bore Ezra's parsimony and ill-will with patient forbearance. Indeed, to Joshua's amazement, Dic Jenkins actually seemed to like his cantankerous employer, or at least to respect and admire him for his craft. Ezra was not only coffin-maker and undertaker, but carpenter to the hamlets, too. It was a constant source of wonder to Joshua that such a brash, insensitive creature could be so delicately skilled at carving wood.

'You fare well, Mr Jenkins?' Joshua asked solicitously.

'I do, sir. I do. Mr Evans is kindness itself, friend and mentor both.' His pale, lantern-jawed face lit up with excitement. 'He has something within.'

'Stop your blathering, man!' Ezra's voice was harsh. 'Attend to the constable's horse.' He was in a state of the greatest distress and agitation and Jenkins fell painfully silent as Joshua, seething with anger, was pushed unceremoniously indoors. Joshua was all set to flay Evans with the lash of his tongue, furious at his high-handed audacity, when Evans murmured with a mixture of humility and pride, ''Tis a showing, sir, an invite.'

'An invite?' Joshua echoed, stupidly at a loss.

Ezra fidgetted uncomfortably. 'A viewing, then.'

Dear Lord! Joshua thought, aghast. Mansel has already sent word to him. He is going to brazenly show me the coffins available, to beg me to see the dead girl decently buried! Surely even Evans could not be so devious and crass? The cold hostility must have shown on Joshua's face for Evans's excitement abruptly vanished and he looked so awkwardly uncertain and downcast that Joshua felt a twinge of shame.

'Well, Mr Evans?' he tried to infuse some cordiality into his tone. 'What is it that you need of me? Some discussion of the funeral arrangements for the girl drowned upon the shore? Some promise of extra payment?'

Ezra was clearly outraged, his small, pinched mouth becoming even more meanly compressed. He walked with painful dignity towards a cloth-covered shape in the centre of the shop, complaining aggrieved, 'You do me an injustice, sir. A grave injustice! It was never in my mind.'

'What then?' Joshua asked, discomfitted and set firmly in the wrong.

Ezra drew aside the cloth to reveal an exquisitely carved cradle of oak, the workmanship so finely executed that Joshua could not restrain a cry of admiration. Ezra's back was rigid with injured pride and he had bristled with undisguised resentment.

'Why, Mr Evans, it is a work of art!' Joshua exclaimed in genuine delight.

Ezra was not wholly appeased, but appeared mollified. ''Twas this I wished to show you, Constable.'

'You carved it, Mr Evans?'

'I did indeed, sir.'

'Why, it is the finest craftsmanship that I have seen.' Joshua lovingly traced the carved flowers and leaves upon it, fingers cherishing the soft patina of the wood, the exquisite symmetry of the design. It was perfect in every detail. 'You are an artist, sir, "he concluded with honesty," a true artist.'

Ezra's mean little ferret face grew flushed with delight. 'It was meant to be a secret, sir, a gift from the villagers to you and Mrs Stradling. Paid for willingly in pence and half-pence by each and every one, from the justice himself to Dic Jenkins there, my humble apprentice.'

'And not in pence alone,' Joshua felt constrained to say, 'but in time and skill, Mr Evans. You have given both most handsomely and I thank you for it. You have spared yourself nothing. It was a generous act.'

Ezra, awkward under such whole-hearted approval, shuffled self-consciously, feet scattering the curls of wood shavings and sawdust upon the floor. 'It was a viewing only,' he said, voice surly to hide his pleasure. 'No more than that, such as I would give to any client.'

'Mrs Stradling will be overjoyed,' Joshua pronounced. 'There will not be a finer cradle in all the hamlets or in the

Vale beyond. It will become a treasure, Mr Evans, a family heirloom and cherished lovingly. Believe it.'

Ezra nodded and sniffed, saying abrasively, 'Mrs Stradling is not to know of it, mind! Not until the presentation.'

'I shall stay silent as the grave.' Even as he uttered the words, Joshua was aware of their clumsiness, but Ezra appeared not to notice. 'Well, Mr Evans, if there is no other business to detain me?' Joshua sought to make good his escape but relished for a brief moment the heady scents of the raw wood and those resinous odours, rich and fragrant, sharp and cloying, essential to the woodcarver's art.

'Business, sir?' Evans's expression of bland innocence changed to wiliness as he mused upon it. 'There is the small matter of the drowned girl . . .' he began.

'Dr Mansel tells me that he has written you instruction.'

'A pauper's funeral, sir? Uncoffined would that be?' 'Ezra's beady eyes were bright with cupidity, busily assessing the worth of it.

'Dr Mansel has full authority. I fear that it is no longer within my province,' Joshua lied. 'Beyond my jurisdiction. Now, sir, if you will excuse me.' His tone was brusque. 'I have much work before me.'

Ezra, acknowledging defeat, stepped aside ungraciously to say, 'As I, sir. As I.'

'Then I will not detain you,' Joshua said pleasantly, 'save to ask if you know anything of the sheep stealing upon the Downs or the smuggling rumoured at the creeks?'

'Know anything?' Ezra demanded sharply.

'Have . . . heard anything, 'Joshua amended, smiling.

Ezra shook his head furiously. 'No, sir. Nor like to. Where would I gain such knowledge?' He added with an execrable attempt at humour, 'My . . . usual clients are scarce in a mood to confide, even were they so minded. I tell you, Constable, that *undertaking* is a lonely occupation, yet every whit as honest and useful as your own.'

'Long may it remain so, Mr Evans.' Joshua said ironically and with no great conviction. 'Long may it remain so.'

To his open amusement, Ezra Evans no longer sought to detain him. Joshua was hustled peremptorily without, with all that haste and urgency with which he had been hurried within.

Despite his desire to return to Thatched Cottage, Joshua found himself frustrated and delayed at every turn. There had been a minor assault at one of the taverns along the dockside where a sailor, imbibing not wisely but too well of the local ale, had been refused further custom. He had responded by clouting the landlord with a pewter tankard for his discourtesy, making aspersions all the while about his parentage. His host had impetuously retaliated in kind, rather than kindness, and a first-class fracas had ensued with the locals taking sides against the interlopers. Joshua had, with the greatest difficulty and at some risk to himself, restored a semblance of order to the place, only to find when he returned to the stables to retrieve his grey, that the saddlebags were emptied of all the goodwill gifts offered for Rebecca. It would amuse her, he knew, in the retelling, although he would confide it to no other. A constable unable to keep track of his own horse would scarcely inspire trust in others or give them confidence!

As he was already in the Port he went in search of his friend, Peter Rawlings, the customs man, to see if there was further news of the suspected smuggling from the bays.

'You think that the drowned girl might in some way be implicated?' he enquired of Joshua.

'I know nothing, Peter, can think nothing, 'he confessed wearily. 'I am clutching at straws.'

'Then you would be better employed clutching something more substantial.' Rawlings said good-naturedly. 'A pint pot might suffice. It would certainly do you no harm, for you look in need of refreshment.'

Joshua did not deny it nor make a foolish objection, so they made their way leisurely to the Ship Aground and settled themselves comfortably in the ingle-nook corner where they could not be overheard.

Rawlings listened intently to Joshua's account of the bringing ashore of the drowned girl, his broad, strong-boned face harsh with concentration. 'And this child, the one at the Crown Inn. You say Mansel declares that she did not give birth to it? That there can be no obvious connection between the two events?' Joshua murmured assent. 'It seems unlikely that the child can be in any way linked with the smugglers,'

Rawlings reasoned aloud, 'although there are certainly known to be both men and women involved.'

'No. It seems unlikely,' Joshua agreed.

'Unless,' Rawlings hesitated, 'unless the child became an encumbrance, a danger to their work even.'

'Would they not have farmed it out?'

'But that would leave them more open to discovery. It would involve others,' Rawlings persisted. 'People talk. Draw conclusions. A poor family suddenly grown prosperous? An unknown child suddenly brought into a village? No, it does not fit.' He paused, reflecting for a moment in silence before exclaiming with an edge of excitement. 'The woman, now, the drowned girl, that is a different matter.'

'A smuggler perhaps?'

'It seems feasible. Someone suspect or unreliable, talkative even. An unnecessary risk to their work and to them?'

'Perhaps,' Joshua was unconvinced and drank his ale moodily, staring into his tankard as if he might find answer there.

'What does our lord and master the justice say?' Rawlings asked with sly humour. 'I'll wager that it was not "Well done thou good and faithful servant"!'

'There is no virtue in betting on a certainty,' Joshua said. 'He is woefully disabled by gout, unable to stir from Tythegston Court.'

'Then we may thank God for small mercies!' Rawlings declared. 'For while he is complaining of that he is unable to complain of us. Besides, it is as well to know exactly where he is at any given time. His energy and enthusiasm are a sore trial and his bumbling interference worse. I have lost count of the times my well laid plans have been wrecked by his over-exuberance.'

'He means well.' Joshua made an effort to be fair.

'Then the Good Lord preserve us from the well meaning!' Rawlings exclaimed fervently. 'It may serve the justice well enough as an epitaph, but I would rather it were not the premature cause of mine!' Their shared laughter was companionable and without malice for, despite the justice's urge to be always in the thick of things, they held him in respect, affection even.

Their conversation turned to making plans for catching the smugglers, then to other workaday matters, a diversion interrupted by the hurried arrival of the harbour master.

Ayde-Buchan glanced about him keenly, patently searching with a purpose. When he sighted Joshua and Peter Rawlings in the ingle-nook, Joshua raised a hand in salute, beckoning him towards them, then nodded to the landlord to bring them more ale. 'I had hoped to see you, Constable, to have a word.'

Joshua and Rawlings made room upon the bench for him to be seated beside them. 'You have news, sir?'

'Little enough, I fear. I have questioned the captains of those boats due to embark upon the next tide. None has knowledge of a lone passenger fitting the description of the drowned woman, nor yet of a woman and young child. They have checked the passenger lists thoroughly and questioned their crews to no avail. I am sorry.'

Joshua tried to hide his disappointment, thanking him, then saying, 'It would have been foolish to expect result. Too easy, I fear.'

'All is not lost,' Ayde-Buchan said firmly. 'There are three ships, small passenger vessels bringing iron ore from Valparaiso, or pit props from Scandinavia, which have already set sail, two bound for Bristol and one from across the Channel at Porlock. If you choose I shall contact their owners, or question the ships' officers upon their return, for they ply constantly between ports.'

Joshua murmured his agreement. 'Should the woman have been put ashore much earlier,' Ayde-Buchan continued, 'by some foreign vessel,' he shrugged helplessly.

'Meanwhile,' Joshua reminded dispiritedly, 'there are still the shore based workers to be questioned, the hauliers upon the horse-drawn tramway, the clerks in the shipping offices, the merchants and traders, labourers, carpenters sail repairers, chandlers, rope makers . . . I fear that it will take me until Michaelmas and beyond!'

Rawlings did not seek to deny it, offering, 'Then I shall gladly question all those in the customs offices and those engaged in the trafficking of coal, minerals and other freight if it will serve to help you.'

So it was agreed.

When Ayde-Buchan returned to his work at the docks,

Rawlings and Joshua finished their ale and took leave of each other.

'Rebecca is recovering well?' Rawlings asked solicitously on parting, 'and your son and heir flourishes?'

'Indeed,' Joshua said, smiling with absurd indulgence.' And the proud father prospers, too. We are altogether a happy and united family. Does it not persuade you to sample the pleasures of matrimony, Peter?' he probed slyly.

'Not while the pleasures of courtship are so freely and generously offered,' Rawlings answered straight-faced. 'When that advantage runs short or age inhibits me, then I might be forced to make choice.'

'Then I wish you the joy I have from mine,' Joshua said handsomely. Rawlings pretended to be downcast, declaring, 'The trouble is, Joshua, that the most perfect and desirable of women are already spoken for, snapped up by connoiseurs such as you.'

'I shall convey to Rebecca your dissatisfaction with all others and your assurance of her superiority. It will serve to cheer and uplift her.' Joshua grinned sheepishly, confessing, 'I could wish myself as swiftly cheered. I am not sanguine about the outcome of this case, Peter, not sanguine at all.'

'You might call in the justice?' Rawlings suggested innocently, keeping well clear of Joshua's upraised arm.

At Thatched Cottage, Joshua's hopes of gentle relaxation and refreshment were put in a flux by Rebecca's plea that he plead for Cavan and Rosa to have charge of the child at the Crown Inn. He alone, she assured him, could persuade the justice of their suitability as surrogate parents. It would be cruelly heartless to deny them such blessing when, with John Jeremiah's birth, they themselves had been so handsomely blessed. To Joshua's credit, fatigue and frustration notwithstanding, he had no real need to be persuaded. His friendship for Cavan and affection for Rosa were spur enough. With scarce a pause to consider, he rode out resignedly for the justice's house, practising in his mind the arguments and inducements most likely to influence him. With a clear ride he would arrive at Tythegston Court before dusk and, more importantly, before the justice sat down to his dinner; a ritual celebration too holy to be frivolously disturbed.

'Well, Stradling?' his greeting was perfunctory. 'I trust that you have brought your bed here, since you seem determined to make an excuse to stay!' Joshua murmured non-commitally. Perversely, the justice grew expansive, declaring with evident satisfaction, 'Rebecca will have told you that Sir Matthew will visit her tomorrow to see his grandson? Is that not a splendid thing?'

Joshua, who had no knowledge of it, mumbled agreement.

'Moreover,' Robert Knight continued jovially, 'Sir Matthew has done me the honour of accepting my modest hospitality and will bring my good friend, Dr Handel Peate, as companion. Is that not splendid?'

'Indeed, sir.'

The justice looked crestfallen, moving his engorged foot gingerly upon the footstool to say querulously, 'If you have ridden all this way to inform me of it then you might have spared yourself the necessity.'

'No, sir, I come upon a different matter.'

'Not more deaths, Stradling?' he asked sharply. 'It would be damnably inconvenient – unfortunate, I mean . . . a tragedy, even,' he corrected himself hastily. 'I would not wish to become over-involved, you understand?'

Joshua explained about Rosa Doonan's visit. Her wish to care for the child abandoned at the Crown Inn.

'Really, Stradling!' he expostulated. 'Have you no initiative? No self-reliance? I should not be bothered with such trivialities.' His voice softened momentarily. 'Rebecca specifically asks my consent, you say?'

'Yes, sir.'

'Then you may tell her that I give it gladly. A brief note by messenger would have sufficed.' He peered at Joshua myopically over his lenses. 'You should surely be beside her, Stradling, at such a sensitive time, not lingering upon the roads?' The justice reached over for his wine glass and waved Joshua away in cheerful dismissal. 'Take care, my boy. Take care,' he murmured and returned to his solitude and his Canary wine.

Chapter Six

Although dusk was falling and both Joshua and his mare were weary from their day's exertions, Joshua did not return directly to Thatched Cottage. Instead he rode through the stone archway to the Crown Inn yard and went immediately in search of Tom Butler. Armed with the justice's consent, he might reasonably have waited to make arrangements for the child's keep until the morrow. Yet he knew that another night of fretting and uncertainty would set Rosa Doonan's nerves raw and distress the Butlers, for they were a tender-hearted couple and had formed an attachment to the child.

Phoebe's plump face creased into incredulous joy at the news. 'The justice is willing for her to stay in Newton village? Well praise be to heaven!' she exclaimed delightedly, all but suffocating Joshua in an impulsive hug and knocking her house-bonnet awry in her excitement.

'Praise be to Joshua and the justice, too!' Tom Butler curtly reminded her of her manners, but his sharpness was no more than an outlet for his own relief and both she and Joshua knew it.

Phoebe impatiently adjusted her muslin bonnet, tucking a few wisps of grey hair beneath. 'Oh, Joshua, I do not mind confessing that it is a sore weight off my mind, for she is the sweetest, most gentle-natured babe and it grieved me deeply that she might be taken to the poorhouse.' She hesitated. 'That poor woman . . . the one drowned at the breakwater . . . You think it might be her child?' Her homely features were sharp with pity. Both Phoebe and Tom Butler were regarding Joshua intently, their anxiety plain. He would not dissemble, for they were entitled to be told.

'It is not yet public knowledge,' he began stiltedly, 'but others will know soon enough.'

'If there is some reason for secrecy,' Tom Butler said, bluff face honestly concerned, 'then it is better that we remain in ignorance. 'Twill not offend us, Joshua. We will ask no more. It was not from idle curiosity that Phoebe spoke, I would have you believe it, but from care for the child.'

'I know that none could have cared for her better, nor given her such affection.'

'Saving her own flesh and blood,' Phoebe said quietly, 'and she is denied that.'

'The child was not that of the dead woman,' Joshua stated flatly. 'She had never borne a child. Dr Mansel will swear to it at the inquest. He has already performed an autopsy upon her.'

'Then . . .' Phoebe's voice trailed away, bewildered. With effort she composed herself to ask bleakly, 'Then you have no clue as to who the child is or from whence she came? Nothing to link her with any other? No real hope that any will come forward to lay claim to her?'

'There is always that hope.'

'But who, then, will take her in?' Phoebe pleaded in distress. 'It will be the care of a lifetime, worse a lifetime of uncertainty, never knowing if or when the child might be reclaimed. Who would shoulder such a burden? I would not have her farmed out to someone who will ill use her, treat her as no more than a beast of burden. She is not deserving of that!' Phoebe's face crumpled into misery, an anguish of tears.

'Now! Now! my love. Do not take on so.' Tom Butler put a brawny arm comfortingly about his wife's shoulders. ''Tis not the end of the world! We will not let her go, I promise you, save to a good and loving home. Young Mary Flynn who has care of Joseph will do well enough. She will care for two infants as sensibly as one. She is a good-natured girl. The extra shillings will be a godsend to her, believe it. And it will not break us neither, for trade is good and we have ridden good times and bad and been no poorer for it in the end.' Phoebe had stopped crying for long enough to settle a loving kiss upon Tom Butler's rough-grained face, hugging him affectionately, and demanding of Joshua, 'Who will the justice release the babe to?'

'To Rosa and Cavan Doonan, if they are willing.'

Phoebe looked at him long and hard, unable to mask her astonishment. Yet she could not mask either the joyous relief that flooded her. When she spoke, it was to say, simply, 'Yes that would be fitting. Rosa is not a girl to go lightly into things. She will make a proper commitment, and Cavan, too. She has rare courage and determination, as the justice saw when Cavan was shot and all but killed by the highwayman, for she nursed him back to health at the justice's house. 'Tis no wonder Rosa came to mind.'

'Cavan has agreed, Joshua?' Tom Butler asked doubtfully.

'I have not yet approached him, but I think he will make no objection. It is at the justice's request.'

Tom Butler shook his head ruefully, unconvinced. ''Tis no small matter to accept another's child. Joseph is kin, and our boy, Reuben's, child, his and Bella's. He is our responsibility by rights, Bella being dead and such and Reuben at sea. Yet it is not easy and grows harder by the year, as Phoebe will testify. I speak plainly and with honesty, admitting what I would not willingly say to any other, for you are a man of good common sense and discretion and will think no worse of me for admitting what is no more than God's honest truth. I tell you, Joshua, that young Joseph is nigh on as dear to me as Reuben was. I'll own that I could not bear now to lose the boy, to have him taken from me, even should Reuben remarry.'

'You think it would be kinder not to ask Doonan and Rosa to care for the babe?'

Tom Butler flushed and shook his head, confusedly, saying, 'I scarce know what to think, Joshua, save that Doonan and Rosa must make up their own minds. Yet, come what may,' he admitted soberly, 'it will be kinder for that poor child to have a home and family. There is no question as to that, 'tis not in doubt.'

'Doonan might share your anxieties. He might well refuse it.'

'I did not say that I would refuse it,' Tom Butler's voice was gruff, his face painfully reddened. Embarrassment rendered him brusque. 'That Doonan is young and active, I'll not deny. For all his hot-headedness and bombast he is kind at heart. An honest man. You could not wish for better. Should he refuse then the child will be made welcome here. She will not go unwanted.' He turned, wiping his hands fiercely upon his apron and, without another word, hurried from the room.

Phoebe Butler murmured quietly to Joshua, 'All that Tom said of Doonan might as easily be said of him. 'Tis the strong, gentle giants who oftimes feel the deepest hurts. They are sensitive to the needs and hurts of others, but will not speak openly of their own. He grieves for Bella, Joshua, and I am powerless to help him. Like many another generous in flesh and spirit, Tom will do no violence to others; the violence he does is to himself.'

Joshua touched her shoulder in awkward understanding, speaking no word of easy sympathy and Phoebe nodded.

'I shall miss the babe, 'she said, 'for she has already found a place in my heart. I hope that she may fill Rosa's heart and hearth as lovingly. She is a warm, affectionate woman, Joshua. A cradle filled is a need filled.'

Joshua nodded. There was not much that escaped Phoebe Butler's keen eyes and keener compassion, he thought.

''Tis not for Rosa, but for you, I fear, Joshua.'

'For me?'

'Aye. You will need more wisdom than Solomon ever knew, should someone lay claim to the babe I mean. In solving one problem that besets you, you will create another. You will likely be cast as the villain of the piece. You will bear the brunt of all the anguish and resentment stirred, and not be easily forgiven.'

'My back is broad, 'Joshua murmured with an attempt at lightness.

'And your heart tender,' Phoebe said firmly,' as tender as Tom's, my dear, but there, it is both virtue and curse as I have claimed so often. Without sympathy, a feeling for others, you would not be the man you are. No, nor the constable you are and we would be the poorer for it – ' she broke off, shamed by her own temerity, to say briskly, 'Well, I had best prepare the child against your returning. Rosa will not want to waste a precious second, nor I to linger over the parting.'

'Doonan might not give his consent,' he reminded.

'He will,' she said with certainty. 'For Rosa's sake and for his own.'

*   *   *

69

At the Doonans small cottage at Newton village, Joshua tethered his grey to the iron ring set into the stone wall and knocked purposefully upon the front door. It was Doonan who hurried to greet him, his broad unlovely face beaming with pleasure at the sight of his visitor. Beneath the profusion of fiery hair, his vivid blue eyes were alight with innocent curiosity.

'Why, Joshua, my friend! You are welcome, truly welcome.' He clasped Joshua's shoulder with the natural exuberance of a friendly bear, shambling beside him as awkwardly. 'What brings you here at this hour? 'Tis good news, I hope?' His ingenuous face grew painfully anxious as he halted to demand uncertainly, 'Rebecca and John are well?'

'Uncommonly well and a joy and delight to me!'

'Yes, I have heard nothing save rapture from Rosa. She has scarce taken breath, for she visited them this very afternoon. It seems the lad is a paragon: Handsome, Intelligent, Sweet-natured.'

'Indeed,' confessed Joshua complacently, 'for it is certain that he takes after me!'

Doonan gave a huge bellow of laughter and a jovial punch with his great fist before hustling Joshua cheerfully within.

'Joshua? A rare pleasure to see you, my dear.' Rosa, who had been painstakingly stitching, her pale hair haloed in the lamplight, set her needlework down and came forward to greet him. She reached up unselfconsciously to settle a kiss upon his cheek, asking, 'There is something you would ask of me? Some commission for Rebecca perhaps?' Her eyes were gently beseeching, cautioning him that Cavan must not know of her plan.

'No, something I would ask of you both. A favour, but I shall not think it amiss if you refuse me.'

'Refuse you, Joshua?' Cavan's face was a picture of outraged astonishment. 'Why should we refuse you?'

'It is no ordinary favour I seek, more a commitment. I would ask you to consider carefully, give no hasty answer. You will need time . . .' Joshua blundered to a halt, aware of Cavan's puzzlement and Rosa's painful uncertainty.

'Well? You had best tell me exactly what favour you seek,' the Irishman instructed practically. 'Then I can make proper answer.' He grinned, adding philosophically, 'If it is brute strength you need, Joshua, to aid you, as in the past, then I am at your disposal. 'Tis certain that it is not my brain or my beauty you seek – although Rosa has more than enough to serve us both.' The gaze he turned upon Rosa was warmly affectionate. 'Well?' he demanded again, 'Am I to get an answer? I swear, Joshua, that your confounded nervousness puts me in a flux,' he grumbled. 'If you will ask me straight out it will do both of us a favour!'

'The babe abandoned at the Crown Inn. I would have you and Rosa care for it,' Joshua said baldly. 'That is, the justice would have you care for it.'

The look of astonishment upon Doonan's face was comical. 'The devil he would!' he exclaimed. 'Rosa? You have knowledge of this?'

'None,' she said with honesty. 'I have seen nothing of the justice.'

'Rosa?' he appealed to her again, 'What do you say, for the onus lies upon you? It is you, my love, who would be called upon to care for it, to make sacrifice.'

'But *you* who must work, always, to provide,' she reminded.

'That is of no account,' he waved it aside impatiently. 'It is not a matter of pence but commitment, as Joshua says.' He turned to Joshua, his blunt face creased in concentration. 'This babe that Ossie found at the inn, a girl child he said?'

'Yes, a babe of some six months.'

'The justice asked for us specially, you say? He thought first of Rosa and me? Why?' he asked sharply.

'Because he trusts you, holds you in esteem. Believes that you will do your honest best for the child.' Joshua answered without hesitation, knowing that he spoke no less than the truth, even if the justice was unaware of it.

Cavan looked at him intently for a long moment, then nodded, satisfied.

'If you would have me ride back tomorrow for answer,' Joshua prompted quietly, 'that you may discuss it alone?'

'Rosa?' She made no answer, but her disappointment was plain. 'No! Be damned to it!' Doonan exclaimed, smiling broadly. 'There is no reason in all the world for delay! 'Tis plain Rosa has set her heart on it, for all that it is surprise and shock to her as to me. No, we will take the babe, Joshua, 'Tis decided.'

'Would you have me bring the child from the inn?' he asked doubtfully.

'I shall fetch her myself,' Doonan said, 'and now, this instant, that she may settle overnight. Rosa, you will wait here upon our coming – give her welcome.' He turned to Joshua, asking abruptly, 'What is the little girl's name?'

'It is not known,' Joshua confessed. 'She was abandoned without note or identity.'

Doonan sniffed and swallowed hard, wiping a vast hand across his mouth before looking to Rosa. ''Tis not fitting that she come here nameless,' he said, his face mutinous and flamed redder than his hair. 'It would be as if she is nobody, does not rightly exist.'

'What would you have us call her, Cavan?' Rosa's voice was low.

'Joy,' he said. ''Tis a proper name. It cannot be shortened nor misunderstood. If she comes, it should be whole-hearted and clear to all. Yes, Joy will do well enough.' He looked anxiously towards Rosa, seeking approval, afraid of rebuff.

'Why, it is a lovely name, Cavan!' she exclaimed. 'A name to be proud of and handsomely chosen.' Her eyes were soft with unshed tears, her voice gentle. 'Do you not think so, Joshua?'

'Yes,' Joshua said. 'It is handsomely chosen.'

Upon the morrow, Joshua walked out from Thatched Cottage to question his friend, Ossie the ostler, at the Crown Inn. He had left Rebecca languorously abed, for she had risen twice in the night to feed John and to comfort him into sleep again. She might have hired a wet-nurse from the village with a babe of her own to suckle the child, but had scorned to do so, welcoming the tender intimacy of the task, their shared closeness. John's nursemaid, Kitty, was a sensible, warm-hearted girl, practical and efficient, but Rebecca was determined that she would not allow her to become a surrogate mother to the child.

Rebecca had suffered from being early deprived of a mother's love, and from a barren and rootless childhood, plagued always by her father's fecklessness. It was she who, from earliest days, had been comforter, working every hour that God gave to earn them a frugal existence. She would not, Joshua knew, decry those years of unremitting toil, working as a shellfish gatherer upon the shore. They had brought her the friendship and affection of Jeremiah, Sophie and the rest, and let her enter their world. They had given her, too, independence and strength of spirit enough to enter Sir Matthew's world; that world into which she had been born, and which her father's selfish intransigence had denied her. Without such hardship Rebecca would not have become the woman she was now; compassionate, honest, assured of her own worth and the worth of every other. It was not surprising, Joshua reflected as he walked the cobbled highway to the Crown Inn, that Rebecca wanted to give freely to John Jeremiah that loving devotion which she had been unfairly denied.

What was it that John Burrell had once confided to him? 'That half the physical ills in the world were caused by lack of affection; the coldness of the uncaring. That love was often salve and remedy when all others had failed.' Joshua was not inclined to doubt it, although, to be fair, John Burrell had then declared, smiling broadly, that most of the other ills were caused by over-indulgence, the greed and slothful excesses of the rich. He was, he had offered, straight-faced, on his way to Tythegston Court, to give honest advice to the justice as how best to lessen his gout. He would preach the self-same restraint and abstemiousness as Robert Knight preached so devoutly from his pulpit and, no doubt, to as little effect!

'Are you not sometimes discouraged, sir?' Joshua had asked, amused.

'No, for what we both preach is a counsel of perfection. We are born into original sin, Joshua, and some are content to remain so. The rest of us may struggle to be rid of it, but we are human and fallible.' He had raised his high silk hat, then stepped into his carriage, a gaunt, desiccated figure. 'It would be vastly uncomfortable treating only saints,' he confessed, taking up the reins. 'They would make me so painfully aware of my own imperfections.'

'But might not they also suffer in silence, sir?' Joshua suggested.

'I shall tell you if ever I have the misfortune to encounter one. But I beg leave to doubt it!' John Burrell had tugged at the reins and, smiling broadly, driven away.

Joshua, cheered by the recollection, walked briskly under the Crown Inn archway into the stable yard. The sweeping boy who had brought him the message about the child, now in Doonan's care, was busily at his work of clearing the cobbles of horse-muck and hay and the residue of chaff that hung stubbornly in the crevices, spilled from the coaches' floors. His fingers upon the broom were blue with cold, wrists pathetically thin beneath the cuffs of his ragged coat, his feet bare. He greeted Joshua with a ready smile of recognition, shyly returning to his task, the steady, rhythmic strokes of his labours following Joshua upon his way.

Ossie came quickly from the stables upon hearing Joshua's footsteps upon the yard, gnarled fist of a face vivid with pleasure, step jaunty. 'Why, Joshua, my friend, it is a rare treat to see you!' he exclaimed. 'Rebecca fares well, and the babe? Jeremiah is over the moon that the boy has been named for him.' He gave a gap-toothed grin, adding, 'The only living creature named for me is that moth-eaten donkey, in the stall yonder, belonging to Elwyn Morris's girl. I have the care and feeding of him.'

'Then it is to be hoped that he rewards you for your pains.'

'Indeed not!' declared Ossie with a chuckle, 'for a more stubborn, cantankerous and wayward animal never drew breath!'

'Then you are admirably suited,' Joshua proclaimed blandly, 'for I have oftimes heard the same complaint of you.'

Ossie's leathery face creased into a smile as he said humorously and without rancour, ''Tis true that neither the donkey nor I are things of great beauty, nor over-endowed with brains. Yet I'll own that his legs are straighter and his back less bent. He has the advantage of me there.'

'Perhaps,' Joshua confirmed, after due consideration.

'Although we may both lay claim to being sturdy, dependable and hard enough workers.'

'Perhaps you work marginally harder,' Joshua conceded handsomely. 'All in all, Ossie, I would grant you the slight edge in wit and nature.'

74

'Damning with faint praise!' exclaimed Ossie, cheerfully unoffended. 'Since the poor creature is dumb, Joshua, his wit is hardly in question. As to nature, we are both what we are, take us or leave us.'

'I will willingly take you as you are, Ossie,' Joshua said magnanimously, 'and thank God for it! You have more humour and good common sense than any man I know.' The tribute was honestly made.

'Then I take it that you have come to pick my brains?'

'If you will allow.'

Ossie grinned, 'It would please me were you to find that I have some, for I sometimes take leave to doubt it! But it is of the babe abandoned here at the inn that you have come to question me?'

'That and the young woman found drowned at the breakwater.'

'Yes, Tom gave me a description of her.' Ossie hesitated. 'But he claimed that the pair were in no wise related,' he protested, bewildered. 'That Dr Mansel had proved it so.'

'He has proved that the dead woman never gave birth to a child.'

'Then you still believe that there might be some relationship, some blood connection?'

'I do not know what to believe, Ossie,' Joshua confessed dispiritedly, 'save that, to my mind, it is an unlikely coincidence. Think . . . an unknown woman is found stabbed then thrown into the sea on the very day when an infant is left abandoned. Moreover, a child well cared for and well dressed, no ordinary pauper child. Why here? Why at a small country inn upon the coast and not upon the main highway? It is the end of a journey.'

'Unless one leaves from the Port,' Ossie hazarded.

'But why from here? It makes no sense.'

'A meeting, then? An assignation with someone whose business is here, within the three hamlets?'

'Unlikely. It is a small close-knot community and nothing is easily kept hid from friends or neighbours. Someone, somewhere, must have knowledge of the dead woman or of the child. That is the only certainty.'

'The dead woman did not arrive upon the public stage,

75

or upon a private coach or hired post-chaise.' Ossie stated emphatically. 'Leastwise, not here at the Crown Inn. I am here day and night to see to the safe disembarking of passengers and to see the horses uncoupled, then fed, watered and rested.'

'But if you were otherwise engaged, Ossie? Say tending a sick horse?'

'It would make no matter,' Ossie insisted stubbornly. 'One of the stable lads would come and search me out, either from the stables or my loft. They have instruction and would not disobey it. No, Joshua, you must look elsewhere.'

'But where?'

'The livery stables would best serve you, or the other inns and taverns, and I shall make discreet enquiries of those who stable their horses here, if you would wish it?'

Joshua murmured his appreciation.

'If you would question the groom and stable lads?' Ossie ventured.

'No. It would be to no purpose.' Joshua glanced up irresolutely, watching the sweeping boy still bent sedulously at his labours, movement as steady and rhythmic as the pendulum of a clock.

Ossie followed his gaze, saying, 'He is a good boy, Joshua, but, perhaps like me and my namesake, a little ponderous and slow-witted. Yet he is none the worse for that. A 'natural' I would call him; one born unfinished in mind and closer to nature. He has a natural affinity with all living things.'

'Should I leave . . . provision for him?' Joshua murmured tentatively, awkwardly ill-at-ease.' Will you see that he is fed, Ossie? That he has some place in the stables to lay his head?'

'That would be a kindness.' Ossie said, 'and none shall know of it, not even the lad himself. He is not best able to fend for himself. I would do more, Joshua,' he confided, 'but . . .,' He grimaced ruefully, leaving it unsaid.

Joshua knew that every last penny that the ostler earned was spent on feeding the poor useless animals bought into his care, those ill-used upon the company stages and run even when blinded or maimed until they could be run no more. Joshua would not speak openly of it, for it was Ossie's secret and it would have grieved him were his charity crudely made known.

'I will return with money enough to aid the lad,' Joshua promised quietly, 'and whatever his future needs I will see them met.' He brushed aside Ossie's muttered thanks, saying awkwardly, 'There, but for the grace of God, go I . . . or my son.'

Ossie did not make answer, but in passing the sweeping lad put a steadying hand to the boy's thin shoulder, saying, 'You have laboured enough, lad. The place is as clean now as a new-made pin.' He took a halfpenny from the pocket of his worn leather breeches. 'Warm yourself with a mug of hot ale, for you have earned it,' adding sharply, to stem the boy's thanks, 'There is a coach due directly, so do not idly linger. You will be required to sweep the yard again, so that those aboard may make fitting descent.'

The lad nodded and turned to do his bidding, bland moon-face suddenly alive with anticipation, scarce coherent in his joy at such an unexpected windfall. Ossie's hand tightened briefly upon the boy's shoulder. 'It was he who found the babe, Joshua.'

The sweeping boy's face was fierce with confusion as he stammered, ''Twas none of my doing, sir, I swear it! 'Twas none of my doing.'

To Joshua's pity he cowered away, head bent, hand raised as if to ward off an expected blow.

'No, it was none of your doing,' Ossie said gently, releasing him. 'And were it not for you the child might have suffered harm. He saw no woman, Joshua, for I have asked him. He is an honest lad and would not lie.'

The boy grimaced, looking anxiously from one to the other, trying to redeem himself for something not even understood. ''Twas a man,' he blurted. 'A man. A working man. 'Tis all I saw.'

'Ossie?' Joshua's face was taut.

'This man,' Ossie could not keep the tension from his voice. 'Did you know him, lad? A man from these parts? One who comes often to the inn?'

The boy, eyes wide with fear and confusion, blurted, 'No, sir, a stranger.'

'Tall or short was he? Thin? Fat? Dark haired or fair? Think, boy, think!' Ossie urged harshly.

'A man,' he said. 'A man, sir, 'tis all I know.' He had begun

77

to tremble uncontrollably, pinched face distorted with pain at his own clumsiness, his inability to recall or understand.

'Did he speak no word?' Ossie asked more gently, shamed by his irritation.

'He said that he would kill me, sir, were I to speak of him to any other.'

Ossie's gaze met Joshua's, anxious and filled with remorse. 'But you could have told me, lad!' he scolded despairingly. 'You could have trusted me.'

The sweeping lad's eyes were alight with brief intelligence as he declared triumphantly, 'You did not ask me, sir! A woman, you said.' His eyes were fixed anxiously upon the ostler's face, fearful lest he contradict him.

'Yes,' Ossie acknowledged wryly. 'A woman I said.'

Chapter Seven

Long after the sweeping boy had scurried away, clutching his halfpenny to buy ale, Joshua and Ossie remained engrossed in conversation within the stable yard.

'You think he spoke the truth, Ossie?' Joshua asked uneasily.

'I would stake my life upon it. He is an honest lad.'

'Yet it will serve no purpose,' 'Joshua said, discouraged, 'for he can give us neither description nor aid.'

'You had best leave it to me,' Ossie suggested equably. 'I shall do my best to learn what he knows. To harry and confuse him would frighten him the more. I fear, Joshua, that it will need time and patience to disarm the poor lad, for he has known little save blows and curses in his short life.'

'It is a tragedy that he is lacking in wits,' Joshua said unhappily.

'Perhaps,' the ostler's expression was wry, 'the *real* tragedy lies in other people's attitudes, their cruelty and baiting of him, as if he were to blame for what God has denied.' He sighed. 'It is the feral savagery of the pack to turn upon the weakest of their kind.'

'It might be kinder, then, to ignore what he has said,' Joshua ventured. 'Not to disturb his mind further. I would not have the boy harmed, Ossie.'

'Nor I, my friend, but it is already too late.' When Joshua looked at him, perplexed, Ossie said, 'Think on it. He has been threatened with death by a villain unknown. One he cannot describe. One who perhaps has seen your comings and goings at the Crown Inn.'

'But surely he must be aware that he is safe? The lad is plainly feeble-minded, whatever outlandish claim he made none would give it credence.'

'You did, Joshua, and so did I.'

'How, then, can I hope to protect him?' Joshua demanded. 'If I could convince the justice, have him taken temporarily to a place of safety . . .'

Ossie shook his head. 'That would do naught save double the boy's misery! He has refuge and company here. He feels secure only with what is familiar to him. Most of all he feels of use, Joshua. His love for the horses is as deep as mine.'

'But his safety!' Joshua persisted. 'Is not that paramount?'

'No.' Ossie spoke with honesty. 'His safety, his life even, would be of small account to him were he denied all that gives it meaning. It would be impossible to explain to him the whys and wherefores. Sorrow and regret would cripple him. Believe it. He would know only that he was banished, and for some wickedness he could not even comprehend. No, he must not be taken from the inn!'

He spoke with such vehemence and conviction that Joshua said quietly, 'What would you have me do?'

'If you will let me watch over him, keep him as near as possible to my side.' Joshua nodded assent. 'Should the man ever appear here to seek him out or threaten him,' Ossie continued, 'then I will send a message at once. You have my word upon it.'

'Then I shall do as you ask, 'Joshua promised, impressed by the ostler's earnestness. 'But there is something in this whole affair which disturbs and puzzles me, Ossie. I am not ashamed to admit it.'

'And that?'

'The reason behind it. It makes no sense. Why should such a man threaten an innocent sweeping boy. Moreover one patently lacking in wits?'

'Perhaps the meeting was so hurried, and fraught with panic to escape undetected, that he was unaware of it?'

'Perhaps.' Joshua was plainly unconvinced. 'No, Ossie, the real nub of the matter lies elsewhere. Why would the leaving of a child, a pauper even, within the yard of an inn so derange him that he would make threat against the lad's life? It has neither rhyme nor reason! Too many such children are abandoned daily through poverty or sickness. It is a tragedy, certainly, but . . .

'But not tragedy enough to provoke violence? Save against authority,' Ossie suggested. 'Yet might not murder be cause enough?'

'Murder?'

'Consider, Joshua. The dead girl . . . the abandoned child.'

'You believe as I do that there is some link between them?'

'I am certain of it,' the ostler said with quiet conviction. 'I would not willingly set the boy's life in jeopardy, Joshua, for he is not deserving of that, and unable to give proper consent to be used so. But if the man returns . . .'

'Then you will send for me upon the instant!' Joshua instructed, warning, 'I want no mock heroics, Ossie, nor threat to life or limb, you understand?'

'Perfectly,' the ostler said, straight-faced, 'a bow-legged ostler, half crippled in body, and a sweeping boy, crippled in mind, are hardly a deterrent to a savage murderer. Perhaps I could induce my namesake the donkey to kick him insensible?' His shrewd intelligent eyes were alight with humour. 'Then there is always the stable cat.' Whistling tunelessly through the gaps in his teeth, he turned at the sound of the post-horn to await the arrival of the morning stage.

Joshua was not easy in his mind about Ossie's involvement, for he could guarantee neither to protect his friend nor the sweeping boy. Moreover, he felt guilt at using the lad as a decoy, a pathetic scapegoat, without his knowledge or consent. Yet in view of Ossie's fierce determination to keep the boy at the Crown Inn, there was little he could do to deter him. If the man who had abandoned the infant *were* also the murderer of the unknown girl, then it was, in the absence of all description or evidence, the only way to trap him. Joshua was not sanguine about the outcome. The chances were that he was already safely away from the three hamlets, for he would scarcely be of a mood to linger. If it was his *own* child whom he had deliberately abandoned, could not the fury he had turned upon the sweeping lad, the only witness to his crime, have been misunderstood? Despair and grief might have driven him to such rage, his own frustration vented upon another. Had Joshua himself been forced, through starvation or poverty, to abandon his son, he knew that all hell itself would not equal the rage for retribution within him. Anguish would render him insane. He shivered involuntarily.

For whom, then, was he searching? Some hapless pauper denied his child? A vicious murderer? Or were they one and the same? He was still dwelling disconsolately upon it when he rode into the small livery stables at the Port.

The new owner, a darkly hirsute man, lean as whipcord and with the bony, equine features of his charges, greeted Joshua civilly. He was, he informed Joshua ingratiatingly, eager to aid the constable in any small way that he was able. He had the greatest respect for the law and those who upheld it, and was honest and fair in all his dealings, as any who knew him would testify. Joshua, who thought that the livery man protested his innocence too vehemently, was not impressed. He was of the opinion that self-praise was small recommendation and that the fellow had something that he was unusually anxious to hide, some minor peccadillo that the authority of Joshua's uniform brought guiltily to mind: a modest degree of overcharging? Dishonest dealing with some horse-trader or gypsy? The secret transportation of tobacco or brandy for his own use? Certainly, the fellow seemed shifty and ill-at-ease, but he scarcely had the makings of a major criminal. He lacked the temperament, the brazen effrontery of the habitual villain. Whatever small misdemeanour he had committed, Joshua was not of a mind to harass him. It was essential that he gain the man's confidence. He must persuade him to speak freely and without reservation. It was the solving of a vicious murder that must take priority over all else.

'In what way, Constable, may I help you?' the livery man demanded uneasily. 'A horse, would it be? I'll own I have nothing as fine as your grey, sir, nor like to have.'

'No, it is another matter altogether.'

The man's bony face seemed to grow even longer and more lugubrious. 'Sir?'

'I am seeking news of a passenger who recently arrived in the hamlets.'

'Passenger, sir?' The man relaxed visibly. 'Then you have come to the right place! I have a prodigious memory for faces, a talent you might say. What manner of man are you seeking?'

82

'No man. A woman, either travelling here alone, or with a young child.'

'You can describe her, sir? There are so many . . .' he gestured helplessly. 'Those travelling to and from the Port, reputable gentlewomen, and others, for where there are men or trade there is a trade in flesh, doxies, field-whores and such . . .' He broke off, rough with embarrassment, to declare piously, 'Not that I would knowingly allow such . . . creatures use of my few poor waggons and carriages, sir, nor condone any such goings on, here or elsewhere.'

So that, thought Joshua, not without reluctant amusement, is why he imagines that I am here, to harry and question him. To demand a share of the profits even! A pimp or procurer then? Or merely a willing dupe ready to turn a blind eye for a modest return? I'll warrant that in his trade with the ladies of the night it yields a better return than his trading in horseflesh. 'Yes, sir,' agreed Joshua urbanely, 'I am sure that you are, as you claim, the very soul of discretion . . . in every instance.'

The livery man, suspecting irony yet finding that Joshua's face was guileless, grew more relaxed and confident. 'This young woman, sir, the one of whom you speak, the woman you are seeking, could you give me fair description? Height, build, colouring, clothing and such?'

Joshua, with memory of the dead girl's livid features seared into his mind, found himself strangely unwilling to speak of her. He had no knowledge of her in life and yet, perversely, in death he felt that to make her the object of a stranger's prurient curiosity was the cruellest betrayal. Yet betray her he must if he hoped to find her murderer. He chose his words carefully, describing her with a cold exactness which secretly shamed him, as if, he thought, he stood in Obadiah Mansel's stead, wielding a scalpel to lacerate and lay bare a life.

'Ah,' the livery man's face grew increasingly enlightened, his interest quickened. 'Ah, yes, sir. I have knowledge of the woman of whom you speak, for I rode out myself to fetch her, as passenger.'

'You are sure of this? You could not be mistaken?'

'Indeed no, Constable, as I say, I have a talent for observing such things. None can fault me. I'll vow that I would make as honest a constable as I am a livery dealer.'

Joshua wisely forebore from comment, demanding, 'She was alone, this woman, or with another, a man perhaps?'

'She had with her the child of whom you spoke, sir. An infant, no more than a babe in arms.'

'Where?' Joshua demanded urgently. 'Where did you take her? The Port? The breakwater, perhaps?'

'Not there, sir, indeed, it was the strangest hiring, a mystery, even.' The livery man's bony face broke into a smile to reveal large, uneven teeth, painfully overcrowded. 'For I was asked to pick her up four miles and more beyond the hamlets.'

'Where exactly?'

'The old Roman road, sir, "the Golden Mile" 'tis called.'

'She was set down by another conveyance? A post chaise perhaps?'

'Indeed I could not tell you, Constable, for she was there and waiting, and in a lonely and God-forsaken spot.' Seeing Joshua's acute disappointment he mumbled defensively, 'It would serve no purpose were I to lie and pretend to such knowledge. I saw nothing, sir, neither chaise nor any lingering close by. She was quite alone, sir, save for the babe.'

'Would you know the child? Recognise it?'

He shook his head, 'Indeed, I would not, sir! They are all alike as peas in a pod. Horses, now, well, that is different. I could give you a description that no man could match.'

'Where did you take her?' Joshua strove to hide his mounting irritation.

'Ah, that I remember well enough. As I say, it was the strangest hiring. To the edge of the dunes, those windswept dunes beyond the churchyard at Newton. I'll own it confused me for 'tis a bleak deserted place with scarcely a living soul, save for the odd fisherman or poacher.'

'You did not ask her whither she was bound?'

He grinned sheepishly, admitting, 'I did, sir, but was given short shrift for my pains, sent away with a flea in my ear, you might say! And she was right. It was none of my affair. Yet the enquiry was from simple kindness, a neighbourly act and no more than that. I would have taken the little luggage she possessed and carried it gladly, or driven her to wherever she was rightly bound, and charged her no extra, for I made that clear.' He paused before venturing, 'Were it not for the babe,

Constable, I might have thought it some assignation or lovers' meeting.'

'Such meetings are not the prerogative of the unwed!' Joshua reminded.

'Indeed, no, sir. A wedding ring is no proof of fidelity or chastity, that I'll not deny, but one thing I can tell you for certain.'

'And that?'

'That she wore no wedding ring, no ring of any kind nor even the mark of it, for I take note of such things. She might well have been searching for her lover, the father of her child, or so I thought after, for she seemed unusually nervous and distraught, as if unsure of her welcome at her journey's end.' He added hesitantly, 'That was but conjecture, you understand, no more than an impression.'

'Then I shall keep it in mind. She had scarcely any luggage, you say?'

'No more than a single tapestry pouch, sir, to carry those requisites for travel and suchlike that a young woman travelling with a babe might need upon the road. That was why I believed that she might have arrived unexpectedly . . . travelling upon impulse.'

'Or that her luggage was sent ahead upon an earlier stage? Collected, perhaps, by some other?'

'Perhaps. Yet, as I say, 'tis all conjecture, sir, and I am only sorry that I cannot be of more positive use.' He fidgetted uncomfortably, toecaps scuffing the loose chaff upon the stable floor, trying to make escape without giving offence. All around was the familiar ceaseless activity of a livery stable, the coughing and snickering of the horses in their stalls, the to-ing and fro-ing of the grooms and stable lads, the clatter of hooves and waggons upon the cobbles. It was, Joshua thought, a scene like no other, and the mingled odours were as primitive and richly evocative. The warm, cloying odours of animal sweat and fresh ordure were strong in the nostrils, with the smells of leather soap and harness, liniments and unguents, and over all the sharp ammonia tang of equine urine, piercing and unmistakable.

'If you will forgive me, sir, I had best attend to my business.' The livery man essayed a tentative, apologetic smile. 'I will end up in the Marshalsea, else. If there is nothing further, sir?' He made to sidle away.

'A moment!' Joshua halted him. 'I have but one more question.'

'Sir?'

'Who arranged the hiring of the coach? Can you recall? A man or a woman. Can you give description?'

'Why, Lord bless you, sir, I wish that I could! I thought it strange at the time, but it seemed . . . honest and above board, so I did not question it. 'Tis not my way to turn away trade however it comes and from wherever.' He broke off, colouring at having so easily betrayed himself, only to confess quickly,' 'Twas a package, sir, left at the stable door, given into the care of the youngest stable-lad. You will learn nothing from him, for I catechised him most severely, thinking it a joke and all. 'Twas some poor vagrant left it upon the instructions, he said, of another, who gave him a sixpence for his pains. I'll wager it was soon enough squandered on ale! No doubt that pauper is long gone, and the sixpence with him!'

'This package? What did it contain?' Joshua demanded curtly.

'Instructions, sir, instructions as to where to pick up the woman, although it made no mention of a child. That and the wherewithal to pay for it, the coins tied into a leather pouch. The exact fare and a shilling for my labour.' His gaunt face was aglow with satisfaction.

'You did not, by any chance, keep the note?'

'No, sir. That I did not, leastways, only until I had picked up the fare as directed. Since I was handsomely paid, and in advance, there seemed no earthly reason to keep it.'

'You keep no records, then?' Joshua asked tersely.

'Indeed I do, sir, and pay my taxes in full and on the nail! No, and do not begrudge them neither, for we must help those who cannot help themselves, as the good book tells us! 'Tis the certain way to heaven, sir.'

Joshua, who would have been cheered by a little certainty on earth, asked without much hope, 'You do not recall the name of the sender? The signature?'

'There was none, sir, but it made no matter, for the payment was just.'

'Indeed,' Joshua agreed drily.

'You will be pleased to know, Constable, that I took no foolish risks, for all that the money was delivered. I feared some skulduggery, a ruse to entrap me, footpads or highwaymen and such. It is true I had none aboard at the time to be robbed of their valuables, but a horse and carriage are temptation enough to those of evil intent. So I took a pistol with me, primed and loaded.'

'Very prudent and very commendable.'

''Twas as well, though, that I was not called upon to use it, for I am the world's worst shot. I would as like as not shoot the horse or myself.'

That would have added farce to tragedy, Joshua thought unfairly. Aloud, he said, 'Then we must be grateful for small mercies, sir. It is providential that you were spared to aid me.'

The livery man's face was so radiant with unalloyed pleasure that Joshua felt guilt added to meanness of spirit. 'If I might see the stable-boy, the one who delivered you the note.'

'I shall send for him upon the instant, sir, and he shall bring you your grey.'

Joshua thanked him civilly for his time and trouble and they parted most amicably, each with honour upheld. He had thought of leaving without having word with the stable-lad, but his meeting with the sweeping boy at the Crown Inn was salutary reminder of what might be lost through negligence or presuming too much. In the event, the stable lad was able to tell him nothing.

As Joshua rode out again upon the grey he was uncertain as to where his next visit and questioning might lie. He now knew with certainty what he had formerly suspected: the dead woman and the child were linked, together if not as mother and child then in some other kinship. He had still to learn what her purpose was in visiting the hamlets and whom she had come to seek. Had she come in innocence and trust, only to find death at a murderer's hands? Was she a deliberate victim of long-planned revenge or merely the random target of one drunk or crazed? And why, and how then, was the child taken to the Crown Inn?

He turned the grey towards the blacksmith's forge at

Nottage. There was much to be done and it would need patient and painstaking effort to unravel the mystery. Yet Ben Clatworthy, the blacksmith, would surely be the first to know if any stranger came by seeking information or aid. The farrier's shop was the centre of country life, the meeting place for horsemen, farmers and villagers alike. None would pass by without a cheery word, a request for some implement mended or made, or simply to pass on the latest scandal or tavern gossip. Jeremiah swore that if the weekly newspaper reading upon the village green were half as well attended as the forge then it would be a small miracle, but if the justice's sermons were as well attended then it would be a miracle beyond belief. None had made claim to the opposite.

Joshua's arrival at the forge had brought both Clatworthy and his apprentice hurrying out to welcome him with disarming pleasure, clearly grateful for a brief respite from the heat and clamour of their labours. Clatworthy placed a stone flagon of ale upon an upturned barrel together with two pewter tankards, and sent the apprentice scurring within to hunt out a third for the constable. It was filled to overflowing by the time Joshua had wearily dismounted.

'Your mare has cast a shoe, Constable?' the smith enquired jovially, passing him the tankard of foaming ale. 'Or is it the pleasure of my company you seek?'

'Pleasure and business both.' Joshua accepted the ale with a nod of gratitude as the apprentice made to secure the grey at an iron ring set into the wall. 'It is about the girl found murdered at the breakwater,' Joshua began.

'Yes, Tom Butler has given me news of it. A bad business, Joshua.' His broad, heat-burned face was grave with concern. 'But how may I best help you?'

'By telling me of any strangers who have come seeking help or advice.'

'There have been fewer of late,' Clatworthy admitted ruefully, 'for there is a blacksmith's and farrier's newly opened near the port to deal with the comings and goings to the quayside and all. The transporting of goods and passengers. The horse-drawn tramway has farriers and smiths of its own and has no need of my services. No, Joshua, it is more likely that since the dead girl was found at the breakwater then her murderer would have made his enquiries there.'

'Perhaps,' Joshua agreed dispiritedly.

'Yet, if the murder were premeditated and not upon impulse,' Clatworthy mused, 'then it would be crass foolishness to enquire openly of any, to make himself remarked.' He hesitated. 'You have enquired at the livery stables? I ask because I am sometimes called upon for my services there.'

'I have, but without result.' Joshua explained briefly all that had transpired, asking, 'What is your honest opinion of the man? The new owner?'

'Curtis?' Clatworthy's antipathy was demonstrated as he spat into the dust, giving vent to his scorn. 'I would trust him as far as . . .' he glanced about him, seeking inspiration, 'as far as I could throw my anvil,' he declared triumphantly. 'And that is more generosity than he rightly deserves. He is tight-fisted and sly in all his dealings, as I have just cause to know.'

'In business? Financial dealings?'

'A man who is corrupt, devious in one area of his life, is not easily to be trusted in any other. A leopard cannot change its spots!'

'No,' Joshua agreed, 'but a man may change his ways.'

'I am not over-impressed by the power of instant conversions,' Clatworthy grunted dismissively,' despite the justice's preaching! They are few and far between. Nor would I bet upon their staying power.'

'You have heard something?' Joshua demanded, 'Something which might incriminate Curtis?'

'Rumour only, but 'tis certain that he is not all that he seems. He prospers too well.' Clatworthy coloured under Joshua's scrutiny and admitted sheepishly, 'Well, perhaps there is some envy involved, some resentment upon my part. I'll not deny it.'

He appears to be a good judge of horseflesh,' Joshua said mildly.

'Upon his own valuation!' the blacksmith said, 'and no other's. Believe me, Joshua, he treats the animals and those he employs with the same arrogance, the same mean-mindedness. He will bleed them dry, work them until they drop. You have no need to take my word for it, you have but to ask Ossie. He has some of Curtis's winded and broken down hacks in his care, and paid dearly to rescue them, although they were bound for the shambles.' He broke off in consternation as a lone rider came into view, riding with a fierce urgency that foretold some crisis. As the little piebald pony clattered to a halt beside them, its hide lathered and steaming, Clatworthy held tightly to the snaffle to steady it.

'Dear heavens, Illtyd! What is amiss? You have ridden this poor creature like a bat out of hell!' Seeing the hayward's stricken face and the blood that spilled unchecked from the corner of his mouth, he was all alarm and contrition. 'Dear God. Illtyd has been attacked.' Quick, Joshua, help him dismount. He is all but falling from the saddle!'

Joshua eased the little hayward carefully to the ground, supporting him gently, bidding him take rest inside, but Illtyd would have none of it, fighting despairingly for breath enough to urge, 'Quick, Joshua! The sheep-stealers are upon the Downs and I have no way to stop them alone. Hurry, I beg you, else there will be more bloodshed!'

'More bloodshed?' Joshua's voice was sharp.

'The shepherd from Grove farm, they have killed him and would have set upon me but . . .' His voice trailed away, face bleak with shock, head held with pained awkwardness upon the wry neck.

'I will ride out at once, if you will tell me where the thieves are heading. Where they are driving the flock?'

'No!' Illtyd, for all his shock and weakness, was adamant. 'I will ride with you . . . that is my right! The Downs are in my care.'

Joshua, recognising that Illtyd was not to be swayed, merely nodded and made to untether his grey as Clatworthy cried out to his apprentice in harsh command, 'Quick, lad! Fetch my horse from the field. Go, now! At once! Do not tarry.' As the lad made swift to obey, Clatworthy instructed, 'Then take the waggon and drive first to the Lamb Inn, then to the Crown at Newton, and the Ancient Briton. Say the rustlers are upon Stormy Downs and every man will be needed. 'Tis murderers we seek!'

'And shall I come then, sir, to aid you?' The lad's face was taut with anxiety and fear of rejection. He all but stopped breathing as he awaited response.

Clatworthy's hesitation was brief. 'Aye, you had best bring those without horses with you upon the waggon,' he agreed brusquely.

The boy's face was so transfigured with pleasure that even the little hayward was forced to laughter as he remounted his piebald, wiping the blood from his mouth with a clenched hand.

'If all of our cares were as soon lifted,' Clatworthy said.

'Amen to that!' said Joshua, reining in his horse. 'Amen to that!'

Chapter Eight

Cavan Doonan, seated beside his friend, Emrys, upon the battered cart, with its pot-bellied cob, was in the best of humour. He was returning to his work at the quarry face, refreshed from a noggin or two of ale at the Lamb Inn and singing lustily. Were it not for his vast size and splendid muscles, he might have been mistaken for some wraith or spectre, so completely shrouded with limestone dust was he. In fact, the whole conveyance, the cob and the occupants of the cart, were of a uniform greyness. It was small wonder, Jeremiah claimed, that the superstition about phantom carriages and horses lived on as harbingers of death. Doonan, in his cups upon Emrys's cart, was an apparition fit to strike the terrors of hell into the justice himself, let alone his poor parishioners.

Emrys was a mild-mannered man, but he found Doonan's tuneless bellowing and corncrake voice a penance beyond enduring and was forced to say so.

'Damnation, man!' he exclaimed. 'Can we not ride in silence? 'Tis wonder the cob does not bolt or expire altogether!'

Doonan continued singing lustily, taking neither notice nor offence, broad face wreathed in beatific smiles.

'Since you have taken possession of the babe from the Crown Inn you have done naught save sing and beam upon all, like some moonstruck idiot. 'Emrys grumbled.' I'll swear that I liked you better of old – morose, quarrelsome and silent!' It was said indulgently and without acrimony, for he was aware of what the child's coming meant to both Rosa and Doonan both.

'Would you have me change the tune?' Doonan offered benignly.

'I would have you end it!' Emrys instructed, 'before it puts an end to me or our friendship! I have heard more talent in a rookery. Aye and more melody. Take telling, Doonan! 'Tis *my* cob and cart. You are here on sufferance. Remember it.'

'Oh, and who is to put me out then? You and that lazy winded old cob of yours?' Doonan demanded good humouredly.' 'Twould take you till Doomsday to shift me and well you know it. You and the militia would have a hard enough job of it.' He flexed his muscles and, grinning provocatively, burst into song again.

'God give me strength!' Emrys exploded irascibly.

'You do well to seek His aid,' Doonan said comfortably, 'for none other could silence me.' Then, 'Hush, man! Listen!' he exclaimed urgently as Emrys strove to make reply. 'What is that infernal racket?'

'Your confounded singing – ' but Emrys, too, was puzzled and alarmed as Doonan leapt down from the cart and rounded the corner of the hill to the quarries.

Emrys abruptly halted the cob as Doonan ran back, shouting wildly, 'It is sheep-stealers, Emrys! A gang of them, mounted and on foot. Quick! Slew the cart around to block the road. They will not be able to pass this way.'

'But if they are armed, Doonan?'

'Then we have limestone enough on the cart to deter them, to send them on their way!'

Emrys was unconvinced but obediently leapt down and dragged the reluctant cob into position, blocking the narrow pathway. It was a scene of the wildest disarray and confusion, with the terrified sheep wild-eyed and leaping in panic, hooves skittering upon the backs of others as the rustlers drove them furiously on. The men on foot were trapped in the heaving, rolling surge of fleeces, those on horseback shrieking and cursing, yet unable to stem or control the tide.

'Get back, damn you! Get back!' Doonan's fierce command served only to confuse them further, and Emrys and the cob were all but swept aside by the sheer pressing weight of the flock, terror lending them rashness. One of the men on foot had been hurled to the road, lost beneath the relentless grey tide of fleeces, his two companions leaping and jostling as agitatedly as the sheep themselves in a vain effort to reach safety. Emrys, clinging helplessly to the reins, saw one of the mounted rustlers raise a pistol and fire blindly towards him and heard the whipcrack of sound as it hit the side of the cart, shattering wood. He all but bolted in panic, hands shaking upon the reins, yet found himself frozen, powerless to move. Then a cold anger took hold of him, a fury lest the cob be harmed. He loosed hold of the reins briefly and dragged a rock from the cart, then hurled it as far as he was able, to the very feet of the horseman. He did not pause to take account but sent another, and another, hurling until the cart was all but emptied. He was dimly aware that Doonan was furiously hurling missiles, too, vast chunks of rough limestone that none but he could have lifted from the floor of the cart. Then, miraculously, as if at a signal, the horsemen turned, and the flock, finding access, turned, too, and streamed before them, fleeing desperately wherever they might find escape.

'What now?' Emrys's voice was high with nervous anxiety but triumph, too. 'Where now, Doonan? Shall we follow behind them in the cart?'

'Aye, but at a safe distance, 'Doonan advised. 'It will not do to play the hero, for I have a family now to consider, Rosa and the babe, Joy.' He began to drag the terrified cob around, turning the cart by brute force. Then he put a brawny hand to Emrys's shoulder. 'Well done,' he said.

Emrys nodded non-committally and clambered aboard, taking up the reins again as if he had not been interrupted. He hoped that Doonan had not observed how treacherously his hands were shaking. He affected a studied nonchalance, claiming, ''Twas less of a threat than your confounded singing! One more verse and I might have leapt towards that bullet, not away from it!' It was a pity that his voice came out as the harshest croak, but Doonan gave a great bellow of appreciative laughter as Emrys stirred the cob into life. Then, skilfully dodging the hurled limestone and the occasional errant sheep, they were upon their way. The cart, relieved of its heavy load, was infinitely lighter. Almost, indeed, as light as Emrys's spirits.

Joshua, Clatworthy and Illtyd, riding furiously from the Newton side of Stormy Downs, hoped to block off the small byways that gave access to the main highway, for it was certain that the flock must be driven towards the coast. The toll-house beyond the justice's house upon the main carriageway would be the greatest deterrent against herding the sheep inland. Each animal would need to be counted by the toll-keeper and a fair price paid, lowering their profit. But the greatest risk came from questioning, and added delay. Every moment wasted would heighten the probability of an alarm being raised and of their capture. Sheep stealing was a hanging offence and neither the law nor the enraged villagers would show them mercy. Besides, as Illtyd had testified, blood had been spilt. It was murderers they now sought.

Joshua did not know if the men were armed, but it seemed likely, for if they were arrested and taken before the justice they would have been assured of the noose. Death upon the gallows or by another's bullet. It made no matter. They had nothing to lose by arming themselves. Joshua, too, rode armed and Clatworthy also, upon his own insistence, although Illtyd steadfastly refused the blacksmith's offer of a rifle and would not be persuaded. He had seen the shepherd bludgeoned to death, he declared, and had been lucky to escape with his life. Were it not for his pony, Faith's, skill and endurance he would, at the very least, have been left maimed or crippled. There had been slaughter enough. He would not willingly add to it.

Joshua, glancing across at the young hayward as he rode beside him, thought that whatever Illtyd lacked in strength and stature he made up for in moral courage. He had the greatest respect and affection for his friend. He would not seek to dissuade him from going unarmed. He had not that right. Yet it seemed enigmatical to Joshua that someone as cruelly misshapen and crippled should speak so forcefully at the prospect of being maimed. Had he, then, accepted his grave disability, gaining strength and assurance in conquering it, believing, even, that it did not exist? Or was his refusal to carry a firearm a proclamation that he would not inflict by design upon others the same violence that nature had accidentally wrought upon him?

'Clatworthy has offered to ride on to the byway that leads to Tythegston Court,' he murmured to Illtyd, 'to block that escape to the main highway. Will you ride with me to where the lanes converge?'

'If you will have me, 'Illtyd said with wry humour,' for I am no great deterrent. Mounted I stand scarcely higher than the rams, and standing I shall be eyeball to eyeball with the sheep. I will at least confuse them.'

Clatworthy said good-naturedly, 'Then it will be diversion enough. Joshua has sent word to those at the Lamb Inn to come by the quarry road, and those from the Crown and Ancient Briton will block off their other escapes. They will not get far.'

'Your apprentice is reliable, Ben?' Joshua probed. 'He will not give garbled message?'

'That he will not! He will not fail us. I would stake my all upon it.' He grinned, acknowledging, 'as well I might!'

Illtyd said, 'You had but to glimpse the lad's face to see how great an adventure it is for him. He will not let us down. It will please him to come thundering down upon the waggon, dealing blow for blow, the one securely in charge.'

'Just so long as he has no such delusions of grandeur back at the forge,' Clatworthy said, grinning, 'for he will soon enough be set in his proper place!' He turned, and spurred his horse onwards, a bluff, kind-hearted man, sturdy and reliable as the iron he worked.

He had been gone but a few minutes, and Joshua and Illtyd cautiously led their horses into a small leafy copse at the point where the two roads forked, dividing into their separate ways. Almost immediately they were alerted by the shouts and cries of the mounted sheep-stealers, the answering calls of those on foot and the scuffling and fierce bleating of the flock, restlessly panic stricken at being so savagely driven.

Joshua leapt from the copse with his pistol drawn, barring their way upon the wider byway, and Illtyd took his place upon the other, shouting and waving his arms frenziedly, vainly trying to drive the animals back whence they had come. All was noise and confusion, a jostling, surging melée of flesh and fleece, haphazard and uncontrollable. Both men knew that they could not hope to turn the tide nor even to stem it. Once breached, the flow would be unstoppable. At best they could hope to cause diversion until help came, at worst they were laying their lives at open risk and to no good purpose. Joshua, fearful more for Illtyd than for himself, fired a warning shot into the air, and the sheep, startled into terror, halted, then broke ranks anew. With eyes rolling and hooves flailing, they stampeded, trampling each other in their fury to escape, leaping into drainage ditches and through gaps in the hedgerows, causing chaos to thieves and rescuers alike.

It was into this scene of madness and mayhem that Doonan and Emrys came, once more blocking the way, upon the ramshackle cart. The big Irishman leapt down, laying about him bellicosely with his fists, so savagely vengeful that he might have subdued the rustlers on his own. Joshua and Illtyd, still separated from him by the ceaseless grey sea of flccccs, wcrc so convulsed with laughter at his antics that they could not have helped, even had they been able to reach him. One of the horsemen, urgently seeking escape, had somehow blundered narrowly past the cart and was immediately away, leaving the others stranded. Joshua had half-turned laughingly towards Illtyd to remind him that the escapee would be rudely stopped upon Stormy Hill, when a warning cry alerted him. One of the horsemen had slewed round in the saddle, pistol levelled firmly at Joshua. Joshua froze, damning himself for a careless fool, already tensing himself against the violence of it. But Emrys wrenched the man bodily from the saddle, raining blows upon him, then wresting the pistol from his grasp.

Doonan paused in belabouring one of the sheep-stealers, face a comical mask of astonishment, to exclaim, 'Well done there, Emrys! But you had best hand that pistol to me before you shoot yourself! 'Tis as much use to you as to your pot-bellied nag, for neither has nous enough to use it!'

Emrys said witheringly, 'That pot-bellied nag, as you call it, has more sense in its backside, Doonan, than you have in the whole of your head! Empty vessels make the most sound!' With exquisite dignity he handed Doonan the pistol and climbed rigidly aboard the cart. ''Tis why you sing as you do!' he added, delivering the ultimate *coup de grace*.

It took no great effort to round up the prisoners, for they were outnumbered ten to one by the public spirited imbibers from the Crown and Ancient Briton. They had come as bidden, and upon any conveyance they could find; horseback, mule, and even a solitary donkey, and piled precariously upon Ben

97

Clatworthy's old cart. The blacksmith had returned from his vigil in the byway to the justice's house to find the capture all but over, with his apprentice lad still in the thick of it and so intoxicated with pride and power that, as Clatworthy complained, he was past all reasoning. With his usual practicality and foresight, Tom Butler had come well equipped, his cart bringing not only his potman and the more brawny and bellicose of his customers to act as guards, but plenty of stout straw ropes to secure the offenders. They would be housed briefly in the cell above the coach house of the Crown Inn, then transported by coach to the more exacting regime of the gaol house at Pyle.

Joshua had thanked, most civilly, all those who had taken part in the capture, his praise for Emrys bringing a flush of such honest pleasure and embarrassment to that good quarryman's face that not even the dusting of stone dust could hide it. Doonan had made some jocular and determinedly provocative remark which soon had the pair sparring again, but it was plain that the Irishman was pleased, for once, to remain in his workmate's shadow.

It had been, Joshua thought as he awaited the arrival of the men from the Lamb Inn at Nottage, a successful enough encounter, and the justice would be well pleased. There had been humour in the exchanges and, once or twice, the makings of a real fiasco, a farce even. But now, with the prisoners bound and taken to the Crown Inn for questioning, the gravity of the whole affair reasserted itself, as the euphoria of the victory waned the reality.

Those who had been transported upon Ben Clatworthy's cart took their leave and walked the long road back to Newton, alive with excited chatter and the success of what had been achieved. Joshua, Illtyd and the blacksmith were not now of a mood to celebrate.

'Shall I take the cart back to the forge, Master?' the apprentice asked.

'No, lad. 'Tis best that you go alone.'

'Walking, Mr Clatworthy, sir?' he asked, puzzled.

'Aye, the cart will be needed here. There is a body to be transported, lad.'

All the lad's joyousness was wiped away, his exuberance

dulled, as he offered hesitantly, 'I will drive the cart, sir, if there is need.'

'No. 'Tis not a job to relish. You are needed at the forge. Best be away, lad.' He put a kindly hand to the boy's shoulder, adding gruffly, 'You have proved steady and reliable, done a real man's work this day. Has he not, Constable Stradling?'

'He has indeed,' Joshua said warmly. 'We would have been the poorer without him.'

Illtyd murmured swift agreement.

The lad coloured with pride, fidgetting in his boots, before blurting impulsively, 'The one who died, 'tis said he worked upon the Downs.'

'Yes, a shepherd,' Illtyd answered quietly, 'an honest man.'

'Is he known to you, sir? His name and all? None has given me his name.'

Joshua, seeing his anguish, hesitated, glancing questioningly towards Clatworthy who looked shamed and stricken as he explained remorsefully, 'His father is under-shepherd to the justice's flocks. In my haste to be gone I had all but given no thought. Oh, but it was remiss of me!' he chided himself, 'damnably remiss!' He turned to his apprentice, saying penitently, 'Nay, lad, there is no cause to take alarm.'

The boy looked anxiously to Joshua for confirmation, but it was Illtyd who answered, voice subdued, 'The shepherd was from Constable Stradling's own farm at Grove. A pauper labourer, and one who walked the six miles each day to and from the poorhouse at Bridgend. A man unknown hereabouts and with no known kith or kin. 'Tis not your father. Be assured!'

The boy's face shone bright with relief, then as transparently with sudden shame at welcoming the death of any man. 'Well, sir, I had soonest be away,' he said awkwardly, 'for it is a good two miles and more and I would not leave the smithy too long unattended.'

They watched him leave in silence, each trapped in his own sadness and in thought of what lay ahead.

'I will take you to where the man lies,' Illtyd offered at last. 'It will grieve me that there are none to mourn him, none to lay claim, for, as I told the lad, he was an honest man, gentle and reliable. He will not be easily replaced.'

99

'There will be many a pauper glad of the work,' Clatworthy said sombrely. 'Eager to fill his shoes. That is the way of things.' He shook his head regretfully. 'What would you have me do, Joshua? Would you have him taken to the poorhouse or to Evans's house in Newton village?'

'To the village,' Joshua said. 'He is worthy of Christian burial. I would not have him lie in a pauper's grave. He is not deserving of that. He has earned more.'

'He has earned death,' Illtyd reminded, 'and he was not deserving of that, either. That is tragedy enough. But the real tragedy was his wasted life, the bleakness of it, for we spoke often.' He reined the piebald into sudden action, and was away.

Clatworthy, staring after him, said, 'Let him be, Joshua. Let him grieve alone a while, recover himself. He is a gentle soul and feels the hurts of others, for he has griefs and hurts of his own and none may share nor even understand them. Theirs was a gentle kinship, the affinity of those deprived, outcasts through no fault of their own. He does not blame you, Joshua, nor any other, save those who murdered him. Best leave him be.'

Clatworthy secured his horse to the tailgate of his waggon, then climbed aboard, cautioning, 'Make no mention of what has been said. 'Tis best forgotten. Illtyd will regret it else.'

When they came upon Illtyd's piebald faith tethered to a gatepost by a field, Clatworthy drove the waggon along the rutted track to where the hayward stood beside the dead man. Illtyd looked up, fine intelligent eyes dark with pain, and nodded and apology as Joshua dismounted.

'If you will ride with Ben to the village, to the undertaker's house, 'he offered quietly, 'then I will take the news to Grove. I know that 'tis your farm, Joshua, and your privilege by rights, but I would count it a favour. Jed was much liked by those upon the farm and they will feel the hurt of it, for he was a gentle soul, kindly, and slow to take offence. They will need to send a labourer to take his place, to protect the sheep from foxes and such . . . and from human carrion!' he said bitterly. 'I'll swear, Joshua, that 'tis not only wild animals who are red in tooth and claw. They kill to survive. It is man's inhumanity that causes the most savage hurt. God help us, for we are unfitted to help ourselves!'

They worked patiently and in near silence at their macabre task, and when the dead man's body was safely loaded upon the cart, Illtyd mounted his piebald to ride to Grove farm.

'They will not escape unscathed, Illtyd. They will get the punishment they deserve.'

Ben Clatworthy nodded, 'An eye for an eye.'

Illtyd said, 'It is too late. Justice comes too late. It comforts the survivor and not the dead.'

Joshua and Clatworthy watched in silence as he rode away. 'It might act as deterrent to others,' Clatworthy said, troubled.

'I have to believe it,' Joshua's voice was low, 'or by God, Ben, all that I do is a useless waste, a foolishness, and not worth a corpse's candle.'

They had scarce reached the cleft in the road that led to the main highway before they heard the urgent clattering of hooves behind them and the vociferous shouts and cries of the riders from Nottage village bidding them halt. It was with some reluctance that Joshua obeyed, for neither he nor the blacksmith was of a mind to let the dead man upon the cart become an object of open curiosity.

'Constable!' It was the landlord of the Lamb Inn who hailed him, face as hot and lathered as the mount he rode. 'A moment, sir! A moment of your time!'

Joshua knew that it ill-behoved him to show abrasiveness, for they were good men all and had come willingly to aid him. Yet he could not suppress a certain aggravation. He tried to make his smile welcoming, his voice light. 'I have good reason to thank you all for coming,' he said. 'It is a rare privilege to have aid upon which to depend.'

Hugh Shell brushed his gratitude aside, murmuring, 'It is our duty, sir, as it is yours, and none would shirk it, else there would be no rule of law within the three hamlets.' His face, polished red from heat and effort, grew redder yet as he blurted triumphantly, 'We have captured the sheep-stealer, sir, the one who sought escape.'

Joshua glanced towards the jostling throng of horsemen

101

behind him, demanding in puzzlement, 'And where is he now? I see no sign of him.'

There was laughter and unrest from Hugh Shell's followers and a burst of excited chatter as the landlord declared emphatically, 'Nor will you, sir!' The laughter redoubled. 'The prisoner is already at the Crown Inn cell.'

'He has not been harmed?'

'Not *he*, sir, but *she*! 'Twas a woman we captured!'

'A woman?'

'Aye. One cleverly disguised in cloak and beaver. And a spitting, clawing hell-cat of a creature with more nerve and savagery than the men who rode with her,' he confessed, not without reluctant admiration. 'I'll wager, Constable, that you will find the questioning more of a trial than the capture itself!'

'Does anyone recognise the woman? Know whence she came?' Joshua demanded 'Have you learnt anything of her?'

'As I say, sir,' Shell ruefully fingered the scratch marks upon his cheek, 'she was scarce in a mood for civilised banter! 'Twas all we could do to transport her to the Crown.'

As Joshua smilingly thanked him and made to rejoin Clatworthy at the cart, Shell called out, 'It seems the reason for her fury, her agitation you might say, was that she feared for her babe, a girl child, seemingly, farmed out unwillingly against her safe return.'

Chapter Nine

Joshua's surprise at hearing that one of the sheep-stealers was a woman was only surpassed by elation that she had been captured and now awaited questioning at the Crown Inn. The most puzzling aspect of the affair was mention of the girl child whom she had farmed out, or perhaps abandoned. Was it the infant found by Ossie? It was a possibility, no more than that. He could set no great store upon it.

Shell had insisted that the woman was fearful less for her own safety than for the child's. Yet it did not altogether ring true. Was it then a ruse to escape punishment? Hardly, for her plea would have been made to the justice and not to those whose influence held no real sway. Joshua felt confused and uncertain. Would a woman claiming to be so intent upon her child's safety have set it deliberately at risk by her own actions? It seemed unlikely. Yet perhaps thieving and violence were all she knew. It did not preclude her from loving another; one dependent upon her for life itself. And the father? A member of the sheep-stealing crew? Joshua knew, now, the intensity of a father's feelings, the strength of commitment it aroused. As for the woman herself, whatever her sins, and murder was now numbered among them, could the birth itself have crazed and deranged her? Birth fever was not unknown, but that was for others like Dr Mansel or Burrel to give opinion. Joshua's initial elation at the woman's capture was now tinged with doubts about the child's identity. If it were the child abandoned at the Crown Inn then the link with the murdered woman at the breakwater could be rigorously explored and that mystery solved. It would please him and the justice, of that much he was sure. Yet it would bring his friends, Doonan and Rosa, only grief and regret, for the child, once identified, must by law be taken from them and put into the Poor Law Guardians care.

103

Oh, it was a damnable mess and no mistake, but he was duty bound to clear it up, whatever the moral and legal implications and at whatever cost to himself and others.

He was unaware that he sighed, but Clatworthy, glancing up from the cart and seeing Joshua's exhaustion and turmoil of mind, said compassionately, 'I will take the body to the village, Joshua, to Ezra Evans's place, and make whatever arrangements you think best. I know that you have trials enough at the Crown Inn without added aggravation.'

'That would be a kindness,' Joshua said. 'I do not mind admitting that I would sooner tackle those at the Crown, thieves and murderers though they be.' He grinned ruefully. 'It would not please the justice were his constable to be convicted of felonious assault, whatever the provocation.'

'Evans would provoke the angel Gabriel himself!' declared Clatworthy feelingly, 'but he will not easily provoke me, believe it! I am three times his size and nigh on twice as devious. Besides, he has need of my services as blacksmith and farrier and dare not offend me for fear I shall call in his dues.' He made a wry face. 'No doubt I shall have need of *his* services at the end! The only consolation is that I shall be blissfully unaware of it, that and the fact that it is my heirs and kinsfolk who must haggle and pay!'

Joshua glanced involuntarily towards the dead flesh upon the cart, murmuring, 'If you will tell Evans that I will pay Jed's funeral expenses, that he will not be a burden upon the parish.'

'Yes, I will tell him.'

Joshua nodded, reining in his horse to ride through the archway of the Crown. 'Illtyd was right,' he said disconsolately. 'All we can do is hope to comfort the living, ourselves, to assuage our guilt, for all else it is too late.'

'No!' Ben Clatworthy's rebuttal was harsh. 'You may not only avenge his murder, Joshua, but prevent such violence upon others. That is reason enough for what you do.' He stirred up the horse, flicking purposefully at the reins, and took the cart, clattering and swaying across the uneven cobbles and into the village beyond. Joshua rode under the arch and Ossie came to stand beside him, holding the grey steady as he dismounted.

'I hear you have done well today.' The ostler's leathery face was creased with concern, eyes bright with compassion.

'Too little and too late, Ossie.'

The ostler did not question or dispute it. 'Aye, that is often the way of things,' he said. ''Tis the privilege and burden of life, I fear. While we live and breathe there is no way around it.'

Joshua's interrogation of the sheep stealers was thorough, and painstakingly made. He needed to learn all that he could of their activities and methods and of all others directly involved, before they were transferred by coach to the gaolhouse at Pyle. They could not have hoped to transport such a large flock without the aid of companions along the shore, skilled sailors who would lie in readiness, anchored off, until both time and tide were right. There were so many isolated creeks and inlets along the eastward shore and as many beyond the common lands to the west, all rocky and perilous to reach, the scene of past villainy and wreckings. Joshua had sent word through Tom Butler to Peter Rawlings at the port, warning him of what had occurred upon Stormy Downs and begging his cooperation. He knew that Rawlings would act at once to halt the sheep-stealers' craft and to take off those who manned them, for if they gained news of the arrests they would be instantly gone. The customs men's cutters were fast and efficient, less ponderous than the cumbersome vessels used to transport livestock, and Joshua could not doubt the outcome.

The men Joshua questioned had been taciturn and aggressive by turns, their hostility a barrier. Joshua had striven to be impartial, coolly objective even, but he feared that his dislike and resentment were plain. It would not do, he thought wryly, to be accused later of intimidation and prejudice, for the murdered man had been in his employ and the flock his own. The crux of the matter was that since the penalty for sheep stealing was, at best, imprisonment then deportation to the colonies, at worst death by hanging, the offenders had little to fear from their truculence. Since all involved would be condemned to a public flogging, then death upon the gibbet for wanton murder, Joshua possessed neither inducement nor bargaining power. His only hope of securing the information he sought was by duplicity. He could give no firm promise of leniency, that much was clear. Yet, if he could somehow persuade one of the thieves that, with cooperation, a plea might be lodged for him and his sentence made lighter, then it might serve to loosen his tongue. They were scum and renegades, Joshua knew, and had loyalty to none but themselves and the saving of their own worthless hides. So it was that by guile and evasion, if not deliberate falsehood, Joshua, little by little, gleaned the information he sought.

He had concentrated first upon the weakest, most craven, of the men; one almost crazed with terror and scarce coherent in his distress. Joshua, alternately abrasive, demanding then unexpectedly patient and placatory, somehow eased himself into the man's confidence. He coaxed, bullied, chided, gave spurious sympathy. In the end he learned what he wished to know, the names and numbers of those involved, the places where they met and the identity of the one who directed the operation, provided instruction, money, and wherewithal. It had came as no surprise to Joshua that he was a respected and well-to-do gentleman of property, lately come to live in the Vale of Glamorgan. That his complicity in the affair would be hard to prove, dangerous even, Joshua was aware. He would first raise the matter with the justice alone, then tactfully canvass Sir Matthew's opinion and Dr Peate's opinion, too. They were privy to many of the hidden secrets in the Vale, their society valued and eagerly sought. They would have heard rumour and speculation and come to conclusions of their own.

For the moment, his immediate task was to alert Rawlings and his men to exactly where the sheep thieves' trow lay moored, in one of the rocky creeks beyond Newton Bay. Joshua had chosen Tom Butler to stand beside him, armed guard upon the prisoners and Butler had been swift to agree. There had been no need to caution him about keeping future silence about anything he heard, for he was the very soul of honest discretion. Yet he would serve as reliable witness in court should corroborative evidence be needed. None could fault him for integrity, nor question his veracity. He was a man respected by all and a great favourite with Joshua and the justice.

With Butler's potman sent post-haste to the port to find where Rawlings and his men were likely to have ridden, and with others beside him to spread out and take message, Joshua felt more sanguine. Yet one last obstacle remained; the questioning of the woman prisoner.

She was, as Joshua soon learnt, foul-mouthed and vindictive, a scheming harridan. He found neither softness nor hint of repentance, her fluent curses and ill-humour as malevolent as those of any of the men. His questioning about the child was met with contemptuous silence and she would not be shaken from it by inducement or threat. She was a handsome, well-fleshed woman, dark-haired and with an arrogance of bearing that spoke of gypsy blood. She might, Joshua thought, have held a tawny animal appeal for any man, even that putative gentleman who lived so richly in the Vale. It was not beyond the bounds of possibility that the child was his bastard. Yet why then would she abandon it? Surely its existence would prove no danger to her. Rather, it would give her further hold.

Joshua tried telling her of the birth of his own son, hoping to establish some common ground, a point of contact between them. She remained obdurate, unimpressed and silent. He tried to persuade her that were the child's whereabouts known, then it could be supervised in her absence, money for its upkeep paid and its welfare made safe. Pleas, promises and threats alike failed to move her. She stayed stubbornly silent, scorn made plain.

In the end he had to admit defeat. She would be taken to Pyle gaolhouse with the others and left to suffer the venom and spleen of her gaolers, for murder wilfully done. She could expect neither leniency nor pity. Her womanhood would be no protection, no defence. Joshua knew that he must visit her at Pyle gaolhouse to seek to establish the child's identity, for it was bound up inexorably with the girl found dead at the breakwater. He was not sanguine about the outcome. It seemed unlikely that he could break her wall of silence or her spirit. Whatever impelled her it was a fear greater than her fear of the gallows. She watched his departure from the cell with disdain, a sneer of contempt, then, with a cynical smile as he turned and came back to the bars, she spat full was

107

his face. Joshua recoiled, wiping the saliva from collar and jacket, unable to control his disgust as Tom Butler clanged the cell door shut, and secured the lock.

'By God, Joshua!' he said when they were safely away and the guard well out of earshot. 'I pity Rosa and Doonan if she proves to be mother to their babe. 'Twill break Rosa's heart to know it.'

'There is only one I have more pity for, one who will be more deeply hurt.'

'The child itself?'

Joshua nodded. 'Should the woman escape hanging and one day gain release, then I hold no hope for its future.'

'But if she is hanged,' Tom Butler persisted, 'then Rosa's and Doonan's way will be clear. All will be resolved.'

'No, it will be neither resolved nor forgotten. The past casts long shadows, Tom. None in the three hamlets will forget, nor forgive. The child will bear the full brunt of the hatred its mother earned by killing one of our own.'

'The sins of the fathers,' Butler murmured, 'unto the third and fourth generation. Oh, but it is a damnably cruel world, Joshua! Cruel and unfair.'

Joshua did not seek to contradict him.

'Either way,' Butler ventured soberly, 'Rosa and Doonan must lose . . . unless,' he suggested hopefully, 'they move away to some place where they are unknown? Begin anew.'

'It would be a high price to pay,' Joshua said, 'for their friends, livelihood and home are here. They would never feel safe, never secure. There would always be fear that someone would come seeking the child, someone with the power to claim it.'

'Its father, or close kin?'

'Yes.'

'But if the woman dies without revealing her name? If you do not persist too strongly, who would know?' Butler's broad face was creased with anxiety. 'The child's best interests would be served, she would find a good home with Rosa and Doonan.'

Joshua said heavily, 'It is the interests of justice I serve, Tom. That before all other.' He was painfully aware that he sounded both pompous and stilted. 'The girl murdered at the breakwater,' he said firmly. 'I owe duty to her. The dead have as much need of protection as the living.'

'I beg leave to doubt it!'

Joshua made no reply.

'There is one thing I do not doubt, Joshua,' Butler put a hand to Joshua's arm, strongly reassuring. 'I do not doubt your compassion and integrity your will to do what is right.'

'Right is not always best or kindest,' Joshua admitted with honesty, 'and it makes friends into enemies.'

Butler nodded gravely. 'In the end,' he said, 'the opinions of others hold little sway, whether friends or enemies. It is a lesson hard-learned and from bitter experience. You first have to satisfy yourself, Joshua. Do what you know to be honest and right. You have to respect yourself to earn the respect of others.'

They had descended the stone steps from the coach house loft and Butler stood indecisively upon the cobbles of the yard, large florid face awkward with concern. 'You have earned the respect of all in the three hamlets. Do not doubt it.' Gruff with embarrassment, he turned abruptly upon his heels and entered the Crown Inn.

Rebecca, loving John Jeremiah as she did, still felt some lack in her life, a sameness verging on boredom. She should, she chided herself severely, be the happiest woman in the three hamlets, in the world even. She had the sweetest, most contented babe that ever breathed, a husband who loved and cherished her, and a home that suited her to perfection. She had loving friends and family, a household staff devoted to her, and no financial worries. Her health was excellent, she was in full possession of her faculties and, since John Jeremiah's birth, had regained all her looks and vitality. Why, then, this sense of unease, this strange dissatisfaction?

The truth was that she had never been used to such Sybaritic idleness. Even at Southerndown Court her life had been filled, for she had insisted upon learning every detail of how life upon a large estate was ordered. She had immersed herself in all aspects of fiscal, domestic and country life, taking much of the strain and responsibility from her grandfather's shoulders. In addition, there had been daily lessons with Dr Handel Peate with Elizabeth Devereaux as a friend and companion. The old gentleman was an inspired tutor, keen in intellect and rich in humour, and Rebecca had valued both his friendship and instruction. Then there had been in addition the usual tutorial instruction in the polite arts required of a gentlewoman of quality. Some, such as drawing and painting, she had excelled at, having a natural talent which had been sedulously fostered. At music and the pianoforte she had been, she conceded, less than competent, her only talent a reasonably mellifluous voice, tuneful if not as clear-pitched as Elizabeth's. At needlework and tapestry she had proved ludicrously inept and not even the finest instruction could alter it. She had once complained, in honest vexation, to Elizabeth that she had as much aptitude for stitching as a giraffe for the pianoforte and Elizabeth, smiling broadly, had not disagreed.

It had been a close friendship, made closer by knowledge of a past shared and overcome, each gaining strength from the other. Roland Devereaux's sister, Mary, a long-time friend of Elizabeth, had come to the hamlets innocently seeking her aid. She had found, instead, death at the hands of Elizabeth's brother, Creighton Crandle, an arrogant brutal creature, selfish and over-indulged. He had paid for his crime but his family had paid a harsher more demanding price. His misery was ended in death, but his father, confused and all but useless in mind, languished still in a prison cell. Elizabeth and her mother, although blameless, had been dispossessed and forced into paupery. It was Rebecca's compassionate plea to her grandfather, Sir Matthew, which had secured their safety and a home at East Lodge. There, Elizabeth's mother, Louisa Crandle, had been nursed back to health and spirits, and Elizabeth had become Rebecca's friend and companion and grown as dear to Sir Matthew as Rebecca herself.

Mary's murder had been a time of such pain and savagery that Rebecca had doubted that the wound would ever be healed. Yet from it, and the suffering, had come a closeness that could never have been foreseen and would never now be broken. It had brought together Joshua and Rebecca and united Elizabeth and Roland Devereaux, first in sympathy, then in loving marriage. It had ultimately, too, led to Rebecca's reunion with Sir Matthew and the beginning of a new life.

Indeed, one might say to the beginning of new human life; John Jeremiah and Mary Devereaux, tenderly named for her dead aunt, were the living proof of it.

Rebecca, reflecting now upon the strangeness of it all, wished fervently that Elizabeth were nearer, that they might take up their good-humoured gossip and bantering as of old. Shared motherhood would forge an even stronger bond between them, the future as great an adventure and as fiercely unpredictable as the past. What she lacked, Rebecca decided, was that very sense of adventure, the stimulus of change and of breaking new ground. Louisa Crandle would have declared frostily that since Rebecca was now a matron, a respectably married gentlewoman, such frivolity ill became her. She must meekly submit to the demands of matrimony and motherhood, accept a predetermined role in society, favouring none, offending none, for that much was demanded of a lady of quality. Rebecca was not sure that she was entirely fitted for the role of a lady of quality. Indeed, if the criteria were to be dictated by the mores of society, then she was adamant that she had no desire to be so. Quality lay in those like Jeremiah and Sophie, Sir Matthew and Dr Peate; a strength of character and compassion which owed little to birth and breeding for it was innate. Poverty or riches were largely irrelevant, as she had learnt early.

Oh, damnation! Rebecca thought. What I lack is real purpose, something to be enthusiastic about, something to absorb me utterly. Yet there were rules which had to be obeyed. She had not been 'churched'. There had been no service of thanksgiving after childbirth, so she must not yet venture into formal society until that moral duty was discharged. 'Society' did not mean only the upper echelons, that rigid hierarchy to which Mrs Louisa Crandle conformed, but to all. The folk of the three hamlets, whether paupers or yeomen, were as rigid in their adherence to this tenet of the faith as were the landed gentry. There was no way around it, for even Joshua and Sir Matthew would not countenance the breaking of it and, as rector, Robert Knight would be scandalised and grieved. No. There was a time to assert her independence and a time to be circumspect. Discretion would serve her better. For the moment she would bide her time. She would not be content to

111

do so, merely wise! Yet, when an opportunity presented itself, she would be ready and waiting to take up a new challenge. She would assert her independence. Allow nothing to stand in her way.

She had always worked with Joshua upon his more demanding cases, sparing all of her time and energy to help find solution. Theirs had been a working partnership from the very day of Mary Devereaux's tragic violation and death. Nothing had changed. She, Rebecca, had not changed, save, as Joshua, to have added responsibility, new life to protect. If Joshua were not prepared to allow her into his investigations then she must simply make investigations on her own account.

For the moment she awaited with impatient excitement the arrival in the three hamlets of her grandfather, and of Dr Handel Peate. She had no doubt that they would find John Jeremiah wholly captivating and superior in every aspect, and would be as absurdly besotted with the child as Joshua and she. She cherished and stored every last compliment about her son and was equally elated if it was stated that he favoured Joshua in looks or that he favoured her. Sophie and Betty Turner declared that he might lose his shining cap of black hair and that all infants were born with eyes of the brightest, clearest blue. Rebecca was not wholly convinced, for who but a fool would seek to change or improve upon perfection? Whatever small changes nature made she would accept them with equanimity, grateful for her son's existence. She would not become one of those obsessed, hideously doting mothers who saw no wrong in her child, believing him incorruptible.

For a moment there came into her mind the arrogant, laughing face of Creighton Crandle, red hair ablaze, all colour and sly vitality, a red-haired fox, bloodied in tooth and claw. A coldness gripped her. A sense of terror and decay. She shook it off with an effort of will that left her exhausted and trembling. It was long ago, she told himself. Time past and safely ended. It was the effect of the birth which so plagued her, a natural weakness which laid her emotions raw. As soon as ever she was 'churched' she would take John Jeremiah and visit Rosa Doonan in the cottage in Newton where Jeremiah had once lived.

From Joshua's account of the babe, she was a beautiful

112

child, fair and fresh-skinned as Rosa herself and as gentle and sweet natured. A perfect miniature of Rosa herself. Yes, Rebecca decided, that was what she would do. It would give her pleasure to take her son and introduce him to Jeremiah, Illtyd, Emily Randall, indeed all of her friends, and savour their compliments and praise at producing such a treasure. Then, with John Burrel's permission, she would drive to Southerndown Court to visit her grandfather, and show John Jeremiah proudly to the tenants and labourers upon the estate and the household staff. Then to visit Elizabeth and Mary at the Dower House and Mrs Crandle at the lodge. Tomorrow, Joshua's parents would arrive to worship their grandson and make their obeisance. Charlotte Stradling, she knew, would be openly besotted with him, and Joshua's father, dour and awkwardly taciturn, his emotions well hid, yet his pride and pleasure in his grandson would be as fierce as her own. With a smile Rebecca went to pay homage to her son, for she could not bear to be long parted from him.

Joshua, upon leaving the Crown Inn, rode into Newton village to visit his old adversary, Ezra the Box. It was not a meeting he looked forward to with any pleasure, but he hoped that Ben Clatworthy's assurances that Jed's funeral expenses would be promptly paid would sweeten Ezra's disposition. He held no great hopes of this for it would have needed a Damascene conversion to make him even tolerably civil. Joshua carefully tethered his horse without the shop, lingering over it as long as he was decently able in order to postpone the meeting. When he finally entered, to his astonishment the undertaker rushed in from the small, ill-furnished room behind the shop, clutching his massive ginger tomcat which he negligently sent sprawling, ignoring its outraged protests. Ezra was smiling broadly, benevolently even, his pointed teeth bared ingratiatingly in his ferret-like face.

'Ben Clatworthy has no doubt told you what is required for Jed Carter's funeral?' Joshua said stiffly.

'Indeed, Constable, a proper Christian funeral, rather than a pauper's burial.'

'I was not aware, sir, that the church estimated our worth on an ability to pay,' Joshua pointed out coldly.

'No, indeed, sir. All are equal in the sight of God,' Evans intoned piously. 'Yet we are not yet in heaven, Constable, and man cannot live by bread alone! More's the pity.'

'If you will render account,' Joshua said firmly, 'it will be paid in full. Let that be an end to it. There is no more to be discussed.' He turned purposefully on his heel, unwilling to betray his aggravation.

'But there is more to be discussed, sir.'

'Indeed? I was not aware of it.'

The ginger tomcat had returned and Ezra moved it aside irritably with the toe of his boot, claiming, 'I have news for you, Constable. News to surprise you.'

'About Jed? Jed Carter?'

'No, sir,' his little ferret face was alive with importance. 'The unknown woman, the one from the breakwater.'

'Dr Mansel has already delivered her to you?'

'Indeed, sir, not an hour since. I am to keep her here until the inquest, embalm her and such, do what I may to tidy her, make her respectable.'

'An unfortunate choice of words!' Joshua could not help himself chiding scathingly.

Ezra was unconcerned. 'I recognised her at once,' he said with satisfaction. 'For I have seen her before, sir, and can give honest account of it. There! I thought it would surprise you. One good turn deserves another!'

Chapter Ten

Sir Matthew's arrival at Newton village was a matter of pride and delight to the cottagers of the three hamlets. It was rarely that a member of the *haut-ton* ventured to so remote and bucolic a place, even to take the sea bathing. The 'quality' were accustomed to taking the waters at more elegantly fashionable resorts such as Bath, where they were certain to meet others of their kind. There, the therapeutic values of their 'cures' might be legitimately countermanded by wining, dining, dancing, gaming and other more voluptuous pursuits. That it was done purely upon a physician's advice added virtue to endeavour. Small wonder, then, if they chose to cleanse themselves comfortably from within rather than without. Spa waters ingested may prove disagreeable, but the icy waters of the Atlantic ocean upon bare flesh are quite insupportable.

When Sir Matthew and his companion, Dr Handel Peate, arrived at Thatched Cottage, a small crowd of awed and admiring onlookers had assembled. Their cheerful banter and chattering had given way to respectful silence as the splendid equipage drew up at the gates. All, from the humblest crossing sweeper to the tradesmen and artisans, were rendered dumb with admiration. The de Breos coach was a miracle of perfection, from the six matched chestnut horses, beautifully caparisoned, to the aged coachman and twin postillions in full livery. They wore the de Breos colours of plum and gold, elegantly designed and richly encrusted with golden threadwork. Even their sartorial splendour did not outdo the glory of the coach itself: solid, imposing and magnificently crested, it was a thing to marvel at, its elliptical springing and slender wheels a miracle of the coach-maker's art.

Sir Matthew was perhaps the most elegantly aristocratic of all, his erect and dignified bearing and his courteous manner impressing even the few scapegraces and drunkards at the fringes of the crowd and keeping them respectfully mute. He had greeted the onlookers most cordially and his companion Dr Peate, known to be a renowned scholar and gentleman of the cloth, had been cheerfully good-humoured. It was, everyone knew, a rare and splendid occasion, for Sir Matthew had come to see not only his granddaughter, Mrs Stradling, but his great-grandson and heir, John Jeremiah Matthew Stradling, and to pay his respects. It was they knew a time of joy for the old gentleman, yet it held a certain poignancy, too. There was not one amongst them who did not know the full story of Rebecca de Breos and rejoice in its triumphant ending. Had she not worked and lived among them as fishermaid, sharing their poverty and the harshness of their lives? Was the child not named for John Burrel and the old fisherman, Jeremiah Fleet, as well as his illustrious forbear? Yes. It was an occasion to treasure and keep bright in the memory. Rebecca Stradling, as they must now think of her, had shown by living and settling amongst them that she thought them of real worth. Neither she nor the constable were boastful and highfalutin', but people of honest stock and always approachable.

As Rebecca waved excitedly to greet the visitors from the parlour casement of Thatched Cottage, Sir Matthew was aware that the cottagers held her in real affection, real esteem. She waved to them, too, cheerfully and unselfconsciously, as much at ease here as at Southerndown Court. If he had regretted the harshness of her early years, their bleak frugality, and wished them undone, he could not wholly grieve them now. His own son, Rebecca's father, had proved weak and unreliable, crushed by adversity, and thrusting upon her childish shoulders the burdens that were rightfully his own. She had borne them bravely and without bitterness or complaint. Sir Matthew, who loved her more deeply than any other in his life, was grateful only that she had been restored to him. She had found an intelligent, loyal and loving helpmate in Joshua Stradling, and he thanked God for that too. He would have no qualms about the future of Southerndown Court, his lands and estates, for they would be in safe keeping until his great-grandson inherited. He smiled at Dr Peate, opaque blue eyes bright with certainty, and Dr Peate nodded delightedly and smiled

116

back serenel. They entered the house together, two venerable gentlemen, honed to spareness by age, yet dignified and erect. Rebecca, watching them from the casement, had been filled with such a rush of tenderness and affection for them that she had all but wept. How small they suddenly seemed, how shrunken and diminished by age, as though time and life itself had drawn strength from them, leaving them dry and spent. She had forgotten how aged they were, how frail and vulnerable.

When she ran forward to greet them it was with such loving joy and tenderness that her care for them could not be in doubt. She embraced her grandfather so fervently that he was forced to take urgent breath before he could speak, and even then his words were lost in the flurry of kisses she settled upon his gaunt cheeks. Dr Peate had been welcomed as wholeheartedly. They had borne the indignity of it with admirable restraint, stoicism even, smiling at each other self-consciously yet with a certain indulgence.

When they had been served suitable refreshment, had exchanged those social pleasantries expected of them and quite exhausted the news of Rebecca's and Joshua's friends, family and acquaintances in the Vale and beyond, Sir Matthew asked quietly, 'Well, my dear, and are we not to see the young gentleman?'

Rebecca might have sent for his nursemaid or asked Ruth to bring him, but did not. She excused herself from their presence and went to fetch him from his crib. She knew that it would be a meeting fraught with both joy and sadness, with hope for the future and regret for what was past and could never be undone. A meeting too private for any other to witness or share.

She brought her sleeping son cradled to her, then put him into her grandfather's arms. Sir Matthew spoke no word but gazed at the child for a long moment, his lean, austere face filled with such a tenderness of pride that Rebecca felt the ache of it at her breastbone, raw as the tears behind her eyes. Sir Matthew smiled at her and nodded and Dr Peate went to stand beside him, frail-boned and with the intent, myopic gaze of an aesthete and scholar. He was, Rebecca thought with affection, not unlike an engaging child himself, so alive with wonder and curiosity and with his nimbus of white, baby-fine hair.

117

Rebecca, watching them, and hearing their extravagant exclamations of delight as John Jeremiah opened his eyes, seeming to gaze back enquiringly at them was touched beyond measure. There was a gentleness between them, that natural affinity between the very old and the very young, fragile and quick-passing, as if all that is to be denied to them must be held, now, in memory alone. She thought that she would never forget the small cameo before her; the two old gentlemen, white-haired and frail-boned as birds, their thin aesthetic faces aglow with pleasure at the dark-haired child. Spring and winter, Rebecca thought, the beginning of life and its ending, each beautiful and inevitable in its own way. She felt a sadness engulf her, a sense of impending loss. She could not imagine that John Jeremiah, so warm in flesh and so newly created, could come to old age, to loneliness and grief, as she and Joshua must, all their fierce loving dwindled to dust.

'He is a fine child, Rebecca, 'Sir Matthew said. 'You will bring him soon to Southerndown Court? Show him the lands and estate that he may learn to love them?'

'Yes, grandfather. We will come, and often,' she promised, 'for it will be a joy to him and home, as it was to me. There will be so much you will enjoy together, so much to share and learn.'

Dr Peate smiled down at John Jeremiah and put a thin, desiccated hand to the child's soft cheek. 'Always so much to learn,' he said regretfully, 'and never enough time. May God grant me grace to instruct him, as I strove to instruct Joshua and Rebecca both.' He added, smiling, 'It would give me fresh purpose in life, new energy, and lend strength to old bones.'

'With two such mentors,' Rebecca declared affectionately, 'he will be rich indeed! The days will always be too short for all he will wish to learn and do.'

'Then he will be well blessed, my dear,' said Dr Peate with pardonable satisfaction, 'for that is the true definition of a happy man.'

Joshua, face to face with Ezra Evans in the undertaker's shop, stared at him in astonishment, scarce able to believe his ears. 'You know the murdered woman? Are able to identify her?' he demanded brusquely.

'Well, not exactly.' Ezra's smile was ingratiating, his manner evasive.

'What does "not exactly" mean, Mr Evans?' he demanded acerbically. 'Either you know her or you do not.'

'In a manner of speaking, 'Ezra prevaricated, sniffing hard.

'No! Not in a *manner* of speaking, but plainly, sir!' Joshua was as aggrieved by the undertaker's shiftiness as by the fact that *he*, of all people, held the key to the dead girl's identity. 'Speak plainly, man!' he expostulated. 'Do you know her or not?'

'I have seen her, sir.'

'Where? And when? Come, man, this is important. Do not hold back!'

Ezra shuffled his feet in the sawdust of the floor, gazing at his boots as if they might give him inspiration. 'The Burrows,' he mumbled almost inaudibly.

'The Burrows? What were you doing upon the Burrows?' Joshua accused. Ezra hesitated, licking dry lips, grimacing slyly. 'There is no reward!' Joshua rebuked firmly.

'It was never in my mind, Constable!' Ezra's outraged innocence might have been convincing in any other. 'I think I may claim to know my duty as a citizen, sir. My debt to the justices and the law.'

Joshua begged leave to doubt it. 'So you were . . . exploring the Burrows?' he prompted, 'bent upon upholding the public good?'

Evans glared at him suspiciously, crafty little face indignant, but he nodded agreement.

'This excursion of yours, it would have nothing to do with the sheep stealers upon Stormy Downs?'

'Sheep stealers! As God is my witness, sir, I would never stoop to such infamy. The very idea is preposterous!' he was all but spluttering in his indignation.

'Oh, I do not accuse you of being implicated, Mr Evans. In no way directly involved.' Joshua's expression was bland. 'I merely thought that you might have, well, observed some suspicious activity having come, perhaps, from Newton Creek?'

'Newton Creek? I was never at Newton Creek! What business would I have at Newton Creek?'

'The same as . . . whatever occupied you at the Burrows,

119

Mr Evans?' Joshua suggested mildly. 'Seeing off poachers, perhaps? As you say, you are a man of integrity and strong public spirit. But that need not concern us now.' Ezra did not seem reassured. 'The dead girl,' Joshua reminded. 'You saw her upon the Burrows?'

'Yes, I saw her,' Ezra agreed truculently.

'Well? Can you enlarge upon it? There must be something more? Was she alone?'

'No.'

'Then who, in heaven's name, was with her?' Joshua could not hide his exasperation. It was, he thought, like attempting to get blood from a stone, a metaphor that was chillingly apposite having regard to Evans's occupation.

'Not who, Constable, but what.' Joshua looked at him in bewilderment. 'There was a child, a babe in arms, but a small one-horse carriage, too, and a man – '

'A man? You can describe him? Recognise him if need be? You will be needed as a witness should he be found and apprehended.'

'There is no need, sir. No need on earth.'

'There is every need!' Joshua refuted abrasively. 'Whatever your . . . reservations, your personal involvement, it makes no matter! Your duty is plain!'

'No,' Ezra gave the merest hint of a smile. 'You misunderstand me, sir. I will give evidence, if that is what you require, but would it not be better were I to point you towards him? Tell you where he may be found?'

'You actually know this man? Then why did you not tell me!' Joshua demanded irately.

'Why, you did not ask me, sir.'

'Hell and damnation!' Joshua exploded, 'do not play the innocent with me, Evans. I know you too well! Who is he and where is he to be found?'

'At the livery stables at the port, Constable, as one would expect. 'Tis the new owner, a man by the name of Curtis. You have heard of him?'

'Yes, I have heard of him.'

'A surly creature. Not a man to be trusted,' Ezra warned. 'Tread carefully, Constable, for he is mean-minded and corrupt. Rumour has it that he is engaged in all kinds of villainy and deceit, a dyed-in-the-wool villain and best avoided.'

Joshua, for once, was speechless. Ezra spoke without irony, face concerned and free from guile. For a moment Joshua almost liked him.

'Should the man, Curtis, be convicted of murder?'

'Yes?'

'Then I might go into the livery business. 'Tis certain it will be sold cheaply.' Ezra's little ferret face was sharp with cupidity.' You will tell me of the arrest, Constable? Give me fair warning?'

'I will always give you fair warning, Mr Evans. Believe it!'

Enmity restored, Joshua went out hurriedly into the street.

His return to the livery stables was swiftly made. Joshua was scarcely aware of the long ride across the sandy acres of Pickett's Lease nor of the noise and bustle of the port, the ships with sails full-bellied in the Channel beyond, a sight that always subtly raised his spirits and gladdened him. Now his rage for Curtis's duplicity all but blinded him of sight and reason and his anger was as much for his own credulity. There was no excusing his incompetence, as the justice would justifiably insist. He must do his best to rectify his carelessness. Learn from experience.

When he rode into the yard of the livery stables, Curtis was engaged upon some business with a customer, a surly, sour-faced man demanding the hire of a gelding. Curtis glanced up and greeted him affably enough, but could not conceal a certain wariness, a hint of unease.

'I will be with you in a moment, Constable. My transaction is all but ended.'

The man intent upon hiring gave Joshua a cursory glance, face set and mutinous, and the haggling continued until a bargain was sealed.

'Now, sir, how may I best help you?' Curtis's dark-grained face was determinedly mild, his manner unruffled. 'You have changed your mind about selling your grey?'

'I have changed my mind about nothing!' Joshua answered curtly.

'How may I best help you?' Curtis repeated, but with less certainty now.

'You may help me by telling the truth!'

'The truth, sir?' His bewilderment seemed genuine.' I do not know of what you complain.'

Joshua did not attempt to dissemble. 'It has come to my notice that the woman we spoke of, the one you claimed to have picked up upon the Golden Mile and set down at the dunes . . .'

'Yes, sir?'

'That you drove with her deep into the heart of the Burrows. No, do not attempt to deny it! You were seen, I have good and reliable witness.' It must be the first time, Joshua thought sheepishly, that Ezra had been so described.

'But I do not deny it.' Curtis declared. 'The dunes, the edge of the Burrows. The Burrows themselves . . . It is all one matter! A splitting of hairs! I do not see the relevance of it. Of what am I accused?' he asked truculently.

'The woman of whom we spoke is dead, murdered,' Joshua said tersely.

'Dear God!' Curtis's outrage was real. 'Am I claimed to have murdered her then! Who has accused me and with what proof? It is a lie, a blatant lie, and I will not stand for it! You had best take me before the justices and I will swear to it.'

'You do not deny that you took her deep into the heart of the Burrows? That you were seen with her and the child?'

'Why should I deny it? It is the truth and I have never sought to hide it, for I took her to where she asked to be driven! I did no more and no less. Now, you had best arrest me or be gone from the livery. Make your choice!' His face was flushed with anger, the outrage of innocence or of a cornered man, Joshua could not be sure.

'Why should she ask to be set down, not at the dunes near the church as you earlier claimed, but deep in the heart of the Burrows? There is neither house there nor help.'

'Hell and damnation!' Curtis exploded into intelligence. 'How am I expected to know? I am not her keeper! As I have told you, her fare was paid. I did as I was directed. No more and no less!'

'Yet you say that you do not know who paid you, 'Joshua

122

persisted. 'Did that not give you cause for suspicion, alarm even?'

'If I suspected all who come here or demand my services then I would end in bankruptcy! I judge men not by the cut of their jibs but their readiness to pay. Now, sir, if you will allow me to earn an honest crust, I will be about my lawful business.' His expression was surly, his stance openly belligerent.

But Joshua stood his ground, asking bluntly, 'Did you not wonder when you left the woman and child whether you were leaving her at risk? Did it not occur to you that she might be intending to take her own life, be at the mercy of wind and weather, or fall prey to some felon?'

'As I have said,' he exclaimed irritably,' I am not her keeper, nor any other's! Let that be an end to it!'

'But in common humanity,' Joshua began, only to be abruptly silenced as Curtis declared scathingly,

'Common humanity pays no bills! Now, sir, either take me before the justices or take your leave. I have work to do if you have not – save to harass those who attend their own business and not others!' He added witheringly, "If that is what I am charged with, then I plead guilty.'

'I seek a murderer,' Joshua said coldly.

'Then you must look elsewhere!'

'I shall look anywhere and everywhere,' Joshua's voice held both purpose and warning. 'I shall not give up. Believe it!'

'Then I wish you joy of your work, Constable!' Curtis's tone was derisive, a veiled insult. 'I'll own that I am oftimes defeated by mine.' To Joshua's enquiring look, he answered, 'Horses are crude, stubborn creatures, stupid and with little to commend them. More trouble than they are worth!'

'The same may be said of men.'

As if Joshua had not spoken, Curtis continued sourly, 'They may be tamed by the whip and the goad!'

'I have more faith in the value of patience, for both horses and men.'

'Then 'tis no wonder you have such little success, Constable,' Curtis taunted, 'that you are forced into harassing those innocent of crime instead of pursuing those who commit it!'

'A warning, sir, 'Joshua said levelly.

'A warning?'

'Yes. It does not do to goad and whip savagery into animals, be they horses or men, for they will become wary and vicious in return, awaiting only the moment to strike back. Contempt for them may reap a harsh reward.' Joshua turned, and strode away before Curtis could answer, leaving him fuming impotently upon the cobbles.

Curtis shouted angrily for a stable boy to bring Joshua's grey and the young lad whom he had earlier berated came running anxiously at his command. Curtis continued blustering and haranguing the boy, making him painfully slow and awkward in his actions and confusing him the more. Joshua saw, to his disgust, that the boy's face bore evidence of a recent whiplash and his bare arms the bruises and scars of old beatings and felt a cold fury rise within him. To openly accuse Curtis, he knew, would but exacerbate the situation, make him more brutal and callously set upon revenge. Joshua delved into the pocket of his breeches and delivered the boy a penny, and felt pity as the lad took it with murmured thanks, then cowered away instinctively, beyond Curtis's reach.

'I thank you for your cooperation, sir,' he said wryly to the livery man.

'I fear you have learned nothing and have had had a wasted journey, Constable.' Curtis's self-satisfaction was clear.

'I think not,' Joshua replied, regarding him steadily. 'I have learned all I wish to know of you, sir, and your business here. Besides, it has reinforced me in my certainty of what we discussed.'

'Discussed?'

'Indeed, sir. I beg you will remember it. It will hold you in good stead for my future visits.' Joshua's gaze veered towards the stable-lad. 'It is wiser to treat all, whether animals or men, with patience and forbearance, else you might reap harsh reward. I bid you good-day, sir, against my return.' He steadied the grey, then rode out purposefully through the archway. He did not look back.

Rosa Doonan, picking up her daughter, Joy, from the make-shift cradle which Cavan had fashioned from the drawer of a linen press, paused to press a kiss to the infant's soft cheek. Oh, but she was a pretty babe, she thought indulgently, and as contented as the day is long. The child's coming had made such a difference to their lives it was past all believing, for she filled their hours as she filled their hearts. Rosa selected some fresh gowns for her from the chest, scented with sweet-smelling lavender, and smiled to see how the little girl smiled and crowed her delight, making no resistance or objection as Rosa dressed her. There were so many fine clothes to choose from for Rebecca, Phoebe Butler and indeed all the good folk of the hamlets had been generosity itself, grudging her nothing.

She had been especially touched when Emily Randall had come calling, bringing with her a hand-sewn christening robe of such exquisite stitchery that Rosa had burst into tears of real pleasure. They had wept and laughed together as true friends might, regretting such foolish mawkishness their sentimentality. Yet Rosa had been truly touched by Emily's generosity, the hours of patient, painstaking labour so freely given. Rosa had known that Emily had stitched christening gowns for Elizabeth Devereaux's babe, Mary, and for Rebecca's John; gowns to be admired and cherished as heirlooms in the years ahead. Yet the gown Emily had made for Joy was every whit as skilfully sewn and as lovingly made. Rosa's warm tears had been for that, too, that Emily had lavished as much care upon their daughter's gift, although she and Cavan and Joy were united only by love, and were not blood kin.

Emily said when Rosa had exclaimed her pleasure and incredulous delight, 'Oh, but it has long lain waiting, my dear, in the small glove chest in my loft above the coach-house. Not simply for any child, but for yours and Cavan's. It was made with Joy's coming in mind.'

Cavan, upon seeing it, had scarce been able to credit its cobweb-fine delicacy, the fragile perfection of it. Indeed he had been too nervous at first to pick it up, as nervous as he had been of holding Joy, feeling his great fists too awkwardly clumsy. Yet, when he had finally been persuaded, he had held both with real tenderness, his calloused palms, roughened by toil, as gentle as any woman's touch.

'It is kind, Emily. A gift to treasure,' he pronounced gruffly. 'It is more than that, it is a gift of acceptance, made from the heart.' He flushed dully to the roots of his fiery hair, a large ungainly man, unused to offering words of affection. Emily,

125

who had been governess and pauper both, did not ask him what he meant. She, too, had been accepted in the three hamlets, generously and unconditionally, and knew the power of it to heal hurt. It was enough that Cavan understood.

Rosa, with Joy dressed, lifted her against her shoulder and bound her firmly to her in a crocheted shawl which Sophie had given to her. Although summer was fading it was a warm sunlit day and the westerly breeze from the sea no more than the lightest caress. Emrys had offered to take her, upon the morrow, to her widowed mother's home in Lias Cottages, the small row of fisherman's dwellings near the port. But today she would venture as far as the village to show Joy to Phoebe Butler and to take tea with her and her little grandson, Joseph, in the private parlour behind the bar.

Rosa, dressed in her very best straw bonnet and matching blue gown, with lightweight slippers instead of the heavy boots that were everyday wear, set off for the village green. If she were too early then she could sit upon one of the benches awhile, providing it was not too chill, and there would surely be someone who would hurry to see her and make much of Joy and her prettiness and her fine-laundered clothes. So alike were she and the babe in their translucent fairness, so near in colouring and features, even that none could take them as other than mother and child. She would take the small track through the edge of the dunes abutting the rear of the cottage, for she would find it quieter there and be in less danger from careless horsemen and carriages than upon the main highway. The air was warm and balmy, clotted with the scents of wild thyme and the sea, the wind-cropped turf springing beneath her feet and lightening her steps. With Joy in her arms and bound snugly to her by the crocheted shawl, Rosa felt truly at peace with herself and the world.

She was emerging onto the highway beside the village green, the Crown Inn already in view, when she heard the urgent clattering of hooves, the fierce galloping of a lone horseman. She had barely time to leap to the side of the pathway upon the roadside verge, shielding Joy jealously, fearful of being trampled underfoot, when she was hurled to the ground. It had the fearful inevitability of nightmare as she saw the horseman turn and come pounding back towards her. The

126

horror was in the obscene black sacking that covered his face with crude slits for eyes and mouth, as if he were some vile creature of the night, inhuman and insubstantial. Yet, as he leant from the saddle to wrest the child from her, the strength and violence were human, the malevolence too. Rosa clung to Joy with a demon's fury, hearing her wild screams echoing the child's bewildered cries. She fought only to save them both. She would have clawed, ripped flesh, killed if need be, to keep them together. She would have hurled herself under the horse's hooves rather than surrender the child. She felt pain engulf her as the blows descended, the fierce, wrenching pull as if her arms were being torn from her body. Then, still whimpering and sobbing aloud, she heard the shocked cries, and the fury of running feet.

Dazed and all but fainting with terror, she saw the horseman stiffen, and his eyes a virulence behind the blackness of the hood and ride off. Then, to her relief, she was raised to her feet, still clutching Joy to her, and gentle arms enfolded them both protectively.

'Dear God!' Tom Butler exclaimed, 'I have never seen the like of it! What madman would behave so, and to a harmless woman and child? I can scarce credit it!'

Ossie and he half led, half carried, her to the safety of the Crown Inn where Phoebe awaited. Shock and fierce indignation at the sight of Rosa's injuries and the child's terrified bewilderment gave way to stark practicality as both were warmed and gently comforted.

'Best send for Dr Burrell,' Tom Butler was instructed, and he went without murmur to do as Phoebe bade him.

As Ossie harnessed and made ready a horse and gig from the stables, Tom Butler said, 'It makes no sense, Ossie. What could he want of a woman with child? And masked so savagely? There are harlots and field-whores aplenty at the docks. And she was clearly carrying neither jewels nor money! Do you think it was the child he wanted?'

Ossie's face was as troubled as Tom Butler's. 'I fear so,' he admitted uneasily. 'Murder has already been done. Best ride out to the quarries, Tom, and bring back Doonan. He had best be told. And Joshua, too.'

'Aye,' Tom Butler said heavily. 'I had best be moving.'

Chapter Eleven

Tom Butler drove the gig immediately to Dr Mansel's house upon Clevis Hill to seek aid for Rosa and Joy. John Burrell responded with urgency, pausing only to hear the gist of the message, then set out briskly on foot for the Crown Inn below. Butler was able to give only the sketchiest details of the attack, although he assured the physician that despite the rough handling and blows which Rosa had suffered, she seemed to have escaped with no bones broken.

'I fear, sir, that it is shock and terror which have most disabled her,' he ventured hesitantly, 'fear for the babe and all. She was shaking like an aspen, scarce able to utter a word.'

'A hooded man, you say?' Burrel demanded curtly.

'Indeed, sir, 'tis no wonder she was disturbed beyond reason. I am not a cowardly man, not given to heathenish fancies, but I'll swear he put the fear of the very devil into me! Ossie fared no better. I have never seen him so put about! On Rosa's account and his own.'

'You did not recognise him, this hooded man?'

'No, that I did not, else he would have felt the full force of my wrath! It was ended so quickly, in a flash, you might say. My care was more for Rosa and the babe.'

Burrell said briskly, 'As mine must be. But where do you go now, Tom? To apprise Joshua?'

'Aye, that. But first to the quarries to have a word with Doonan.'

Burrel smiled wryly, shaking his head and saying, 'Whoever the man might be, villain or lunatic, I do not fancy his chances, should Doonan find him. He would fare better before the justices. *That* he might at least survive!' With a terse nod, he was away, boot soles crunching upon the small stones of

the carriageway, leather satchel clasped close, before Butler
had even made for the highway.

As Dr Burrel had forecast, Doonan was almost beside himself
with rage and distress when he heard of the brutal attack upon
Rosa and Joy. He abandoned his work upon the quarry face
without so much as a by your leave, and none in authority
had thought fit to halt his departure. Indeed, it was certain
that none would have been able, for work regulations and all
else, save Rosa and the babe, were dismissed from his mind.
Butler would have driven him to the Crown in the gig and then
set off in search of Joshua, but Emrys, seeing Doonan's blind
fury, thought it politic to take him there upon the cart, leaving
Tom Butler free to track down the constable.
  There had been none of the customary ribbing and joshing
upon the way, for Doonan was profoundly set in gloom and
Emrys had little heart for banter. Doonan's broad square-
jawed face had been set hard with anxiety and he looked
pallid beneath his filming of stone-dust, cheeks, lips and even
the blazing red of his hair leeched of all colour. Neither he
nor Emrys had washed themselves at the buckets of icy
water which the quarry lads brought from the nearby stream.
All along the highway Doonan had muttered imprecations
beneath his breath, cursing Rosa's assailant for his savagery
while promising that *he* would earn a much harsher return.
Had not Emrys been painfully aware of Doonan's distress
and the gravity of the assault upon Rosa and the child, he
might have been struck by the humour in the situation. The
Irishman's rage had stirred the old cob into violent reaction
as though, by exerting himself to unnatural limits, he might
somehow escape the floods of vituperation. They must, Emrys
thought, have been as bizarre a sight as the hooded horseman;
the wild-eyed Irishman mumbling curses, the pot-bellied nag
fleeing like a bat out of hell and he, at the reins, like some
ghastly spectre. Small wonder if those passing drew back in
alarm, fearing they saw the phantom funeral cart, harbinger
of death and disaster.
  Their arrival at the Crown Inn could scarcely have been less
auspicious, yet within order and calm had been miraculously
restored. John Burrell, satisfied that no lasting injury had been

129

done, had tended Rosa's scratches and grazes and given her a salve of arnica to ease the worst of her bruises and a potion to calm her nerves. Joy he had declared to be mercifully uninjured and none the worse for her experience. It would, he assured Rosa, be soon forgot. So it was that Cavan Doonan hurried into the parlour of the inn, hob-nailed boots clattering upon the flagstones and erupted into a scene of tranquil ease.

Rosa, Phoebe Butler and Dr Burrell looked up in surprise from their conversation and dishes of tea and spice cakes, for all the world like elderly dowagers deploring the unheralded arrival of a disruptive small boy. Doonan, weak with relief yet, perversely, outraged to find all so irritatingly normal and unconcerned, gave vent to his feelings with extraordinary vigour. Rosa, recognising the true cause of his frustration, ran to be with him, hugging him close despite her finery, her tears making runnels in the whiteness of stone-dust, and soon he was reassuring her and murmuring endearments, anger spent.

Burrell finally convinced him that neither Rosa nor Joy had taken harm, and Phoebe Butler bustled upstairs to where Joy was being cared for with young Joseph, to bring her for inspection. Her pleasure at seeing Doonan made plain, and bashfully reciprocated, he was induced to take a measure of ale before returning, upon Rosa's insistence, to the quarry face. John Burrell had promised to return to Clevis Hill to pick up his carriage and to drive Rosa and her daughter home, and to see them safely settled. So, to the approval of all, it was arranged. He would call again upon the morrow to make sure that mother and child had suffered no ill-effects, he promised, and Doonan offered him gruff thanks, trying to salve his earlier surliness. Then he hurried off to Ossie's little room above the stable where the ostler and Emrys were seated upon a stark wooden bench, supping tankards of ale. He refused all offers of refreshment, joking with heavy humour that they had best return to their labours at breaking stone, else it would be they who were 'stony broke'! Emrys had heard it said so many times before that he was hard put to summon up laughter, but laugh he did, and Ossie laughed appreciatively with him, for they knew what effort it had cost the big Irishman. They valued his friendship as he valued theirs.

Once settled aboard the cart and seated beside Emrys,

Doonan said, as they cleared the archway from the stable yard, 'Damned if I would bestir myself so swiftly again, Emrys.'

'Would you not, Doonan?'

'No, 'twas a storm in a teacup.'

'Indeed?' Emrys's voice was carefully neutral.

'Sitting there, they were, without a care in the world . . . like . . . like gentry at some bloody conversazione!'

Emrys hastily hid a smile, saying with commendable gravity, 'Yet it must have been a relief to you, Doonan?'

'Aye, I will not deny it.' He hesitated before blurting, 'They are all of life to me, Emrys, Rosa and the babe.'

'Yes, I am certain.'

''Twas Joy he was after!' Doonan exclaimed wretchedly.' Although I cannot tell Rosa, nor fathom the whys and where-fores of it!'

'You can tell Joshua what you fear.'

'Yes, 'though he will have small hope of success. We have neither a description of the man nor reason for what he did.' he groaned audibly. 'Oh, but it is a damnable mess, Emrys! I swear I will not have a moment's peace until he is trapped and safely behind bars.' Emrys nodded agreement. 'If I find him, then it will be the worse for him!' Doonan threatened abrasively. 'I will murder him, I swear it! Kill him with my bare hands!'

''Tis best to leave it to the law, to proper justice.' Emrys advised temperately.

'Justice? What justice is in terrorising women and babes? 'tis a coward's way, that of a bully and blackguard.'

'I'll not deny it, but it will serve no purpose to take things into your own hands, to extract violent revenge. It is not the villain who will suffer but Rosa and the babe, were you to end upon the gallows. Think, man! Ponder upon it! Would you leave them unprotected and destitute?'

Doonan sighed, confessing, 'Aye, you are right, Emrys. My hot-headedness was ever my failing and might well be the ruin of me. But I shall speak to Joshua.' He hesitated, admitting clumsily, 'You sometimes have sense enough, Emrys, I'll not deny it, although God alone knows where you learnt it, for you have neither chick nor child, like me. No family responsibility.'

131

With admirable forbearance, Emrys said, 'I learnt it at my mother's knee. Unlike some others.'

'Well, 'Realising that he had gone too far been insensitive even Doonan tried to make amends. 'Well, I don't mean you have *no* responsibility, nothing at all,' he mumbled, adding with sudden inspiration, 'you have the old cob!'

'Aye,' Emrys said drily. 'And I reckon I have the best of the bargain. He has more intelligence than some, is always patient and reliable, and easier to feed. Besides, he never throws a tantrum, or answers back!'

Doonan considered for a moment, suggesting sheepishly, 'And he never sings?'

'No,' agreed Emrys, grinning widely. 'He *never* sings.'

Honour and amity were restored.

Tom Butler's quest to find Joshua finally succeeded when he saw the constable riding furiously across the wide sandy acres of Pickett's Lease after quitting the livery stables. He was, Butler thought, either in a rage or a desperate hurry, for he rode like a fiend possessed. The grey, given her head, galloped with vigorous abandon, grateful to be unconfined. She was a magnificent animal, Butler thought admiringly, all easy strong-muscled grace, her hooves thudding upon the springing turf, mane and tail streaming in the wind. Joshua was an equally impressive sight, tall in the saddle, his splendid uniform and helmet adding a dashing devil-may-care distinction. There was a natural affinity between horse and rider, a careless arrogance. Butler found himself strangely moved by the rapport between the two, their easy understanding and companionship, the fleeting perfection of the sight. He hesitated before calling out to Joshua, not wanting to disturb the sheer harmony of the scene, the unselfconscious idyll.

Startled, Joshua reined in the grey beside the gig. 'Tom? Is it by chance we meet?' His face was anxious.

'No, I fear there is trouble, Joshua. I have come deliberately seeking you.'

Joshua dismounted and went to stand beside him, listening intently and with growing dismay as Butler explained what had occurred.

'Rosa and the babe are safe and unharmed? You are sure of it? You are keeping nothing hidden, nothing back?'

'No. I have told you all I know, little enough in all conscience! It was all so swift and confusing.'

'You did not recognise him, Tom? Neither you nor Ossie? There was no . . . mannerism, no impression of build, nor way of riding? Nothing to give you clue?'

'Nothing,' Butler admitted despondently. 'He neither spoke nor even turned at our coming, made no attempt to battle with us, although with the horse and all he clearly had the upper hand. I have thought about it since, here, alone, upon Pickett's Lease.'

'And what opinion have you come to?'

'That his main concern was to keep his identity secret.'

'Someone known to us, then? A villager or someone in authority in the port?'

'Perhaps, someone at least easily recognised in future.' He paused, wondering whether Joshua might think him foolish, before confessing with diffidence, 'I thought perhaps someone disfigured in some way, scarred perhaps or otherwise marked. 'Tis but a suggestion . . . 'He trailed off shamefacedly.

'Yes, it is the most likely reason, 'Joshua said matter-of-factly.' If so, we have even greater cause for concern.'

'How so?'

'Because there is something deeper that impels him, some reason for secrecy beyond whatever purpose he had in assaulting Rosa and the babe.'

'The woman murdered at the breakwater?'

'I fear so. He would have persevered else, taken Rosa or the child at whatever cost. He would not have allowed two unarmed men to halt him.'

'You think he will return, Joshua?' Tom Butler's square-jawed face was tense, eyes wary.

'I am certain of it. Yet how can I offer Rosa total protection? Explain my fears for her without increasing her terror and making her a prisoner in her own home? It would ruin both Doonan's life and her own.'

'There are many good men in the three hamlets unable to find honest labour through no fault of their own, men I have known for a lifetime and would trust implicitly and with my own life or any other's. If the justice and the vestry would be prepared to pay a small sum . . . see them armed, if need be?'

'The justice will not quibble,' Joshua promised firmly. 'I have but to convince him that Rosa's life is at risk.'

'Then I will speak to them in confidence,' Butler said, 'tell them what is involved and bid them report to you in secret. There is a room available at the Crown if it will serve you better, Joshua, for there their comings and goings will cause no disquiet.'

'Yes, I shall be glad of that, Tom,' Joshua said warmly, 'as I am grateful for your help to Rosa and the child.'

''twas but a neighbourly action. I did no more than would any red blooded man, incensed by such mindless violence. It does not bear dwelling upon! It was the act of a coward and madman to assault a helpless woman and babe. What sort of man are we dealing with, Joshua? What drives him?'

'When we know that,' Joshua said ruefully, 'we will know all, and there will be no further need for hesitation or conjecture. The damnable truth of it is, Tom, that we do not even know whom it is that we seek. We can neither describe him nor say what manner of man. A man in authority, cloaked in respectability, or an outright villain who would be known and recognised by all? I do not know how best to instruct those who will defend Rosa . . . what best to say.'

'Say that they must suspect all and trust no one,' Tom Butler said firmly, 'that no man may be judged above suspicion, no man exempted.

'It will cause anguish and mistrust in the three hamlets, 'Joshua reminded soberly, 'but, yes, it is the only way. Better mistrust than that violence should come again to Rosa and the child. There is already one death to avenge.' He remounted the grey and solemnly turned and saluted Tom Butler, then rode off towards Newton village and Doonan's small cottage

Joshua did not know if he had been able to reassure Rosa that the attack must have been the work of a passing stranger, a lone highwayman, bent upon easy theft. Even to his own ears it sounded a thin and unlikely story, for a woman and child would scarcely offer rich pickings. Money and jewels might be more easily come by upon the highway where a single coach might offer valuables and coins in plenty at barely more risk. Besides, what common thief, whether footpad or horseman, would attack so foolishly, in broad daylight, and within sight of a busy inn and village green? He would be courting disaster and for such little gain. Then there was the bizarre theatricality of the hood. A scarf as mask, perhaps, to briefly conceal a high-wayman's identity, that was commonplace; easily explained if captured or as easily disposed of. Joshua had never before come across the idiosyncracy of a hood. It was an aberration, an eccentricity which disturbed him. Was it meant to terrify or to conceal? A freak even. He dared not dwell too closely upon it in questioning Rosa lest he put her in terror of some strange, unholy ritual, the precursor of violation and rape.

'You think he will return, Joshua?' she pleaded for reassurance.

'As long as he remains in the three hamlets then he is a danger to all,' he said carefully. 'But I will set men to keep a watch upon the highways and byways. They will do so unobtrusively and he will soon enough be caught.'

'You believe he is still here, then?' her voice was high with anxiety.

'I believe that   if he is wise, then he will have left this place. But I cannot swear to it, Rosa,' he said with honesty.

'What shall I do, Joshua? I cannot become a prisoner in my own home!' she said despairingly, then, with a touch of her old spirit,' I *will* not! Else he will have succeeded in all he set out to do . . . to terrify and render me helpless.'

'If you and Cavan will allow it then I will set a man on guard here, in your own house, someone already known to you, a man reliable and trustworthy and, if you choose, he will accompany you wherever you choose to go.'

Joshua saw the conflict within her reflected upon her face then, slowly, resolved. 'It will not please Cavan,' she said, 'for he will think it a slight, a slur upon his manhood that he is unable to protect Joy and me.'

'If you would have me reason with him?'

She smiled despite the painful stiffening of her face where the blows had fallen. 'Reason and Cavan do not go together, Joshua, when fists might rule, as well you know. But to me and to Joy he is all sweet concern and gentleness. I shall persuade him of the need for it, never fear.'

'If you would prefer to have Cavan here beside you,' he offered, 'I will speak to the justice and see that it is arranged. Those at the quarries would not deny him. I am certain of that.'

'As I am certain that it would drive me to distraction, if not to Bedlam!' Rosa exclaimed with humour. 'One infant I can cope with, Joshua, but two might be sorer trial than that creature in the hood! Do not even consider it, I beg of you, if you value my friendship!'

Joshua, glancing at her pretty, determined little face, disfigured now with swellings and bruising, said truthfully, 'I value both your friendship and your courage, Rosa. Believe it!'

Rosa nodded, then turned aside to tuck the blankets more firmly around Joy in her makeshift cot so that he would not see the tears that started so treacherously to her eyes. She blinked rapidly to disperse them, seeing her child through a mist that shimmered and blurred her vision, fighting for control. When she turned to escort Joshua to the door of the cottage she felt almost calm again, quietly composed.

'I will send Stenner from Thatched Cottage at once to stay with you until Cavan returns,' Joshua promised, 'and he shall bring Betty Turner here in the gig upon some pretext or other. Their coming will not give rise to comment nor alarm Cavan as strangers might. It will seem no more than a visit from friends, eager to admire your lovely daughter.' His voice softened as he looked at the child, adding, 'A joy by name and by nature.'

Rosa reached up and settled a gentle kiss upon his cheek, aware of the painful stiffening of her own, and watched him mount the grey and ride swiftly away. Then the tears began in earnest and she sobbed painfully and unseen until she could weep no more. She could tell no one, not even Cavan, of what she really suspected, that whoever had attacked her had killed the unknown girl at the breakwater. He came either to revenge himself upon her or to steal back Joy. He had killed once and would not be satisfied until the child was once more in his power. What he would do with the child was past all thinking about, a horror she could not even dwell upon for the sickness of despair that gripped her. None must take Joy from her that she was certain. She was certain of little else save that to keep Joy safe she would kill any man or woman who sought to harm her. Was that why the murdered girl had died? Trying to protect another's child? If it proved to be so then Rosa would keep her always in grateful memory, her own and in Joy's when she was able to know and understand. Rosa would not believe that her daughter might someday be reclaimed by another. Could not. It would be too cruel a price, even for such happiness as Joy had brought her.

Upon leaving Doonan's cottage, in a reflective mood, Joshua rode at once through Newton village and thence to Thatched Cottage to tell Rebecca what had transpired. He would tell her all, certain of her discretion before Rosa and others, lest she wrongly fear that she and John Jeremiah were as cruelly at risk. He would need to confide the truth to Stenner and Mrs Turner, too, or at least as much as it was politic to know without giving unnecessary alarm or spreading their unease to Rosa. Rebecca would, doubtless, find some convincing reason for the housekeeper's visit, a message or invitation to Rosa, or a small gift for her daughter, perhaps, as Rebecca was as yet unable to visit her friend. Joshua, trained and experienced as he was in observation, would have freely acknowledged that in affairs of the heart he was woefully unobservant. In fact Rebecca often challenged him upon it, accusing him of being either deliberately obtuse or wilfully blind. Yet, to his secret pleasure, he had noticed that Stenner and Betty Turner seemed to have grown unusually companionable of late. They had both known deprivation and paupery, and Betty Turner and young Thomas had suffered intolerable cruelty and neglect. It would be a blessing to all three were friendship to develop into lasting affection. A loving family life would ease away the old hurts and soften those scars remaining. It would certainly do no harm to give them added opportunity to be together. He felt quite absurdly pleased with himself at devising such a feasible ploy, and one, moreover, designed to protect Rosa and to set his own mind to ease. None would suspect any ulterior motive from his involvement nor accuse him of it.

Rebecca, who was circumspect, gratefully welcomed his initiative. It was, she assured him, a quite remarkable plan and one she wholeheartedly supported. In fact it stopped little short of genius. She obligingly furnished victuals from the kitchen and added a prettily embroidered cot-cover for Joy to the list of small gifts. Joshua had all but blurted out news of the cradle from the villagers which Ezra had shown him, asking if John Jeremiah's crib might be spared to Rosa, whose daughter's makeshift cradle was no more than an empty drawer. Yet, fortunately, good sense reasserted itself and he said nothing of it. It would have served only to distress Rebecca and to spoil the surprise which the cottagers had so generously planned. It would have surprised Joshua to know that Rebecca, far from thinking him unobservant in matters of the heart, as she sometimes claimed, thought him a true romantic: Sensitive, Warm-hearted, Intuitive even. Yet it would have served no purpose to tell him openly, save to embarrass and make him self-conscious or diminish him before others. So the polite fiction was maintained to the benefit of all.

Joshua, once Stenner and Betty Turner had left in the gig for Rosa's cottage, found brief time to relax and see his son, and to hear from Rebecca of the excitements of the day, notably Sir Matthew's and Dr Peate's arrival. They had known that he was not able to be present at Thatched Cottage because of his duties as constable and, indeed, would have found it a cause for opprobrium had their visit encouraged any such neglect. They were two gentlemen with the highest standards of ethics and morality and expected the self-same discipline in others. Joshua respected them both, moreover, he held them in the greatest affection and would not willingly court their bad opinion.

For the moment he was more than content to relax in the comforting warmth of hearth and home and in Rebecca's company. Too soon he must prepare to don what Rebecca still called his 'gentleman's clothes' and set out, alone, for the justice's house at Tythegston to share an all-male dinner with Robert Knight, Sir Matthew and the redoubtable Dr Peate. Rebecca was excused on account of her recent motherhood, not yet being churched and accepted back into polite society. Strangely enough she had not cavilled at this nor made even a modest objection, declaring that she would, instead, have Sophie and Emily Randall for company, and would certainly have invited Rosa, too, had she not been made aware of the assault upon her. Whatever transpired, Rebecca insisted, she would visit Rosa, and soon, and Joshua solemnly promised that he would make time to accompany her.

So it was that, to his hedonistic delight, he stepped into a hip-bath, refreshingly scented with fresh rosemary, his gentleman's apparel set out upon a wooden butler stand before a roaring fire. It was a more than usually civilised way of life, he thought, sybaritic even, and he would not have willingly exchanged it for the bleak coldness of the unmarried state. Dressed in his finest doeskin inexpressibles, his fine hand-made hessian boots, his frilled shirt and neckerchief and the grey coat with its collar of quilted velvet, he continued his 'preening and tittivating', as Rebecca styled it, at the gentleman's toilet stand which she had bought for him.

'My dear Joshua,' she exclaimed when she saw him resplendent in his finery, 'I'll vow that you will be the most handsome and distinguished gentleman at the justice's soirée.'

Joshua grinned, saying, 'Since I shall be the only gentleman present who has not used up his three score years and ten, Leyshon included, I will not deny it.'

'Pride goeth before a fall, sir,' she reminded. 'Besides, handsome is as handsome does.'

'Then I shall kiss you most handsomely.' Joshua demonstrated his proficiency to the extreme satisfaction of both.

'Joshua?'

'Yes, my love.'

'I would find you handsome were you three and twenty, or three and seventy, 'Rebecca said shamelessly. 'You are quite the most elegant, handsome and distinguished gentleman it has ever been my good fortune to meet. 'Tis no wonder I accepted you.'

'And you, ma'am, are the most accomplished flatterer and brazen wench I have ever encountered, 'tis no wonder I courted you!'

With an arm about her waist and amidst her laughing denials, Joshua generously allowed her to escort him into the stable yard.

At the Crown Inn archway, Ossie lingered indecisively,

seamed walnut face clenched in concern. He was not sure what troubled him nor how could he explain it to others. Indeed, he did not know if he should mention it at all, since it was all so nebulous, scarce more than a feeling of something gravely amiss.

Even as he reflected, Joshua rode by upon the grey, handsomely attired in his gentleman's finery and set for the justice's house, Tythegston Court, to take dinner. He waved cheerfully to the other and called out a teasing greeting, and Ossie instinctively responded in kind, so that Joshua rode on, smiling broadly, raising his high silk hat in extravagant deference.

Perhaps I should have halted him, Ossie thought, told him of my fears. Yet what did they amount to? What credence could he put upon them? The only witness had been the sweeping boy and he, as even the most charitable knew, was lacking in wits and in words, scarce able to make himself understood, save to the horses in the stables. Yet he had been almost demented with terror, so anguished and incoherent with shock and distress that Ossie was afraid that he might throw a fit of some kind, an apoplexy even. Ossie had tried to pacify him, make sense of his ramblings, but he could not be calmed, sobbing and shaking most violently. All he could say was, 'Blaze! Like Blaze!'

'Who?' Ossie had urged him, 'who, lad?' But in vain, for the boy was too terrified to make explanation. Ossie had ushered him within the Crown Inn and Tom Butler had given him a tankard of ale, spiced and made hot with a poker, but had been unable to wrest sense from the boy. Yet Ossie was certain that something or someone had come to terrorise the sweeping lad and he felt an overwhelming sense of impotence at not understanding or being able to act upon it.

Tomorrow, he vowed to himself, he would seek Joshua out, tell him of his fears. Perhaps Joshua would be better able to question the lad, for he would be calmer then, the terror receded. But what terror? What blaze?

Ossie took a hunk of bread and some strong cheese from his bleak loft above the stables, his own frugal supper, and carried it down to the stables below where the lad made his bed beside the horses. It was the only comfort he could give; comfort for the body. A broken mind and spirit is harder to heal.

Chapter Twelve

The dinner party at Tythegston Court, contrary to Joshua's expressed opinion to Rebecca, turned out to be a lively and stimulating affair, for the three elderly gentlemen were excellent raconteurs and the justice's cellar their equal in quality. If the conversation occasionally veered towards the formal and polite arts, it was leavened by such outrageous wit and mimicry that even the imperturbable Leyshon was observed stifling a smile as he went stoically about his duties.

It was a most eloquent and convivial gathering, the pristine napery, gleaming crystal and silver and the glowing candles a fitting background for the sartorial elegance of the gentlemen themselves. The food proved excellent and the toasts to Rebecca and John Jeremiah Matthew Stradling made with the greatest good humour and gallantry. Indeed, as Joshua would have been the first to admit, while his own energy ebbed and his senses grew agreeably relaxed by wine, his fellow companions grew increasingly lively and loquacious. It was true, he reminded himself, that he had been hard at work all day while they were at leisure. Yet that was not the real nub of it. His fatigue sprang not from over-exertion but from knowledge of failure, his inability to act. It drained and demoralised him. Once he found himself stifling a yawn, a solecism quite insupportable in such distinguished and eloquent company. He had joked with Rebecca, he recalled guiltily, about the advanced ages of Sir Matthew, Dr Peate and the justice, not to mention the redoubtable Leyshon, who considered them mere striplings, scarce entering their prime. Why, then, did he feel that he was the geriatric and not they?

Sir Matthew, seeing the strain and tiredness that beset the young constable, skilfully turned the conversation to the affairs of the three hamlets and Robert Knight's part in them, and gradually, almost imperceptibly, Joshua was drawn in and his opinion sought.

'The young woman who was murdered at the breakwater,' Sir Matthew asked when they were settled over their port. 'You say she has no connection with the infant abandoned at the inn?'

'No,' the response was Robert Knight's. 'Burrell will swear to it as, indeed, he must, at the inquest to be held Tuesday week. It is my firm opinion,' he stated sententiously, 'that the dead woman and the child were in no wise related. That the affairs are coincidental and no more.'

'Joshua?' Sir Matthew regarded him quizzically. 'You do not agree?'

'No. I am convinced that there is something hidden, something that links them,' he admitted ruefully. 'Yet what it is I am unable to say.' He told them of the attack upon Rosa and Joy and his fears for them, and made his plea to Robert Knight for aid to protect them.

'Yes! Yes! Of course you must do what you think fit.' The justice was dismissive, feeling that he had been unfairly compromised, set at a disadvantage. 'That alters the whole complexion of the affair,' he grumbled. 'Without the facts, Stradling, I can scarcely make considered judgement. It was remiss, damnably remiss!'

'The attack has but recently occurred,' Joshua found himself saying defensively. 'It was while I was engaged in questioning the owner of the livery stables at the port.'

'The livery? What aberration sent you there? Upon whose information?'

'The undertaker's, sir. Evans the Box.'

'The man is a charlatan and a rogue!' Robert Knight declared abrasively. 'A mean, grasping creature, devoid of all human charity.' He recollected himself guiltily, aware of his own deficiency. 'And what did you learn of this . . . livery man?'

'Curtis,' Joshua supplied. 'He admitted that he had taken the woman and child to the Burrows, as Evans will be prepared to swear.'

'Swear?' the justice was sceptical. 'He would swear that his own mother was a renegade, sir, if it suited his own purpose. I would place no more reliance upon him than . . . than upon a weathercock! He changes direction with every fresh wind that blows!'

Dr Peate smiled conspiratorially at Joshua, asking innocently, 'This man, Curtis, he admitted it, you say?'

'Admitted what?' the justice persisted, 'that he transported her to the place requested? What crime is that? What could you charge him with? Telling the truth? If you ask me, Stradling, it was a wasted journey. As like as not it was *Evans* who was up to no good! Poaching, no doubt, or bent upon smuggling.' Joshua did not deny it. 'Rawlings has not contacted you about the smugglers?' Robert Knight demanded irascibly. 'He has found no further evidence?'

'No, sir.'

'I am surrounded by dolts and nincompoops, villains and incompetents!' The justice raised his eyes heavenwards, piously long-suffering.

'I am sorry, sir, that you judge us so,' Dr Peate's precise, cultured tones were warm with amusement.

'No! No!' To his credit the justice flushed then delightedly joined in the laughter, explaining, shamefacedly, 'This attack upon Rosa Doonan has unnerved and distressed me, for I feel in some wise responsible.' In answer to Sir Matthew's questioning glance, he confessed, 'It was I who gave her permission to keep the child.'

'Upon *my* insistence, sir.'

The justice brushed Joshua's interruption aside, declaring, 'I would not have her harmed. I did not realise the implications . . . what dangers were involved.'

'It would do greater harm were you now to remove the child,' the calm, measured voice of Sir Matthew reasoned.

'But to a place of safety?' the justice insisted.

'There would be no place of safety. Nowhere on earth that a determined man could not breach. A foundling home or poorhouse would not protect the child and only add grief to the Doonans' loss. It would be the greatest cruelty and to no purpose.' He paused, adding briskly, 'Besides, you have freely given Joshua permission to hire protection for Rosa and the child.'

'Yes,' the justice admitted reluctantly, but he was clearly unconvinced.

Dr Peate, sensing his indecision, strove to change the course of the conversation. 'I understand, Joshua, that you have been successful in apprehending the sheep stealers upon Stormy Downs? A very creditable endeavour.' The justice remained silent.

'It was purely with the help of the villagers, Dr Peate,' Joshua admitted. 'They were magnificent in every way.' He repeated the story of the capture and Doonan's and Emrys's part in it to appreciative chuckles from his listeners and a spate of hilarious suggestions as to how it might otherwise have been conducted, or ended. The company grew increasingly more relaxed and congenial, inspired by port and good humour.

'This woman,' Dr Peate ventured, 'the one dressed in men's clothing. Robert made mention that she claimed to have given birth to a child.'

'Yes,' Joshua admitted uneasily. 'Yet I have no proof that it is true. I questioned her thoroughly, and those with her, but to no purpose.'

'A ruse, perhaps, to seek leniency?' Sir Matthew suggested.

'I honestly do not know, but I shall ride out tomorrow to Pyle gaolhouse, to learn what I may. A cell and the threat of hanging might prove a deterrent enough to loosen tongues.'

'Or stiffen the resolve,' the justice predicted gloomily. 'They have little to gain save the wrath of their fellows.'

'Or their own skins,' Sir Matthew reminded. 'That is incentive enough.'

'Yes,' Dr Peate conceded. 'It is often claimed that there is honour among thieves. I beg leave to doubt it! A man who will steal for gain will betray for gain.'

Sir Matthew said quietly, 'If the woman has a child and loves it, as she claims, then I think that you will be hard-pressed, Joshua, to break her. The maternal instinct is strong enough to withstand all, even the threat of death and separation. To protect the child, whatever her sins and failings, she will sacrifice all.' He hesitated. 'Mr Knight . . . Robert, has confided to me that you suspect the possible involvement of Sir Peter Henshawe in the Vale of Glamorgan.' He shook his head regretfully. 'It will be hard to prove.'

'Indeed,' Dr Peate agreed. 'He is accepted as a gentleman

of the highest calibre and widely respected. His philanthropy is well-known and there will be none willing to offend him.'

The justice grunted, 'It is all academic, sir. A nonsense, a mere figment of the imagination. Where is the proof? The say-so of a sheep-stealer and villain? What force would that have in a court of law? What credence?'

'Yet the accusation was laid.'

'Precisely, by a villain wanting only to save his own hide! Joshua has no evidence that it was not a name remembered and chosen at random. Why, such accusation might as easily be laid against any one of us here present, as a diversion . . . a ploy. Besides, although Rawlings, my customs man, took prisoner three men awaiting the sheep thieves, and anchored off Newton Creek they made no such allegation.'

'If Joshua can find another to substantiate such accusation,' Sir Matthew declared firmly, 'I will act without delay. Respectability and philanthropy are no defence against corruption. They might well be a deliberate cover. Meanwhile, Dr Peate and I will learn whatever we can of Henshawe and his business activities, for we may do so in seeming innocence and with none suspecting our involvement.'

Joshua thanked him while the justice mumbled polite approval without any real enthusiasm, feeling that the initiative was slipping away from him.

'I was about to suggest,' Sir Matthew said equably, 'that a likeness be made of the woman murdered at the breakwater, a drawing, perhaps, that might be easily reproduced and distributed with some small reward attached?'

The justice bristled, saying, 'Of course. A capital idea. Why have you not thought of it, Stradling? Not put it into practice?' He hesitated, confessing, 'Rebecca has drawn such likenesses in the past, but it would not be seemly now, of course. One could not ask it of her. It is quite out of the question. But Dr Mansel, now. Perhaps as Home Office pathologist he might take on the task.'

'Can he draw, sir? Is he capable?' Joshua asked, puzzled.

'Capable, Stradling? Of course he is capable. Does he not need to draw diagrams for anatomical usage and such?' he asked vaguely. 'Yes, that shall be arranged at once, before the inquest and burial, else it will be too late! You had best take word to him, Stradling. Tonight. When you leave.' Joshua nodded resignedly. 'Oh, and you had best tell the undertaker, Evans.'

'I do not think that Dr Mansel will find much comfort at Evans's house, sir.'

'Comfort? Comfort?' demanded the justice with acerbity. 'There is less comfort for the corpse! It is his duty, sir, part of the Hippocratic oath: "First, do no harm",' he quoted sententiously. 'Comfort, indeed! We must all sacrifice our comfort in the interests of others.' He passed the port to Dr Peate and motioned to Leyshon to offer the humidor with his choicest cigars. Dr Peate raised a quizzical eyebrow at the manservant before gravely accepting one and saying with convincing innocence to the justice, 'I concur wholeheartedly, sir. As gentlemen of the cloth it is incumbent upon us to set example to others. God grant us the strength of mind and will to do so.'

'Amen to that, sir,' the justice said, not a whit disconcerted. 'Amen to that.'

Long after Joshua had taken his leave of them the three elderly gentlemen lingered beside the library fire, sampling the justice's brandy and reviving old memories and reliving old times, for they had been friends since early adulthood.

'Joshua is a young man of rare intelligence and honesty of purpose,' Dr Peate ventured. 'You are fortunate that you have him in your employ.'

Robert Knight's dark, protuberant eyes glimmered with humour behind his gold-framed glasses. 'Indeed,' he agreed. 'I am not unaware of his powers of persuasion. I sometimes have the bizarre delusion that it is he who is employing me.' He laughed unaffectedly, admitting, 'There is a constant battle for supremacy between us; a conflict of wits and will. It adds spice to an otherwise unendurably placid existence.'

'I believe, Robert, that he relishes it as much as you,' Dr Peate approved. 'That he is fully aware of your regard for him.'

'Oh, I do hope not!' the justice exclaimed, 'for I am at the greatest pains to hide it. It would serve no purpose to turn the boy's head with praise and flattery, however well meant. No. We are both more comfortable with an armed neutrality,

146

occasional hostility even. It keeps us on our mettle.' As Sir Matthew laughed appreciatively, he continued, 'I tell you honestly, Matthew, that you are well blessed in Joshua, and in Rebecca, too. Now there is another generation in young John Stradling, a chance to link future with past. There is a closeness of blood, a continuity; a chance to redeem those errors and disappointments too long endured. I would give much of what I own, all even, to secure such a succession.'

Sir Matthew put a comforting hand to his friend's arm, saying soberly, 'I know that having lost your young nephew so bitterly in death, Robert, the future must sometimes seem bleak indeed, as bleak as mine with my own son's defection and death, for we were never reconciled. I regret it. The wasted life and the wasted time.' He shook his head, saying, 'There is no pain deeper than the pain of regret, for things done or left undone, said, or left unsaid.'

Dr Peate nodded. 'Yes. I sometimes think that the whole of humanities griefs can be encompassed in those two sad words, 'If only.'

There was a silence before he said, with deliberate lightness, 'Your land and all that you own is entailed and will continue through future generations. What little I own will be of no consequence to any and die with me.'

'No!' Sir Matthew's denial was sharp.' It is your teaching and your example which have formed the lives of others, those like Joshua and Rebecca. You have given them faith and stability, a recognition of their own true worth. A line of blood stretches through but one family, weakening perhaps with generations. Those whom you have instructed will know no such boundaries, and who can judge the ultimate value of the good which you have done?'

Dr Peate's thin, childlike face was at first grave, then radiant with unconcealed pleasure, as Robert Knight added with gruff awkwardness, 'I am grateful for your loyalty and friendship. There, it is said, and I will not repeat it, for it will not bear the retelling. Age and drink render a man maudlin. That is the crux of it. They make poor companions. Yet you have been close friends and companions to me these many years, I am grateful for that.'

Robert Knight sniffed audibly to hide his embarrassment

at so crassly revealing his true feelings. He would regret it upon the morrow, he knew, for it was not the behaviour of a civilised gentleman; a justice, squire and man of the cloth. Yet our friends are privileged to witness the best and worst in us, and to recall only that which is good. They were all three, old, and their time remaining was best used to advantage. Dr Peate had said that 'If only,' was the saddest phrase in the language; the tragedy of words spoken, or left unsaid . . . No. He would not, after all, regret it. It was no more than the truth. They had based their lives and living upon it. They were beyond the need for pretence.

Joshua, riding along the main highway from Tythegston Court, silvered now by the paleness of moonlight, should have felt comfortably at ease. That he did not owed nothing to the vagaries of the evening, for he had dined and wined superlatively and enjoyed the stimulating company and conversation of friends. Besides, he had heard his own doubts and fears debated by others and benefited from their objectivity and clarity of mind. In addition, Sir Matthew had promised him help in investigating Sir Peter Henshawe's putative involvement in the sheep stealing encounter upon Stormy Downs. Dr Peate, too, had declared his willingness to help. Even the justice's habitual abrasiveness had been tempered, then overcome. Altogether it had been less of an ordeal than he had, at first, feared. He realised, now, that he had been remiss in not warning the justice of the attack upon Rosa and in springing it upon him when his opinion had already been given. It had served to diminish Robert Knight's authority before Sir Matthew and Dr Peate, made him look foolishly autocratic, inflexible in mind. Joshua was sorry for that but had known no way to prevent it, for the justice had brushed his tentative explanations irascibly aside, declaring, 'This is neither the time nor place for a discussion of mundanities, Stradling! This is a social occasion, a rare opportunity to welcome my friends. It will surely keep until tomorrow? I would not burden others with trivia.' He had hesitated only briefly, to demand, 'There have been no more deaths? Murders?'
    'No, sir, but . . .'
    'But me no buts! Short of plague, pestilence, earthquake,

tempest, or violent deaths, I will hear no more of the affairs of the three hamlets. We are not a gathering of peasants with no thought of the world beyond. Sir Matthew and Dr Peate are scarce deserving of that.' The implication was that Joshua might well be.

Rebuffed, if not chastened, Joshua had not pursued the matter. The result, as he now knew, was once again to incur Robert Knight's displeasure. It seemed, he thought philosophically, that there was no way of avoiding it since sins of commission or omission stirred the same wrath. His role, whether active or passive, was predetermined. He was the justice's scapegoat. He had best accept it. Yet, deep down, he had a liking and respect for that abrasive and volatile gentleman and knew that, however grudgingly, it was returned. Their verbal skirmishing was no more than a battle of wits, the cut and thrust of polemic, rapier keen yet meant only to taunt and draw blood, not fatally wound.

Joshua suddenly felt a lifting of spirits. The road ahead was a stretched ribbon of moonlight dappled with the shadows of hedgerows and trees, the grey's hooves ringing clear as a tocsin upon the night air. For a moment he was at one with nature and could forget the doubts and uncertainties that plagued him, the realisation of all that needed to be done. The sudden harsh cry of a nightjar lacerated the air and in a moment his mood was gone, the sense of oppression returned. He would have welcomed a swift return to Thatched Cottage and to the warmth of a shared bed, Rebecca's flesh and soft embrace. He could not return yet awhile, for he had the justice's commissions to fulfil. The prospect gave him little pleasure. Dr Mansel would scarcely be overjoyed at being roused at such an hour and burdened with the task of spending an hour or so sketching a cadaver, and in the company of the odious Ezra the Box. He could only hope that he would not follow the mores of the Ancient Greeks and slay the bearer of bad tidings, metaphorically if not in the flesh! As for taking the justice's command to Ezra, to be slain might be a more welcome fate. It was too late in the day to keep up the fiction of even the barest civility.

Even as he pondered, he heard behind him the unmistakable sound of a light-weight carriage taking the corner to the Clevis

Hill. There were few enough gentlemen's carriages in the three hamlets and it aroused his curiosity to hear one being driven so late into the night. A casual visitor to the Crown or the Ancient Briton would have secured a room for the night long since, for the roads were no place for a lone traveller after dark. He reined in the grey and waited.

The carriage which came into view was Dr Mansel's familiar curricle, open to the night air and balanced upon two slender wheels. Mansel drew up the twin horses beside Joshua, the whale-oil lamps strangely diminished by the moon's glow.

'Joshua? Abroad at such an hour?' His opaque green eyes beneath the craggy brows were alive with curiosity.' I see that it is a social outing that has beckoned, unlike my own.'

'Dinner with the justice and Sir Matthew and their friend, Dr Peate,' Joshua confirmed. 'But I have come seeking you, sir. It is the greatest good fortune that I have met you.'

'Dear Lord, Joshua!' Mansel exclaimed feelingly, 'not another corpse or disaster! I have scarce left the last one.'

'You have been called out to a death, sir?'

'No! No!' Mansel exclaimed. 'I had in mind the girl murdered at the breakwater. But, yes, I have been called out urgently to attend a man injured by a gun shot.'

'A shooting, you say? Where, sir?' Joshua demanded abruptly. 'Who was involved?'

'There are no sinister implications,' Mansel said, smiling. 'I do not think it need trouble you. Indeed, it was scarce worth the bother of harnessing up the curricle.'

'An accident, then?'

'Undoubtedly. A flesh wound only, superficial, and of his own carelessness. I might have been spared the effort and clung to my beauty sleep.'

'Who, sir? Who is involved?' Joshua's voice was unusually sharp and Mansel looked at him in open astonishment.

'Someone newly come to the hamlets. I do not know if you have knowledge of him? He owns the livery stables at the port, a man by the name of Curtis?'

'Curtis! Hell and damnation!' Joshua exploded forcibly. 'Then I had best be off to interrogate him.'

Mansel raised his eyebrows expressively, saying equably, 'I do not think that there is need for urgency. Believe me, Joshua, he will live 'til morning and, like as not, to his full three score years and ten! He is ludicrously hale and hearty, more's the pity, for he is a crass, insensitive creature and would be no great loss.'

'I take it that he made no great impression upon you, sir?'

'Then you take it correctly. It would be hard to make any impression upon *his* thick hide, even with gunshot! A more churlish, self-opinionated rascal I have never met. He offered me neither gratitude nor respect for my pains. I might have stayed safely abed.'

'Then I shall defer the pleasure until tomorrow,' Joshua said, not without relief, 'for I could not guarantee the warmth of my own reception.'

Mansel looked at him quizzically, but did not pursue the matter, asking instead, 'But you said that you had come seeking me, Joshua. What is it that you require of me? Or is it at the justice's behest?'

'The justice's,' Joshua explained about the need for a drawing of the murdered girl and the promised reward.

Mansel broke into a great gust of laughter which almost set the horses bolting in panic, then shook his head incredulously. 'Dear Heaven!' he exclaimed, grinning. 'I thought that I had heard it all! He wants me to sketch the cadaver, you say? Are you sure that you heard aright? You have not wined too well?'

'No.' Joshua was grinning as foolishly. 'I fear that he is set on it. Nothing will dissuade him.'

'Then I shall oblige.'

'I shall apprise him of it, sir, as soon as ever I am able.'

Mansel nodded, saying, 'There is but one small impediment.'

'And that, sir?'

'That at medical diagrams, sketches of organs and their functions, none can fault me. A likeness, now, well, that is a different matter.'

'Then you will not be eager to accept the commission?' Joshua could not wholly conceal his disappointment.

'On the contrary, it will give me the richest amusement, notwithstanding a certain macabre quality.'

'But if you cannot promise a convincing likeness, sir?'

'Ah, that is the nub of it. But believe me, Joshua, I am

151

reasonably competent, if without Rebecca's artistic distinction. I shall do creditably enough, never fear. No, my amusement will lie in making two sets of drawings – one fastidiously correct in every detail and prepared solely for the justice.'

'And the other?'

'Of the execrable Ezra. Should he even attempt to harass or aggravate me with his importunate whinings I shall threaten to fasten one upon every tree, giving promise of a reward should he be first vigorously assaulted, then apprehended and brought to me.'

'I do not think that such a venture would be strictly legal, sir,' said Joshua, straight-faced.

'No more are Ezra's,' responded Mansel. For a brief moment the light of the moon lit up his amused, intelligent face, silvering his profligate eyebrows and the aureole of fly-away hair, wispy as thistledown. Then, as suddenly, the laughter was gone, his expression sombre. 'I will make as honest a likeness of the dead girl as I am able,' he promised. 'Whoever she may be and whatever her story, she is deserving of that. She was not deserving of the death that came to her, the manner and violence of it. It is all that I can now do. I would have her killer apprehended and brought to justice.'

'As I, sir,' Joshua agreed.

'I never get used to the waste of it.' Mansel's hands were clenched hard upon the reins, delicate and strangely sensitive for so well-fleshed a man. 'The waste that is death, I mean. It is more than a severing of flesh and bone, a stilling of blood. It is an ending of all.'

Joshua knew that it was of his dead wife that Mansel spoke and did not know how best to answer him.

'Well, I had best be moving,' Mansel murmured awkwardly. 'Will you visit Ezra tonight? Give him news of my errand?'

'No. I will reserve that pleasure for tomorrow when I am better able to face the encounter. If wining and dining have not prepared me, I can but hope that sleep does! I do not view the prospect with any great fervour.'

Mansel smiled, 'And I, sir, would place the rigours of a post-mortem operation well below the rigours of Ezra's company, for at least my companions, then, have the virtue of silence!' He took up the reins, stirring the horses into life, but immediately calming them again to say unexpectedly, 'I was called out just after dusk, to Weare House, you recall it?'

'The annexe to Pyle Inn and set upon the shore?'

'Yes. There are patients there, travellers arriving for the sea-bathing before the season ends.'

'There is something there needing my attention? Some difficulty?'

'No, none. It might be nothing of import, you understand, but Burrell has told me of the attack upon Rosa and I know that you seek the killer of the murdered girl.'

'You saw someone suspicious?' Joshua demanded. 'Some activity, perhaps?'

'Lights, Joshua, lights only, but far beyond Weare House, out beyond Newton Creek. Not steady but moving and bobbing, like hand-held lanterns. It might be no more than fishermen setting their nightlines, dependent upon the turn of the tide.'

'Perhaps.'

'I could not rightly tell where, you understand. Upon the cliffs, beyond even. Dusk was falling and making distances deceptive and the lights awkwardly moving,' he apologised. 'The moon was not yet high.'

'After you left Weare House? Or before?'

'Before. When I quitted the house, after an hour or so, for I was persuaded to pause there for refreshment, the lights were gone. All was darkness again.'

'You spoke of it to no one?'

'No one.'

'Then, please, I beg of you, keep silent upon it.'

'If you think it wise,' he hesitated, blurting shamefacedly, 'I would have come searching for you or sent word but was summoned at once to Stormy Downs and thence from my bed to attend Curtis. In the confusion and flurry, I forgot.'

'It makes no matter. They will be long gone,' Joshua said, 'but I will keep watch or ride out now, to learn what I may.'

'I think it might serve you better to change from your gentleman's finery,' Mansel advised, smiling widely. 'It could set you to severe disadvantage. They might seek to rob you, hoping for rich pickings from such a fine macaroni, a dandy even!'

'Then it is to be hoped that it will lull them into a sense of

153

false security! Such a harmless Beau Brummel would scarcely wish to soil his fine clothes, much less soil his hands! It is all part of my strategy, sir; a skilful deception.' Joshua grinned and raised his high silk hat in extravagant salute, then firmly turned the grey towards Weare House and the sea.

Chapter Thirteen

Joshua's nocturnal visit to the rocky creeks beyond Newton point elicited nothing of purpose, for the incoming tide had done its work well. It had washed away all traces of human activity, the frilled edges of foam at the water's edge a phosphorescent glow in the moonlight. Beyond, upon the ridge of dry sand, there was a tangle of flotsam and jetsam cast high. All the detritus of nature sucked clean and spewed out as if by some peevish giant; bladderwrack and feathers, driftwood and cork, cuttlefish bone and egg cases, dried to brittleness and long forsaken. Amongst them tiny seawater creatures moved unseen, scavenging relentlessly, the living preying upon the dead.

Joshua, standing disconsolately beside the grey upon the wind-drifted dunes, wished that all the detritus of flawed humanity could have been gathered as neatly and as easily and cleanly disposed of. There was nothing here for him. It was true that in the cleft between the dunes there was sign of past activity not yet swept into order by the wind from the sea. Yet what did a flurry of sand and footprints signify? Fishermen dragging their boats into the sea, eager to cast their nets while the moonlight held? Cottagers setting their nightlines to eke out a frugal living, like Jeremiah, or simply to feed their families? Whatever Dr Mansel had seen, there was no vestige of it now; neither light nor movement.

Joshua remounted the grey. The tiredness which had earlier plagued him had returned and with it a sense of futility. He would venture no further along the coast for, with the tide high, his way would be barred by the swift race of the river estuary; fiercely impenetrable in full spate. Tomorrow he would speak of his suspicions to Peter Rawlings, the exciseman, beg him to keep watch. It might amount to a little harmless smuggling, no more than that. A small haul of tobacco and brandy for the cottagers' own use and from which the local excisemen obligingly looked away, even if they were not fully prepared to turn a blind eye. Joshua, setting the grey to return across the rough track through the dunes, smiled wryly. If Ezra the Box were involved, his arrest would cause more chaos and disaster than the sheep stealers and smugglers combined. A place without undertaker or carpenter would soon feel his loss, and he and the justice would be inconvenienced more than most. And Dr Mansel and Burrell, too, dealing as they must with cadavers. Well, guilty or not, Joshua was certain that the justice would be ill-inclined to plead for him the Queen's pardon. At least Mansel would be spared the ordeal of having Ezra as unwilling host and he, Joshua, would hear no more of his cantankerous whining. Strangely, the prospect served only to depress him. He urged the grey onward. Was it the heady pride of fatherhood which mellowed him, he wondered, or merely the caution of age? He set the horse to a gallop, and vowed to forget Ezra and all else which plagued him.

Joshua slept the sleep of exhaustion, dead to the world and all its sins, the moment his head touched the pillow. Rebecca, who had determined to stay awake to catechise him about the justice's soiree, had already succumbed. She was slumbering soundly, blue-black hair a darkness against the stark whiteness of the bed linen. Joshua sank gratefully into the goose-down mattress beside her, luxuriating in its womb-like comfort, feeling drowsily secure. He was vaguely aware of John Jeremiah's cries for attention and of Rebecca leaving their bed but, try as he might, he could not fully awaken, trapped uneasily beneath the membrane of sleep. He awakened early, mind restlessly exploring the demands of the day until, unable to suffer it more, he crept from bed, hurriedly donned his constable's uniform and, in stockinged feet, found his way silently below.

None in the house was yet stirring, for it was barely dawn as Joshua put on his riding boots and helmet and eased his way quietly without. It was a clear, crisp morning, the sky streaked with a softness of gold, saffron and red, growing steadily more vivid and lighter and with the promise of a fine day. Joshua felt the need for solitude, a quietness to calm and ease his

156

mind, and walked first across the village green, then, on an impulse, into the churchyard of the little Norman church of Saint John the Baptist. The church itself was of weathered stone so softened by age that it seemed to have grown from the landscape, formed by nature like the sea-smoothed pebbles upon the shore. There was a solidity about it, a permanence that was balm to the spirit, as if the devotions of those who had loved and worshipped there had seeped into its very fabric, permeating the very stones themselves.

Joshua, gazing at the square embattlemented tower, the lichened roof, the deep hewn windows and the grey tide of gravestones which lapped it, felt his anxieties ease. Seven hundred years and more of living and loving, of birth and death, of small sorrows and joys, were all about him. They had come and gone as inevitably as those who had borne them, with nothing to show save a plot of rich earth. Even their names died with them, obliterated by time, as forgotten as they. Yet there was no pathos in it, simply a rightness, the calm certainty of nature reclaiming its own to give life to those who came after. The resurrection preached within lay as surely without, in the springing green turf, the salt-laden air, the trees casting their leafy dappled shade. Joshua, quietly refreshed in mind, strode back through the churchyard and across the village green to the Crown Inn and into the stable yard.

Ossie, who had seen him passing, showed no surprise that Joshua had sought him out. His deep-scored face was warm with pleasure as he greeted him and bade him share ale with him in his small loft above the stables. It was such a sparsely furnished hide-away, so bleak and comfortless that Joshua sometimes wondered how the ostler endured such deprivation. Yet the reason was clear to all who knew him . . . He practised self-abnegation that the animals he cared for might be housed and fed, for he would turn no needful creature from his door, be it human or animal . . . It was strange, Joshua thought, that all who were distressed in body or mind gravitated instinctively there, for there was no comfort in so barren a place, only in Ossie's caring.

'I have been keeping a watch for you, Joshua,' Ossie said, placing a tankard of ale before him upon the wooden board.

'There is something troubling you, Ossie?'

*   *   *

157

'Rather something troubling another, one who can find no way of telling it, of making himself understood.'

'A dumb animal, you mean?' Joshua asked, bewildered.

'No, yet it is locked within him as uselessly.'

'Of whom are we speaking, Ossie? Someone known to me?'

'The sweeping boy in the yard.' He glanced through the single bare window onto the cobbles below and Joshua, following his gaze, saw the lad painstakingly clearing the horse-muck, yard-broom clutched jealously, as though someone might wrest it from him.

'What troubles him, Ossie? Of whom or what is he afraid?'

'That is the devil of it, Joshua! I have asked and asked him, to no real purpose. He is too weak-minded to explain, unable to put into words what ails him.' He hesitated. 'If you could speak to him, Joshua, he might respond to you, for he knows that you think well of him and would do him no harm. You have the lure of your grey mare, which he so admires, and the authority of your uniform. I beg you will at least try, for he is a gentle harmless creature and I grieve to see him so stricken.'

'What has he confided, Ossie? That someone has threatened or harmed him?'

'Nothing save the word "blaze", and once,' *like* blaze'. Then he fled to the stables unable to utter more. I tell you, Joshua, the boy is nigh out of his wits with terror.'

'I will speak to him,' Joshua promised. 'And now, Ossie, when no other is in sight to harass or distract him. If you will come with me, lend me support to win his confidence? I would not further distress him.'

The boy looked up from his sweeping, then nodded shyly to Joshua, thin face wary until he saw that Ossie would remain beside him. Little by little Joshua won his confidence, chatting quietly of the grey and promising that he would bring the mare to the Crown Inn that the boy might better inspect her, help groom her even if Ossie gave leave. Yet when Joshua asked what had earlier disturbed him, the boy's face stayed blankly expressionless, wiped of all understanding.

'You spoke of a blaze,' Joshua probed gently. 'You spoke of it to Ossie, you recall? A fire somewhere? A lantern? What was it that frightened you so?'

'No!' The lad's face crumpled in real terror and he trembled so violently that Joshua was remorseful and almost as anguished as he. Then the poor creature glanced despairingly about the yard, hurling his broom to the cobbles and with a wild, eldritch cry that made Joshua's blood run cold, was away across the yard and out through the arch. Joshua would have run after him, fearful for his safety, but Ossie put a restraining hand upon his arm.

'Leave him be, Joshua,' he said quietly, 'leave him be. He is confused and frightened, unable to find words. They are locked inside him with whatever terrors so bedevil him. It will serve no purpose to question him more, save to send him from the one place where he can find food and shelter, a place to lay his head. He is safe here.'

'Are you sure of that, Ossie?' The question was harshly asked.

'No . . . no more than you. There is something which threatens the lad, something to which he is unable to put name. I do not know if it is horror or his own benighted mind which renders him useless.' He shook his head despairingly.

'If he should confide in you . . .?'

'Then I shall tell you upon the instant. You have my word upon it. Something evil and unknown has reduced him to such terror, Joshua. I wish to God that I might help him but I do not know how, or even where to begin.'

'What is it that he might have seen or imagined, Ossie?' Joshua persisted. 'Is the boy terrified of fire? Has he seen moving lights perhaps? Thought them corpse's candles, harbingers of death? Old beliefs and superstitions die hard.'

Ossie said carefully, 'I do not think that he has wits enough to understand such things, Joshua, even were they said deliberately to silence him. No, it is not the supernatural that he fears but something human and malign.'

'The girl's murderer?'

'I fear so, or some other bent upon death and destruction.'

Joshua asked tensely, 'Then you will have to care for the boy, Ossie? There is little I can do to protect him. The presence of a stranger, even a guard, would unsettle him the more. He might flee in his terror, towards whatever sets him at risk.'

'I will watch over him, Joshua.' The ostler's weather-beaten fist of a face was clenched in concern, voice firm. 'Whoever or whatever seeks to harm him must first harm me.' He stood, firmly determined, upon the cobbles, a small shrunken ostler with bent back and legs awkwardly bowed from childhood. He was, Joshua thought, a gallant fierce little fighting cock, one who would go on battling until the last drop of blood was spilled, his or another's. One could not hope for a stronger ally or a more dependable friend. He could not speak such thoughts aloud.

'Take care, Ossie.'

Ossie looked at him hard, then nodded and turned abruptly away. With shoulders painfully hunched he made his slow way back across the cobbles to the stables beyond.

Joshua had returned to Thatched Cottage still pondering uneasily upon whom or what had caused the sweeping boy's turmoil of mind. He was no nearer a solution. The poor creature was clearly incapable of coherent speech or thought. If Ossie was unable to reassure the lad, or patiently unlock his mind, then Joshua despaired of ever learning the truth of it. There was nothing to link the incident with the death of the girl at the breakwater, nor yet with the woman at Pyle Gaol house. Now there was the added complication of Curtis's gun wound. Joshua felt instinctively that they were in some way intertwined. That it would need more than conjecture to convince the justice, he was fully aware. Like Dr Mansel, he demanded hard facts and supporting evidence to make accurate assessment. It was one of life's little ironies, he supposed, that the justice's role as rector required absolute faith in an unknown God, and Mansel's role as physician, faith in his own finite powers and those of providence! It would have served Joshua better had they shown such unquestioning faith in him. Moodily, and without much hope of such a miracle, he walked across the yard of Thatched Cottage and within.

Sight of his son, now awake and hugely contented, restored him to humour, and a trencherman's breakfast, cooked by the excellent Betty Turner, continued the good work. Rebecca's cheerful and uncritical presence throughout the meal was balm to his jaded spirits, and the list of interrogations and duties to be completed before the day's end no longer seemed impossible to achieve. He had all but forgotten the meeting at the Crown Inn which Tom Butler had arranged, to make permanent provision for Rosa's protection. That must be added to his tasks, as well as the statutory report to the justice and a visit to the port to apprise Peter Rawlings of his fears that the smugglers were active beyond Newton Creek.

'I do not think,' he murmured apologetically to Rebecca, 'that I shall be here in the hamlets for the churching. It will not please the justice..'

'It would please him less were you to neglect your duties!' Rebecca said airily. 'I do not give a fig for the justice's sensibilities nor any other's!' she declared stoutly. 'Well, save yours,' she amended. 'Besides, the churching is no more than a formality, Joshua. A ritual. I defy anyone to convince me that my John Jeremiah is born into original sin or inherits the sins of the father, whatever *they* may be!'

'As far as I am aware, my love, my sole indiscretion lay in marrying you,' Joshua teased, skilfully sidestepping, then grasping her upraised arm before imprisoning her close to his chest. He settled an affectionate kiss upon her pretty, mutinous face, saying as she rebelliously struggled free, 'Now, if it were *your* sins and omissions in question, Rebecca, I fear the justice would be hard pressed to list them before Michaelmas. The entire congregation would faint from hunger or horror before he was half done.'

'Ah, but what a time they would have of it, Joshua!' she declared irrepressibly. 'I'll vow it would be his best attended sermon ever, as well as the longest!' She linked an arm affectionately through his and escorted him cheerfully into the stable yard.

Upon leaving Thatched Cottage, Joshua's first brief call was at the Crown Inn. There he made arrangements with Tom Butler for a meeting with those volunteers paid to protect Rosa and to patrol the highways and byways of the three hamlets. A time was set against Joshua's returning from Pyle gaolhouse and, he was grateful to leave the necessary organisation in the landlord's capable hands. Tom Butler's guarantee of the men's good character and discretion would be recommendation enough, for he was an honest man and a fine judge of such honesty in others.

There was no immediate urgency to ride out to see Rawlings, and Mansel had declared that Curtis was in no great danger or discomfort from his gunshot wound. Consequently, Joshua determined to return via the port and to settle both issues during a single visit. For the moment, his priority must be to learn what he could of the sheep-stealers, in particular the woman who rode with them. She was a taciturn creature, ill-bred and hostile, yet others might be persuaded to speak more freely. If he could prove some link with Sir Peter Henshawe in the Vale, or find out whether the child she claimed to have farmed out actually existed, then it would serve him well. Even to prove her a liar would give Rosa and Doonan some peace of mind, although it would advance his search for Rosa's assailant no further.

So it was that, in a spirit of patient optimism, Joshua set out from Newton. He followed the wide, leafy carriageway skirting the great meadow pool, past the walled Elizabethan manor house, Nottage Court, and thence through the small farming village of Nottage and on to the stony track which led through Kenfig dunes. The westerly wind from the sea was strong with the smells of seaweed and wet sand, invigorating, yet upon the flesh no more than a pleasing warmth. In the old language, the ancients called it 'the breath from the ox's nostrils', so gently and moistly it blew. Yet cruelly, and without warning, it could scourge the unwary, lashing with gales and intemperate rain. It spared nothing that stood before it. Neither man nor beast could find protection, nor even the great sailing ships that dared pit their man-made strength against it. It shredded sails, snapped masts and boards as effortlessly as kindling, and dashed them, splintered, upon the rocks. The sea was graveyard for the unwary and the westerly gales their executioners; their sole monuments those crucified wrecks and ribbed spars that rose, like dark skeletons, for a brief resurrection before final oblivion.

Now, however, the sea was no more than a plucked greyness tipped with pale foam, the breeze a benison. Beneath the grey's hooves, the creeping thyme sent up a sharply crushed odour and the air was heavy with the oil of gorse flowers, their saffron

162

blooms smelling of coconut and bruised grass. Joshua inhaled the mingled fragrances, the grey, graceful and strong-muscled, moving smoothly beneath him.

The shot when it rang out was so violently unexpected that the mare reared in sudden terror, forelegs raking the air, and Joshua was all but thrown to the stony pathway. In the split second that he steadied the grey he reached instinctively for the rifle in the leather holster at the mare's side and leapt down to defend himself. The shot came from behind an outcrop of rock, screened by thornbushes and stunted willows, with a spreading of dunes beyond.

Joshua flung himself bodily to the rough turf behind a boulder, as fearful for the grey's safety as for his own. Whoever the attacker might be, his first thought would be to disable or drive away his victim's mount, leaving him vulnerable. To have shown himself openly would have made Joshua an easy target, for there was no protection between where he now lay and the rocks where the gunman hid. Joshua screamed urgent command to the grey and, with the obedience of long training, it fled, galloping fiercely beyond range of the marksman. Joshua steadied his rifle upon the flat surface of the boulder, awaiting opportunity to fire. There was neither sound nor movement, his adversary as wary and loath to disclose himself as he. It was to be a battle of nerves, then? Joshua, waiting impotently, felt his neck muscles grow tense, his jaw stiffen, the stress of uncertainty laying emotion raw. He dared not relax nor lessen his vigilance, eyes trained always upon the lone outcrop of rock. So intent was his gaze that his eyes blurred with the pain of it and he felt the sweat bead his lip and hairline and trickle at his nape. Then, with a wild cry, the gunman showed himself, firing even as he rose, a bullet ricocheting from the surface of the boulder as Joshua fired blindly, instinctively, in return. Joshua was in a turmoil of conflicting emotions, his every instinct to risk all. Yet cold reason was against it. He could not hope to reach the outcrop unhindered, nor even the sparse protection of scrub and willow before being gunned down. What, then? He could call out for the grey, yet it was too great a risk to take, exposing them both to certain reprisal and the marksman's aim . . .

In the split second of indecision, the gunman took his

163

chance, rising and firing again, and Joshua returned fire instinctively. Yet, even as he pulled the trigger, he was aware that this was no ordinary thief or footpad but a man obscenely hooded, as Rosa and the others had described. The moment seemed frozen, etched in stone, and Joshua with it, for he could summon neither wits nor will. Then, in one swift movement, his adversary had leapt into the saddle of his waiting mount! Joshua expected him to come thundering towards him, bent upon shooting him down, and ran from the shelter of the boulder, the better to take aim. It would be a battle now for survival, for neither could hope to escape unscathed. Even as he braced himself, the gunman shot wildly, then veered his mount towards the dunes and the rocky shore beyond, swallowed up in the fastness of maram and sand.

Joshua called frantically for the grey and it came swiftly to his command. That it would be less than useless to give chase, he knew, for the man was plainly no stranger to the dunes and shore. Upon the soft dunes and sandy hollows, his trail would be clear, but once upon the common lands or the tangle of wild lanes abutting the shore there would be no hope of tracking him. He would then have the advantage, once more the attacker, with Joshua the one pursued . . .

Joshua remounted the grey and urged it back towards the stony byway, praising it aloud for its courage and intelligence, while deprecating his own. Yet, the more he dwelt upon the encounter, the more certain he became that his attacker had turned away for some purpose. What had impelled him to do so when he had Joshua so clearly in his sights and could have shot him with impunity? Was it risk to his own neck that had stayed him? Fear that his identity might be disclosed? That argued that it was someone Joshua would have known and identified to others. Or was it that whatever villainy the gunman was engaged in was more vital than killing a mere constable who might hinder or set his plans awry? Self-preservation was the game and, for the moment, both had succeeded. There were winners and losers, and survivors. Joshua knew that survival did not put an end to the game. It would continue until one or the other lost. It would have helped, he thought wryly, were he to *know* his adversary.

*   *   *

Stenner had risen early and, upon Joshua's instruction, taken the gig to Cavan Doonan's cottage on the fringes of the Burrows. The senseless assault upon Rosa and her daughter was the talk of the three hamlets and all who spoke of it were astonished and outraged. It could only be the work of some itinerant stranger, they declared, for none in the three hamlets would stoop to such infamy. It was cowardly and unprovoked. While such a villain was at large, no woman or child was safe from such mindless violence. None could rest easy.

It was known that their constable had been charged by the justice to hire men to patrol the highways and byways. Tom Butler had said so, and that the men had been named and chosen for Mr Stradling to instruct. Yet so many of the ancients and those without hope of paid labour had declared themselves willing to help that Tom Butler agreed to call a special meeting of the villagers, that their skills might be put to advantage. He would make arrangements for it, he promised, immediately upon the constable's return.

Stenner, halting the gig without Doonan's cottage, knew that he would prove poor deterrent to a man of strength committed to violence. He was no more than a makeshift, a token protector. That he had come armed was upon Mr Stradling's insistence, for he was not altogether easy in the company of guns. He had come ostensibly to take Rosa and the babe upon an outing in the gig, to the Crown Inn, where they might be safe in Doonan's absence. Upon the constable's return, permanent protection would be arranged and the byways patrolled and made safe. He had fully expected to travel there alone, for that was Mr Stradling's instruction, but almost at the moment of his leaving the yard of Thatched Cottage, Betty Turner came bustling out to join him. She was laden with cloth-covered baskets, neatly packed with mouth-watering delicacies, freshly baked, their fragrance so warm and richly aromatic that Stenner felt a churning in his stomach and saliva forming at the corners of his lips.

As he helped her into the driving seat beside him, she confided that Mrs Stradling had been insistent upon her coming. She would give Rosa the company she needed and there was food enough for all three, so that Mrs Doonan need not feel obliged to send out for victuals. Stenner did not remind

165

her that there would be refreshment aplenty at the Crown Inn, for it would have seemed churlishly ungrateful. Besides, none could turn as light a hand to pastry as Betty Turner and only a fool would spurn such a privilege. It was a privilege, too, to have such a companion beside him, Stenner thought, for she was a comely woman, handsome in all her ways and with no simpering foolishness like some, nor silly airs and graces. To tell the truth, Stenner admitted to himself, although he would never dare to declare it to her or any other, he had grown to love Betty Turner dearly and her son, young Thomas too. Yet he must keep it well hid for she was far beyond him in skill and intelligence, superior in all her ways. To declare himself would certainly offend her, or make him an object of derision or pity, and ruin the easy friendship they knew. No, he was not of a mind to confess it, for it would mean an end to all. He would be forced to leave Mr Stradling's employ, return to his existence as pauper. He would be lower in value than the beasts he tended and none would call him friend.

Even as he helped Betty Turner to dismount from the gig, Rosa Doonan hurried out to greet them, pretty face wreathed in smiles of welcome. She had put a friendly arm about Betty's shoulders, exclaiming excitedly at her coming and at the delicacies so generously offered. Stenner had watched them indulgently, amused by their innocent prattling, and steadied the horse to unharness it from the gig and take it to the safety of the stall in the outhouse.

He had put the gig to rest upon the cobbled yard and settled the horse and watered it, and was about to make his way back when something alerted him. He felt a prickling at the nape of his neck, a certainty of danger that set his nerves on edge. The Burrows stretched endlessly about him, pristine, untrod, acres of wind-drifted sand, silvered with maram. The dry-stone wall, raised breast high, was solid protection from the sea gales and encroaching sand, the small wicket gate set into it the only breach in its defences. His hand tightened upon the pistol he held, feeling its cold metallic hardness, but it brought him no comfort. He did not know what ailed him, what nervousness made his hand shake so violently. His mouth was dry and his heart beating so suffocatingly that he felt it not only at his ribs, but pulsing at his throat. Yet he forced himself towards the gate.

There was neither sound nor movement without save for the stirring of maram and, far away, the rhythmic surge of the sea, soft as a whisper. At the furthermost corner of the yard there was a sudden swift movement, and Stenner spun around in fear, pistol cocked and levelled. In those brief seconds, when he saw the hooded man, he fired blindly, impelled by such a rage of fury that he felt no fear. His response had been immediate, involuntary even, and he knew that the gunman had been as horrified and shocked as he. He knew that he had found his target by the scream of pain as the marauder fled, arm held uselessly. Coldly, and with savage intent, Stenner fired after him. He saw the gunman awkwardly swing himself into the saddle and urge his mount away, to be swallowed into the sea of dunes, lost from sight.

Stenner felt no thrill of achievement, no false pride in himself. He felt only a great lassitude, an emptiness deep as the tremors which engulfed him. The pistol stayed clutched in his shaking hand, the smell of cordite stinging his nostrils and whipping tears to his eyes. Thank God, he thought foolishly, that it was not some innocent creature I shot at so wildly, some foraging animal, else I would have been a laughing stock, the butt of all. He would have gone within to reassure the womenfolk, but his legs would not carry him, and, to his shame, he sank down uselessly upon the cobbles of the yard.

Chapter Fourteen

It had taken but a few brief moments after the crack of gunfire for Betty Turner and Rosa to gather their wits and come running, panic-stricken, into the yard. At sight of Stenner lying upon the cobbles, Betty, believing him wounded, let out a scream of anguish. She stood for a second, swaying helplessly, face drained of all colour, scarce able to breathe for the wrenching of pain within her. Then, in a rush, she was kneeling beside him, cradling him to her, stroking his hair, kissing him frenziedly and muttering such tender endearments as he had never thought to hear. The tears were running unhindered down her cheeks, splashing from mouth and chin and none, not even Stenner himself, could have doubted her love for him. He tried to reassure her and Rosa both, but the words would not come for the shameful chattering of his teeth, his jaws clamping rigidly together.

'Oh, my dear, my dear man, I had thought you dead,' she exclaimed wretchedly. 'Are you wounded? Badly hurt?' She did not wait for answer, but cradled him to her again, most tenderly, grateful only that he lived.

Stenner thought that he had never known such a richness of pleasure in all of his life and prayed that, if he were dreaming, it might last for ever and never be broken. All was noise and confusion now, with Betty and Rosa trying to question and be heard between their weeping, and the terrified horse in the outhouse, fidgeting and neighing and all but breaking down the door in its efforts to be free. It was that which calmed Stenner and set him firmly in command again, of himself and those in his care. With Rosa's and Betty's help, he scrambled awkwardly to his feet, pistol still clasped in his clenched fist as if it could never be prised from him and went to settle the horse, clutching it still,

168

gentling it, speaking with confident reassurance, making it secure.

So it was that he shepherded the two anxious women indoors, gentling, easing their fears in that same natural way. A man valued and loved, who had defended his own and won.

'You believe that you wounded him?' Betty Turner asked when all was explained to them.

'I am sure of it, but how badly I do not know.'

'He did not attempt to return fire?' she persisted anxiously.

'No, for he was disabled by the wound to his arm.'

'He will not return, then,' Rosa's voice was high-pitched with fear as she held Joy protectively to her.

'No. I am sure of it. He will be well clear of the Burrows. Believe it. He will put as many miles as he can between us for fear of discovery.' Stenner, for all his firm assurance, was not wholly convinced. It might have been no more than a flesh wound, he thought disconsolately, and what better time to return than when two terrified women were guarded only by a poor apology of a pauper with more luck than skill, more anger than courage. 'I will go back into the yard,' he said quietly, 'keep watch at the gate, for it will make a good vantage point. None can approach without my knowledge. I shall have the pistol to deter any who will not declare themselves. It would not be wise to drive to the Crown Inn. But if we do not arrive as promised, Tom Butler will come seeking the reason and, as like as not, bring others with him.'

'Then you had best eat and drink,' Betty Turner said practically, 'for you will need to keep your strength up.'

All his gentle protests failed to sway her. She was firm upon it. 'I shall take my victuals into the yard,' he promised at last, in order to placate her.

'Then I shall come with you!'

'I do not think it wise.'

'Was it wise that you set yourself so bravely at risk to defend us?' she demanded abruptly. 'It is not wisdom but affection that impels me. I would be beside you, whatever comes, that is the truth of it. 'The colour which had been drained from her came seeping back in a swift flush, deeper and darker than the redness of her hair.' I cannot say it

169

any more plainly, Abel George Stenner, so let that be an end to it.'

He nodded. 'When Mr Stradling comes,' he said, 'he will set up a search party. Seek retribution. He will know what best to do.'

'He will do no better than you.' Betty Turner said briskly. 'You are a man of rare courage, George Stenner, and none can deny it. Mr Stradling least of all.' He looked at her enquiringly, not understanding. 'He chose you to protect us both,' she declared stoutly. 'He would not have chosen lightly. He knows your value, your courage and loyalty. You are a man to be trusted, George Stenner. A man to rely on, not just for the moment, but always. I have known it from the first and have never felt need to change my opinion. Now, shall we venture without? Into the yard?'

He nodded and, holding the pistol steady, walked boldly beside her, erect and proud, as to the manor born.

The rest of Joshua's journey to Pyle gaolhouse was mercifully without hindrance. Apart from a certain dishevillment which he strove manfully to set to rights, he was physically none the worse for his adventure. Moreover, the grey was lavishly admired by the ostler at the inn where he stabled her, so Joshua's equanimity was further restored. If vicarious pride counted as one of the seven deadly sins, Joshua reflected, then he must plead guilty in full measure.

As to the guilty within the gaolhouse, it was a foregone conclusion. The justice was scrupulous in declaring that every man, or woman for that matter, must be adjudged innocent until lawfully proven guilty. As a principle, Joshua was prepared to accept the legality of it, if not the veracity. Long association with villains like Ezra the Box had strained both his credulity and his patience. He was no longer a naive innocent, trusting in the ultimate good of mankind. As in all of nature there were the good, bad and indifferent. Those aspiring to perfection and those fatally flawed. The trouble was that saints were thin on the ground. In fact, scarcer than hen's teeth, while the sinners flourished like the green bay tree. Still, those within the gaolhouse could scarcely claim purity of spirit or action! They had been caught *in flagrante delicto*. Evidence was against them. Any judge convinced of their innocence would need to be not only deprived of all his senses but a Bedlamite to boot! Their only hope of leniency was to inform upon some other, someone mighty and influential enough to earn them reprieve, someone of the status of Sir Peter Henshawe. In a spirit of resolve, Joshua went within to try and perform such miracle.

The gaoler, a surly wall-eyed fellow, slovenly in speech and dress, greeted him without any great enthusiasm. He was, Joshua thought, as unprepossessing as any of those immured within and barely civil. Perhaps close association with the dregs and leavings of humanity had demoralised him and he had sunk into a lethargy deep as theirs. In any event, he set no great example, save as one of the great unwashed. Joshua was not unusually squeamish, but the odour of sweat, filth and neglect which arose from the man and his clothing offended his nostrils. He was relieved when the fellow motioned him to a room where he might interview the prisoners, promising to stand guard without the door.

The prisoners brought to him and interviewed separately were less truculent than before, not needing to bluster and prove themselves before their companions. Yet, at the name of Sir Peter Henshawe, they relapsed into their former sullenness, unwilling to cooperate. It had been hard to judge the reason for their reluctance. Some seemed genuinely ignorant of his involvement, unable to recognise his name. Others, Joshua was convinced, were driven to deny it from fear of reprisal. Although they strove to hide it under a mask of hostility, their unease was all too plain. It was evident in their pallor and sweating, their evasiveness and false aggression. Yet, try as he might, Joshua could not beat them down into confessing.

He fared no better with the men whom Rawlings had captured at Newton Creek. Their cold hostility and dumb insolence were clearly a pre-arranged tactic and, for the moment, he had to acknowledge defeat. Should one break, then he knew that *all* would be drawn in, each eager to exonerate himself and accuse others. None claimed to have knowledge of the woman sheep stealer, or would admit that she had a child. As far as he could judge, for they were liars, thieves and cut-throats all, the father of the putative child was not among their number. His questioning on the subject had

171

been treated with unconcern, indifference even, and he knew that it was from the woman herself that he would be forced to gain proof of the child's identity and where it now lived.

When she was seated opposite him in the spare, windowless room, Joshua was forced to concede that, despite the rough masculinity of her clothing and her unkemptness, there was a restless, feral quality about her that was strangely disturbing. Her darkness and vitality were the inheritance of another race, Mediterranean or Middle Eastern, for her colouring was almost swarthy. She had a remnant, perhaps, of gypsy blood, with all the natural grace and arrogance of a pure-bred itinerant people. Certainly she showed no deference to his authority, facing him as an equal in her own eyes, if not as his superior.

'You claim, I believe, to have a young child, a daughter?'

'I do not claim, 'her voice was deep and with an accent that was unfamiliar to him, but not unpleasing. 'I *have* a daughter.'

'A child of what age?'

'What is your interest? How can it concern you?'

'I would wish to guarantee her safety, see that she is cared for, whatever comes.'

She grinned, saying mockingly, 'I wish I could believe in such charity, such selfless concern. It does you credit, sir.' Adding insolently, 'You will get your reward in heaven!'

'And you, ma'am, upon earth,' Joshua reminded quietly. 'Does it not trouble you that your child will always be in the care and protection of others? Others not of your own kin?'

'She has that care, will have always. It is promised. I would not rest easy else.' Her voice faltered and died away.

'And can you depend upon it?'

'Yes. I can depend upon it!' There was a hint of anger in her quick response, a desperation. Was she, Joshua wondered, seeking to convince herself?

'But for how long?' he persisted cruelly. 'A week? A month? A year? How will you be sure?'

'Hell and damnation!' She sprang from her chair, hands clenched to strike him. 'Will you give me no peace? Would you destroy me?' He saw the glint of tears, knuckled away roughly before her fists dropped uselessly to her sides. 'I have no more to say.' Her voice was painfully controlled

172

again, rigidly impersonal. 'You had best summon the gaoler, for you will learn nothing more of me or mine.'

There was, Joshua thought, a dignity about her, despite her distress. Almost against his will he felt a stirring of pity. He said impulsively, 'I would have you believe that my aim is to see the child cared for, to ensure her future. I speak not only as a constable but as a father and a man.'

She looked at him for a long moment, dark eyes intent, then nodded, admitting, voice low, 'My daughter is all that is now left to me. I have been made firm promise, binding, and for life. Should it prove false then you have my oath that I will be revenged. From prison or the grave itself, it will make no matter. If I have need of your help, will you give it?'

'Yes, I will give it.'

Her darkly intelligent eyes stared challengingly into Joshua's as she said with a humour which lightened them, and lifted the soft edge of her mouth, 'In some other life, Constable, and in some other place . . .?'

'We might have been friends, ma'am.'

'Or more than friends?'

His amusement was ungrudging, and as light as her own.

She turned and walked to the door, knocking upon it peremptorily to alert the gaoler, asking unexpectedly, 'What is it that you wish to learn of my daughter?' and warning, 'I will not give you news of her whereabouts or kin, cannot.'

'Her age, ma'am?'

'Nigh on two years, sir. She is more an infant than babe. I fear it will not help you.'

'It may help others,' Joshua murmured. 'More deeply than you can know.'

On the solitary journey from Pyle to the port, Joshua had time to reflect upon the woman at the gaolhouse and the curious contradictions in her nature. It was a strange dichotomy, he thought: aggression, fearlessness and passion on one part, tenderness and loyalty to her child on the other. Yet, in deliberately choosing the life she led, she was denying the child the very stability she sought for her. What violence drove her? What was the catalyst? What inheritance from the past, or childhood hurt, had forced her to such recklessness with

173

her own life and the lives of others? Revenge? He would never know.

She would certainly be hanged for the murder of Jed Carter, an innocent shepherd, who could have posed no danger to those viciously armed. It was a mindless savagery, killing for killing's sake, the feral bloodlust of the pack. He knew nothing about the woman, not even her name or from whence she came. Yet, for a brief moment, when humour ousted prejudice, there had been a rapport between them, an understanding. It had flared briefly and died. He was no nearer a solution as to the whereabouts of her child or to the identity of the man who financed and ordered them, the 'respectable gentleman' who lived upon theft from others, sanctioning murder, yet keeping his own hands free of blood. Joshua had deliberately kept the name of Sir Peter Henshawe from her, forbearing to ask the questions he had asked others lest it forewarn her. He must await news now from Sir Matthew and Dr Peate, for they would surely hear rumour of his business interests and know the foundation of his wealth. They would make discreet enquiries and arouse no suspicion.

It was strange, Joshua thought, that she had appealed to him for aid for the child, should someone betray her trust. Whom did she suspect? Was she fearful that after her death someone would renege upon a promise given? He, Joshua, had not made his vow to her lightly, but from awkward pity and for the child's sake. It would have grieved him were his own son so placed; left at the mercy of those who, perhaps, reared him for money and denied him love. Well, he had learned something from the encounter. The child which Rosa and Doonan had taken into their home was not the child of the woman in Pyle gaolhouse. That child was an infant nigh on three years and not a young babe. The information had been given freely and without dissembling and he did not doubt the truth of it. For the time being, at least, Rosa and Doonan might keep their Joy, no longer fearful that she was the child of a thief and murderer all too soon to be hanged.

There was but one impediment. Someone else had need of their child and was willing to maim Rosa if need be and abduct the babe. He had already shown his savagery near the Crown Inn, and Joshua could not doubt that the hooded man who had

174

fired upon him in the dunes at Kenfig was one and the same. It was a web of deceit and violence stretching ever wider, the strands strong and unbroken, with some ruthless predator at its core, someone prepared to bide his time before feeding upon the unwary; immobilising, killing, drawing blood. Joshua would have given much to know his adversary. He knew only that he was a chosen victim. His vigilance must be not only for others, but for himself.

Rebecca, leaving the parish church of Saint John the Baptist after the service of churching, paused upon the village green with John Jeremiah clasped in her arms. Indeed, she could scarcely have done otherwise, for their way was impeded by an indulgent throng, each and every one of them rapturously singing the child's praises. Sophie Fleet and Ruth were preening themselves importantly, and even the rector, Robert Knight, was smiling besottedly at his godson and making such fatuous faces and noises that it was a wonder that the entire congregation did not think him unbalanced. There was great argument as to which parent he favoured, his eyes, ears, mouth and colouring were debated at length, and occasionally with such acrimony that Robert Knight was forced to mediate. Nonetheless, it was a charmingly rustic scene, with the womenfolk dressed in their most becoming finery and with a delightful holy day atmosphere.

At the sound of a carriage fiercely rounding the corner from the Burrows, there was an immediate pause in the conversation, a quickening of curiosity. In a moment the carriage drew to a violent halt at the Crown Inn and Tom Butler leapt down and came running, breathless and perspiring freely, rubicund face aglow with concern. Even as he reached them Rebecca saw the gig from Thatched Cottage draw up urgently beside the inn with Stenner, pale-faced, at the reins and Betty Turner beside him. Rosa, stricken-faced and with Joy clutched protectively in her arms, was clambering down and looking about her anxiously, scarce taking in the scene upon the village green in her concern and agitation.

'Butler?' The justice's voice was harsh. 'What is it? What has occurred?'

'There has been another attack upon Rosa, sir. There. At the Burrows.'

'In her own home?' The justice was appalled. 'She has not been harmed? Is not hurt? Or the child?'

'No, sir. Thank God, and I say it devoutly! But for Stenner's bravery she might well have been molested or shot!'

'Stenner? He was armed, then?' the justice asked, in confusion.

'He was, sir.'

'Upon whose authority?'

'Mr Stradling's, sir. It is as well that he was. He was able to shoot at the attacker and wound him.'

'The devil he was!' the justice exclaimed, not without admiration. 'Did he recognise the assailant? The gunman?'

'No, sir, for he was hooded as before.'

'The sheer damned insolence of the fellow! To attack again, openly, and so soon. It beggars belief! The man must be a half-wit, an imbecile!'

'No, sir, I fear that is the danger.' Tom Butler's face was anxiously set, voice troubled. 'I think that he is a man of intelligence and cunning, with but one purpose in mind. He will not rest until he has achieved it.'

The justice grunted non-committally before rallying and declaring stoutly, 'Then he will have the law to reckon with. Constable Stradling has my authority to hire as many strong men as he is able. There will be no unseemly quibbling from the vestrymen! Nor will it end there. If necessary I shall set up a hue and cry. Send for the militia if needs be. He will be stopped once and for all! I will not have my hamlets terrorised or the cottagers' lives set at risk.' The justice's plump face grew empurpled with choler, protuberant eyes almost starting from their sockets with honest wrath. Then, belatedly remembering Rebecca and John Jeremiah and the occasion which had brought them to church, he subsided into shamefaced embarrassment.

'You and the ladies had best be off home, my dear,' he advised, 'and you shall go in my coach, travelling in safety.' As Rebecca made to protest, he held up a hand to silence her. 'No, I will brook no argument. I will not hear another word! It is not safe to walk the roads while such a . . .' he groped for a suitable epithet. 'while such a reptile walks free,' he asserted triumphantly. He called for his coachman and gave firm instruction that Mrs Stradling and her friends were to be delivered to Thatched Cottage at once and that he must, on no account, return until they were safely within.

Rebecca, knowing that his concern was real and that to defy him would be headstrong foolishness, for argument's sake gave in with good grace. She thanked him gravely and settled an affectionate kiss upon his flushed cheek, making it redden the more with pleasure and embarrassment. She would have infinitely preferred to have hurried over to the Crown Inn, to gain first-hand knowledge of the affair from Rosa, but knew that she must not. As a newly churched matron it ill became her to behave with the scapegrace fecklessness of old. John Jeremiah's safety was her first concern. She must not forget it. Besides, she would learn all that had occurred, verbatim, from Betty Turner, even if Stenner's modesty forbade him to boast. It had not escaped her that, before entering the Crown Inn with Rosa and Joy, Betty had put a gently possessive hand to Stenner's arm and whispered reassurance, her homely face alight with tenderness.

'Well now, my dear,' the justice said benignly as he saw Rebecca settled into his coach. 'It behoves me to take extra good care of my godson, for in all too few years I can but hope that he will take heed for me. My concern for you both is naught but self-preservation. A care for my own ageing and decrepit hide.' He shut the door of the coach with a flourish and turned to Tom Butler, who still hovered nearby. 'I will come at once to the Crown,' he said, 'to hear the full story from you and Stenner and to decide what is to be done. You have seen Constable Stradling? Know where he may be reached?'

'I believe, sir, that he travelled to the gaolhouse at Pyle to interview the prisoners and hopes to return by way of the port. There is a meeting planned at the inn in an hour or so.'

'Then I will wait upon his return.' The justice strode purposefully across the green and called out peremptorily to Stenner, who came running meekly from beside the gig, pistol clasped awkwardly to him. 'Well done, Stenner! Good man!' the justice enthused. 'You are a credit to the hamlets, sir, and to those who employ you. More, you are a credit to yourself.'

He coughed and cleared his throat loudly, then self-consciously put a hand to Stenner's shoulder. 'I shall not forget it. No, I shall not forget. You will be rewarded, never fear.'

Stenner's lean face was warm with surprise and pleasure but the words he would have uttered stayed locked fast within his throat. He might have protested that he wanted no reward, that he had done what was needful from duty and affection alone. He murmured his thanks to the justice, gaze dropped low, his words scarce audible. Yet, within, he felt such a fierce glow of pride that it all but devoured him. The justice's words would burn bright for always. Most of all, it pleased him that the justice had addressed him as 'sir'. He had spoken not as to a pauper born but as an equal. Stenner felt every last inch a hero and gentleman as he walked with the justice within.

When Joshua arrived at the port his spirits quickly lifted, for it was such a bustling, joyous, colourful scene that he could not long remain aloof from it. Everywhere there was activity and excitement with a cheerfully haphazard mixing of men and womenfolk, all busily intent upon their errands and tasks. Sailors and craftsmen, hauliers and dockside labourers rubbed shoulders with passengers, officials and crew. The quays were piled high with produce, familiar or strange, humdrum or exotic. Small mountains of iron ore, limestone and pit-props mingled with gleaming, jet black hillocks of coal. Cheese, butter and bales of wool from the Downs lay alongside rainbows of cloth and aromatic spices. The smells of fish and coffee beans, tea and fruits a pervasive richness against the astringent iodine tang of the sea. Everywhere there were horses, those led by patient hauliers, their faces blacker than the coal they worked, were great, plodding creatures, chained and firm-muscled. They had to be strong for they drew the vast iron trams, piled high with coal and ores on the twelve-hour journey to the distant valleys beyond the sea. The carriage horses and those from the livery stables beyond were lighter, more graceful creatures, slender of leg and chosen for stamina and speed. Private equipages with matched and elegant horses trotted alongside the sturdy dray horses and the poor broken-down hacks that drew the carriers' carts. Here, Joshua thought, all the world and its wares came together and were blended into one. It was a crucible, a melting pot, like those of the flourishing new iron foundries beyond.

His hopes of meeting his good friend, Peter Rawlings, and taking modest refreshment at the Ship Aground were swiftly dashed. The excise officer, he was told by one of Rawlings's subordinates, was absent upon some investigation upon the rocky coast beyond Sker; a wild and savage place where wrecks and smugglers were commonplace. He would not, it was feared, be back before nightfall. Joshua demanded paper and quill and left a hastily scribbled message for him about the suspected smuggling beyond Newton Creek. He carefully sealed it with melted wax, making the firm impression of his ring before the wax hardened to ensure that it was read by no other. It was an act of discretion he had early learnt, and he knew that the justice and Rawlings would approve it.

With little real enthusiasm he then made his way across the horse-drawn tramway to the edges of the inner dock where the livery stables lay, to interview Curtis. It was no more than a routine enquiry such as he would have made after any firearm injury, accidental or not. Dr Mansel had firmly assured him that there were no suspicious circumstances and that the wound was accidentally self-inflicted. Yet he felt an uneasiness. Was it linked with his dislike of the man? He could not be sure. Curtis was certainly a surly, unlikeable fellow, and his treatment of animals and men did nothing to endear him to Joshua. As he led the grey into the livery yard the same thin stable-lad came forward timidly to take the snaffle rein.

'Your employer, Mr Curtis, is here?' he demanded quietly. 'I would speak with him.'

The boy stared at him gaunt-faced, fidgeting uneasily, before blurting, 'No, sir. He is not here. He is gone.'

'Where may I find him?' The lad looked at him helplessly. 'I know that he has suffered an accident, a wounding,' Joshua said patiently. 'His house, lad, where is his house?'

'No, sir.' The stable-lad's hand tightened upon the snaffle. 'You misunderstand me. He is gone. Gone away from here. Disappeared.'

'When?'

'I cannot say, sir. None saw him go nor can make guess at the reason.

179

Chapter Fifteen

Joshua's return to Newton across the sand-drifted acres of Pickett's Lease found him morbidly introspective and filled with misgivings. For once, the sight of the great sailing ships lying off and awaiting the tide failed to stir in him a sense of awe and adventure, that excoriating revival of childhood dreams. He was as unaware of them as of the great schooners and brigs, the barques and barquetines, sailing the sea roads beyond, passage stately and serene, their sails proud-breasted as swans in the wind.

He needed time to reflect, he thought, to try and set things to order in his mind. All was a kaleidoscope of colour and shape, changing patterns without form or substance, elusive and incomplete. If the pieces could somehow fall into shape, remain constant, then he might hope to make sense of it all. It was with a groan of despair that he recognised the justice's coach in the stable yard of the Crown Inn, and realised that his meeting with the paid volunteers would be attended by Robert Knight. He would claim to be there in a supervisory capacity, declaring that he would remain aloof, a mere observer. Yet Joshua knew that he would question and harry, carp and make suggestion, castigate and criticise incessantly. It was an immutable fact of life, like death and taxes. Since it could not be avoided, it were best endured.

The justice greeted Joshua with surprising enthusiasm, spilling out the story of Rosa's ordeal and congratulating him upon his foresight and perspicacity in sending out Stenner armed. When Joshua, in turn, told him of the attack upon him in the dunes at Kenfig, the justice was less impressed, his disgruntlement made plain.

'You allowed him to escape, Stradling? How, sir? Did it not occur to you that, knowing the coast was clear, he would make tracks for Newton? That Rosa's life would be set at risk? Where were you bound? Upon what errand?' he demanded.

'To question the prisoners at Pyle gaolhouse. The sheep stealers, sir.'

'Oh. And what did you elicit? A full confession it is to be hoped and the avowed implication of . . .' Conscious that his tirade might be overheard, he broke off, to add discreetly,' of that certain person of whose identity we are both aware.'

'No, sir. I was given no such assurance, but I plan to return. I have hopes that . . .'

'Hopes! Fiddlesticks, Stradling! Piffle! Hopes carry no weight in law! Facts are what are needed. Facts, sir! Did you learn nothing at all?' he demanded incredulously.

'I learned that Rosa's child is not, as I feared, the daughter of the woman at the gaolhouse.'

'And is this fact or hope, sir?'

'Fact. I am convinced of it.'

'Well,' the justice appeared mollified. 'At least it will give the Doonans peace of mind upon that score. Yet the threat to them remains. How do you explain it, Stradling? Who else is involved in this bizarre affair?'

'I do not know, sir,' he admitted tersely.

'But it is your business to know!' the justice reminded curtly. 'It is what you are paid for, sir. I hope that you are aware of it!' The justice grunted. 'Well, a fine kettle of fish, Stradling. A fine kettle of fish. We are no closer to a solution. I might add that I use the term "we" loosely, for no blame devolves upon me!' he claimed sententiously.

'No, sir. Any blame is mine alone.'

Robert Knight glanced at him sharply for signs of insolence but, finding none, redoubled his attack. 'The child is not that of the woman at Pyle gaolhouse nor that of the woman murdered at the port. Mansel will swear to it. How, then, in heaven's name, is the infant involved, for involved she is, and at the heart of the matter? But *what* matter, Stradling? That is the crux of it!'

'There are three matters, sir. I do not know whether they stand alone or are inter-related.'

'Three matters?' he demanded testily. 'I am aware of

only two. The murder and the sheep stealing. What other is involved?'

'There has been rumour of smuggling beyond Newton Creek.'

'Yes, yes, I am aware of that, but there is no evidence that it is more than that. We are a coastal parish, Stradling. Smuggling, wrecking even, are inevitable hazards. These outbreaks are sporadic. Isolated. How can they equate with murder, sheep stealing and the abandoning of a child? No. You are clutching at straws, sir. Bring me proof! Any proof. Idle speculation will scarce suffice!' He glared at Joshua, demanding abrasively, 'Are there any more events, or facts, of which I should be aware? Or am I now in full possession of the little evidence gleaned?'

'Curtis, the owner of the livery stables at the port was wounded by a pistol shot, sir.'

'So? Dr Mansel assures me that it was an accident and of no significance. Have you checked upon it? Made enquiry?'

'I have, sir, but Curtis has disappeared.'

'Disappeared?' Under any other circumstances the justice's outrage would have amused Joshua. 'How disappeared? When?'

'During the night, sir, after Dr Mansel attended to his arm. He left without word or warning and none has seen him since.'

'Well, he is free to come and go as he pleases. He is neither a criminal nor a wanted man! Perhaps he has set out upon some journey, to collect a passenger by coach or to see a horse-dealer. After all, that is his lawful occupation,' he added drily.

'With a pistol wound to his arm, sir, he would scarcely be in a fit state to do so.'

The justice sought irritably for answer. 'Well, perhaps someone has taken him, upon his own request.'

'Perhaps, sir.'

'Really, Stradling!' he rebuked testily. 'I do not know why you have such a down upon this man! It is more like a vendetta, an obsession even. You surely cannot seriously think that he has been abducted?' When Joshua made no denial, the justice said grudgingly, 'Well, if you are so stubbornly set upon persecuting the fellow you had best continue your enquiries, although your time would be better spent elsewhere. I tell you, here and now, that there is no mystery about it. It is all a figment of your imagination, no more than that! Do as you wish. I wash my hands of Curtis and the whole affair.'

Joshua would have given much to believe it.

'Now,' the justice continued sarcastically. 'Is there anything else which you have accidentally omitted from mentioning? Whether fact or fiction? I shall be obliged, sir, if in future you will keep me informed. As justice, squire and rector of the three hamlets it ill-behoves me to remain so ignorant.' Realising his mistake too late, he rounded furiously upon Joshua, chiding, 'If you would see an example of devotion to duty, heroism even, you had best turn to your groom, Stenner. It is salutary, sir, that a man in lowly employ, an ex-pauper even, could so bravely risk his all in the protection of others.'

'Indeed, sir,' Joshua agreed. 'He is a man of the greatest loyalty and courage, unfailingly honest and industrious to a fault.' The generosity of the tribute did not altogether please the justice who mumbled defensively. 'I find no fault with your conscientiousness, Stradling, nor your devotion to duty, your intelligence even. It is your methods which confuse me.' Joshua wisely forebore from comment. 'I think that your man, Stenner, should be given some official recognition from the vestrymen, some public acknowledgement of his bravery. A parchment scroll and medal, or a more tangible reward would you think?'

'He is certainly deserving of it.'

'Well, I shall put it in hand. We had best go within and choose our volunteers to patrol the highways and act as guard over Rosa Doonan.'

'Yes, sir.' Joshua made to accompany him to the room which Tom Butler had prepared.

'Not, you understand, that I shall have any interest or firm views upon the matter. I shall in no wise commend or otherwise interfere. That is not my way. I believe that the labourer is worthy of his hire,' he remarked obtusely. Then, with a complete change of tactics, he confided, with voice and face softened to almost fatuous gentleness, 'Upon my soul, Joshua, my boy, you have a rare prize in Rebecca. A jewel.

183

A gem. And a fine son. A family of whom to be proud! I hope
that you recognise what bounty it is, what a rare privilege.'
He paused, sniffed and polished his lenses with a silk kerchief
from his coat pocket, first breathing heavily upon the glass,
then looked hard at Joshua.

'Oh, I do, sir,' he answered devoutly. 'I do, sir.'

The justice nodded and ushered him peremptorily within.
He knew that it had been only a momentary lapse upon the
justice's part to address him as 'Joshua'. A social nicety. Once
within he would be once more his low constable and addressed
as such. 'Stradling' was all he might expect. Theirs was a curious
balancing act between formality and friendship, and neither
had yet conquered the art. Like his long-time feud with Ezra,
his relationship with the justice was fragile, and frequently
volatile, but a battle of intellect rather than wits. Both his
adversaries were possessed of a singular merit. Whatever the
aggravation, they were never dull.

Obadiah Mansel was not in the best of humours. It had been
a tiring day and the distances he had been forced to drive
excessive and his patients, when he finally tracked them down,
were cantankerous and demanding. It seemed that no sooner
had he travelled to the far ends of Stormy Downs than he was
summoned to the far reaches of Sker, or to the wilds of Nottage,
no sooner had he returned, exhausted and disgruntled, than he
was urgently summoned to Stormy Downs again. He did not
know if it was the maliciousness of fate or of his patients which
irked him the more. The trouble was that he was growing old
and wearied, and not even John Burrell's selfless help could
halt the passage of time. The fee for a doctor's visit was beyond
the means of most and the poor sent for him only in the direst
emergency, turning first to the wise women and conjurors for
aid. He saw only those in extremis, their fate already sealed. He
was like the wingless and featherless bird of death, so feared by
the villagers, a harbinger of loss. His presence but a preliminary
to Ezra Evans's calling, tight-lipped and mercenary, with his
funeral cart.

As Mansel halted the gig outside Evans's shop in Newton
village and handed the reins to Dic Jenkins, the undertaker's
self-effacing apprentice, he wondered what aberration had

made him concede to the justice's request. It was a bizarre notion. It was enough to treat the living, without having to immortalise, in charcoal, the dead. Yet it was no more macabre a pursuit than performing a post-mortem, and that was the work which, as pathologist, he had chosen to do. Yet, try as he might, he was never fully innured against the randomness of death, its violence, and finality. It was a just phrase 'The grim reaper'. As stalks of corn fell to the sickle, so are we cut down without pity, or hope of reprieve, whether at God's discretion, or the whim of our fellow men.

The unknown girl within had died from another's violation. In a moment of savagery more than flesh had been destroyed. It was a destruction of youth and hope, of existence itself. Why, he thought dispiritedly, did death always seem so much more poignant in the young? Perhaps because their dreams were intact, their innocence too cruel a reminder of what might be achieved rather than what must be endured. Mansel set his hand upon the latch, lifted it resolutely, and walked within. Young or old, death, as with Madeleine, his wife, was the ending of all, save memory in others. A life is all we have. The dead girl was deserving of having her death atoned, her murderer brought to justice. It was little enough to do. He would not cavil at it.

Ezra crept forward from the darker recesses of the shop, actually rubbing his hands unctuously, manner ingratiating. His smile vanished, to be replaced by a frown of annoyance as he recognised who had entered. Upon hearing the gig drawing up on the cobblestones without he had hoped for the arrival of some wealthy client, and had sent Dic Jenkins scurrying to attend. A glimpse of Dr Mansel's high silk hat and his evident sartorial splendour had further lifted his hopes. Ezra was a mean-minded and calculating little creature and had been forewarned about the physician's errand and could see no financial gain in such an endeavour and did not attempt to hide his disappointment. Indeed, he could not.

'Well, sir?' he surveyed Dr Mansel discouragingly. 'I suppose you have come to draw the corpse?'

'No, sir! I have come to create a likeness of someone in life!' He knew that he had answered abrasively, but the barb did not penetrate Ezra's thick hide.

'Indeed. Living or dead, they are grist to our mills, sir. We are, in a manner of speaking, in the same trade.'

The insolence of it so outraged Mansel that, for a moment, he was unable to make reply. 'I do not think, Mr Evans,' he said coldly, 'that attempting to render assistance, to save life, can be properly equated with . . . burying the dead.'

'Ah, but there you are wrong, sir.' Ezra was not a whit put down. 'You may work brief good, I do not deny it. Give respite, even, but they all come to me in the end.'

'If you will show me where the girl is to be found,' Mansel ordered brusquely, 'I will not detain you.'

Ezra smiled at him, his small ferret face alive with cupidity as he asked with seeming innocence, 'Your patients are well, sir? Flourishing, all, it is to be hoped?'

The audacity of it made Mansel gasp aloud. The man was a ghoul! His insensitivity was past bearing. 'My patients, sir, are my own affair and the concern of no other. Their faith in my confidentiality, as in my competence, are not in question! It is as well that your clients are less demanding!'

'The dead woman is in the outhouse. Across the yard. Next to the old cob's stable,' Ezra murmured, aggrieved. 'I will come with you. Show you the way, then sit beside you as you work.'

'Indeed you will not!'

'I would have you know, sir, that I am an artist in my own right!' Ezra reminded stiffly.

'Then I suggest you persevere with it and leave me to mine!' Mansel was aware of the ungraciousness of the rebuke but could not regret it.

'You had best have a care for your health, sir,' Ezra said spitefully. 'The outhouse is cold, as it needs to be, harbouring corpses and all. You might take a chill or an ague.'

'Then I shall be well able to treat myself.'

Ezra looked disgruntled, saying petulantly, 'Well, you had best be careful where you are stepping, crossing the cobbled yard; the old cob is not careful where he leaves his droppings. He is no respecter of persons, high or low.'

'Perhaps he learns by example!' Mansel muttered beneath his breath. Aloud, he said crisply, 'Have no fear, Mr Evans, horse-droppings are easily avoided. *Their* contamination is quickly dispersed by the good, clean air.' With a flourish of his silk hat, he strode briskly without.

Dr Mansel completed his unenviable task in less time than he had anticipated, mercifully free from Ezra's odious presence. So engrossed in his work was he that he was as oblivious to the cold as to his unsalubrious surroundings. He felt that he had captured a reasonable likeness of the dead girl, more than that, the essential quality of her. It had not been easy, for the face of one dead is wiped of all vitality, all emotion. The transformation of death is akin to a rebirth, Mansel thought. The old miraculously grow young again, the hurts and cares of everyday living eased away. The young are trapped for ever in their innocence; waxen grave lilies or marbled cherubim upon an age-old tomb. How much, he wondered, was owed to the embalmer's art? Perhaps, as Ezra claimed, he, too, was an artist. Yet he lacked all the artist's sensitivity, indeed any sensitivity at all! He had almost touted for custom, Mansel recalled, believing him to be a profitable source of commissions. Why, the man was no better than a vampire! Even a body-snatcher would at least have respect for those living, if not for the dead! His sketching done, Mansel hurriedly left the yard by the back way to avoid another unseemly wrangle with the unsavoury little man. As he climbed triumphantly into his gig, Ezra came hurrying from within, the shop bell jangling viciously behind him.

'Dr Mansel, sir! A moment of your time! I have a proposition to put to you.'

With a swift word of thanks to Dic Jenkins at the reins, Mansel stirred the horse into life and was away, gig wheels rattling upon the cobblestones, the carriage all but overturning in his haste. He dared not dwell upon what Ezra's proposition might be. An arrangement to purchase news of those in imminent danger of demise? Second hand coffins? Mansel heaved a sigh of relief that he had escaped unhindered. His cares dropped from him. He would take the drawing to Joshua Stradling's house and bid him have copies made for distribution. He was not sanguine about the outcome. It seemed too remote a chance that a stranger to the three hamlets would be seen and recognised, but he had done what was asked

187

of him and felt more at ease with himself. There was one good thing about his visit to Ezra; however fractious or demanding his patients, in future they would seem very saints and martyrs. Mansel chuckled aloud. No, there were two good things. It would stiffen his determination to stay alive. He would prefer that the undertaker suffered from *his* ministrations rather than he from Ezra's, artist or not! When he finally succumbed, then he would, mercifully, be past caring.

Rebecca, impatiently awaiting Joshua's return from his meeting with the justice, learnt from Betty Turner of the alarms and excursions of the day. She spoke most spiritedly of Stenner's courage and tenacity in driving off the hooded gunman and in protecting Rosa, Joy and her, and of the real debt they owed to him. Her plain, no-nonsense face was flushed with pride in his achievement, its stippling of freckles all but hidden in the fierce surge of colour to her skin. If Rebecca had ever questioned the depth of affection which Betty felt for him, she could doubt it no more. Her love was as vividly unmistakable as her glowing red hair and with as little hope of concealment. Rebecca secretly rejoiced with her that she had so firmly thrown off all shadow of the past.

"Tis not only that he is a hero, ma'am,' Betty Turner said proudly, 'and he is that right enough, for none, not even Constable Stradling himself, could have bettered him. No, 'tis his modesty and kindness to all that are the real marks of his quality. He is a good and gentle man.'

'He is a gentleman in every sense of the word,' Rebecca agreed warmly. 'For it is a quality that is born within and has nothing to do with rank or title or accident of birth. Yes. He is a fine man, Betty, and we are the richer for knowing him.'

'My Thomas will be pleased, ma'am,' Betty confessed shyly, 'for they are as comfortable and close as kin.' Her face clouded briefly. 'Indeed, ma'am, they are closer than kin, for they have chosen their friendship and let it grow.'

'Then that is the best test of all,' Rebecca said quietly, 'for real love oft grows from such friendship, whether that of a child for another, or a woman for a man.'

Betty Turner did not pretend to misunderstand. 'Yes,' she said simply, ''tis firm foundation, I am thinking, for passion without friendship is swift to grow but slow to root. It flares and dies in one brief flowering. As I have cause to know.' There was silence between them until Betty Turner said, with grave honesty, 'Yet there is good in all things, even those that give the greatest hurt.'

'I am not sure,' Rebecca admitted uncertainly.

'Oh, but *I* am sure, ma'am! We can learn from the cruelties of the past, the evil endured, and turn it to advantage. The bad gives us a yardstick to measure the good. More, to appreciate it. Whether the good comes early or late, it makes no matter. The miracle is that it comes at all. We must accept it and be grateful.'

'And will you accept George Stenner, Betty, should he ask?'

'I will, Mrs Stradling, and gladly. Not just because he is the hero of the moment, although I cannot fault him for that. No, 'tis because of what he has been to me through all the long months of bitterness and hurt when we were abandoned. He has been a rock and a refuge. A man to trust and respect.'

'Then that is a firm foundation, Betty.'

'Yes.' Betty hesitated, then declared confidently and with head held high, 'And I love him. If there is some doubt of it in his mind then there is none in mine. He is not second best or a substitute for what is lost and can never be recovered. He is the man my heart and mind would choose to love above all others. And I shall prove it to him and give him new pride in himself and knowledge of his true worth.' She spoke with such certainty of the rightness of it that Rebecca felt a quickening of spirits as joyous as Betty's own. Yet she felt, too, a regret for what had been endured; for cruelty and betrayal, for wounds laid raw. Perhaps past suffering would bind the little family more closely together, give them, as Betty hoped, the sensitivity to know how richly they were blessed. Yet, it was a cruel old way of learning. But life itself was a harsh teacher, with no pretensions to be fair.

Rebecca, grateful for the fact that Joshua's life and her own were now in gentler, calmer waters, went upstairs to marvel at her son. As she held him close, relishing the soft warmth of his skin and the milky fragrance of it, she felt a sadness that she was no longer able to know the closeness of him at her breast, the

189

intimate tenderness of feeding him. It had grieved her when the midwife and John Burrell said that she had best find a wet nurse from the village. She had felt her role usurped, her rights as a mother unfairly violated. Yet there was no alternative. She had accepted the finality of it and hired a young woman from Newton village to nurture the child. She had tried to tell herself that it was a blessing in disguise, for it would give her time to do those things long neglected. It gave opportunity to roam further afield and to help Joshua in his investigations, as of old, with or without his consent or knowledge. Yet, she was not wholly convinced.

As she laid John Jeremiah to rest in his crib, the sound of a coach drawing up on the cobbles without Thatched Cottage sent her hurrying to the casement, alight with curiosity. It was the justice, she felt sure, come to speak to her of the churching and to seize the opportunity to see his godson, for he was as besotted with the child as was Joshua himself. But it was the smaller de Breos coach she saw, with its familiar crest and livery of plum and gold.

Her disappointment that it was not a surprise visit from Sir Matthew and Dr Peate or Elizabeth Devereaux was acute, but she strove to hide it from the messenger who delivered the sealed envelope to her for Joshua's safekeeping. There was, too, an affectionate letter for her from her grandfather, which she bore off in triumph to read avidly and alone. He wrote so naturally and vividly of the estate and those who dwelt and worked upon it, that she might almost feel herself to be at Southerndown Court. His phrasing and descriptions, she thought, were as elegantly fashioned as he, and his observations rich with affectionate humour. It was with regret, and a warmth of affection for the old gentleman that she set the letter aside to be re-read at leisure.

Even as she rose to await Joshua's coming, she heard the familiar clatter of the grey's hooves as he rode into the yard, then the unmistakable rattle and creak of the gig as Stenner brought it to a halt. When Joshua entered it was a grief to her to see how strained and fatigued he was, his uniform dishevilled from the trials of the day, his boots scuffed and muddied. He rubbed a hand tiredly across his eyes, confessing ruefully:

190

'I had best make myself presentable, Rebecca, bathe and change my linen, for I am scarce human.'

'Or all too human, my dear, for you drive yourself far too harshly.' She walked to where he stood before the fire, linking an arm through his and reaching up to settle a swift kiss upon his cheek. 'I shall not ask you how the day has gone,' she said, 'for I have already heard of Stenner's defence of Rosa.'

'Heard? But how?' He clapped a hand to his forehead, saying contritely, 'The churching! I had all but forgot. I am so bound up in my own affairs that I had not the thought to enquire.'

'You are forgiven,' Rebecca promised, smiling,' for it went smoothly enough, with John Jeremiah the very model of perfection and like to expire from a surfeit of praise and flattery. From the justice, most of all!'

'Then I could wish that a little had rubbed off on me,' Joshua confessed, 'for I fear that I am definitely *persona non grata* to Robert Knight, although Stenner is rightly lauded.'

As he turned towards the hall staircase Rebecca said, 'Oh, in my haste to see you it all but slipped my mind! There is a sealed letter for you from grandfather to be expressly delivered into your hands. It came by coach not half an hour since. Will I keep it against your return?'

'No!' He was back in an instant, immediately alert, all tiredness fallen from him as he tore open the envelope.

'Is it bad news?' Rebecca demanded, 'for it came so urgently.'

'No. It is the best news I have had in many a long day! It gives me a lever, Rebecca. A way to prise open the woman's defences, the one at Pyle gaolhouse. To make her talk.'

'How, Joshua?'

'The child she spoke of has been traced, it seems.'

'I do not see how that can serve you,' she said, perplexed.

'It has been snatched from the house where it was farmed out. Violently abducted.'

'Dear heavens!' Rebecca was all concern. 'That poor woman! The poor creature will be distraught. I pray to God that no one will harm it! It would break her heart, Joshua.'

'Then I must hope that it will break her silence, too.'

191

Chapter Sixteen

Joshua spent a restless night, mind a maelstrom of swirling thoughts, his dreams disturbed and fragmented. If he had hoped to awaken miraculously refreshed and with new clarity of mind, then he was to be disappointed. Despite the evidence from Sir Matthew the picture was no clearer. It was, he thought dispiritedly, like attempting to piece together a peculiarly abstruse and complicated puzzle without knowing the finished design. One worked blindly, by instinct, dependent upon chance. If pieces were accidentally missing or deliberately withheld then it was a challenge with little hope of success. Joshua, who was not easily defeated, was painfully aware of his human fallibility. It would need a miracle to solve the case, he reflected, and the Almighty was not always so accommodating.

Rebecca was still asleep, so Joshua tried to slip quietly from their bed without disturbing her. She murmured, and stretched out a detaining hand, face flushed and heavy from sleep, then gave up the struggle to surface. Joshua washed briskly in cold water from the washstand ewer, completed a sketchy toilet, then swiftly dressed and, with riding boots in hand, crept downstairs. He was due at the courthouse at Pyle to attend the inquest upon the murdered girl at 9 o'clock. He would make an early start that he might first see the woman sheep stealer and give her Sir Matthew's news.

He could hear Betty Turner moving purposefully in the kitchen, already preparing for the day. He did not disturb her, but strode into the yard to fetch the grey. He could take breakfast at some inn or tavern upon the way, or when his ordeal at the courthouse was over. Knowledge of what he must do and say robbed him of appetite. The woman, he knew, was no more than a common thief, a murderer if not by the act then

192

by association. Yet, against all his inclination, like Rebecca, he could not but be moved by her love for her child. He felt pity for her as well as contempt, a strangely disturbing mixture of emotions that he tried vainly to quell.

Once set firmly upon the highway to Nottage, he had leisure to think more constructively. Where, he wondered, had Sir Matthew learned of the woman's identity and the abduction of her child? It seemed surprising that one of the privileged classes, one of the landed gentry should have access to such mundane information. Knowledge of Sir Peter Henshawe's business affairs was to be expected, for they were common currency among men of such standing. Sir Matthew might obtain such details legally and without arousing the least suspicion. Dr Peate, a celebrated clergyman and scholar, would certainly be aware of the spiritual and emotional needs of the family and be a frequent guest. But news of the common sheep stealers and the woman at Pyle? No doubt Sir Matthew had once more called upon the services of Rhys, his water bailiff. Joshua had found cause to be grateful to the estate worker in the past. Rhys was, by virtue of the work he did, adept at tracking others unseen. Poachers and vagrants took issue with him at their peril. The water bailiff was a well-known and popular figure at the inns and ale houses of the Vale and might move freely without arousing mistrust. In addition, his brother was boot-black at the local tavern and others of his family similarly suited elsewhere. They were privy to all the gossip and comings and goings throughout the Vale, and a small fee might procure their services. As justice of the peace Sir Matthew would also have access to information not freely attainable to others, and hear rumours too. All in all he was a valuable ally as well as a cultured and amenable old gentleman and Joshua was grateful, most of all, for his undemanding love for Rebecca. It was a bond that held them close, and with John Jeremiah's birth, was irrevocably strengthened.

The guard at the gaolhouse was conscientious and helpful, unlike his surly predecessor, and the woman Joshua sought was brought at once to the stark inhospitable room set aside for such interviews. She showed neither curiosity nor alarm at Joshua's presence, her face coldly expressionless as she silently took the chair offered to her. They regarded each other for a moment across the scarred and ink-stained table, with Joshua wondering how best to begin.

'Well, ma'am,' he said at length, 'I think we may dispense with the preliminary skirmishing, for it serves no purpose.'

She gazed at him suspiciously, wary, but still making no response.

'I know your name, ma'am, and much else about you.'

She stared at him sceptically, mouth wryly amused.

'You are one, Corinne Blackstock, born in Spitalfields, London. A member of a strolling company of actors lately appearing in the Vale of Glamorgan.'

'Am I, sir?' Her tone was insolent, deliberately provocative, but there was no mistaking her unease. 'Then you had best prove it.'

'I have documents, ma'am. Signed and witnessed. And there are those eager and willing to come forward and identify you. As I said, let us dispense with skirmishing and evasion. It serves no purpose. There is too much at stake.'

'Since all that is at stake is mine, sir, *my* freedom, *my* life, I fail to see why it should concern you!'

'It concerns me, Miss Blackstock, because there is another involved.'

'If you seek news of him then you had best look elsewhere! I will not betray him!' she exclaimed contemptuously. 'Let that be an end to it! I have nothing to lose.'

'Ah, ma'am, but you have already lost that which you hold most dear, that is the crux of it.'

'What have I lost? What, sir? My freedom? It is of little account to me. I took the risks offered and will pay the price.'

'No, ma'am, it is not of your freedom that I speak.'

'What, then?' her puzzlement was genuine, voice sharp-edged with fear. 'You think I have lost him, too? That he will desert me? He will do what needs to be done, never fear!'

'I speak of your child, ma'am, your daughter.'

'My daughter? How is she involved? It is some trick to unnerve me, to make me confess all! What do you know of my daughter save the little I have told you? You lie! Confess it!'

Joshua, seeing her rising panic, felt no triumph, only a sickness of shame at what he was forced to do. It would

194

destroy the only comfort that was left to her, her solace and hope.

'Your daughter, ma'am, is named Anna and was farmed out to a cowherd and his wife at Wick in the Vale, a kindly couple by the name of Prosser.'

'Was?' she exclaimed in anguish. 'She was, you said? In God's name, where is she now? If you have harmed a hair of her head then I swear that you will pay dearly! What gave you the right to take her from those she loved?'

'I did not take her, ma'am, would not. I have a child of my own.'

'Who, then?' There was no mistaking her terror and confusion. She had torn herself from the chair and hurled herself furiously towards him, fingers digging deep into his arm, the table between them no barrier. 'For the love of God, I beg you, tell me where she is.' Her rage had given way to pleading, her voice so low that it could scarce be heard. 'Please, I beg you in all humility to assure me that she is safe, that she will not be harmed.'

'I cannot give you that assurance.'

'Why, sir?'

'Because I have news that the child is dead, was taken at the command of one who feared that others might gain knowledge of his dealings, associate him with his child, and with you.'

'No!' the denial was ripped from her. 'No! It is a trick to destroy me, to incriminate others! Confess it!'

Joshua's awkward pity showed that he spoke the truth, but he could find no words to comfort her or absolve him from shame.

'You know, then, who has taken her?' She could not bring herself to utter the word 'killed' or accept its finality. 'You know his name?'

'I do, ma'am, as all else about him. But I must needs ask you to confirm it, for there is no other way.'

She had sunk back into her chair, hands clasped hard to her mouth, as if she would hold in the terror that assailed her, the scream of grief from within. Then she buried her face in her arms upon the table and wept as though her heart must break and dissolve as painfully as she. Joshua would willingly have laid a compassionate hand upon her shoulders to try and

195

staunch her grief, but knew that he must not. Human contact was forbidden and he must wait in silence. When she looked up her face was ugly in its hopelessness, all beauty and vivacity drained away with her daughter's life. She was empty of all emotion, even hatred for the one who had betrayed her and his own child. Hers was an emptiness of spirit so deep that Joshua felt the loneliness of it within himself and the raw scald of tears at his eyes.

'Sir Peter Henshawe,' the name was quietly spoken.

'You will give evidence against him, if need be?'

'I will give evidence.'

'It may well save your life, ma'am,' he blurted clumsily.

'Save my life, sir?' Her mouth twisted wryly. 'I would not wish it prolonged. I have little enough to live for.' He nodded, unspeaking. 'Now, sir, if you will have me returned to my cell.'

Joshua called out to the gaoler and he entered and led the woman away. When he returned, Joshua gave him a gold guinea, saying abruptly, 'The prisoner has lately lost a child, an infant. I beg that you treat her as kindly as you are able, bring her what small treats you may to raise her spirits, whatever is needful.'

'I will, sir.'

Joshua dug deeply into his pocket and offered the man a half-sovereign saying, 'If you will accept this, sir, for your pains.'

'No pains, sir, common humanity. But I thank you humbly.'

Joshua knew that it had been no more than a futile gesture on his part, a way to salve his own shame and hurt. Yet she might find in it some small proof of his caring. He had little heart for the inquest before him. There had been too much death, too much violence and betrayal. Yet he had to believe that what he did was of worth, else it was all an illusion and not worth a corpse's candle. He could find solace in bringing the guilty to justice, in avenging the dead. The woman within the cell could find no comfort in revenge, no solace, no hope. She had lost the two human souls who gave meaning to her life. It was tragedy enough. That the man she loved and trusted had killed the child of his own creation and loving was tragedy past all enduring.

John Burrell had taken a copy of the likeness, which Hansel

196

had made of the dead girl and scrutinised it carefully. Mansel, seemingly absorbed in studying a water colour painting upon the study wall was, as Burrell was uncomfortably aware, watching him covertly, awaiting opinion. Burrell was amazed at the skill and sensitivity of the drawing, the depth of perception shown. Mansel had captured, not the frozen emptiness of the dead, but the character and verve of one living and in warm-blooded flesh.

'It is a remarkable achievement,' he praised warmly. 'As fine a likeness as any I have ever seen. You have missed your vocation, Mansel!'

Mansel's plump cheeks were suffused with colour, pleasure and embarrassment as he confessed ruefully, 'I think, sir, that I might have fared better as artist than physician! To create life from death is of more value than creating death from life. Of late,' he added feelingly, 'I seem to deal more with the dead than the living!'

Burrell said with a dry smile, 'I fear that is in the very nature of things. Those who survive our ministrations take living for granted. Those who die are proof of our failure. More, they are remembered as saints and paragons whatever their dispositions! It holds out great hope for our future, do you not agree? In years to come you will be remembered as a great physician, a saviour of the afflicted, your memory revered by all. Does that not comfort you?'

Mansel grinned, saying, 'No, sir, it does not, for I shall be past caring. A little credit and faith in the here and now would serve me better.'

'Well, I give you full credit for the likeness of the murdered girl! None could improve upon it.'

'Save the man who robbed her of life,' Mansel reminded. He shook his head despairingly, exclaiming, 'Oh, it is a savage old world, Burrell!'

'But the only one we have, so I had best be about my business in it.' Burrel said crisply, adding, more charitably, 'Shall I take the likeness with me, Mansel? Who knows? Someone, somewhere, might recognise her.'

'If you will, although I hold out as little hope as Joshua Stradling. She was not a cottager, else she would have been known to us or to those upon the outlying holdings and farms.

197

Nor was she a pauper, for he has made enquiries of Walter Bevan, the relieving officer to the poor. No, it is my opinion that she came here from afar, upon some ship or private coach. Whoever killed her has long departed, leaving his track well covered.'

'You will be required at the inquest this morning?' Burrell asked.

'Yes, I shall take the curricle and leave in half an hour or so.'

'It will be no more than a formality while her identity remains unknown.'

'Indeed, a mere formality, as the other inquest next Thursday into Jed Carter's death. Known or unknown, it makes no matter. A poor enough epitaph, Burrell, God knows!'

'Perhaps He is the only one who knows, understands, and forgives all,' Burrell reminded with wry humour.

'Then I do not envy Him!' Mansel said. 'The inquest will prove punishment enough. To judge others for all eternity must be very hell itself!'

Burrell set out on horseback for the Weare Bathing House upon the isolated beach beyond the dunes at Newton. The guests were those from the busy coaching inn at Pyle, who used it as a convenient annexe when braving the Atlantic waters. At summer's end, they would be few and intrepid and ordered there upon a physician's decree, for the curative properties of seawater were becoming increasingly used in treating disorders of the bones and diseases of the skin. It was Burrell's private opinion that if it were the doctors who were ordered to present their flesh to the icy blasts, it would be a short-lived fad. Or perhaps it would be *they* who were short-lived. It was a peculiarly Puritan ethic, he considered, that such suffering and bodily chastisement set one into a state of grace. It was more likely that they set one into a state of numbness, if not decay. Still, he had been summoned to Weare House to treat a guest who complained of some chill or trembling ague, which was hardly surprising. He would attend the patient well and do whatever he was able. Such rich visitors were few and far between, and their generous fees helped to subsidise those more greatly in need and without the wherewithal to buy it.

As he reached the bottom of Clevis Hill, he changed his mind about riding direct to Weare House and decided instead to visit Emily Randall in the loft above the coach-house. It was ridiculously early in the morning, and those at the bathing house would scarcely have stirred from bed. Even if his patient were confined to his, then it would hardly inconvenience him to rest a while longer. Emily would cerainly be awake and dressed, and preparing for her day's teaching at the school.

She was a gentle, warm-hearted woman, with a serenity that comforted. An easy woman to be with. Yet she was possessed of a sharp intellect and mocking humour that added spice to their friendship. He had grown to depend upon her, John Burrell thought. To value her nearness. No, that was not altogether true. He respected Emily for her spirit and courage and loved her dearly. What was it, then, that held him back from declaring it openly? There was none save she with whom he would wish to share the life remaining; none who could stir him to such laughter and tenderness, passion even. Yet he could not make that final commitment, would not. The shadows of the past always came to blot out the present. A blackness fierce and all-pervasive, that he could not inflict upon another. He had tried, in vain, to exorcise the horror of it, the memorics that held him jealously in thrall. The regrets and self-recrimination, that murderous rage for revenge, were gone now, stilled by the passing of time. Enemies had become friends, old griefs as pale and elusive as the sad ghosts of the past. All that remained was a darkness of spirit. It fell upon him at random, stifling as a cloak, cutting out light and reason, rendering him a useless cowering thing until the black depression lifted. How could he explain it to another when he could not explain it to himself? How could he inflict it upon another? It was more than flesh and blood should be called upon to bear. Burrell hesitated and all but turned and rode out of the Crown Inn yard, but already Ossie was beside him, taking his mount, smiling good-humouredly, greeting him with honest pleasure that he instinctively returned.

As the ostler, murmuring words of reassurance, led the animal away, Burrell mounted the stone steps to Emily's loft.

'Why, John, what a pleasure to see you, my dear. I bid you come in.' Her warmth of welcome was as unfeigned as Ossie's. 'There is nothing amiss? No special reason for the call?'

'No reason in all the world, save a need for your company. A yearning for friendship.'

'Then that is the best reason of all.' She smiled delightedly and motioned him to a wheel-backed chair beside the fire, leaving her school books where she had set them in order upon the scrubbed table, and coming to settle herself beside him. 'There is something I would ask you about, John. I am in need of advice from one clear-sighted and objective.'

'Then I am not sure that I am your man,' he said, mouth lifting in amusement, 'although it is a description which pleases me.' He paused, thin intelligent face intent. 'It is a medical query which you pose me?'

'No, a question of a future.'

'Indeed?' Try as he might he could not keep a certain stiffness from his tone, a wariness.

'The future of a child.'

'Rosa's child?'

'No, another. One in my care and of whom I have great hopes, John. An intelligent boy with the prospect of becoming a fine scholar.'

'If?' he asked tersely.

'If a way can be found to persuade him and others where his future lies.'

'Dafydd Crocutt,' he said. 'You have in mind Dafydd Crocutt, Elwyn Morris's boy?'

'Yes.'

'Would you have me speak to Morris? Seek to persuade him?'

'No. The obstacle is not Elwyn Morris. He loves the boy. I have known him from our poorhouse days, and he will do what is best for Dafydd, of that I am sure.'

'You mean that the boy himself is unwilling? I cannot believe that he still hankers after that poor, arid apology of a farm upon Stormy Downs. Besides, Joshua has already bought it, on the promise that Dafydd may one day buy it back, work it as owner.'

'Yes, it is all that remains to him of his father's life now. He will guard it jealously, whatever comes, feeling it his duty to farm it for his father's sake.'

Burrell was silent for a moment, thinking of what Mansel had told him of Jem Crocutt's death. It had been of a savagery past belief. A merciless crucifixion by the wreckers who believed his life a danger to them when he stumbled upon their murderous ravages at Sker. He had been nailed to the great downbeam of the barn by the tines of his own pitchfork and left to die, impaled like some bloodless insect. It had been his eight-year old son who had found him and borne the hurt of it since.

'If it is the boy's wish to farm such a useless place, Emily?'

'No, it is not his wish, John. It is an obligation. A vow that he made upon Crocutt's death. How can it be binding? He was but eight years old.'

'I do not see,' he said carefully, 'how I might help. What have you in mind?'

'Raising the wherewithal to further educate him. To give him the opportunity he merits, to give him a chance in life. A choice . . .'

'And where would this . . . venture take him?'

'To the grammar school at Cowbridge. If the money can be raised!'

He stifled a smile, saying with mock gravity, 'May I take it, Miss Randall, that you are not importuning me for immoral purposes?'

'For the most moral of purposes, sir. To benefit another.'

'Then I admit to a feeling of grave disappointment, I had hoped that it might have benefited me.'

Emily flinched as though he had struck out at her, and he wished the foolish words unsaid. He said abruptly, 'I have money saved. A little, and useless to me, for all my needs are met. But Elwyn Morris is a proud man, Emily, and would not accept it. I do not see how it could be done without giving offence. Unless . . .?'

'Unless?' Emily repeated forcefully.

'Unless by way of scholarship, one endowed by some benefactor unknown. A venerable gentleman, who wishes to share his bounty with others.'

'Why, John, that is a capital idea!' Emily ran from her chair and hugged him, setting an ecstatic kiss upon his cheek, unselfconscious in her delight at his cleverness.

'There is but one impediment, Emily.' He saw the joyousness fade from her and was ashamed.

'An impediment, John?' she asked anxiously.

'Yes, it will mean being denied security, accepting less.'

'If you feel that I ask too much of you,' she said, pained and confused. 'That I have thrust it upon you too quickly and without thought.'

'No, my dear. It is you who will be deprived and must bear responsibility.'

She looked at him in bewilderment. 'I fear that I do not understand. You are not leaving the hamlets? Will not be forced away?'

'No, I will stay, Emily, for as long as ever you have need of me. Damn it, Emily! Can you not understand? Can you not help me out? I am asking you to marry me.'

'Then I accept,' she said calmly, 'although, I'll warrant it is not the most elegant proposal ever made, nor the most flattering. But it will suffice.'

Her mouth curved into a smile and he found himself smiling involuntarily in response, then laughing helplessly as they clung foolishly together, unable to utter a sensible word. Then he kissed her soundly and with a warmth of passion that left her in no doubt of his reason for asking her.

'Emily,' he began, face suddenly grown uncertain, 'there are things I should confess to you, things about me that you should know.'

She set a gentle hand to his lips, saying, 'I know you, John Burrell, better than you know yourself. Your strengths and weaknesses, your doubts and fears. You forget the letters that you sent in friendship to Jeremiah Fleet, when you faced the cholera epidemic, believing that you would not survive. I read those letters to him, for Jeremiah could neither read nor write. You poured out your heart and soul, as to one unknown. It was a cleansing, my dear, of old wounds, a catharsis. I learnt more of you then than of any other upon earth. I loved you as I love you now, wholly and for ever.'

'But there are dark places within me, Emily, some blackness of spirit of which, I fear, I shall never be rid.'

'I would take the whole man, John,' she said simply. 'The man complete and unaltered, for that is the man I love. What cannot be healed must be shared, my dear. For that is what loving is, a sharing of joy and griefs.'

'You will not regret it, Emily, I swear to you. I will forget the past. No longer let it torture and cripple me.'

'I would hope, John, that you will always remember,' she said quietly, 'for it has made you what you are. I cannot wholly regret the cruelty of it, nor of the paupery I have known. It has given us understanding, a deeper, richer loving, the kinder for coming so late.'

John Burrell took her into his arms again and kissed her with the greatest tenderness, and she returned his kisses with a fervour that stirred and delighted him, so generously were they given.

'Young Dafydd Crocutt will be delighted,' she ventured practically when she was fitted to speak again. 'And Elwyn Morris and Eira, too. He was always a brave, intelligent child, and a favourite of mine.'

'I hope, ma'am, that he will not oust me in your affections.'

'Indeed not! Yet he has been successful in guiding us into matrimony when I had all but despaired. I shall show him no favours, for that would be unseemly.'

'And unfair?'

'And unfair. Yet I might cherish a fondness for him secretly.'

'As you secretly cherished a fondness for me?'

'I do not deny that I pursued you openly and quite shamelessly,' she confided artlessly. 'I was vastly relieved when you stopped running.'

John Burrell's lean, saturnine face was bright with humour. 'As I, my dear. I regret only that it took me so long!'

Chapter Seventeen

The inquest upon the murdered woman was, as Burrell predicted, no more than a formality. Dr Mansel and Joshua gave their evidence clearly and succinctly, and the dockside labourer, who had found the body, with such paralytic nervousness that his tension had affected all. A verdict was returned that the victim had been murdered by person or persons unknown. The crux of it was, as the justice said scathingly to Joshua afterwards, that the woman herself remained unknown. It was a sad commentary upon Joshua's efficiency as constable, he was adjured, and even reflected unfavourably upon the justice himself. It must be rectified, and soon.

Joshua listened to the tirade in silence, knowing that the justice's frustration was no greater than his own. Dr Mansel, impatiently awaiting the arrival of the ostler with his curricle, was a reluctant witness to the scene, and tried to divert the justice's wrath. His social pleasantries were coldly, if civilly, received and exchanged, then the justice renewed his attack with added vigour. The glance of embarrassed commiseration which Mansel gave the constable spoke volumes.

It was Joshua who startled the justice into silence. 'If you have time to step into the courthouse cells, sir, to see the prisoner?'

'Why, sir? What benefit would it confer? If your questioning has failed then you must persevere, not expect others to do your work for you!'

'My aim was to save you a journey, sir.'

'A journey? What journey?' he demanded irately. 'I swear you talk in riddles, Stradling! Clarity, man! Speak clearly!'

'A return journey, sir.'

'Why should I return?'

'To take a signed deposition from the woman, sir. She has confessed freely.'

Joshua was aware of Mansel's bubbling laughter, instantly smothered, and of the justice's rising irritation.

'She has confessed to the sheep stealing, you mean?' The justice lowered his voice. 'Since she was caught red-handed, she could scarcely deny it!'

'No, sir. She has confessed freely to all, including the murder of Jed Carter and the involvement of that . . . that anonymous gentleman in the Vale. She has incriminated him and will give evidence under oath. Her proof is irrefutable.'

'The devil it is!' The justice was momentarily at a loss. He glanced suspiciously towards Mansel, who was staring with bland innocence towards the stables, then took Joshua's arm in a firm grip and drew him urgently aside. 'Now, sir! Give account of yourself!' he commanded frigidly. 'It ill becomes you to keep me in ignorance, to make me a laughing stock before all. Your proof, sir, that this is not some devious ploy upon the part of the prisoner to escape more leniently.'

'Joshua handed him Sir Matthew's letter which he scrutinised in silence. When he handed it back, his face was carefully expressionless.

'We had best go within,' he said curtly. 'You may tell me, briefly and concisely, what has occurred, that I may be better prepared to deal with the woman. Sir Peter Henshawe is the father of the infant, Sir Matthew implies, and has had the child abducted and murdered. Oh, it is infamous, Stradling! Past all belief! The man is a monster without soul or feeling. It will please me to see him hanged! I cannot conceive of a more heinous crime, nor one so undeserving of forgiveness.' He faltered, belatedly remembering his role as priest as well as justice, conceding, 'Well, of course, absolution is in God's province alone, although we must show *some* Christian charity to wrongdoers, even those seemingly beyond redemption. I'll swear though, Joshua, that I shall be hard pressed to offer him charity, much less forgiveness.'

'As you say, sir, perfection is God's attribute, alone.'

The justice looked at him keenly, then relaxed, his tentative smile erupting into appreciative laughter. 'Yet we must all aspire to it. You, sir, most of all!' With a chuckle at his own sagacity, he hurried Joshua cheerfully within.

With a signed confession from Corinne Blackstock and corroborative evidence from the other sheep stealers, who were cravenly intent upon saving their own skins, Robert Knight was satisfied that he could swear out a warrant for Sir Peter Henshawe's immediate arrest. He would, he vowed to Joshua, send immediate word to Sir Matthew, begging his urgent cooperation to see the man caught and brought to justice. His cheerfulness upon entering that part of the courthouse which housed the cells was grimly abated, his manner strained.

'Well, sir, it is ended!' Joshua said.

'No, Stradling! It is not ended for that poor benighted creature within and I cannot but pity her, notwithstanding the violence she has done. She was not deserving of the death of her child nor so cruel a betrayal.' His rich vibrant voice was filled with compassion. 'Yet my heart goes out to poor Jed Carter, too, for he lost all, even life itself. Oh, it is a damnable tragedy, Joshua, wrought by man's greed and rapacity! Henshawe will have much to answer for, here and beyond in a final judgement.' He stumped ahead of Joshua, plump-jowled face anxiously set, shoulders hunched dejectedly.

'Would you have me send for your coachman, sir? Have the carriage brought to you?'

'No, leave it a while, Joshua. I need time for reflection, time to compose myself.'

Joshua hesitated, saying tentatively, 'If you would take refreshment, sir? A glass of Madeira, perhaps, I would willingly accompany you to the Pyle Inn, for I have not eaten since dinner.'

'No,' he smiled wearily. 'Your abstinence does you credit, sir, as your devotion to duty. You have done well, Joshua, and I regret my earlier outburst. It was ill-mannered and without cause, save for my devilish irascibility and the ravages of gout. I beg you will forgive me.'

Joshua, grieved to see him so humbled, nodded awkward acceptance. 'I will return within,' the justice said. 'The woman has need of me for what little spiritual help I may give! You said that you wished to spare me a visit, Joshua. Yet I return, now, of my own volition. I lack the words and emotions to bring her comfort,' he admitted, 'for I cannot easily reach out to others, a sad deficiency in a priest.' He turned sharply and walked within.

Joshua went to retrieve the grey from the stables, mind upon the woman within the gaolhouse and the justice's lack of belief in himself. He would find the words, Joshua thought, but would they bring comfort? Were they any more than empty rhetoric? A salve for a wound too deep and raw to be reached? He did not doubt that the justice would return. Yet, perhaps, it was the comforter who had the greater need to be comforted.

After leaving the coach-house loft, John Burrell again postponed his promised visit to Weare House and set off on foot towards Newton village. He was a great favourite with Ossie, whose unfailing good humour endeared him to all.

'It will be the briefest of visits,' he assured the ostler, 'and the exercise will stand me in good stead.' He grinned, adding tongue-in-cheek, 'I had best try walking some of the fat from these old bones.'

Since he was as lean and high-strung as a thoroughbred racehorse, Ossie replied, straight-faced, 'Since that is your considered opinion as a physician, sir, I will not contradict you. But a word of practical advice.' Burrel regarded him quizzically. 'I bid you have a care for the cracks in the cobblestones, sir, and avoid the culverts and ditches, for it would grieve us to lose your custom.' Whistling boldly between the gaps in his teeth, he made his way cheerfully across the yard.

Burrell's exchanges with Ossie were always a pleasure to him, for the ostler was one of the few people with whom he was able to relax and be comfortably at ease. The years Burrell had spent in prison had, he knew, made him morbidly introspective, unable to reach out to others, his remoteness as a physician a necessary defence. Yet, with Ossie there was no such barrier. Indeed, there were no barriers of class and occupation, for Ossie admitted to none. As with his beloved animals he judged all as equals and treated them accordingly. Sir Matthew and the sweeping boy in the yard were accepted for

207

themselves and afforded the dignity owed to them. It was a rare trait, Burrell thought, but as natural to Ossie as his nearness to the soil and his good common sense. An hour with Ossie was balm to the spirit, Burrell declared to Mansel, and of more practical use than all of their pills and potions.

Now, as he turned into the driveway of Thatched Cottage, Burrell rehearsed in his mind what he must ask and say. It was no ordinary social visit or a routine visit to examine his godson, John Jeremiah, although he would find an excuse to visit the boy. Rebecca, whose affection for Burrell had caused her to name her son after him, greeted him as always with genuine pleasure. They were bound always by the vicissitudes of the past, their shared understanding an unbreakable bond between them. They were always direct and honest with each other, for there had never been need to dissemble.

'Oh, John, my dear! Come in, I beg of you. Is it John Jeremiah you have come to see? I will take you at once to his room, and then you must take some refreshment with me.'

'No, Rebecca, I have not come to see John Jeremiah. I have come particularly to see you, and in Joshua's absence.'

'Why?' She was immediately alarmed. 'Is Joshua sick? Suffered some accident? I beg you tell me!'

'No, my dear,' he hastened to reassure her. 'It is a matter of business only. I spoke clumsily and without thought. There is a proposition I would put to you.'

'I'll own you intrigue me, John.' Rebecca motioned him to sit down beside her. 'What does this proposition entail?'

He explained to her Emily's plans for Dafydd Crocutt's future. 'Why?' she exclaimed enthusiastically, 'that is a marvellous idea, and one which has my wholehearted support! If Emily is so certain that Dafydd has a future as an exceptional scholar then there is no better recommendation.' Her intelligent blue eyes were alight with curiosity as she asked, 'But how may I help? How may I become involved? Is it to Dafydd you would have me speak, or to his stepfather? His mother would not, I know, stand in Dafydd's way, for she has only the harshest memories of Grove farm.' She broke off, sensing his awkwardness, to ask gently, 'Is it money you require from me, John? The wherewithal to fund the scholarship?'

He flushed, fidgeting, and glancing uneasily at his boots, to murmur, 'It is a loan I need, you understand? I would wish to endow the bursary myself and will pay back the money and interest annually from what I earn as Mansel's partner. I would not ask, save that if a scholarship is to be endowed then the whole of the capital must be presented at once. It is beyond my reach to offer such a sum. Yet, if I delay, then the boy will suffer. It will be too late.'

'Oh, my dear John.' He sat anxious and straight-backed, fearing her refusal. 'I will help the boy gladly, and none shall ever learn of it from me, save Joshua,' she amended, 'for I would not wish such secrets to come between us.'

'You do not think that he will make objection, feel I have unfairly pressured you?' he probed anxiously.

'No. He admires Dafydd for his courage and tenacity, his loyalty to Jem Crocutt's memory. But he would not have him sacrifice himself and his future. That would be too high a price to pay. Besides, Joshua was a pupil at the school, and would feel it a kindness upon your part.'

'As it is upon yours, Rebecca.'

'No,' she protested with stark honesty, 'for it will not be a burden upon me. It will in no wise affect my life. It is you, John, who must bear the brunt of it, the commitment and self-denial. I admire you for that. The money is all I may offer. You are giving of yourself.' He looked as if he might have spoken but, instead, took her hand in his, holding it gently and gazing at her with undisguised affection, the bond between them beyond the need for words. Rebecca did not seek to free her hand.

'Grandfather has set aside money for me,' she said, voice low. 'I know that he and Dr Peate, too, would think it well used in such an endeavour. I shall ask the advice of his notary in the Vale, John, and travel there tomorrow, for it might take some time in the setting up of such a bequest.' Burrell hesitated, and Rebecca thought he wished to make some objection, for he was clearly ill at ease, painfully uncertain. 'There is something troubling you?' she asked anxiously, 'something you would wish changed?'

'No,' he was awkward in his embarrassment. 'Rather there is something I would have you do, if you agree, Rebecca . . . and others.'

'What is it you would have me do?'

'I would like the bursary to be in Dr Handel Peate's name, if he would not think it impertinent of me to make such suggestion. I know from what Illtyd, Joshua and others have told me that he was a tutor at the school and a man greatly loved and respected.' Colour flamed beneath his skin as he murmured, 'It would be a tribute, a gift to a fine man whose memory and work would endure beyond him.' As Rebecca had not spoken, he blurted uncomfortably, 'If you think it will distress him, give him offence?'

'No, my dear. I think it will please him more than you will ever know. It will be the only memorial he would choose to leave others, a continuation of all he has sacrificed and striven to do, a tribute from one good and honest man to another.' She set a kiss to his gaunt cheek before saying decisively, 'I will see that all is arranged, John, never fear. It shall be done without the knowledge of any, save those intimately involved. What is not known cannot be revealed, even by accident. Were Dafydd and Elwyn Morris to discover our involvement, it would grieve and humiliate them before others, and make your own position untenable. It would sour relationships and make Elwyn Morris desperate to repay the debt. He is a proud man and would feel himself a failure for being unable to provide for his stepson's needs.'

'There is one other whose needs will be affected, Rebecca. One who is involved more than any other.'

'Emily?'

He nodded.

'But of course, John. It is at Emily's instigation. The whole idea is hers.'

'I have asked her to marry me, Rebecca. To be my wife. You are the first to learn of it!'

'Oh, my dear. How glad I am!' Rebecca leapt up, dragging him upright with her, waltzing him around in her excitement, hugging him close. 'Oh, my dear! It is the greatest good news! I cannot tell you how pleased I am! Emily is the kindest of friends and I love her dearly.'

'As I, Rebecca.' His dark saturnine face was aglow with pleasure at her delight in his news. 'But you had best wait until she confides in you,' he suggested, smiling. 'I would not rob her of the pleasure of such unconfined joy! It will hearten her as it heartens me.' His face grew suddenly more serious as he said with quiet gravity, 'We have come a long way together, Rebecca, from the days when I was thought to be a villain and murderer. Every man was against me, every hand save yours. So much has changed. Our lives have changed, and we have changed.'

'No, John. *We* have not changed,' she said with conviction, 'for I always knew you for a good and honest man, one to be admired and trusted. Our lives have changed, but for the better. We cannot regret the past, for it has shaped us and brought us to where we are. You have the promise of a loving future with Emily now, and I the blessing of Joshua and John Jeremiah. We are rich in friendship.'

'Yes,' he said gravely. 'We are rich in that.' He hesitated, saying diffidently, 'There is one thing that troubles me still, Rebecca.' She looked at him questioningly. 'I will know how to approach Elwyn Morris, before all is arranged and set in motion. I will make casual mention of the merits of the school and the scholarship endowed by Dr Peate, and Emily, too, will convince him of the worth of it. That Joshua was a pupil there will stand us in good stead, for Elwyn Morris greatly respects and admires him.'

'It is Dafydd who you think must be convinced?'

'Yes. I fear it will not be easy, for his mind is set upon farming those few barren acres which Jem Crocutt left – more blight than inheritance. He will feel that he has betrayed his father's memory by leaving here. He will sacrifice the dream for the substance, and sacrifice himself if need be.'

'There is one whom he loves and respects above all others,' Rebecca said, 'his dearest friend and mentor, as he was mine.'

'The old fisherman? Jeremiah Fleet?'

'Yes. If you will allow me to have word with Jeremiah, tell him of what is involved. Confide all to him. He will tell no other, believe it. I would trust him with my life.'

'As I once had cause to,' Burrel reminded quietly. 'I do not doubt, Rebecca, that he will salvage Dafydd's life as he salvaged and rebuilt the poor wreckage of mine.'

Richard Turberville, the young curate at Maudlam, was

211

beloved by his parishioners, for he was a gentle and godly man. He lived, from choice, in the direst poverty, that he might better share the burdens and deprivations of his flock. What he practised as Christian humility was often viewed with considerably less charity in the parishes beyond. His brother clergy, whose benefices were often the gift of family, lived in comparative affluence and deplored such eccentricity. It made them feel uncomfortable. What irritated them most was that there was no real reason for Turberville to behave in such a bizarre manner. It was well known that he might have lived like a lord, for his family were the owners of Ewenny Priory, with its rich farmlands and holdings. Turberville, if asked, might have responded that it was the Lord whom he was attempting, in his simple way, to emulate. Such presumption would only have enraged them further. He was an irritant, a thorn in the flesh. Yet what could not be cured must be patiently endured.

The bishop, who had little patience with the curate and his outlandish ideas, but did not openly wish to offend the Turbervilles, found the ideal solution. Richard Turberville was banished to the poorest, most neglected, parish in the diocese and conveniently forgotten. Amongst the poor and labouring classes, whose only fight was for survival, such arcane notions could do little harm, the bishop reasoned. There would be no preferment for the young curate. He was disruptive and iconoclastic at best, unhinged at worst. Yet it surprised him that the young curate had the affection and loyalty of his entire flock, and even of a few wealthy traditionalists like Robert Knight of Tythegston. Of course, the people of Maudlam were of the common herd, still untutored and heathenish in their ways and with few expectations. Rhetoric and pedantry would scarcely impress them. But Robert Knight was a different matter. His approval of the young curate was to be greatly deplored. To encourage such extreme behaviour was to encourage anarchy. If young Turberville wished to practise self-abnegation, and live in poverty, then he would be better enclosed in a monastery. The bishop decided to speak firmly to his friend and colleague Robert Knight about it and see if he could bring some influence to bear. The bishop was not sanguine about the power of conversion. There was little pressure he could exert upon Knight, for he was wealthy,

212

powerful and stubborn enough to resist both commands and blandishments. In his own way he was as much of a rebel as young Turberville. The bishop turned his mind to more spiritual and less mundane matters and, once again, Richard Turberville was providentially forgotten.

Now, as he harnessed the mule to the cart in the yard behind his tumbledown cottage, Turberville's long, bony face was creased in perplexity. It would have surprised the bishop to know that it was the poverty and squalor of his own life that troubled the curate. Not upon his own account, for he scarcely noticed the inconveniences of it. He was a natural ascetic, concerned more with the survival of the spirit than the flesh. Yet it was of the flesh he was thinking now. Not his own miserable hide but the flesh of one dear to him and whose welfare concerned him more than his own. He loved Ruth Priday, Rebecca Stradling's serving maid, and had foolishly asked her to marry him. The foolishness lay not in his choice, for she was the gentlest, most loving of creatures, but in his own temerity. How could he, in all conscience, ask her to live in such an unspeakable hovel and share in a life of penury? He saw it now with new eyes, eyes made sharper by love, and saw it for the mean dwelling that it was. Yet he would not take help from his family. The money accrued in his name from birth, he had renounced entirely, giving it, by stealth, to those in greatest need. He could not renege upon such commitment, nor yet upon his commitment to Ruth. He loved her dearly. Life without her would be a penance to be endured and a greater deprivation than any he had known. He did not know if he had strength enough to bear it.

Her savage violation and rape by the brute who had beaten her, and left her for dead, had left her for a time insensible and robbed of speech. It was Turberville who had patiently coaxed her back to living and a trust in others; a victory bitter and hard won. He had fallen in love with her. It had been, from the first, inevitable, for the pity between them was a bond, fragile but ever tightening, that strengthened and drew them close. Turberville had been unwilling to speak his love, knowing the terrors and mistrust which still bedevilled her, although her speech and understanding had returned. It was at her father's, Joe Priday's, request that he had spoken of his fears for her future to Joshua, who had relentlessly tracked down her assailant and seen him gaoled. Joshua had asked his fiancee, Rebecca de Breos, to find work for Ruth at Southerndown Court, and she had generously taken her as her personal maid. The separation had all but broken Turberville's will. He knew an anguish of flesh as well as mind. Yet he had not spoken his love lest it drive her more cruelly from him.

Months later, when he had been murderously set upon by a stranger within his own church, it was Ruth who had come to nurse him, and she who had openly declared her love for him and her willingness to share his future, whatever came.

'Whatever came,' the words returned now to haunt him. He was committed to God, committed always to His service, and the service of others. Was it fair, he wondered, to consign another to such relentless self-sacrifice, to penury, and the sordidness that such deprivation entailed? He had prayed, long and hard about it, begging God most earnestly to show him the way, to tell him what was required of him. There had been no sign, no miraculous enlightenment. If God had spoken, then it was no more than a whisper heard within, the certainty that he, alone, must make decision.

Turberville harnessed the mule to the cart and set out for Newton village. He would take Ruth on a long-planned drive to the seashore, he thought; tell her of the doubts that assailed him, his agony of mind. As he passed by the stone-built forge with its roof of turf, the blacksmith, Joe Priday, left his toil at the anvil and came out to exchange a cheerful greeting as the lowly equipage passed by. Priday's face was seared with heat from the fire, skin polished as a burn. His black curls, thickly springing, were damp with sweat, brawny arms bared. He called out, smiling:

'I beg you will give my love to Ruth, sir, tell her that I rejoice in her good fortune, that I eagerly await her coming.'

'I will, sir, I will,' Richard Turberville called back, voice borne away with the wind from the sea, and lost in the rattle of cart-wheels upon the stony track.

I will take the path through the dunes, he thought, then skirt the great pool, and try to set my mind to ease. There is a peace and tranquillity in such loneliness, a balm for the spirit. He felt a lessening of hurt as he drove deep within the dunes,

214

a pleasure in such isolation. No sign of animal or man, only the occasional windhover and the plaintive, near-human, cry of a far off curlew. Yet, when the cart took the track through a cleft in the dunes he knew that it was human pain he heard, human grief.

The man forsaken upon the sandy wastes before him might have been mistaken for a bundle of bloodied rags, had there not been some tremor of movement, a thread of terrified sound. Richard Turberville leapt awkwardly from the cart and stumbled towards him, bootsoles sinking into the drifted sand as he strove to reach him. When he neared the poor creature, pity and anguish turned swiftly into shock, for the man was bound at wrists and ankles with straw ropes that had flayed his skin to raw flesh in his efforts to free himself.

'Dear God in heaven!' the exclamation was piously made. 'What savagery is this? Who in God's name could wreak such havoc?'

The man was a mass of bloodied bruises and weals, his features scarce recognisable as human. Turberville was at first fearful that the victim was no longer breathing, that his life had ebbed in those few brief moments since he had leapt from the cart to aid him. Yet, when he set his hand within the man's coat, there seemed still the barest flicker of life, the presence of a heartbeat.

What was he to do? The poor wretch was barely breathing, and he dared not delay by returning to Maudlam. There was none there who could treat his wounds. He must drive on to Newton as he planned. Pray God that either Dr Mansel or Burrell would be there at the Clevis to tend him. He had wasted a few precious seconds in trying to loosen the bonds that oppressed the man, but to no avail. He must linger no more. Although Turberville was a tall man, well honed by walking and weather, he all but despaired of lifting the stranger into the cart, for he was so awkwardly bound and as much a dead weight as a corpse. When finally he managed to set him clumsily upon the boards, Turberville's breath was raw in his throat, his heart beating so fiercely at his ribs that he could hear its agonised thudding.

With scarce a moment to recover, he set the mule to follow the thin thread of track and then, where the paths converged, towards the main highway. When he saw the grey ahead with Joshua's unmistakable figure in the saddle, he strove to call out to him, his voice a pitiful croak.

Joshua had not at first heard him, but he turned abruptly in the saddle at the sound of the cart's rattling, then halted, and came swiftly riding back, face uncertain beneath his fine helmet.

'Richard? Are you bound for Newton?' His expression hardened at the sight of the bloodied figure within the cart, and he leapt from his mare in agitation, scarcely able to believe it.

'You know the man, Joshua?' Turberville asked, bewildered.

'Curtis!' Joshua said, stricken. 'Dear God, Richard. They have murdered Curtis!'

Chapter Eighteen

Joshua had ridden ahead of Richard Turberville and the cart with its gruesome burden to forewarn the two doctors upon Clevis Hill of the urgent need for their services. He had seen assaults and injuries enough to know that Curtis had very little hope of survival. The beating he had suffered and the shock of being left bound and helpless might well prove more than he could physically or mentally bear. What manner of man, he wondered despairingly, as he rode through the pillared gateway of Mansel's house, could wreak such mindless savagery upon another of his kind? It was degrading. Inhuman. A perversion too debased to comprehend. It no longer mattered that his own antipathy towards the stricken man had been instinctive. What mattered now was that Curtis should be given ease and comfort. It was with overwhelming relief that Joshua saw Mansel's curricle at the door, about to be driven by the groom to the coach-house.

'Dr Mansel is within?' he called out sharply.

'Yes, sir. He has newly arrived from Pyle. The inquest.'

Joshua hastily dismounted and, leaving the grey standing, hurried within, calling urgently, 'Dr Mansel! Quick, sir! A moment of your time.'

Mansel, surprised, and bewildered, emerged from the library. 'Constable Stradling,' he said, bemused, 'I have but lately left you at the courthouse. Does it concern the inquest? Is there some irregularity or doubt?'

'None, sir. It is your professional services I seek. I have urgent need of a doctor!'

'You, sir?' Mansel's opaque eyes were confused.

'No, sir. A man found brutally attacked upon Kenfig dunes. Bound hand and foot and left to die.'

'Where is he, sir? Where may I find him?' Immediately he

was all efficiency and solicitude. 'Would you have me ride out with you? I will order my coach to be brought.'

'No, sir. It was Richard Turberville who found him and brings him here, now, upon his cart.'

Mansel, despite his concern, essayed a dry smile, saying, 'Well, sir, if he has survived such a journey then my hopes are high. Either Turberville or I must render him service.'

'I would prefer that it were you, sir,' Joshua said crisply, 'for I shall have need of him as witness.'

'You know the man, Joshua?'

'Curtis, sir. The owner of the livery at the port.'

'The devil it is! He whom you were seeking? The man I attended with the gunshot wound?'

'Yes, sir, the same.'

'Dear heaven, Joshua!' Mansel's pale-washed eyes were aglow with mischievous humour. 'He has not yet settled my earlier account! I had best try to keep him alive and breathing, for my own sake as well as his!' He grinned, adding, 'I think, sir, that you might well be an asset to my practice, finding me patients wherever you travel. Having them delivered to my very door.'

'Indeed, sir, a lucrative source of income for us both!'

'If you could vary them a little,' Mansel said, eyes twinkling, 'it would suit me better. To tend the same patient twice in so short a space of time seems a little excessive. It might even throw doubt upon my competence.'

Even as he spoke there was the sound of Turberville's cart, wheels scattering the gravel and drawing to a violent halt, and Mansel was all quick alertness and action.

Seeing Curtis upon the cart so violently beaten and, with feet and ankles viciously bound he let out a savage oath, momentarily losing composure. In a split second he was back in command, calling tersely for help from his groom and the yard servants. Then, with the assistance of Joshua and Richard Turberville, he had Curtis borne carefully within and set upon the examination table of his surgery. Mansel dismissed the servants but curtly bade Joshua and Turberville to stay. It took him but a few brief moments to cut the straw ropes which bound Curtis, muttering fiercely the while. When it was accomplished, Joshua offered, uneasily.

'If you would have us remain, sir? Render what assistance we may?'

'No,' Mansel grimaced expressively. 'I know, sir, how often you have spurned my kind offers to attend at postmortems, that as entertainment its value soon palls. Besides,' he added slyly, 'I shall have work enough to attend the victim's need, much less the bystanders'. No, sir, you may safely retreat.' Joshua's relief made Mansel smile. 'But you, sir,' Mansel said to Richard Turberville, 'may be of the greatest assistance in John Burrell's absence, if you feel able to aid me?'

'I will not say "with the greatest pleasure', sir, 'Richard Turberville said, 'but with the keenest commitment. Yes, I am ready and able to do whatever you ask of me.'

Mansel nodded, motioning dismissively to Joshua. As he gratefully made his escape, Joshua heard Richard Turberville say ruefully, 'I shall keep my prayers in abeyance, sir, dependent upon your earthly competence. It would please me better were your ministrations needed rather than mine.'

'It is as well, Mr Turberville's, to keep them in reserve,' Mansel answered. 'At least you have the advantage of me.'

'How so?' Turberville's voice was puzzled.

'I am left to my own devices, sir. The sole arbiter. You may always appeal to higher authority, when all else fails.'

Their companionable laughter followed Joshua without.

Joshua, while appreciating the offer by Mansel's housekeeper to rest awhile and take refreshment, made good his apologies and excuses, and walked out into the garden to retrieve the grey. He was at a loss as to the best course to follow, for the finding of Curtis so gravely injured had set his plans awkwardly awry. To the best of his knowledge, Robert Knight was still at the gaolhouse at Pyle, giving what comfort he might to Corinne Blackstock. His own search for Curtis was dramatically ended, and who knew what the immediate conclusion might be? There seemed little point in hovering ineffectually at Clevis. He would be better employed elsewhere.

Even as he strode from the house towards the stables, the urgent clatter of hooves gave him reason to pause. Someone feverishly seeking Dr Mansel's aid, he thought, only to be cruelly denied such help. It would be both crisis and personal tragedy, for the services of a doctor were not lightly sought. He lingered for a moment, prompted by concern and curiosity, only to see that the lone rider was John Burrell and he was in a lather of excitement.

'Joshua!' he hailed him cheerfully.' Oh, it is providential, sir. I had never thought to see you here. You are the very man I have been fruitlessly seeking! What brings you here?' Joshua told him of Curtis and his own and Turberville's part in the affair. 'And Mansel? He has returned from the inquest?'

'Yes, sir, and treating him now with Turberville's aid.'

'Then I had best add my efforts to theirs.' He called out sharply to a groom to bring Joshua's horse and take his own, and a stable boy came abruptly running to do his bidding.

'This man, Curtis, you say, he was bound and savagely beaten?'

'Yes. It is not certain if he will survive.'

'Then it was attempted murder?'

Joshua nodded, saying grimly, 'It might well be murder itself!'

'You fear that it might be bound up with the murdered girl? With the attacks upon Rosa?'

'I honestly do not know,' Joshua confessed dispiritedly. 'I have learned that the sheep stealers upon Stormy Downs are in no wise involved. Beyond that, I am certain of nothing, save my own incompetence. If you will excuse me, sir,' he said ruefully, 'I had best be away, for here I am neither use nor ornament.'

'Burrell, glancing towards the classical statuary adorning the lawns and shrubbery, grinned, saying lightly, 'Use, I doubt. Ornament? Most certainly. You would make a welcome antidote to Mansel's invincible gods and goddesses.'

'Human, and all too fallible?'

'Indeed, as are we all.'

The stable boy was returning with Joshua's grey, and as he made to leave to take the reins of his horse, Burrell said quietly, 'You have not asked me, Joshua, why I was seeking you. There is a small personal matter of which Rebecca will apprise you, but it does not need immediate attention, unlike the other.'

'The other, sir?'

'The copy of the likeness Mansel made, that of the murdered girl.'

'You have news of her?' Joshua could not suppress his excitement and heard it in the pitch of his voice. 'How, sir?' he demanded.

'There is a patient of mine at Weare House, a gentleman from Somerset by name of Mark Gould. He recognised the dead woman instantly and will put a name to her, if you will ride out and interview him. It had best be soon for he leaves later today upon the Somerset Maid, and will sail with the tide.' He paused, amused by Joshua's expression. 'From your surprise, Joshua, I might well number myself among those heathen gods, as Thor, maker of thunderbolts!' He turned to go, murmuring, 'Mansel will be pleased that his drawing has brought results.'

'As I, sir,' Joshua agreed fervently. 'As I!'

'It is all owed to the benefits of scholarship,' Burrell added obscurely, 'the capacity to reason, evaluate and explore.' At Joshua's look of startled incomprehension, he said, smiling, 'Ask Rebecca. She will convince you of the virtue of it, I am sure.'

Joshua, although intrigued by Burrell's veiled reference to Rebecca's part in the affair, resisted the temptation to return to Thatched Cottage to question her about it. His immediate need was to ride out to Weare House and see the visitor from Somerset, whom John Burrell had treated, and who claimed to recognise the dead woman from Mansel's drawing of her. Mark Gould, he had given as the gentleman's name. It meant nothing to Joshua. Gould was clearly a stranger to the place, a transient visitor, stay brief and uncertain as the swallows, and as dependent upon the weather and tides.

The ride through the dunes to the bays had been brisk and stimulating, for he had given the grey her head. The smells of the sea and sand were strong in her nostrils, for the westerly wind had risen now, its keen edge sharpened with iodine and salt. The sand, wet from the retreating tide, was firm beneath the horse's hooves, their indents deep crescents behind it. Joshua turned her, briefly, to the edge of the sea, the rippling water at her heels a sudden veil, translucent as glass, then shattering into droplets of spray, swift as the gulls

221

above them. Their cries, Joshua thought, were as mournful and plaintive as the cries of those lost at sea and, for a moment, memories of the wreckers at Sker came flooding back, harshly disturbing, to haunt him. Abruptly he reined the grey in and set her towards the square house of red brick in the lee of the dunes upon the foreshore.

It was a squat, utilitarian structure, with no claim to distinction or beauty, yet it served its purpose well. It was meant to withstand the rigours of the winter gales that hurled Atlantic breakers upon the shore, fierce waves that battered and beat upon the land, their force as fiercely destructive as upon the sea. Ships which had not found harbour were sucked down remorselessly, then spewed up on the shore, no more than a tangle of splintered driftwood; the flotsam and jetsam of things living and dead, of seaweed, and flesh and bone.

Joshua watched the sea now in its end of summer calmness, the clear ripples edged with milky foam, and thought how wanton and capricious it was, how unpredictable. 'A mistress', Roland Devereaux had described it,' one who, whatever her moods and revenges, held one in thrall'.

Now Joshua's task was to identify a woman whom he had seen only in the calmness of death, to put living flesh upon dead bones, to resurrect whatever she had once been to others: daughter? wife? mistress? friend? Was she good or evil? Loved or hated? From whence had she come? Who had feared or coveted her enough to risk murder? He hoped that Mark Gould, a stranger to him might provide answer, if not answer then a key to where the mystery lay.

Joshua dismounted as a whey-faced ostler came forward to take charge of his mount as, with murmured thanks, and a word of encouragement to the grey, Joshua entered Weare House.

The manager of Weare House, one employed and appointed by the owners of Pyle Inn, was unknown to Joshua, for the work was seasonal and changes often made. He introduced himself and greeted Joshua civilly, confiding that Dr Burrell had told him to expect the constable's coming. He was, Joshua thought, a dapper, effete little fellow, a regular little dandipratt. He walked and talked nervously, eyes gazing restlessly all about him. Jeremiah, who had met him often on his forays to the shore, had dismissed him as, 'Grasshopper legged and grasshopper minded' and Joshua, witnessing the man's quick, jerky movements and speech, decided that it described him exactly.

He took Joshua to the main drawing room where Mark Gould lay supine upon a sofa, a cushion at his head, a warm travelling rug covering him from chest to feet. The manager made brief introduction, then, exclaiming that time was unfairly pressing, went distractedly upon his way. He clasped a hand nervously to his brow before leaving, and Gould raised his eyebrows expressively heavenwards, mouth pursed. Such dramatics, his look inferred, were best left to those of a theatrical bent and not to servants at bathing houses. He motioned Joshua to be seated at a chair beside him saying, 'I trust, Constable Stradling, that I may be able to help you. Dr Burrell has told me what is involved.'

'I shall try, sir, to keep my questions brief,' Joshua promised,' for I can see that you are unwell and I would not wish to overtax you.'

Gould, a bluff, grizzled gentlemen of middle years, smiled broadly, saying good-humouredly, 'Believe me, sir, I welcome such intrusion. It will relieve the tedium of my stay, the unbearable monotony. I was sent here upon the doctor's advice and would wish the same "cure" upon him, for I will return to Porlock in worse order than when I left it!'

'You do not think highly, sir, of the efficacy of sea-bathing then?' Joshua asked, tongue-in-cheek.

'I do not!' The denial was emphatic.' It has nothing to recommend it, save to those whose fortunes are founded upon its promotion. Quacks and charlatans and the owners of bathing houses and inns! It is cold, disagreeable and more likely to kill than cure.'

'Then I am glad, sir, that you have been spared for long enough to enlighten me.'

Gould grinned appreciatively then broke into irrepressible laughter, declaring, 'You will have seen, Constable Stradling, that this so-called holiday has improved neither my temper nor my health. I beg you will take it as the ramblings of an invalid and make concessions for such tiresome display. Now, how may I help you?'

223

'You recognised the woman in the drawing, sir, or so Dr Burrell informs me.'

'Yes, I have seen her before, six months or so ago, in Porlock.'

'You can identify her, Mr Gould? Put name to her?'

'Ah, now, there you have me. I cannot give you her Christian name, but the surname stayed in my mind because it is so strange a name, Yeo.' He grinned self-consciously, explaining,' It was a chance meeting, you understand, at the house of an acquaintance with whom I had little in common, save prospect of business. The boredom was intense and the food and refreshment execrable. Conversation fared no better. The young woman entered briefly with a young child, a babe in arms, and I heard the gentleman who employed her address her as "Miss Yeo".'

'Yes, it is an unusual name,' Joshua conceded. 'One not easily mistaken or forgotten.'

Gould smiled, admitting engagingly, 'I'll own that, but for the boredom, I might not, even now, have recalled it, for I set myself to occupying myself with thinking of other surnames beginning with Y, and words to rhyme with it. A puerile occupation,' he said dryly, 'but it may yet bear fruit if it serves to aid you.'

'This young woman, Miss Yeo; she was some kind of nursery nurse, you think? A servant with the house?'

'I can only speculate, and with hindsight, for I thought no more of her at the time. But, yes, that was my impression.' He hesitated, continuing, 'Yet from her demeanour, her confidence, she might have been some poor relation, employed from obligation. I cannot be sure.'

'And the gentleman, sir, who employed her? You have his name and address?'

'Yes, I anticipated your request, and earlier asked for a quill and ink to be brought. Here is the name of the man concerned and where he lived.'

Joshua took the paper, glancing at Gould questioningly as he did so. 'Lived, you say, sir? He is no longer in residence in Porlock?'

'No, Constable Stradling, I fear not. His business was unsound. A fly-by-night venture, as unreliable as he. I am grateful that I was not persuaded to invest in such chicanery. I am a down-to-earth man, not easily impressed by such trumpery!'

'You do not know, sir, where he might now be found? Where he removed to from Porlock?'

'No. I fear not. To be truthful, sir, Porlock was well rid of him!' Seeing Joshua's downcast expression, he said appeasingly, 'It should not be too difficult to trace him, Constable Stradling. A name like Augustus Scurlock is as unusual as "Yeo". It is not easily forgotten or mistaken for some other.'

Joshua said resignedly, 'Yet, if his business affairs are suspect, sir, and he is a fly-by-night as you say, I do not hold out too much hope of his veracity. A name is easily changed.'

'Then I had best give you an accurate description of the man, for I will not call him gentleman. It is a soubriquet to be earned rather than bestowed lightly, do you not agree?'

'I do, sir.'

'He is of middle height, slight in build and of age, somewhere between thirty and thirty five years. His hair is pale in colour, not unlike your own, and artlessly arranged to cover a thinness at the crown. His skin is pallid, waxy even, as though he spends little time outdoors. I suspect that it is the pallor of one whose nights are spent at the gaming tables or at other less salubrious pursuits! Eyes dark, but whether blue or brown I cannot rightly say, for I notice such things only in women.' He gave a self-deprecating chuckle, adding, 'His wife, now, was an altogether different kettle of fish! A rare beauty, and with none of his stridence or showiness. A gentlewoman, certainly, but who and what her antecedents were, I cannot tell you.'

'And a description of Mrs Scurlock, sir?'

'As I say, a beauty, Constable Stradling. Almost as tall as Scurlock himself, of slim build and regular features. Eyes blue, hair pale gold, her complexion flawless. I can best describe it as 'English Rose', but even that does not do full justice, for there was a warmth about it, a bloom which was indescribable. In short, sir, she was exquisite!' He hesitated, saying apologetically, 'If my description has given impression that she was insipid, a timidly, self-effacing creature, then I malign her. She had spirit, intelligence and grace, as well as beauty.'

'I think, sir, that you have described her exactly,' Joshua assured him, smiling widely. 'I regret that I have not yet met this . . . paragon of all the virtues!'

'Now there, sir, you malign me!' Gould rebuked. 'I did not make guess as to her virtue or virtues! Yet, I'll own, it puzzles me that she should have wed a man like Scurlock, if wed they were. A boor as well as a scoundrel and cheat, as was later proved.'

'It is not uncommon for women to be attracted to such creatures, 'Joshua observed, 'to defend and love them even. They are won over by those very faults and deficiencies they have been warned about from the cradle.'

Gould grunted assent. 'Like moths to a flame,' he agreed, 'with as little hope of escaping unscathed. Perhaps it is that very danger which drives them. The need to risk all.'

Joshua's mind went briefly to Corinne Blackstock at Pyle gaolhouse and he answered quietly, 'Such loyalty demands too high a price.'

'I hope, sir, that it was not the price demanded of the woman in the drawing which Dr Burrell showed, Miss Yeo.' Gould said soberly. 'Betrayal is enough to bear, but to murder is to rob one of all. I hope that you will find the brute responsible, Constable Stradling, and bring him swiftly to justice.'

'I thank you for that, sir, and your ready help,' Joshua said. 'I wish you a safe journey, sir, and comfort at your journey's end.'

'I feel that I shall have earned it,' Gould confessed, straight-faced, 'by the very barbarism and deprivation suffered here. Were a gale to blow up and the lifeboats to be launched, I would make no effort to board one, Constable Stradling. I would sooner go down with the ship. I have had my fill of salt-water bathing. It is a much overrated pastime, believe it.'

As Joshua made to go, Gould said, 'I did not ask you to take refreshment, sir. It was remiss of me. Your presence is the only entertainment I have been offered upon this benighted holiday! Will you allow me to remedy the deficiency now?'

'I thank you, but beg you will excuse me, 'Joshua made

apology. 'There is a matter of the greatest urgency awaiting me at Dr Burrell's house, a man mortally wounded.'

Gould raised his eyebrows, saying, 'It is my hope, sir, that he fares more comfortably than I, that he will not be prescribed sea water for his ills! The ale here is little better than it, in taste and strength. You were wise to refuse it. I bid you good day.' Amused, despite himself, Joshua saluted, and went out, smiling, to retrieve his grey.

It had been a bloody and oftimes harrowing experience for Richard Turberville, assisting Dr Mansel at his work in cleaning and stitching the violence done to Curtis. The gunshot wound had been painstakingly tended and redressed and, although Turberville was not a squeamish man, he had once or twice felt nausea and faintness bedevilling him, and had been like to disgrace himself. Mansel had done all that was required with exemplary skill and confidence, so immersed in the intricacy of his work that he was all but unconscious of Turberville's presence. The curate had stood by conscientiously, handing the surgeon whatever was required by him and helping at tasks which brought the sweat to his eyes and sickness burning to his throat. Yet he had not renege upon the promise to aid Mansel, nor even thought to. He was only grateful that, throughout the ordeal, Curtis was sunk deep into unconsciousness and that he had not needed to minister quantities of brandy to him to deaden pain and thought. Had Curtis screamed aloud, Turberville knew he might have fled the room and the sound of it. When all was safely over, he was relieved that both he and the patient had survived the hurt of it and for Mansel's single-mindedness and skill.

'What will happen to him now, sir?' he asked Mansel. 'Where will he go? Who will tend him?'

'He will stay here,' Mansel said, divesting himself of his gown at the sink and scouring the blood away. 'Burrell and I will watch over him and will hire a reliable nurse from Newton village to render full-time care. Then he will be transported to the hospital when he is fitted to stand the journey.'

'Will Joshua set guard over him there?' Turberville asked anxiously. 'For his life is clearly at stake? None but a madman would have inflicted such injuries upon him.'

227

'None but a madman, or one sane enough to value his own hide above any others!' Mansel corrected. 'But you may rest assured that Joshua will set guard upon him with the justice's blessing' He smiled before adding, 'I thank you for the help you gave me, sir, and for the quiet unobtrusiveness of your presence. You are ideally suited to my profession.'

'I'll own, sir, that I feel better suited to my own!' Turberville said fervently. 'I am grateful that your skills invalidate the need for my further involvement.'

Mansel nodded, saying quietly, 'I would not specify that your prayers, your offices even, will not be needed.'

'Now that is in God's hands,' Turberville agreed quietly. 'You have done what you were able, sir, and I pray that Curtis will live to thank you for it.'

'His survival will be thanks enough.' Even as he spoke there was a commotion without, and Burrell entered, hurrying to Mansel's side with the briefest acknowledgement to Turberville and the blurted information that the justice, Robert Knight, was seeking him. In moments the two physicians were deep in discussion, and with his presence forgotten Richard Turberville made good his escape.

He would, he decided, go at once to Thatched Cottage where Ruth would be awaiting him, worrying perhaps at his lateness, for the picnic had been long planned. It was a grief that he would be forced to tell her of his doubts and misgivings, and he did not relish the hurt it would bring to them both.

He had barely left Dr Mansel's house upon the mule and cart when he heard the rumbling of a coach behind him and Robert Knight's harshly stentorian call for him to halt, which he did, reluctantly.

'Turberville! Wait, sir! I would have word with you.'

Turberville, still physically and emotionally drained from his ordeal with Curtis, tried to gather his senses and show some enthusiasm for this new interruption. He would have clambered down from the cart, but the justice had already opened the door to his coach and, with the help of a footman from the box, was hurrying importantly towards him, plump face wreathed in smiles.

Turberville, who had known Robert Knight from childhood, liked and respected the elderly gentleman, but with his picnic

228

with Ruth already in peril, he was not of a mood to linger. He knew full well what such a cheerful countenance boded. The justice was about to make some demand upon his time and services: A visit to comfort a prisoner at Pyle or Cowbridge gaolhouse; a plea to take mass when his gout disabled him or to conduct a funeral service in his stead. Turberville, whose qualities of patience and forbearance were legendary, prepared himself to accept whatever request might be made.

'My dear Turberville,' Robert Knight was beaming expansively, protuberant eyes almost lost in the folds of flesh. 'Oh, but I am so glad that I have so providentially come upon you.'

'As I, sir,' Turberville said courteously.

'A request, sir, for your services.'

'With the greatest pleasure, sir. I shall assist in any way I am able.'

'Ah, yes!' The justice's smile widened, dewlaps quivering. 'To assist is the very word. This is scarcely the time and place, sir, but I will ask you nonetheless.'

'Ask me, sir?' Turberville echoed politely.

'Yes. Age and infirmity begin to defeat me.' At Turberville's gentle denial, he said imperiously, 'No! No! Hear me out. I have come to ask, sir, if you will assist me as curate to the parish. The living is in my gift, of course, the choice is mine, although the bishop concurs. He will raise no objection. Well, sir? Will it suit you?'

'It is a gift from God, sir! The very answer to a prayer!'

'Then there is no more to be said,' Robert Knight declared with immense satisfaction. 'It is clearly God's will and our own, sir.' He broke into a rumble of dry laughter as he added, 'The bishop, I regret to say, was denied such divine inspiration. He took a little earthly convincing.'

229

Chapter Nineteen

Ossie, seeing the young curate from Maudlam passing the Crown Inn on his ramshackle cart, shouted a cheerful greeting, only to be almost swept from his crooked legs by the speed of its passing. He stared after it, scratching his head in wonderment. Some terrible calamity was the first thought that came to mind. An accident, then? Someone dying and in need of spiritual consolation? Yet the curate's long, bony face had been wreathed in smiles. Transfigured by joy. Radiant, even. What monumental news had so transfigured him? It was not news of financial gain, for young Turberville was the most unworldly of men. Like the ostler himself, he was inured to deprivation, spared all envy of others. Ossie, who knew of his love for Ruth Priday and the tragedy which had drawn them close, hoped that it was vicarious pleasure which made Turberville so restless, hope for their future together. They had suffered much and were deserving of happiness.

Ossie, thinking of the speed with which the mule and cart had passed by, grinned, then laughed aloud, shaking his head indulgently at such wanton abandonment. Young Turberville had hurtled past like a bat out of hell, a not unworthy description! Ossie only hoped that if he were about to propose marriage, then he was not considering the cart as a wedding carriage. There were limits to a young woman's tolerance and the discomforts she would bear. Yes, even one as sweet-natured and biddable as Ruth, he thought, amused. Then memory of what she had already borne and survived came swiftly to sober him. Nothing that she faced in future could ever remotely approach the horror and betrayal of trust which she had already endured, the breaking of innocence. Yet, whatever vicissitudes lay before her, she would not face them alone. Richard Turberville would share in her sorrows, rejoice in her happiness, love and protect her as he loved and protected all others, for he was a man to be trusted, a man touched by God.

Ossie, glancing towards the sweeping boy, engrossed in his toil in the stable yard, wished, despairingly, that God's touch had extended to the weakest of his creatures – one who remained locked in a useless mind. Yet, perhaps, after all, the sweeping boy was the happier. He had neither the intellect to berate God and himself for what he was not nor the fervour to change and convert others. No doubt, as the rector preached so eloquently from his pulpit, the reward of the meek and downtrodden would be great in heaven. Oh, but a foretaste of it on earth would make life sweeter. He touched the sweeping boy companionably on his ragged sleeve as he passed by, and offered him a word of praise for his industry. The lad looked at him, puzzled, then gave a wide, delighted smile of recognition.

'Blaze!' he said, pointing towards the archway, then more urgently and insistently, 'Blaze!'

Ossie looked towards the archway, but saw nothing save the comings and goings of a stable lad with the Crown Inn horses.

'Yes,' said Ossie, kindly, his mind as clouded with bewilderment as the boy's own, and returned to his horses whom he understood without the awkward need for words.

Ruth had waited patiently for Richard Turberville in the garden of Thatched Cottage, for their picnic together promised to be a memorable affair. Betty Turner had packed a basket with homemade pies and other delectable victuals and added a stone flagon of her best nettle beer. The young curate, she declared severely to Ruth, was in dire need of sustenance, for he was naught but a bag of skin and bones, a veritable scarecrow of a fellow! It was plain to any with half an eye that he neglected himself sorely. It was all very well saving the souls of others and ministering to the spirit. After all it was incumbent upon him to do so. But it would serve no purpose were he to starve himself. He had need of a healthy body, for his soul might take him far in the next world, but little enough distance in this. Ruth meekly accepted the good sense of it and the picnic

231

basket, which would lavishly feed the entire population of the three hamlets with leftover victuals to spare.

'Why, you are as pretty as a picture, my dear,' Betty Turner assured her delightedly, as indeed she was in her bonnet and gown of rose-pink poplin and the matching slippers so delicately made. Ruth, herself, Betty Turner thought admiringly, had much of that same delicacy of colouring and feature, a refinement as gentle as her character and spirit. Yet, within, she had strength beyond imagining, a courage which had enabled her to survive all, leaving the essential core of her untouched by bitterness or hate. She would make a good companion for Richard Turberville, Betty Turner thought, as well as a loving wife.

Ruth had tried always to better herself, to prepare herself for helping him with his work in the parish. First, learning to read and write with Emily's help, then mastering her lessons so well that now she was sometimes called upon to help Emily as teacher in the schoolroom, as well as attend to Mrs Stradling's needs. Yes, she would be an asset to young Mr Turberville, there was no doubt of it.

'You had best not linger too long in the cold air,' Betty Turner adjured her. 'You will not wish to take a chill. I had best fetch your cloak from within.' When she returned with it, it was to ask anxiously, 'You do not think that he will have forgotten? The time already grows late.'

'No, he will not forget. He will not disappoint me.'

'But if something has occurred to delay him? The picnic will be ruined and all . . .'

'I shall wait here quietly until he comes for me,' Ruth said serenely. 'Whenever it might be. He would not forgo our meeting without good cause, Betty, believe it. Your cooking is too strong a lure! I'll vow that you will keep him well fed until Michaelmas and beyond, and none will eat better.'

Betty Turner, flushed and delighted by such honest praise, went, proudly smiling, within, and Ruth settled herself upon the stone bench, the better to see his arrival in the cart.

An hour and more went by, and Betty Turner, peering surreptitiously through the window of the scullery, began to fret and grow restless. Yet Ruth, she saw, was seated still upon the bench, hands lightly clasped, face serene and showing no signs of impatience or distress. At the sound of the mule and cart, she had arisen and went running towards it to unlatch the gate, the picnic basket left, neglected, upon the bench. Oh, but young Turberville was a gangling, raw-boned fellow, awkwardly unprepossessing, for all he was high born, Betty thought. He had neither airs nor graces, nor a penny to bless himself with, but he was a good kindly man, honest and to be trusted, and that was what mattered when passion and all else had fled. Yet, in seeing the fervour with which he greeted Ruth, swinging her around ecstatically and settling a loving kiss to her cheek, Betty knew that his love for her held both passion and tenderness, and felt herself strangely saddened and moved. He lifted Ruth effortlessly into the poor, makeshift cart, the scarecrow mule pulling it, as bony and clumsily fashioned as he. Yet Ruth was gazing at Turberville with such fierce adoration that Betty felt the scald of tears behind her eyes and, feeling an interloper, turned swiftly away.

Richard Turberville came into the garden and carried the picnic basket carefully wihtout and set it upon the cart. He was, he knew, smiling quite absurdly, as unable to control the muscles of his face as the joy that surged within him. He did not know if he could long contain the news of the curacy which Robert Knight had offered him, without blurting it aloud. God had blessed him beyond measure and given him the answer he sought. He took his hand from the reins, and closed his gaunt, raw-boned fist briefly upon Ruth's small fingers.

Ossie, glancing from the Crown Inn archway unobserved, saw Ruth gaze into Turberville's eyes with such a warmth of tenderness that he felt his own spirits rise. She was as softly appealing as a rose, he thought, with that same sweet fragrance and purity, a thing of rare beauty. None of the fine ladies in their elegant coaches, who visited the Crown, could hold a candle to her for loveliness. She would not look out of place anywhere on earth. The miracle was that the place she had chosen was at Richard Turberville's side, upon that decrepit and broken-down cart. That was the joy of this life. Its promise and its meaning.

Richard Turberville drove the mule-cart along the well worn track past the church and the Healing Well and deep into the

233

windswept dunes. The maram grass, silvered by movement and light, had the shadowy swiftness of the clouds overhead, and the sky held a clear-washed brightness, so intense that it pained the eyes. They drove in silence, relishing the rare tranquillity and the joy of being together, a closeness without the need for speech. There were few sounds, familiar and comforting. Above the plodding of the mule and the creaking of the cart came the rhythmic suck and drag of the tide and the cries of the sea birds, softened by distance, haunting and mocking as the sighs of the wind.

When they came at last to the edges of the dunes, the sea lay before them, blue as Bristol glass, borrowing its brightness from the sky, the breeze plucking its surface to points of shimmering light. Turberville halted the mule and descended from the box, and lifted Ruth from the cart, swinging her lightly to the sand. Her bonnet strings had come untied and she took off her bonnet, clutching it tight for fear the wind should snatch it away. It set her pale hair flying beyond her, whipping her cheeks to warm colour, and she stood, entranced, seeing the curved sickle of the bay paled to gold in the sunlight, and the black arms of rock, jealously enfolding it. An elusive strand of hair blew across her eyes, and Turberville smilingly brushed it aside with his long, awkward fingers, revelling in the keenness of her pleasure, the childlike innocence of her joy.

He found a sheltered hollow under the dunes where they might sit free from the rigours of the wind yet still watch the encroaching tide and the feverish scavenging of the sea birds along the water's edge. They were, Ruth thought, like fussy old gentlemen, stiff-legged and pompous, irritably quarrelsome, and each suspicious of his neighbour and jealously guarding his own domain. Yet, upon the wing, all clumsiness was gone as they swooped and circled endlessly or glided effortlessly upon the wind, things of such transient beauty that they brought tears to her throat.

Richard Turberville had carried an ancient blanket from the cart and set it upon the dry soft sand, and placed the picnic basket upon it, then returned briefly to feed and water the old mule and see it comfortably settled.

They ate and drank their fill of Betty Turner's good victuals, laughing and teasing the while, sharing the fragile happiness

234

that all young lovers do. When all was neatly gathered and packed away, Turberville took the basket back to the cart and set it upon the boards as Ruth stood up to stroke the few crumbs remaining from her gown.

'No, do not put your bonnet on, Ruth.' Turberville had returned quietly to stand beside her. 'I would remember you always this way, with the wind in your hair and the brightness of the day upon you.'

She took his hand in hers, sinking down upon the blanket, and drawing him down beside her. 'Oh, it has been the best of days!' she exclaimed, 'with nothing to mar it. I shall remember it always, keep a picture in my mind.' She saw the sudden hurt upon his face and felt a coldness within her as she asked, 'What has happened, Richard? What has occurred to so distress you?'

He told her of finding the beaten man in the dunes and of his aiding Dr Mansel.

'It is of my own assault you thought? It brought it clear to your mind again?'

'Yes,' the admission was reluctantly made. 'It made it real again. I relived the full horror of it.'

Ruth said, voice low, 'And you have sought a way to tell me that you cannot expunge it from your mind? That it will haunt you always? Stand always between us?'

'No!' he grasped her wrist crying, impassionedly, 'No, my love, you misunderstand me! It was never in my mind! I beg you will believe it!'

'I feared that you would always blame me,' she said, voice muffled, 'hold me to account. You have been so sad and preoccupied of late.'

'How could I blame you for the sins of another?' He held her to him so fiercely that she could scarcely breathe, stroking her hair, kissing her, murmuring endearments. 'How could you dream that I could harbour such thoughts? I love you wholeheartedly and for all of my life and beyond, my love, if God wills it.' His eyes were heavy with hurt, mouth ugly with caring. 'No, my dear,' he said with gentleness, 'I love you the more for the courage you have shown, the will to survive without hatred or bitterness, the corrosion of spirit. You are all of my love and joy, Ruth. I could not face a life without you. No, my grief was for what you have suffered and the knowledge that I must resurrect it in your mind as well as my own else you would learn of the assault from others.'

Ruth said hesitantly, 'But you have been so stern and remote, I feared you wished to tell me that your care for me was ended, that there could be no future before us.'

'No. What ailed me was a personal grief. A matter now resolved. It need no longer bedevil me.'

'Then I am glad,' Ruth said simply, 'for you have seemed different today, more light-hearted and carefree, as in earlier days.'

'That is because I have received news from Robert Knight.'

'From the justice?'

'Yes, news that concerns you directly. I hope that it may bring you the same warmth of pleasure that it has brought to me.' He told her of Robert Knight's offer of a curacy, stumbling and tonguetied in his excitement to please her, thoughts barely coherent. The quick joy that illumined her face heartened him, but he saw it die away uncertainly, with no word spoken.

'It does not please you?' he asked, greatly distressed. 'I had thought it would bring you happiness, Ruth. It is a way to live comfortably, to be always together. 'He was wretchedly downcast, not attempting to hide his misery. 'What is it that troubles you?'

'The reason,my dear, for your acceptance' she said with honesty. 'It would grieve me were you to sacrifice all you believe, all you have achieved, for my sake alone. I would not wish to bear responsibility for the hurt it might bring you, the recrimination and regret.'

'Oh, but there will be no regret!' he promised. 'I believe that it is God's will that I move forward, as well as my own. He has given me challenge and answer, Ruth. I beg that you will now give me yours. 'He took her hand gently in his own thin hands, asking with a wealth of tenderness, 'Will you do me the very great honour to be my wife, Ruth? To take me for what I am, and walk beside me upon the way, whatever God wills and whatever comes?'

'Oh, my dear,' she said, eyes bright with tears of happiness,' I would wish no other road and no other beside me. Yes I will wed you, and willingly. I could envisage no life without you. I would be always bereft,' She put her arms gently around his neck and drew him towards her with a tenderness and passion that he wholly returned.

When, at last, he drew reluctantly away, it was to confess, 'I have thought little in the past of what I have renounced, Ruth. Home and title to the estates, a life of ease; in denying it for myself I have denied you.'

'Oh, my dear man.' Ruth chided, smiling. 'You have denied me nothing. Had you not renounced your former life and become a priest at Maudlam I could not even have met you, much less become your wife! There would have been too great a gulf between us; a chasm that could never be bridged. You would have been unaware even of my existence. Is that not so?' He had to admit to the truth of it. 'Then, in choosing poverty, you have found instead the greatest riches!' she teased mischievously, 'for you have found a rare treasure in me! Confess it!'

Although Turberville laughed with her, his eyes grew serious, his manner subdued, as he said with honesty, 'You are the greatest of treasures, Ruth. I shall give thanks to God every day of my life for the blessing of it. I shall cherish and protect you all of my life and none shall harm you. You have my sacred word and promise.'

Much moved, Ruth said gently, 'What harm was done to me no longer has the power to wound, to grieve and draw blood. I cannot believe that it was God's will, for He would not have been so cruel. Yet, I believe that it was God's will that you came, with compassion, to heal me with the promise of that love we now share. I can regret nothing of the past, Richard.'

'And you shall regret nothing of the future, my dear love,' he promised as, taking her hand, he drew her to stand beside him then, with an arm firmly about her waist, he took her, running and breathless, to the water's edge. She had left her bonnet upon the sand and her hair blew wild and free. The salt air was rich with the odours of seaweed and sand and harsh with the cries of sea birds. The sea shimmered before them, an endless ebb and flow, rhythmic and strong as their heartbeats and the warm surging of blood. It was a promise of life, Richard Turberville thought, a timeless resurrection, older than life itself, yet always new. The beauty of it, and the gentle presence of Ruth beside him filled him with such joy that he feared his heart must break within him. He was a man wholly fulfilled, wholly content. He could ask for nothing more.

Joshua, who had ridden to Tythegston Court meaning to apprise the justice of the murderous attack upon Curtis, and to give him the good news that the dead girl had been identified, was disappointed. As Leyshon explained, shaking his head regretfully, 'I fear he is not here, Constable. He left upon an impulse as soon as ever he returned from the inquest at Pyle.'

'He left no word as to where he might be found?'

'None, sir.' Leyshon's thin, parchment-dry face was troubled as he confessed, 'I'll own, Mr Stradling, 'tis unlike Mr Knight to leave so abruptly and without a word as to his whereabouts. He is most punctilious, sir, as you know, keeping me informed always lest someone comes seeking him urgently to attend a dying man or such.'

'You would not hazard a guess as to his state of mind, Leyshon?'

Leyshon grimaced, showing his ruined teeth as he admitted dryly, 'I would need to be soothsayer and conjuror both, sir! The justice's expression is no barometer to his feelings. He is a gentleman always firmly in control.'

Joshua nodded. 'I might wish myself that same virtue,' Joshua said feelingly. 'I had best be away, Leyshon. Will you tell him that I called upon a matter of some urgency, and will make early return.'

Leyshon paused, holding up an admonitory hand, head cocked and listening intently. He smiled broadly as the crunching of coach-wheels upon the gravel of the driveway grew louder and the justice's coach came into view. 'You may tell him yourself, sir, if you still have mind to,' he said cheerfully. 'It will save you the necessity of a return.' As the justice stepped down from the coach, clearly self-satisfied and beaming benignly, Leyshon murmured beneath his breath, 'Now that, sir, needs neither soothsayer nor barometer to predict. The justice is in the best of humours, weather set fair. I see no sign of approaching storm or tempest.'

238

'I would not wager my all upon it, Leyshon,' Joshua cautioned ruefully, 'the weather may swiftly turn about.'

'Ah, Stradling,' The justice's smile was benevolent, good humour all-embracing. 'I have just discharged the most pleasing duty, sir, brought happiness and ease to myself and another. Come within,' he invited genially, 'that we may celebrate the occasion with some of my best Canary wine.' Joshua dutifully followed him within, hoping that the Canary wine would fortify him and continue to sweeten the justice's disposition.

The news of the offer to Turberville, received and discussed with the greatest enthusiasm and accord and all other social pleasantries exhausted, Joshua told the justice of the attack upon Curtis, awaiting some explosion of wrath.

'Yes! Yes!' he exclaimed testily. 'Turberville has told me of the circumstances and that Mansel will minister to him until some more permanent arrangement may be made. A hospital bed will be found for him when he is fit enough to be moved.'

'If he survives, sir.'

'Of course "if he survives". You have a talent for stating the obvious, Stradling.' He helped himself morosely to more Canary wine. 'Did I not warn you of the man, Stradling?'

'Warn me, sir?'

'That this man, Curtis, was an innocent pawn in the game, that your suspicions of him were unworthy, bordering upon the obsessive even. Well?' he demanded.

'I am not altogether sure, sir, that . . .'

'Not sure! Not sure!' he repeated testily. 'That is your weakness. Your failing. Your persecution of the poor creature might well have been his undoing.' Joshua did not venture to enquire as to how that might be. 'Admit it, sir!' the justice commanded. 'You are no great judge of character. You rely too much upon outward appearances and your so-called intuition. It can lead you astray, sir, damnably astray! People are not always what they seem on the surface. You understand me?'

'Yes, sir. Perfectly. Richard Turberville, for example,' Joshua cited innocently.

'Turberville? What has Turberville to do with it?'

'He dresses himself in the clothing of the poor, lives humbly

239

as one of them, a wretchedly deprived fellow without, but a veritable saint within. Yes, sir, I take your meaning.'

The justice looked non-plussed, then irritable, but could hardly decry Turberville's generosity of spirit. After all, he had just appointed him as curate. If Stradling had hoped to make him suffer by such invidious comparison, then he would be disappointed. 'Of course, Stradling,' he said equably, 'that was precisely my point. My acumen in such affairs is undisputed. I am not easily hoodwinked nor deflected from my path.' He smiled, confident that he had turned things to his own advantage but could not, for the life of him, remember how Turberville had come into the conversation. 'The crux of the matter is, Stradling,' he said severely, 'that you vacillate, cannot make up your mind. Is there anything, sir, which you *are* sure of?'

'The identity of the murdered woman, sir.'

'The devil you are! Why was I not told of it?'

'I have just this moment returned from Weare House at Dr Burrell's instigation. A patient of his from Porlock has identified the woman as a Miss Yeo, a nursery nurse or governess. I came here directly I knew.'

Robert Knight appeared mollified but could not resist grunting, 'The wheat from the chaff, Stradling! Learn to separate the wheat from the chaff.'

'I will try, sir,' he pronounced, straight-faced, and caught a flicker of amusement upon the justice's face, swiftly suppressed.

'You know what this means, Stradling?' Robert Knight demanded. 'You must make enquiries at Porlock. Take yourself to Somerset, and find out whatever you may.'

'But the inquest upon Jed Carter, sir? It is but two days off and I will be summoned to give evidence.'

'That is damnably inconvenient, Stradling!' His frown implied that Joshua had arranged it deliberately to thwart him. 'Well,' he conceded grudgingly,' I suppose a few days will be neither here nor there, since so much time has been wasted already.'

'Not entirely wasted, sir,' Joshua protested mildly. 'The sheep stealers and murderers of Jed Carter are safely in Pyle gaolhouse awaiting trial, Sir Peter Henshawe will be

240

brought to book and also charged with the murder of Corinne Blackstock's child.'

'Perhaps! Perhaps! We must not prejudge these things, Stradling. The law must be seen to be impartial,' he rebuked tetchily. 'But, yes, there has been some little progress. I will not deny it. But there might have been more had you not been pursuing some vendetta against an innocent man!'

Damning with faint praise, Joshua thought, amused despite himself.

'I hope, sir, that you will set adequate guard upon Curtis,' the justice persisted. 'He is the only man who can give clue to his assailants.' He peered myopically over the frame of his eye-glasses, protuberant brown eyes hugely magnified behind the lenses. 'Since you have signally failed to find the killer of the dead woman, we might, at least, set guard upon a victim still living, in the hope that he might fare better!' Joshua did not reply. 'It does you no credit,' the justice mumbled, 'no credit at all. The place will soon be knee deep in corpses. It will scarce be safe to venture abroad. We will be prisoners in our own homes, sir, fearful to cross our own doorsteps!'

'If you would have me set a guard upon the court, sir?'

'The court?' he echoed incredulously. 'I was speaking metaphorically, Stradling. My concern is not for my own hide, but other people's safety! My words are not to be taken literally.'

'No, sir?'

'Not when I am speaking metaphorically,' the justice said, repressing the smallest of grins. 'I know that your only intention is to divert me, Stradling, to throw me off my stride, but I will have none of it, you understand?'

'Perfectly, sir.'

'You must learn to accept criticism gracefully, in the manner in which it is offered!' Robert Knight adjured.

'Indeed, sir. I shall look to you always for good example.' Joshua's face was admirably guileless, his tone bland.

The justice's eyes twinkled and a smile twitched the corners of his mouth, then he broke into a low rumble of laughter, dark jowls shaking. 'Be damned, Stradling, if you did not get the better of me in that exchange,' he admitted. He poured Joshua a generous glass of Canary wine and refilled his own, saying good-humouredly, 'You must not take all criticism so

241

personally, Joshua. Learn to abstract the generalisation from your personal experience, it will serve you well.'

'I bow to your greater wisdom and experience, sir,' Joshua conceded, straight-faced, as the justice's low rumbling laughter erupted anew.

Chapter Twenty

Rebecca, dressed in her most elegant finery, set off for Southerndown Court in the small coach with Stenner proudly at the reins. Her first real outing since John Jeremiah's birth was not taken without misgivings, although the prospect of seeing her grandfather, Elizabeth Devereaux and Dr Peate helped, in some measure, to soften her anxiety at leaving her son. She had given so many orders to the nursery-nurse, the wet nurse and to Ruth and Betty, that their heads were spinning with the confusion of them, and it had needed every ounce of their forbearance and tact to humour her. She left a veritable encyclopedia of instructions behind her, including names of those who were to be called immediately in case of emergency, and where they might be found. Ruth did not remind her that she alone, of all the household save Joshua, was able to read or write. Even so, Rebecca was slow in leaving. Had she not had a definite mission to fulfil she might well have changed her mind and remained at Thatched Cottage, but her promise to John Burreil had been binding, her word given. Joshua, helping her into the coach and seeing the conflict within her reflected upon her face, tried to ease her mind.

'John Jeremiah will be in excellent hands, my love,' he assured her. 'He will scarce notice your absence.'

It was not, he realised at once, the right thing to say, and damned himself for a simpleton. She was plainly discomposed.

'Would you have me send for Sophie?' he asked. 'Beg her stay until your return?'

'No, I am a fool and a ninny!' she confessed, smiling shamefacedly.

'You are a mother, Rebecca, John Jeremiah's mother,' he corrected gently, reaching up impulsively to kiss her

243

cheek. 'You will have the most affectionate of welcomes at Southerndown Court, and may boast about and laud our son and heir to your heart's content.'

'I shall be preaching to the converted,' she reminded him, 'for Grandfather and Dr Peate are as besotted with him as we. Besides,' she added with mock severity, 'there will be no need on earth to exaggerate. John Jeremiah is perfect in every way.'

'As you, my love, as you,' he reiterated, making her such a ridiculously excessive bow that she was constrained, first to smile, then laugh aloud, despite her misgivings. As he nodded instruction to Stenner to set the horses in motion, he glimpsed her strained white face through the window of the coach, expression anxious and irresolute, and gave her a reassuring salute and wink before he turned reluctantly away. The outing would do her good, he thought, for she had been confined to the house too long, and had not fully recovered her health and enthusiasm since the birth. Elizabeth's company would draw her out of herself, for they were the closest of friends now drawn even more firmly together by shared motherhood.

Rebecca had sent a messenger to forewarn Sir Matthew of her coming, begging that Dr Peate might also be invited. It had pleased Joshua inordinately to hear from Rebecca of John Burrell's plan for a bursary in his old tutor's name. He held that learned gentleman in the greatest affection, for he had been friend and mentor since Joshua's earliest days. He had not only instructed him and given him a zest for learning, but helped strengthen and shape his character and views. If it had disappointed him that Joshua had forgone the opportunity of studying at Oxford University, then he had been careful to conceal it, praising him always for what he had achieved in his work as constable. It was, Rebecca thought, the essence of all that Dr Handel Peate believed and taught. He valued learning, but valued humanity more. The worth of the individual, whatever his attainments and position in life, was paramount. His affection and respect for Illtyd, who had painstakingly learnt to read and write, was as honest as his affectionate respect for Sir Matthew, his friend and intellectual equal. Rebecca and Elizabeth, too, had learned to appreciate his skills as a tutor and his compassionate understanding. It seemed fitting that John Burrell, a man of the keenest intelligence and one who had suffered so grievously, should have sacrificed the little he possessed to perpetuate the memory of another. Those whom Dr Peate had taught valued and revered him, but it had taken a man of equal quality to recognise his true worth and offer help, in his name, to future generations. She knew that Dr Peate would not spurn the gesture as empty charity. He would know the self-sacrifice it cost, and value the gift and the giver the more.

She hoped that John Burrell would be able to convince Elwyn Morris of the advantages of such a bursary to Dafydd without wounding Morris's pride, or making him feel that he had failed the boy in not being able to provide. Morris had been a pauper for many years and suffered the grudging parsimony of others, the bitter taste of charity meanly bestowed. If he refused to accept the need for the scholarship, John Burrell had declared to Rebecca, then he would not withdraw his financial aid, but ask that the bursary be awarded to another child, one intelligent but disadvantaged, and of Dr Peate's choosing. Rebecca hoped that it was Dafydd who would benefit, for she was deeply fond of the boy and respected him for his courage and industry. Yet it was Dafydd himself who might prove the real stumbling block to John Burrell's plans. He was fiercely independent, and believed that to abandon his plans to farm at Grove would be to betray his father's memory, and all of the past. It would be a hard decision for a boy, barely eleven years old, and one not without grief and soul-searching, whatever the outcome . . . Yet, if any on earth could persuade him of the rightness of it, it would be Jeremiah. Dafydd had worshipped the old fisherman from his earliest days, and it was to Jeremiah he had turned in times of adversity, knowing that his fears and self-recriminations would be eased, his confidences always kept. Jeremiah was a man of the soundest common sense; one of infinite compassion and integrity. A good man, as Rebecca, above all others, had cause to know. He had been father and protector to her, as he had proved to be to Dafydd. Yes, Jeremiah would listen to the boy, then discuss things calmly and sensibly, putting forward no binding conclusion, but allowing him to discuss and evaluate, and make sensible choice. Rebecca hoped that

245

it would be the right one. The sadness was that the misguided reasoning and loyalty of a child might cripple the future of the man he would become. There would be regret and bitterness for what was lost to him, and no joy in what he had thought gained. It was a choice to tax the wisdom of Solomon, much less a bewildered boy. Rebecca turned her thoughts to less vexing affairs; the blossoming romances between Ruth and Richard Turberville, John Burrell and Emily, and Stenner and Betty. It was strange, she thought, how such love had grown from tragedy or danger, the fear of loss. Yet, perhaps, it needed such sharply cruel reminder of what must be sacrificed to prove its worth. Elizabeth, she knew, was as much a romantic at heart as she, and would delight in hearing of the liaisons and all other news of the friends in the three hamlets. Perhaps it was their own good fortune in securing such exemplary and wholly satisfactory husbands which made them look so kindly upon others in love, wishing them that same fulfilment – a joyousness further enhanced by Mary and John Jeremiah. She stifled a guilty pang at being absent from her son and took herself sternly to task. She must make for herself a life beyond John Jeremiah's immediate needs, else she would be in danger of smothering him with over-protectiveness. They both had a need to breathe and grow freely, to loosen the bonds was not to sever them, merely to bring ease and comfort. They would still be held together, but without painful restriction and chafing restraints. So resolved, Rebecca leaned forward in the carriage, gazing appreciatively out of the window, determined upon enjoying every second of her newfound freedom and every familiar scene and landmark upon the way.

They were approaching the bend in the river beyond the old water mill, its wooden paddle-wheel churning the water to a sea of foam and relentlessly driving the great grinding stones within. The rich pasturelands and wooded hills, made fertile by the river silt and the subterranean streams which flowed into it, were as green as those marshy islets flung from the river bed. They stood proud from the mudflats of the estuary, a haunt for long-legged wading birds and foraging gulls, their stark whiteness and restless movement mimicking the scudding clouds overhead. Beyond, on the salt-washed pastures, sheep and cattle richly grazed, somnolent and slow moving, the sheep scarce distinguishable from the boulders and honed rocks edging the sea beyond. To the right of the river, the wind-sculpted pale-sanded dunes rose, mile upon mile, range upon range, silver-grey grasses caressed by the wind as a hand strokes fur. Rebecca, who loved this wild place, seeing it anew felt the pains of an exile returning, that mingling of joy and sadness which is every exile's lot. Pride. Regret. Sorrow for what is gone and can never be recaptured more, the lonely returning of the dispossessed. Overhead a flight of swans passed in graceful flight, the slow beat of their wings a threnody, their purity against the blue of the sky bringing sudden hurt to her throat. They followed the line of the river to deeper waters and to richer new pastures beyond. Rebecca, straining for a glimpse of their passing, watched until they were out of sight. They were so sure in their flight, she thought, and without doubt or hesitation, secure in the company of their own kind. They would go wherever need or urge took them, free as the air they rode.

Her time for lone adventuring was over. Love for Joshua and John Jeremiah held her close, flightless and earthbound, and she could not regret it. She would follow Joshua wherever the future took him.

The tide below began its long race to the river, swirled in the curve of the dunes as the river ran more fiercely now to embrace and mingle with the sea. It was an ever changing scene, yet immutable in its constancy; swift passing as life itself, with that same passion and tranquillity, tenderness and rage. Yes, she was privileged to share it with Joshua and John Jeremiah. She wished for Ruth and Richard Turberville, Emily and John Burrell, and Stenner and Betty Turner, that same good fortune, the sharing of flesh and tenderness, of pity and hope. The gift of love returned. As the coach took the curve of the carriageway into Southerndown Court, she felt a lightening of spirits. She would be welcomed here, as of old, and with undemanding love, warm and unchanging. Yet, at the day's end, she would be going home. There would be demands, but she would welcome them. The past was another country and, like the flight of the swans, the future was unknown and uncharted. It was hers and Joshua's to explore.

*   *   *

247

From the moment the coach rounded the curve of the carriage-way and Rebecca saw again the familiar facade of the court, she felt a mounting excitement. It was, she thought, so elegant and serene a place, with its perfect symmetry and austere simplicity of style: ageless and spare, as her grandfather, Sir Matthew himself, and as dignified and mellow. She knew and loved every inch of this place; its shrubberies and arbours, the terraces and parterres, the secret hidden gardens and the wide sweep of lawns to the sea. It pleased her that this house and estate had been a familiar refuge to her forebears and were part of her history; a history and belonging that had so nearly been denied. John Jeremiah would feel for it that pride and affection which she and Sir Matthew now shared. It would be a perfect world in which a small boy might go adventuring and develop in strength and spirit. A place to sharpen the curiosity and grow.

Sir Matthew, upon hearing the halting of the small coach beneath the porte-cochere, hurried forward to greet her, thin aesthetic face warm with pleasure, and with the diminutive figure of Dr Peate beside him. Rebecca embraced each in turn, hugging and kissing them impulsively, and they returned her impetuous affection with restrained dignity, smiling indulgently the while. She linked her arms affectionately in theirs and they escorted her within, giving smiling response to her frivolous chatter, delighted to be once more in her company. Sir Matthew, despite his advanced age, was a truly commanding figure, she thought proudly, so spare-fleshed and upright, his features undeniably patrician. There was an air of authority about him, that natural self-reliance of those well born. As for Dr Peate, he was what he had always been, the archetypal scholar, frail, and stooped through bending too long at his books. There was a childlike quality about him, the appealing curiosity of the very young, untouched by sophistication. His eyes were widely blue, bright with intelligence and good humour, and his sparse white hair long and fine as a babe's. He was tolerant, gentle, and compassionate, and Rebecca loved him almost as dearly as she loved Sir Matthew. Now, though, her arms entwined in theirs, she was aware anew of the painful frailness of them. They seemed shrunken and diminished, as though made sere by age, then eroded as time and nature weaken and erode all. She knew, for a stark moment, what the

248

loss of them would mean, the grief of it. Then she resolutely put such morbid thoughts aside and walked confidently within.

To her great surprise and pleasure Sir Matthew had made a celebration of her coming, despite the scant notice she had been able to give. Elizabeth and her mother, Mrs Louisa Crandle, she had hoped to see present, but Joshua's parents had been hastily summoned and Aled, Joshua's brother, with his fiancee, Miss Georgina Picton besides. Georgina Picton was the prettiest and gayest of creatures, and without affectation or that simpering foolishness so many young gentlewomen essayed, believing it fashionable. Her doll-like fragility and paleness of colouring might, in another, have seemed tiresomely vapid, but it was spiced by such sharp intelligence and gentle humour that she was altogether irresistible. Rebecca, who loved Aled, and thought of him as a favourite brother, was relieved that he had found so gentle and loving a companion. His past liaisons had been disastrous, and Philip Stradling had long despaired of his son's restlessness and profligate ways. Now, with his betrothal to Georgina Picton, a charming creature and a considerable heiress in her own right, he was wholly restored to favour, a circumstance which, by his relaxed and unselfconscious merriment, he was enjoying to the full.

Philip Stradling came forward self-consciously to greet her, his abrupt, taciturn manner, as Rebecca knew, no more than a shield to hide the extraordinary shyness before others. He was a large, square-jawed man, dark jowled and powerfully made. A man more at ease upon his farms and with others of his kind than in the delicacy of the drawing room. He had much of the clumsy awkwardness of the prize bulls he reared, but a forbidding exterior masked a gentle sensitivity, and Rebecca, who had grown to love him and to appreciate his true worth, was no longer in awe of him. Like Charlotte, his wife, she discounted his habitual gruffness, and could, to Joshua's and Aled's outspoken astonishment, 'wrap him around her little finger with the greatest of ease'. It was plain to all that Miss Georgina Picton was already well set to emulate that feat.

'And how is my grandson, ma'am?' he demanded curtly to cover his ungentlemanly pride.

'He prospers, sir, as one would expect from such healthy and distinguished forebears,' Rebecca said shamelessly. 'Joshua

249

agrees with me that John Jeremiah has a decided resemblance to you. A quite startling likeness.'

Sir Matthew and Dr Peate exchanged the most knowing of glances and Charlotte Stradling's lips curved into a smile at this outrageous canard, but Philip Stadling was plainly delighted. 'You hear that, Charlotte!' he exclaimed, 'the boy takes after me, is that not splendid?' He realised, even as he spoke, the indelicacy of the claim and looked briefly downcast.

'Splendid, my dear! Absolutely splendid!' Charlotte Stradling concurred to the murmured agreement of the others, and Philip Stradling grinned sheepishly and visibly relaxed. Almost upon that instant Elizabeth Devereaux arrived with Mrs Louisa Crandle, and there was such a babble of excited congratulations and chatter from the ladies present that the gentlemen could barely make themselves heard in the ensuing hubbub. John Jeremiah was so lavishly praised by his grandmother for his looks, disposition, intelligence and charm, that Rebecca wondered how on earth she could have given birth to such a paragon of virtue not, of course, that she was prepared to dispute it. It pleased Rebecca when Louisa Crandle put in an immediate claim for her granddaughter, Mary's, superiority in every particular. She was, she declared, unblushing, the sweetest-natured and most forward of infants and, like as not, to become a beauty, for she was most delicately made, her colouring quite remarkable. She would undoubtedly be slender and with a natural grace, for it was apparent, even now, in her every gesture. Elizabeth and Rebecca exchanged amused glances, allowing the two gentlewomen to argue their claims unhindered. Yet Rebecca was not slow to observe that Mary's birth had drawn Elizabeth and her mother closer in understanding and affection, when all else had failed.

Mrs Crandle, whose love had been for her feckless and murderous son, and who had never forgiven Elizabeth for her part in his downfall, now seemed reconciled to Creighton's death. Her maternal affection had been transferred to Elizabeth's child. Mary gave her new status and reason to live, and her faded prettiness seemed to have revived and intensified, and some of her former charm to have returned.

Rebecca, in all the light-hearted prattling and exchanges of news, asked no word of Hugo Crandle, for to Louisa Crandle her husband was as dead as her son. She would make no mention of him, nor admit his existence. A poor bewildered husk, empty of understanding, he lived now in a prison for those criminally insane. Elizabeth, whom he loved, visited him constantly, but always without recognition or response. Yet she would not forsake him, her love and loyalty to him as fierce as his own had once been for her. When Elizabeth and she were alone, Rebecca would ask her how he fared and whether there was progress, for Elizabeth believed, against all the odds, that he would one day recover. Yet it was Joshua's contention, and Sir Matthew's and Dr Peate's, too, that should he do so, it would be the greatest tragedy. He would then be aware of all that had occurred, his son's violent death and his own guilt and imprisonment. Sometimes such cruel uselessness of mind was a man's salvation when the realities of life became too burdensome to bear.

Seated now at Sir Matthew's luncheon table with the elegantly attired and high-spirited company, all such griefs and tribulations could be briefly forgot. It was a scene of exceptional elegance, the pristine white napery, glowing silver and gleaming crystal, not a whit more sparkling and impressive than the assembled guests. The wine flowed as freely as the conversation and the food was of a variety and excellence that could not be surpassed. Rebecca, gazing appreciatively at the animated faces around her, and the silver and crystal epergnes spilling their exquisitely arranged flowers and fruits, thought how gracious and civilised it all was, a world and lifetime away from the murder and intrigue of Joshua's work in the three hamlets.

Rebecca had earlier confided that she had a need to see Sir Matthew and Dr Peate alone, and when the meal was ended and the ladies and Aled and Philip Stradling had adjourned, replete, to the drawing room to continue their conversation, Sir Matthew called her aside. Dr Peate followed them docilely to the library, believing that it was news of John Jeremiah's christening, with a possible request for his services at Newton or the small family chapel at Southerndown Court, that he was about to hear. Rebecca explained haltingly of Dr Burrell's plan for a bursary at Cowbridge Grammar school, and his wish that it be set up in Dr Peate's name. She was not altogether sure

251

that he would approve the scheme and awaited his reaction uncertainly.

He stared at her in silence for a long moment, face drained of all colour and expression, and she feared, from his stillness, that she had angered him. He would think her presumptuous, she thought dispiritedly, believe it an imposition. 'Oh, my dear Rebecca!' His face was alive with honest delight. 'I cannot tell you what joy such a prospect gives me. It pleases me more than I can say. To be remembered in such a way is beyond my wildest expectations. I can scarce speak coherently, for I am so overcome.'

'Then you will accept, sir?'

'Accept, and gladly. It is a kindness of John Burrell to give thought to me. He is a man who has suffered long,' he murmured, 'and I know what added denial it will cost him to set up such an award. I shall value it the more for what he must sacrifice, as for the knowledge that he feels me worthy of it.' His thin, child-like face was aglow with warm colour, his eyes preternaturally bright, and Sir Matthew, grasping his friend's hand firmly, said quietly, 'I congratulate you, sir, for the generosity of your acceptance. I would have expected no less of a response and it pleases me that Burrell has offered you so practical and enduring a tribute, for you are deserving of it above all others.' He and Dr Peate stared at each other for a moment, solemn and unspeaking, their years of friendship and affection a warmth between them, an unbroken bond. Then Sir Matthew said with deliberate briskness to Rebecca, 'Was there not someone you wished to suggest to Dr Peate, my dear, as worthy of such a bursary?'

Dr Peate listened in silence as Rebecca told him of Emily's conviction that Dafydd merited such an award, and of the tragedy of Jem Crocutt's death, and what Dafydd had witnessed and been forced to endure.

'I hope that he may be persuaded to accept,' he said simply, 'freed from the demands and dark shadows of the past. Education would be the surest way to release him. I should like to live to see it, and to know that John Burrell wrought such good in my name.'

Rebecca reached over to kiss his withered cheek, saying with honesty, 'Then it will serve only to continue the good which you have done, sir. You are respected and loved by all those whom you have taught and guided, and none will forget the debt owed to you.'

Much moved by her tribute and the affection with which it was made, Dr Peate said quietly, 'There are no debts between friends, Rebecca, only help freely given. I hope that I may always count those I have instructed as friends, for then I shall be rich indeed.' There was a silence before Sir Matthew said crisply, 'We had best drink a toast to Dr John Burrell for his foresight and generosity, and to yours, sir, in accepting such honour. It is well deserved.' He poured out three glasses of Canary wine, and Rebecca and he solemnly raised their glasses and drank to their companion as he surveyed them, serenely contented and bright-eyed.

They lingered awhile making desultory conversation, talking of those in the Vale and in the three hamlets whom they knew as friends.

'I could have wished Illtyd to have been the first recipient of my bursary,' Dr Peate said unexpectedly, 'for he would be a worthy scholar. He has striven so hard, and overcome so much. I have never known another with a keener mind and with so much fortitude.'

'Indeed,' Sir Matthew agreed warmly. 'He is an example to all. He has a natural intelligence and curiosity, a serenity of spirit which is rare. It pleases me that he comes sometimes to make use of my library and, more, that he gives me the pleasure of his conversation and company. Yet he will not intrude, coming and going so unobtrusively that I am scarce aware of his presence and must go and seek him out.' He turned suddenly to Rebecca, saying, 'I would always have him made welcome here, my dear, whatever comes.'

Rebecca, startled by the intensity with which he spoke, said confusedly, 'But he knows, Grandfather, that you take pleasure in his company. Illtyd will come here gratefully for as long as ever he is able.'

Sir Matthew hesitated as if he might speak further, then shook his head, saying abruptly, 'I have a letter I would have you take to Joshua. It informs him that Sir Peter Henshawe has been arrested on charges of murder and fraud upon my instructions as magistrate and awaits trial at Cowbridge gaolhouse.'

253

'The murder!' Rebecca blurted, unable to hide her distress. 'It is the murder of the child? The child of the woman at Pyle courthouse?'

'I fear so, my dear,' Sir Matthew admitted, advising quietly, 'It is best not to dwell too much upon it. It will serve no purpose save to distress you the more.' He added worriedly, 'I would not have confided it to you, but feared you would hear it from another source. It is the talk of the Vale, the rumour and gossip I would have you prepared.'

'The man's depravity is frightening!' Dr Peate murmured. 'Past all belief! To cold bloodedly order the murder of one's own child to save his own worthless skin! It is his soul he had best have a care to saving. I'll own that were I asked to visit him as priest, my Christian compassion would be sorely strained. My grief would be for that poor innocent he destroyed.' He ended ruefully, 'That speaks of a sad deficiency in me, as well as in him.'

'It speaks of human reaction,' Sir Matthew said firmly, 'for even you, sir, make no claim to be a saint, although you are the nearest I have met to one.'

As Dr Peate modestly strove to deny it, he continued, good-humouredly, 'I am grateful, sir, that you are *not* a saint. You would make vastly uncomfortable company. I should always be reminded of my own frailties, and your perfection would certainly irritate me.' He saw that Rebecca, who had become pale and painfully distressed at mention of the murder of Sir Peter Henshawe's child, was now restored to calmness. 'We had best rejoin the others, my dear,' he prompted gently, 'for there will be much you will want to discuss with them before you take your leave.'

'Yes. Joshua will be agog for news of Roland's voyaging and of Aled's engagement to Georgina Picton. It will please him, I know. I shall invite them to Thatched Cottage, that I may learn to know her better.'

'And that she may worship at John Jeremiah's shrine,' amended Dr Peate, smiling.

'Certainly,' agreed Sir Matthew benignly, 'for it will show her discrimination as well as our own, and set her in good stead for the future.' He turned anxiously to Rebecca, saying, 'You will not forget the letter for Joshua, my dear? It is of the greatest importance.'

'No, Grandfather, I will not forget.'

'As I must not forget to tell Philip Stradling that there are poachers active in the Vale. Not opportunist cottagers who can do no great harm, but gangs, well organised, and which present real threat.'

'I do not think that Mr Stradling will be unduly perturbed!' Dr Peate ventured, amused. 'I would expect him to return any such impertinence with interest! I fancy that it is the poachers who would need to be on their guard, and they who would need protection!'

With much good-humoured bantering, and with the future of the scholarship agreeably decided, they made their way back to the rest of the company, and it was with real regret that Rebecca finally took her leave. She promised to return and to bring Joshua and John Jeremiah with her as soon as she was able.

As Stenner returned with the coach, she made Sir Matthew and Dr Peate their private good-byes, kissing each of them, and holding them close, reluctant to be out of their company. Rebecca waved until they were hidden from sight, and found her eyes unaccountably blurred with tears that, even though alone in the carriage, she would not let fall. She did not know what so distressed her. Their gentle companionship, perhaps, or their growing frailness. Or was it simply the weakness that comes with childbirth; that restless emotion and depth of feeling? She opened her eyelids wide, blinking away the tears, chiding herself for such foolishness, but the mood would not be dispelled.

As the small coach took the hill from the Clevis and rounded the corner past the Crown Inn, Rebecca looked for Ossie to give him greeting but saw no sign of him. He was engaged at some task in the stables, she thought in disappointment, for the ostler would never knowingly let her pass by unheeded.

Ossie was indeed within the stables, tending the handsome piebald mare which belonged to one of the vestrymen, and the sweeping boy from the yard was at his side, body rigid with excitement, face aglow. He is a good lad, Ossie thought, for all his slowness of mind, and the vestryman had asked that the boy help in the grooming, for he was a bluff, good-natured fellow and knew the lad's fondness for the horse.

'Blaze!' he had cried out ecstatically upon catching glimpse of the mare. 'Blaze!' and the vestryman had smiled and nodded approvingly, saying, 'Yes. Blaze is her name. I wonder that you recall it!'

Ossie wondered, too, and when they were safely alone, and could not be overheard, tried to question the boy. His patient gentleness availed him nothing for the boy could utter no sensible word. Ossie knew the vestryman for an honest man, and held no suspicion against him. The lad had greeted him, smiling openly, and had clearly been pleased to see both him and his mare. It was not the horse that he feared, nor its owner. What, then? Some other rider upon a similar horse? An unknown mount with a blaze of white upon its forehead? No, he could not believe it to be so, for the lad, for all his lack of wits, could distinguish every private horse which entered the stable yard, and could put face to its owner.

He would tell Joshua of what had occurred, Ossie decided, and seek his opinion. The boy could scarcely be called a witness, for he was unable to give account of himself or others. Why, then, did Ossie feel that the boy held the key to the mysteries that bedevilled the hamlets? It was more than mere supposition. It was a certainty. He prayed God that no other suspected, save he, or the lad's life would not be worth a corpse's candle.

Chapter Twenty-One

Upon the morrow, early, Joshua rode out to Pyle courthouse for the inquest of Jed Carter. It was a depressing occasion, made melancholy by the setting as well as the circumstances, for there was a grim, impersonal quality to such investigations which always caught Joshua on the raw. Part of the sadness lay in that Jed Carter commanded more attention in death than he had ever known in life. He had been a good man, an honest worker, and Grove farm would feel his loss. But there would be a dozen such paupers, workless and destitute, eager to take his place. There would be few who would long remember him for what he was, only for the violence of his death. He had neither kith nor kin to mourn him, and those few paupers who followed his coffin to the grave would count his murder of less account than the pence they were paid. It was an irony that would not have been lost upon Jed Carter, nor would he have grudged them their bounty. Life and death are common coinage to all. The living must survive as best they can.

He turned the grey into the stable yard of the courthouse and, with a curt word to the ostler, went within. Identification had been duly established and the legal formalities endured. The verdict was unlawful murder; the hearing to be resumed at a date after the trial of those sheep stealers already held within the prison cells. Joshua had expected such a result but was not of a mind to linger to discuss it. However, the justice was not to be denied.

'Stradling, my boy, a moment of your time!' he called peremptorily, and Joshua halted with as good a grace as he could muster, awaiting the inevitable catechism. 'I have news for you, Stradling, splendid news!' His plump-jowled face was aquiver with importance. 'I have received a personal message from Sir Matthew in the Vale. He has ordered the arrest of Sir

Peter Henshawe who is incarcerated at Cowbridge gaol. Well? What have you to say to that, sir? I can see that you are plainly astonished,' he exclaimed with satisfaction.

'I am all but speechless, sir,' Joshua's hand closed over Sir Matthew's letter, held safe in his pocket.

'Hmm!' The justice's grunt was derisive, his smile triumphant. 'Did I not tell you the man was a scoundrel? A villain of the first water? I suspected skullduggery all along. I am not easily deceived. No, sir, I am not easily deceived!'

'No, sir,' Joshua assented readily. 'You are a fair judge of character.'

'I have a modest talent for rooting out the truth,' the justice agreed complacently. 'Some experience and acuteness of perception,' He broke off to say encouragingly. 'But you will learn, Stradling, you will learn. Do not doubt it!' Joshua, who had already mastered the arts of diplomacy and prevarication, was not minded to disagree. 'You had best tell that poor creature within the gaol that Henshawe has been detained, for what little comfort it may bring her. She is troubled in mind and spirit, Stradling, gravely troubled.'

Joshua said hesitantly and with due deference, 'Would she not benefit more from a visit from you, sir, in your capacity as clergyman?'

'I think not, Stradling.' The response was cool.

'My awkward clumsiness might do more harm than good,' Joshua mumbled self-effacingly. 'I could not hope to speak with your conviction, sir, your authority. As you rightly remind me, I lack your experience and . . . acuteness of perception.'

The justice looked nonplussed. 'Well, perhaps a brief word,' he conceded reluctantly, 'if you think it is my Christian duty.'

'It would be grossly impertinent of me to advise you, sir,' Joshua said, 'as to where your Christian duty lies.'

'Quite! Quite!' the justice conceded. 'Well, I had best go within and give the poor creature the benefit of my presence and whatever small comfort I may.'

'I am sure that she will appreciate it, sir.'

'As you, Stradling, I do not doubt,' the justice observed dryly. 'Do not think, sir, that I am wholly unaware of your attempts to outwit and manipulate me.'

Joshua had the grace to look embarrassed, blurting, 'I

truly believed that you would bring her greater comfort than I, sir.'

'Yes. I am aware of that, too, else you would most certainly be standing in my stead!' He permitted himself a wry smile, demanding, 'Where do you intend to go now, sir, or am I not permitted to enquire? It seems that there is some permanent conspiracy afoot to keep me in ignorance of your movements!'

'To the docks, sir, to make arrangements with Peter Rawlings to keep watch upon the smugglers off Newton Point.'

The justice grunted non-committally. 'And Curtis? What news of him? Or have you not seen fit to enquire?'

'He is still at Dr Mansel's house, sir. Deeply unconscious and still too weakened to be moved elsewhere.'

'You have set guard upon him?'

'Yes, sir, on your firm instruction.' The justice raised his eyebrows expressively but said nothing. 'If you have no further command for me, sir?' Joshua said hopefully.

'Command, Stradling? I hope that I am not an autocrat! I request, sir, not command, trusting to your intelligence and initiative,' the justice rebuked testily. 'However . . .'

'Yes, sir?'

'You will present yourself at St John's Parish church this afternoon at 3 o'clock precisely.'

'The church, sir?'

'That is what I said. You will bring Rebecca, of course, upon some pretext or other. I leave the details to you, for it seems you are adept at such evasions . . . prevarication, invention, call it what you will.'

'And the true purpose, sir?'

'There is to be a modest presentation from the people of the three hamlets to celebrate my godson's birth. A recognition of Rebecca's value to the three hamlets in providing the school and so forth.' He hesitated before amending gruffly, 'I mean Rebecca's value and your own, of course.' Lest Joshua think him indulgent, he added sternly, 'You will say nothing of the real reason! You will pretend innocence. I have your word upon it, sir?'

'You have my word.'

259

'You will see that your groom, Stenner, is also present.'

'Stenner, sir?'

'Yes. At my instigation the vestrymen wish to honour his bravery, to give him some tangible reward.'

'Then that is generous of you, sir.'

The justice brushed it aside with a show of irritation, demanding, 'Is there anyone whom you believe Stenner might choose to have beside him? A kinsman, or friend?'

'I understand that he is betrothed to Betty Turner, sir, and that they hope soon to be wed.'

'Capital! Capital!' the justice declared. 'You will endeavour to see that she attends, Joshua?'

'I will, sir.'

The justice, struck by sudden inspiration, glowed with good humour. 'I have thought of the ideal solution, sir, a brilliant idea. I wonder it has not occurred to you.' Joshua waited apprehensively. 'Why, it is near to genius,' the justice continued, 'quite breathtaking in its simplicity. You must tell Rebecca that she attends the presentation to Stenner, and Stenner that he attends the presentation to her. They must both be sworn to the greatest secrecy. You understand? Absolute discretion is essential if the plan is to succeed!'

'I shall be as silent as the grave,' Joshua promised. 'But what of the people of the three hamlets, sir? Those cottagers who have contributed to the presentations?'

'Oh, that is all arranged,' the justice said airily. 'Already in hand. It was originally planned for tomorrow, and all had been notified and requested to attend, but you will be away in Porlock upon your official business as constable.'

'But how did you overcome it, sir?'

'Why, with the town crier, Joshua, how else?' the justice declared with immense satisfaction. 'He has been dispatched to every last outpost of the hamlets, to the most isolated cottages, the outlying farms and holdings. A masterstroke, was it not, sir? I warned you that I am not easily defeated.' Serenely he took his leave, plump face wreathed in smiles, step jaunty, and disappeared triumphantly within.

Emily Randall had approached her old friend, Elwyn Morris, informally and seemingly by accident, although, in fact, she had carefully engineered their meeting. She thought it wiser to speak to him casually on his return from his work upon the horse-drawn tramrod, rather than make an official visit to his house, Crabtree Cottage. His wife, Eira, would have welcomed her most courteously, she knew, and the children would have been excited at the prospect of a visitor, particularly one who taught Dafydd and his step sister, Haulwen, at the village school. Yet she had no wish to antagonise Elwyn Morris nor to unfairly raise the hopes of the family by making the bursary a major issue. Besides, in the end, the choice must be Dafydd's to make, and she would not willingly increase the pressures upon him or alienate him. He was a sensitive, intelligent boy, mature beyond his years but nevertheless a child. To coerce him into acceptance against his will would be a disaster. All she could do would be to set the advantages fairly before him, then hope that he made the decision that was right for him and for his future.

Elwyn Morris was always delighted to see Emily, for he liked and respected her from their days in the poorhouse as, by the same token, she admired him. He was one of the few paupers who was able to read and write, and his kindness towards those who had need of his advice, and his selfless devotion to bettering conditions for them had often brought him into conflict with authority. Punishment for his so-called 'insubordination' was frequently severe and he had been castigated by the workmaster, Littlepage, as insolent and rebellious. Yet neither punishment nor censure had broken his resolve and, in time, conditions had grown marginally better.

He had shown the same resolve in searching for his daughter, Haulwen, lost to him upon his wife's death, when the infant had been 'farmed out' he knew not where. As a pauper he had no rights in claiming her, and none could even tell him where she might be. Yet he had persevered, never losing hope nor his fierce determination to find her. When he at last came upon her in a remote hill-top farm, where the old woman who had reared her had died, the reunion had been all that he had hoped. Emily could not forget how, even with Haulwen's life at stake, and his own, he had chosen to give evidence against the wreckers, and had survived their threats, to see them hanged. He had married the widow of Jem Crocutt, so viciously crucified by them, and taken Dafydd and the rest of her brood as his own, working and caring for them every hour that God gave. It had grieved him sorely that Dafydd, despite all his efforts to please the boy, treated him with active dislike. It was plain that he felt that Morris had usurped his dead father's place, and would not betray Jem Crocutt's memory by acceptance of him. Yet now, at last, they were the firmest friends and, of all the children, Dafydd was the dearest to him and the closest to him in nature and temperament. It was a relationship hard won, and he would not willingly imperil it.

Emily was not sanguine about Morris's approval for the scholarship for, although Dafydd could not attend the school for another full year, when he would be twelve years of age, it would mean long separation from his family. It would mean for Dafydd hardship and self-discipline, too, and perhaps a growing away from those who loved him. His life would change while theirs remained as simple and lowly as always.

Yet, when they met upon the Green before the church, Elwyn Morris listened intently to the news of the bursary, which Emily gave, saying, 'Well, 'tis a rare opportunity, Emily, I do not doubt. A God-given chance for a boy to make something of his life.' He asked, tentatively, 'And you think that Dafydd might have a real chance to win it?'

'Yes, I do, indeed. He is a born scholar, Elwyn, with a natural aptitude, a quick and lively mind. Yes. I think he might well have a chance.' He shook his head despairingly, biting at his lip, coal dust settled in the deep lines and hollows of his face. The whites of his eyes showed luminous against the grime, the irises warmly brown and alive with intelligence.

'I do not know, Emily,' he confessed. 'It is so big a step.'

'No bigger than that from the poorhouse to where you stand now,' she reminded quietly. 'You have succeeded by your own efforts, as Dafydd might.'

'Perhaps.'

'What is it that you fear, Elwyn?'

'That Dafydd might think that he is not loved or needed at home. It has taken me a long, hard time to win his confidence, Emily. I would not jeopardise it.'

'He is a bright, sensible boy and would soon be persuaded otherwise.'

262

'But I will not persuade him, Emily. I have not the right.'

'And Eira?'

'She will not stand in his way if his mind is set upon it.'

'And you, Elwyn?'

'It would give me the greatest pleasure in all of my life to see him take such an opportunity,' he said simply. 'He has progressed beyond me already, Emily. I have given him the little room in the attic where he may study in peace, away from the noise of the others.'

'Yes, he has told me of it.'

'It is his own special place. He is not like the others. He has a need to be alone. He is a clever boy, I know, and would succeed at his studies, be a credit to himself and us.'

'But . . .?'

'But he is loyal and stubborn both. He would sacrifice all if he thought it denied him Jem Crocutt's memory. It is not I whom you have to convince, Emily, but Dafydd himself.'

'Then you will give him your blessing?'

'Aye. Willingly, if that is what he chooses to do.' He hesitated, saying with shy awkwardness, 'It means much to me that you will recommend him, Emily, upon his own merits I thank you for that and for the schooling you have given him. Wherever he goes in life, it will hold him in good stead.'

She nodded and put a hand to his work-grimed sleeve, saying with gentleness, 'We have travelled a long road from the poorhouse, Elwyn, and have much to be grateful for. Our lives are kinder now.'

'Yes. Yes, indeed. I had never thought to find such joy in life, and that is a fact. I have home and family and the comfort of work and friends. I am richer than I had ever dared to hope.'

'Then I would wish the same for Dafydd,' Emily declared, 'for he is deserving of a future bright enough to wipe out the tragedies of his past.'

'He will not grow away from us,' Elwyn Morris said, voicing his unspoken fear. 'He is a good sensible boy and will never look down upon us, or despise us for what we are and what we are not.'

'No. He will hold you in respect and affection always,' Emily said with conviction. 'He will take you for example, Elwyn, when all else is forgot, believe it.'

263

He nodded his gratitude and walked, unspeaking, beside her upon the way.

Dafydd Crocutt walked from Newton village and across the long cart track through the dunes to the bay where the jagged black rocks erupted from the sea. He needed time to think, away from the distractions of everyday life and the clamorous demands of his siblings. His teacher, Mistress Emily Randall, had given him news of a scholarship to be granted to the most promising student in the County of Glamorgan. It had bedevilled his mind ever since. She said that if he applied himself diligently to his studies and chose to apply, then she would willingly coach him to the standard required. Moreover, she would make personal recommendation to the authorities on his behalf. She did not doubt that he was capable of winning the award.

Walking now across the acres of wind-drifted sand, he knew a churning in his stomach, a rising sickness. He tasted the sourness of it in his mouth and grimaced wryly. He did not know how he really felt about the prospect of entering for the scholarship, or how he might explain his reservations to others. He had felt, at first, a shamefaced joy that Mistress Randall thought so highly of him. He was proud that she placed him above all others, for he was eager, always, to please her. He loved his lessons at school and worked at them sedulously, for they brought him a joy and fulfilment not to be found elsewhere. Well, he amended silently, only when fishing with Mr Fleet or riding with him upon the fishcart and discussing things as man to man. Sometimes, too, upon the farm, he felt happiness surge within him, a peacefulness that came from toiling near the earth. Yet, of late, the land seemed to belong to him less and less, as if with his father's death and the coming of the paupers to tend it, he was being distanced from all that he strove so hard to retain – in fact as in memory. It was as though the land would wait no longer for his coming and rejected him as useless and alien. It prospered, certainly, and Constable Stradling had promised him that when he was able he might buy it back and farm it for himself. It pleased Dafydd that it prospered, yet it grieved him, too. It seemed to decry his father's husbandry, his poor attempts to wrest a

264

living from the barren soil. It proved that it could flourish in Dafydd's absence. It paid no heed to his fierce determination to rescue it, the oath he had sworn upon his father's death, to make it all that Jem Crocutt had striven towards.

Jeremiah, watching Dafydd's coming from his vantage point beside the cob and cart, saw by the slack droop of the boy's shoulders and his slow progress that he was troubled in mind. He knew, well enough, what ailed him. Would Dafydd brave it out, he wondered, or return by the way he had come? With a sharp command to Charity to lie still and make no sound of welcome, Jeremiah busied himself in raking the cockles from their sandy beds, not glancing up, seemingly oblivious to all save the task in hand. When Charity could stand the repression no more, he barked frenziedly, and ran leaping and cavorting towards the boy, breathless in his fury to welcome him. Jeremiah looked up, straightening his back with a grunt and giving a casual wave of acknowledgement.

'You have come to help me at the cockling, lad?'

'If you will have me, sir.' His boot scuffed idly at a pebble.

'Aye. You are welcome. It will ease my poor bones and give me company.'

'You have Charity, Mr Fleet, and the cob.'

'Aye, but the old cob is a lazy varmint and Charity, there, is neither use nor ornament. He is a lotus eater, lad, not cut out for the hurly-burly of a fisherman's life like you.'

'I do not think I shall be very good company today, Mr Fleet.'

'Will you not, lad?' He looked at him keenly. 'Would you have me work beside you in silence, then? I will not take offence. It is sometimes better so.'

'No, Mr Fleet, sir.' Dafydd's voice was anguished. 'I would have you listen, sir, and then, if you will, advise me.'

Jeremiah laid down his rake upon the sand, saying gently, 'Then you had best begin, lad, and tell me what so distresses you.'

'There is a scholarship, sir, to be awarded to the grammar school at Cowbridge.'

'Indeed? A fine school.' Jeremiah approved. 'I believe Constable Stradling was a pupil there.'

'Yes. Mistress Randall has told me she will put my name forward, sir, if I have a mind to it.'

265

'And have you a mind to it?' The question was casually made.

'Well, that is the crux of it, sir. I do not know if I am able.'

'If you were not able,' Jeremiah reasoned, 'Mistress Randall would not have promised to support you. That much is clear.'

'I do not mean that I am not able to do the work, sir, for I would make certain of that. I would work at it until I drop.'

'What, then?'

'I do not know if I am able to accept a scholarship, even were it offered.'

'You think your stepfather might feel slighted and hurt, forbid you even?'

'No, sir.' his voice was low. 'He would want whatever is best for me. He treats me as his own.'

'The extra expense, then? Is that what deters you?'

'No, Mr Fleet. Whatever the cost, he would find it. He would work every hour under the sun, and I have a little saved from my work at Grove for books and such.'

Jeremiah's faded blue eyes were compassionate in the grey-bearded face as he reached out to touch Dafydd's shoulder, saying, 'What is it, then, that holds you back?'

'The farm, sir.' Dafydd blurted. 'My promise to buy back Grove farm. I made promise upon my father's coffin. It is binding upon me. I swore an oath.'

'Well,' Jeremiah considered for a moment. 'Why should a sound education deny you that? In my opinion, 'tis more likely to stand you in good stead.'

'But if I do not return to farm Grove, sir, I shall have broken my oath!' he exclaimed despairingly. 'My father's spirit would have no rest, no more would I!'

'Now, now, lad,' Jeremiah's grip tightened upon Dafydd's shoulder. 'That is naught but heathen foolishness. Think no more upon it! It is unworthy of you. I knew your father well,' he said gruffly. 'A good and honest man, his only aim in life to make things better for his wife and family. It would grieve him sorely to see you downcast.'

'But there is no way around it, Mr Fleet. I made promise!' he insisted.

'To whom, lad? To yourself, no other. It is you who must release yourself, for no other living is involved.'

266

'I cannot, sir. There is no way,' he said despairingly.

'Yes. There is a way.'

'How, sir?'

'When you have finished your education at Cowbridge Grammar School, you will have the knowledge and way to make a living at any profession you choose. Then, you may do as Constable Stradling has done.'

'Buy Grove Farm, do you mean?'

'I do indeed, lad. 'Twould be the ideal solution and one your father would have wanted, believe me. You have a young brother, do you not?'

'Yes. Huw, sir.'

'Then the farm is his inheritance as much as yours. Like as not, the love of the soil is in his blood, born into him. Could you not buy it for his safe-keeping?'

'Yes, sir,' Dafydd murmured doubtfully then, brightening, he confessed, 'I think it might serve us both well.' He hesitated, 'But should he not *want* to go farming?'

'Then there are the girls to be considered. One or other might wish to marry a farmer and to make Grove her home. Then there are the paupers to be considered. It is already home to them, and in keeping Grove a working farm, both Mr Stradling and you have given them new life, a chance to prove themselves. That is reason enough and one which your father would have approved with all his heart.'

'You think, then, that I should try for the scholarship, Mr Fleet?'

'I think that you must do what your heart and mind tell you, my boy.'

'You think my father would be glad of it, the scholarship, I mean?'

'I am sure of it. 'Twas the proudest moment in all of my life when Illtyd taught himself to read and write, me being no scholar, never having learnt and all. When Rebecca gave me the lovely new cart as a leaving present, she had my name painted upon the side. Will you not read it to me, boy? Read aloud what it says?'

'It says, sir, 'Jeremiah Fleet and Son, Purveyor of Crustaceans to the Gentry'.'

'Aye. *And son*,' he smiled. 'Oh, it is a rare gift to have a son

267

who is a scholar. It lifts the heart. I feel the lack of it in myself, and grieve it sorely. Your father would have such pride in you, Dafydd! And Elwyn Morris, too, for you are son to him and none could treat you better.'

Dafydd said tentatively, 'I do not think there is a lack of learning in you, Mr Fleet. You are the best man I know and the finest fisherman. I count myself lucky to be your friend.'

'As I you, lad. As I you.' Jeremiah's face was warm with pleasure, eyes preternaturally bright as he cleared his throat, to say, 'That is what you must remember, lad, that however humble your occupation, or however exalted, you must do it always in the best way you can. 'Tis the doing of it that matters and not who or what you are.'

'Yes, Mr Fleet. I will remember, sir.' He hesitated before admitting shamefacedly, 'I shall miss you, sir, if I win the scholarship, I mean. I shall miss you more than any other.'

'Then your returning will be the sweeter, lad, for 'tis said absence makes the heart grow fonder. Distance cannot break a friendship, only strengthen the knot.'

'Yes, sir.' Dafydd was not wholly convinced.

'Besides,' Jeremiah said cheerfully, 'the old cob and I will visit you upon the cart when we are able. Aye, and Charity, too, if he has a mind to travel.' The bull terrier, hearing his name, thumped his tail hard upon the wet sand, wedge-shaped head cocked enquiringly, eyes alert. ''Twill not be the handsomest equipage,' Jeremiah admitted, smiling.

'But it will be the most welcome, sir,' Dafydd said with honesty.

'Aye, and you will not mistake it.'

'No, sir. I would not mistake it for any other upon earth, for I will remember what is painted upon its side and hope to make you proud of me, as Illtyd did.'

'I am proud of you already,' Jeremiah said. 'Whatever you had decided, it would not have altered that.'

Dafydd nodded, but did not speak, for there were no words to tell Jeremiah how it pleased him.

'Oh, but it will be the greatest adventure!' Jeremiah said. 'So much to learn and so much to experience, a whole world of excitement beyond the three hamlets, with other men's thoughts and writings to guide you. And one day, perhaps, such writings of your own. Oh, but I shall walk with you in spirit, every inch of the way, my boy, and relive it with you every returning.' He sniffed and wiped a gnarled hand across his mouth, saying jocularly, 'But the cockles are not inclined to wait upon such a distinguished scholar, nor my customers neither. 'Tis better to work than starve, so we had best be working.'

'Yes, Mr Fleet, sir.' Dafydd ran to the cart and took up a sieve and a spare wooden rake and set to work companionably beside him, scraping the cockles from their sandy beds. 'You are a true gentleman, Mr Fleet,' he ventured, not pausing in his labours.

Jeremiah hid a smile, fearful of wounding the boy's feelings. 'And you will be a scholar and gentleman both,' he returned gravely as they went patiently about their work, secure in each other's company.

Chapter Twenty-Two

Rebecca, sworn to secrecy by Joshua over the vestrymen's presentation to Stenner had found no difficulty in persuading both Betty Turner and Ruth to accompany her to church. She had invented some implausible story about the rector wishing to make an urgent announcement to his entire flock, and neither of them had seen fit to question the truth of it, nor why he had not simply delivered the message from his pulpit of a Sunday. They had speculated wildly upon the content of such an announcement and Rebecca had obligingly joined in the debate, as determined to deceive them as they were to hoodwink her. To her relief Stenner, although normally the most shy and reclusive of men, had readily agreed to not only drive them in the coach but to accompany them within. It pleased Rebecca that his 'understanding' with Betty Turner and his revenge upon the hooded gunman seemed to have given him new confidence and authority, a realisation of his own worth. The award from the vestrymen, official recognition of his courage would, she hoped, raise him even higher in the esteem of others.

Determined to do Stenner justice, Rebecca dressed with special care for the occasion, choosing her prettiest gown of sapphire blue silk with the matching pelisse which Joshua declared to be a perfect compliment to her vivid blue eyes. She surveyed herself critically in the looking glass, adjusting the ribbons of her toning bonnet, and taking up the gloves and reticule which were an exact match for the pretty slippers, hand-fashioned for her by the elderly cordwainer in the village. Yes, she thought, satisfied, she had recovered her colour and slenderness since John Jeremiah's birth and looked well enough. She would do Stenner credit. She would not disgrace him.

Joshua, despite her entreaties that he wear his 'gentlemen's' clothes, could not be persuaded. He could spare half an hour at most from his duties he insisted, for there was much to be done before his journey to Porlock. He had an urgent meeting planned with Rawlings at the port, for the search for the smugglers continued and would do so in his absence. Besides, he must make further enquiries about Curtis, and clear up all other duties outstanding before he left. Villainy, like the poor, was ever with us, he reminded Rebecca. He would hardly impress either the offenders or the justice, should he arrive sporting a ruffled silk shirt and doeskin inexpressibles with hessian boots! No, his uniform would serve him better. So it was agreed.

At the small cottage on the edge of the Burrows, Rosa Doonan prepared Joy for her visit to St John's church. She was in the best of spirits, for Cavan and Emrys were being granted an hour's leave from the quarries upon the Downs, and would drive the cart to the cottage, then walk with her there. There had been no fresh sighting of the hooded man since his attack upon Joshua, and Rosa knew that the highways and byways of the three hamlets were still being carefully watched by the justice's paid men. They were armed upon Robert Knight's firm instruction, and would not hesitate to shoot if the need arose. Their value lay in that they were virtually indistinguishable from all others engaged in following their mundane everyday tasks, for the frugal vestrymen would not see them idle. They were set to mending the highways and clearing the ditches and verges, so that the hamlets reaped double benefit from their hiring.

Rosa had grown to recognise and greet many of them and she felt safe, knowing that they kept watch upon her and her child. The terror of the attack and attempt to abduct Joy had now receded and she tried to banish it altogether from her mind. To immure herself inside the cottage, and Joy with her, would have ruined her own life, and given him victory over her. He would have succeeded in his reign of terror, his attempts to demoralise her and made her a trapped and feeble thing. Rosa was a young woman of spirit, and would not give him that satisfaction, whoever he might be. At first, after Stenner's attack upon the man, she had remained safely within

271

the confines of house and yard, but gradually she ventured further afield, each excursion with Joy a fresh triumph.

Her mother, the widow Howarth, who kept a small lodging house for seafarers near the docks had begged her to leave the isolated cottage and stay with her until the madman was captured and gaoled, as he deserved. Rosa had thanked her but refused to do so, unwilling to leave Cavan to fend for himself or to deny him Joy's company.

Like Rosa and the widow Howarth, too, Cavan was devoted to the child, cherishing her every smile and exploratory word, every awkward attempt at walking. She was, he declared to any who would listen, the very light and joy of his life, as befitted her name. His tenderness towards the child, despite his massive size and clumsy ministrations, was touching to see. She laughed gleefully aloud whenever he swung her joyously in the air, singing the while in his harsh tuneless voice which Emrys so hated. Yet, even Emrys would not remonstrate with him, for he was as enchanted with her innocent delight as all others. He and Cavan vied with each other in lavishing small gifts and sweetmeats upon her, and Rosa had to be strictly impartial in her efforts to stop them from over-indulging the child. Had not Joy been of the sweetest and most placid disposition and unfailingly good-humoured, Rosa feared that she might have been turned into a monster. As it was, she blossomed under the limitless affection which was poured upon her, and returned it one hundredfold. She grew more like Rosa in features and mannerisms with each passing day, their pale, translucent skin and corn-gold hair a sight to soften the heart of the most crabbed misogynist, and make him fall under their spell.

Rosa knew that the justice's presentation of the cradle to Rebecca and Joshua would be a popular and well attended affair, with a cheerful, holy day atmosphere – the more enjoyable for the surprise it would afford Rebecca. Tom Butler had been instructed by the justice to provide victuals and refreshments for the vestrymen and thirty or so of the Stradlings' friends, and she and Cavan and Emrys had been formally invited. It would prove the most splendid diversion, Rosa was sure, and it would please her to show off Joy before her friends and admirers, and feel part of the life of the three hamlets once more, instead of an unwilling outcast.

272

She dressed Joy in the delicate rose pink dress and bonnet, with the matching fringed shawl which Mrs Howarth had extravagantly ordered made for her by the seamstress in Newton village, and set her to lie upon a warm blanket upon the bedroom floor. Then, when she was certain that the child could come to no harm, she set about her own preparations. Cavan and Emrys had promised to be here upon the hour, which gave her less than a quarter of an hour to be ready. They would wash away the worst of the stonedust grime at the quarries, they had promised, and would need no more than a modest titivating before climbing into their Sunday suits, which Rosa had ironed and set out for them.

The urgent knocking upon the back door of the house sent her hurtling downstairs, her dressing barely completed. Oh, but it was typical of Cavan to behave so, she thought indulgently, and always with time at a premium. He treated the forgetting of his key with the same careless inconsequence that he treated all else. It was too bad of him to be so thoughtless. Emrys or not, she would take him to task for his negligence, chide him severely. But surely she would have heard the sound of the cob and cart, the familiar clatter of their boot studs, their voices raised in bickering? She froze in uncertainty, wondering whether to cry out and demand who stood there. Yet she knew that terror would betray her, her voice pitched sharp with hysteria. For a moment she was incapable of thought or action, unable even to summon strength to flee, then common sense reasserted itself.

It was Morgan, the man who stood watch upon the dunes outside the cottage yard. He came, sometimes, to check upon her safety, but more often than not with some small offering for Joy that he had carved or whittled, or a fresh baked sweetmeat from his wife. He had become a familiar visitor, a friend almost, and would oftimes bring his bread and cheese within at her invitation to eat at the kitchen table and share a homely brew.

Rosa, chiding herself for her foolishness, drew back the bolt and opened the door a crack. Morgan stood there, awkward and apologetic, shuffling his sand-caked boots, a small package clutched in his outstretched hand. Then, seeing Rosa's distress, her face drained of all colour, he blurted contritely:

'Oh, it was foolish of me to hammer so loudly upon the door, but I could not get answer, and for a moment . . .' his voice trailed off helplessly. 'I beg you will forgive me, Mrs Doonan, ma'am. I had no wish to frighten or offend you.'

'Nor have you, 'Rosa said, 'for I am grateful always for your company, and for the protection you offer.'

'But you are pale, ma'am,' he persisted anxiously. 'None has tried to harass you, nor gain entrance? You have caught no glimpse of the man?'

'No,' she strove to reassure him. 'There is naught amiss, I swear it. I was upstairs, do you see, preparing for the outing to the church, and did not at first hear you. I hurried, too quickly, lest you be concerned. That is all. You have my word upon it.' She put a hand to his sleeve, smiling easily now, and saying, 'Will you not come inside? Warm yourself at the fire? You may keep watch from the window of the house as easily.'

'No, ma'am, it is better not, though I thank you most kindly.' His broad, wind-burnt cheeks grew redder yet as he added, self-consciously, 'I have brought the babe a rattle from a pedlar's tray, a small thing and of no great account. But it has bells that jingle and ribbons and a teething ring of bone.' He thrust the awkwardly wrapped parcel of Bristol brown paper towards her, blinking his eyes anxiously as she unwrapped it.

'Why, it is the prettiest thing!' she exclaimed in genuine delight. 'Joy will love it and play with it constantly. It is the kindest of gifts and one she will cherish, as I cherish the kindness that prompted it. But I shall not give it to her yet a while, Mr Morgan.'

'No, ma'am?' He tried to hide his disappointment, eyes downcast.

'No, for you must give it to her yourself at the very first opportunity, that she may know the giver and return that pleasure given to her. She will thank you as best she is able.'

Morgan's face was aglow with warmth as he blurted self-consciously, 'The pedlar was an old man, left invalid from the wars. A gentleman born, ma'am, for he could read and write, or so he claimed. There is an engraving upon the handle it seems . . . but I must take his word for it, not being schooled and all. It says, "Joy to the Babe". 'Tis my wish, too, and I thought it fitting.'

'It is fitting and I thank you for it, for I know it is truly meant.' She reached up impulsively and kissed his flushed cheek, saying with a smile, 'And I must take his word for it, too, sir, for like you I can neither read nor write. But, with God's good grace, one day Joy will, and you will be always kindly in her memory. She will cherish the gift and the giver.'

As he turned to leave, the unmistakable rattle of the quarry cart heralded Doonan's and Emrys's coming, with Doonan's raucous singing and Emrys's anguished protests rising above the creaking of the wheels and boards.

'You have company now, ma'am, and will be safe,' Morgan said, opening the gate to the small paved yard that the cob and cart might enter, and returning Doonan's extravagant salute with a bow and a flourish before he returned to the sand-drifted wastes beyond. He watched the two men dismount from the cart, jostling and ribbing each other good-humouredly, full of exuberant male nonsense and mock aggression as they took the cob and cart to the shelter of the stone outhouse beyond. He watched them walking briskly to the house, and their unfeigned pleasure at the sight of Rosa returning in all her finery with the babe, Joy, clasped in her arms. Then, smiling, he turned away to scan the dunes beyond.

Where the far high wall of the yard met the bleak wind-swept side of the cottage, the unseen watcher bided his time. It had been a foolishness to come. Yet, if he did not act soon he would lose opportunity. All his patient waiting and scheming would be laid to waste. Worse, his own life, and those who served him would be forfeit, cruelly set at risk. Yet he could not abandon all that he had striven for. Would not! The flesh wound which so plagued him had been cleaned and tended, and he thanked God that it had not festered and grown corrupt. A few days, now, and all would be over, his task here completed, and he might safely leave. With the child in his keeping, none would ever know how or when it had been done. He would be safe from discovery, free from detection. He would never return to this God-forsaken place, but find opportunity elsewhere.

It had been a mistake to come here today. He knew now that the men upon the streets were armed and would suspect any stranger, shoot him down if need be. He had chosen his time badly, believing that all would be at the church, their attention

275

taken, their guard lifted. He had thought the woman to be alone with the child, the guard upon the dunes far enough away to be no threat to him. He had not counted upon the two men upon the cart returning. Yet, with the stable empty and none save the woman here, he would have safe place to hide until fresh opportunity came. His hand tightened upon the hood of black cloth in his pocket. It had served him well. None could describe him, not even that dolt of a village constable. It had amused him to provoke and attack the creature, to set his wits against a cloddish provincial with more brawn than brains. It was, he thought, amused, an uneven battle and one that he was bound to win. There was small enough merit in beating so unworthy an adversary.

His hand moved from his pocket to the pistol belted beneath the cloth of his coat, and he felt the reassuring coldness of it to his touch. It would give him no satisfaction to kill the woman when he kidnapped the child. Yet, kill her he would if need be, and it was certain that she would not surrender the babe willingly. She was spirited and bold, but boldness was no match against the cool mastery of gun and bullet. With an effort he stretched his cramped limbs, and carefully replaced the small stone he had removed from the wall to give him clear sight of the yard. Then, with a glance about him, he was away as swiftly and silently as he had come.

The little parish church of St John the Baptist was already filled to overflowing with parishioners, and Joshua and Rebecca could scarce make progress across the village green for the greetings and congratulations of their many friends and acquaintances. A pew had been set aside for them within the church, with places for Betty Turner, Ruth and Stenner, too. Rebecca was delighted that he appeared so relaxed. He was clearly unsuspecting of the honour planned, the vestrymen's presentation. Her meaningful glance towards him, and the conspiratorial smile she gave Joshua was handsomely returned, embellished with a wink of complicity. Already there was an air of expectancy among those assembled, a cheerful festive atmosphere over all. Rebecca was determined to enjoy it.

She glanced about her, smiling and nodding at those friends whom she had not met and exchanged greetings with upon the green. Sophie and Jeremiah were seated parallel to them on the opposite side of the aisle with Sophie in her best sprigged gown, and Jeremiah seated beside her, handsome and commanding as an Old Testament prophet. Illtyd, who shared their pew, gave Rebecca a discreet nod and the widest of smiles, his arresting blue eyes so bright with humour and intelligence that they defied the ugliness of his body; the awkwardness that crippled him. Of all those present, Rebecca thought, he was the most deserving of praise and recognition. He had achieved all that he had set out to do in life, never recognising his infirmities, and never soured by bitterness or envy for others. It was no wonder that all who knew him held him in affection and respect and took courage from him.

Rebecca glanced surreptitiously behind her and saw Rosa and her daughter, Joy, as pretty and fresh as spring flowers in their finery. No, she thought affectionately, as pinkly fragrant as summer roses and as gentle upon the eye. Doonan, seated beside them, seemed even more massive and hard-muscled by contrast, a great shambling creature, clumsy as a bear. Yet there was no mistaking his pride in Rosa and the babe and his tenderness for them. Emrys, scrubbed and polished and in his Sunday best, was scarce recognisable without the veiling of stone dust. His hair shone white as snow, his cheeks burnished red as apples, the skin drawn so tight from rubbing that it seemed it must split apart as widely as his smile at being one of the Doonan family. He was so proud to be seen with them, Rebecca thought, that it was a joy to see it.

At the rear of the church she saw Emily marshalling her small flock of pupils, and marvelled anew at the control she had over them, for she appeared never to raise her voice nor threaten punishment. Perhaps her own serenity and gentle encouragement inspired them, too, for well-earned praise is always more incentive than the goad. Dafydd seemed well in control, already standing a full head and shoulders above the rest, his calm authority giving firm promise of the man he would become. Dr Peate had been pleased to receive confirmation that he would enter for the scholarship, and she knew that Elwyn Morris would support Dafydd every step of the way. He could have no better friend or mentor, and none as quietly proud of his achievements. Elwyn's daughter, Haulwen, dark-eyed and as brashly exuberant as he was self-effacing, waved cheerfully to Rebecca, and Rebecca, smiling, waved back. Thomas Turner, Betty's son, catching a glimpse of them seated in the pew, beamed importantly, telling any who would listen that they were his kith and kin until shushed into silence by Dafydd. Thomas subsided with good grace, smile still wide, freckles stippled as a trout's under his thatch of red hair.

Wherever Rebecca glanced there were friends and acquaintances: Dr Burrell and Dr Mansel, elegant in their gentlemen's finery; a scowling Ezra the Box and Dic Jenkins, his lantern-jawed apprentice; Tom Butler and Phoebe, in her best grey coal-scuttle bonnet, with Ossie, face seamed as a walnut, seated beside them; Sophie's friend, Hannah, together with her husband, the cartwright from Nottage; and Ben Clatworthy, the farrier and smith, uncomfortable in his Sunday best; Peter Rawlings and the harbour master, Ayde-Buchan, from the port, and vestrymen and tradesmen, artisans and labourers, all willing and eager to honour Stenner and give him their friendly support. It was a day that he would never forget, Rebecca thought. It would live bright in the memory.

There was a sudden murmur of excitement as Robert Knight appeared from the vestry, austerely authoritative in his clerical dress. The murmur was guiltily stifled at his severe glance over the rims of his eyeglasses, all unseemly whispering quelled.

'I have three splendid duties to perform this morning,' he began expansively. 'Three presentations which will give me and, I dare to hope you, the greatest personal pleasure.'

Three? Surprise rippled like a breeze through a cornfield, and speculation grew.

Robert Knight held up a hand to admonish them, then strode back towards the vestry, drawing the heavy velvet curtain aside. 'First,' he said, 'it is my privilege to present to you your new curate, the Reverend Richard Turberville, who will become friend and comforter to you all, as he has been to those at Maudlam this many a long year.'

Richard Turberville stepped awkwardly into the light, a pale etiolated figure, smiling, and gazing around him abstractedly as if not quite certain that he had strayed into the right place. He was a shambling, loose-limbed fellow, with his long equine face, untidy and unprepossessing, and the congregation stared

278

at him in disbelief. Yet, when he spoke, the power and resonance of his voice, his very simplicity, stilled all doubts. Here was a man of God and a man of the people, a man to respect and love.

Robert Knight's well prepared eulogy of his young curate's achievements, his high academic qualifications and experience, was listened to in polite silence. Robert Knight was preaching to the converted. Richard Turberville's quiet words had struck to the very heart of things, and to the hearts of those present. It had brought him acceptance. His shy smile for Ruth was one of gentle devotion, as much a promise as his promise to those he was committed to serve. Ruth, with treacherous tears in her eyes, smiled back, her love for him proved before all. He had brought her triumphantly through a darkness deeper than the Valley of the Shadow of Death. Given her new life and hope. He would offer such hope to others, sharing their sorrows and joys, giving always of himself, sparing himself nothing. It would be both joy and privilege to walk beside him. When he came to sit beside Ruth, he took her hand in his and held it firmly, as though her very touch gave him that strength he needed and as if he would never let it go.

There was a satisfied silence in the church, then an air of growing expectancy as Robert Knight cleared his throat, to announce importantly, 'My second presentation is to a man whose bravery and public spirited defence of a helpless woman and child has stirred the admiration of us all. He risked his life to defend them, without thought of the dangers or hope of reward. The vestrymen of the three hamlets have been so impressed by his bravery that they have agreed to give him a not inconsiderable sum of money, as a material means to show their appreciation. In addition, there is to be a silver cup, suitably inscribed, to mark the occasion. I call upon the gentleman in question, Abel George Stenner, to come forward.'

Stenner, so pale and trembling that he appeared to be on the verge of fainting, had to be helped to his feet by Joshua. He glanced about him wildly, as though seeking some means of escape, but Betty Turner squeezed his hand to ease its coldness and murmured some words of affectionate pride. Yet, for a while, he stood numbed and unmoving, until Thomas Turner's voice rang out uninhibited before all, tense with pride and excitement, childishly clear.

'He will be my father! He has promised! He is the best man I know!'

Neither Emily nor Dafydd sought to quieten him, and the laughter from the congregation was spontaneous and kind, with no hint of reproach. George Stenner smiled involuntarily then laughed aloud and, forgetting his nervousness, walked with pride and confidence to where Robert Knight stood waiting.

The rector held out a hand, smiling broadly, and repeating delightedly, so that all might hear and take note, 'He is the best man I know! There you have it. The perfect tribute; the perfect speech, and made publicly by one who has reason to know. My well rehearsed speech is superfluous, sir,' he said, eyes twinkling, 'for one cannot improve upon perfection. Brief. To the point. From the heart. To follow it would be an impertinence. I will, however, call upon another to make the presentation, one more closely involved than I. I ask Mrs Rosa Doonan to come and present the awards.'

Rosa came forward, pink with pleasure, and holding Joy in her arms. The rector solemnly took the infant from her as a vestryman handed her the leather pouch of coins and the engraved cup to present. Rosa had not been forewarned and had no speech ready, but the few words she spoke were painfully honest, and no others were needed.

'I thank you, sir, from the bottom of my heart, for Joy and for me. You are the best of men and the bravest of men.' She kissed him warmly, and without affectation before all, Cavan Doonan's loud rumble of praise and agreement overshadowing the gentler approval shown. Betty Turner was crying openly and without shame, and Rebecca felt Joshua's grip tighten upon her fingers, for he was as moved with pride as she, as Rosa and Joy returned to their place, and Stenner came to sit once more beside them.

Robert Knight, beaming benificently upon the congregation, held up a hand for silence, declaring as the cheerful murmuring subsided, 'Now to the third presentation of the day, and one in which I have to declare a personal interest. I refer, as many of you will know, to the presentation to Mrs Rebecca Stradling,

280

wife of our constable, Joshua Stradling, and mother of my godson, John Jeremiah.'

Rebecca, shocked and briefly taken aback, glanced enquiringly to Joshua for enlightenment, but he merely smiled and helped her to her feet, thrusting her determinedly towards the justice, who was by now smiling so broadly that his jaw muscles must have ached.

His protuberant brown eyes were soft with mischievous affection behind his lenses, his amusement plain, as he declared, 'It is the wish of the vestrymen and the entire population of the three hamlets that we honour you for the good you have done, ma'am. You have provided us with a schoolroom and an excellent and dedicated teacher in Miss Emily Randall, and have helped those in need in countless ways, oftimes, unknown, seeking neither recognition nor praise.'

Rebecca, flushed and clearly discomfitted, made to demur, but he continued unabashed, 'I have chosen a friend and admirer of yours, ma'am, to make the presentation.'

Rebecca glanced about her uncertainly as the justice, admirably straight-faced, beckoned Ezra Evans from his pew and bade him stand beside her. Ezra, bustling with sly importance, thrust himself forward, little ferret face undeniably pleased, teeth bared in an ingratiating smile. 'Mrs Stradling, ma'am.'

'Mr Evans, sir.'

The exchange was hesitantly made as two of the older vestrymen came from behind the red velvet curtain that screened off the vestry, carrying a wooden cradle with the careful reverence it deserved. Rebecca could not help exclaiming aloud at the sheer beauty of it; the superb matching and graining of the wood, its flawless sheen and the exquisite artistry of the carving. A labour of love indeed.

'Why, Mr Evans!' she declared with honesty.'It is the most beautiful cradle I have ever seen! What care you have lavished upon it. What weeks and months of careful work. I have never seen its like.'

'Nor will you, ma'am.' Ezra's voice was low, meant for her ears alone, 'for it is carved with special pride and love. I will not carve another.'

'It will be a joy for my son, but not for him alone, sir, but for countless generations to come. It will be treasured, sir, a family heirloom.' She reached towards him unselfconsciously and settled an impulsive kiss upon his cheek. Colour flooded his sallowness of skin as he grunted and nodded curtly, then sniffed and cleared his throat.

'It comes, Rebecca, with the gratitude and affection of all in the three hamlets,' Robert Knight said quietly, 'for each and every one has contributed some small sum.'

'Then I am grateful, sir, and will treasure it always, as I shall treasure the generosity of spirit that inspired the gift. It will remind me always of my friends of the three hamlets, wherever I may be.'

'I hope, ma'am, that you will long remain among us,' Robert Knight said briskly, 'and Constable Stradling, too, for his selfless work for the cottagers and his defence of us cannot be overstated. We of the three hamlets owe him a debt of real gratitude.' He glanced slyly towards the pew where Joshua was seated, adding, 'Even if we sometimes appear slow to acknowledge such a debt.'

Joshua's lips curved into an appreciative smile as he met Robert Knight's amused glance, mocking and faintly challenging. Behind him he thought he heard Peter Rawlings' familiar bellow of laughter turned discreetly into a cough, but could not be sure.

'Since we are so fortuitously assembled,' the rector continued, 'and in a mood of friendship and celebration, it behoves us to bow our heads in prayer and thanksgiving to God, from Whom all such love and blessings flow. He is here among us. An honoured guest. Shall we offer Him now our gratitude and humble devotion.'

Those within the church were filled with a warmth of fellowship, a kinship that would spill over into their daily lives, and those who knew Joshua and Rebecca best were grateful that their generosity and service to the three hamlets had been publicly recognised, and the debt owed to them partially repaid. The celebrations held in their honour and in Stenner's at the Crown Inn promised to be a relaxed and joyous affair, and even the presence of the cantankerous Ezra would not be allowed to spoil it although, to some, his temporary mellowness seemed even harder to bear.

It proved opportunity, too, for another. One who had watched and waited and seen Dr Mansel's and Dr Burrell's bustling arrival at the church from his concealed vantage point in the dunes. With the house emptied of all but unarmed servants, and those upon the highways and byways relaxed and in festive mood, Curtis would be unsuspecting and unguarded. There was little enough time to strike, but strike he must, or bear the consequences.

Chapter Twenty-three

Joshua could not avoid attending the party which the justice and the vestrymen had arranged at the Crown Inn. Since it was to honour Rebecca and George Stenner, he felt doubly committed. Nothing short of the direst catastrophe would have excused him, and he was human and fallible enough to pray that he might be spared that. There were unsolved crimes enough in the hamlets and he was not sanguine that his errand to Porlock would yield any fresh clues. At least it would remove him from the justice's censure, however briefly. The trouble was that it would also remove him from Rebecca and John Jeremiah and the comforts of shared bed and home. As a young unfettered constable, a few short years ago, he would have welcomed such a diversion and counted it an adventure. Now he looked upon it as a penance to be borne. He was growing old and settled, he thought, amused, a regular stick in the mud! Responsibilities sobered him. Once he would have risked life and limb without caution. Indeed, the very thought of danger would have spurred him to wilder excesses. Yet now his thought was all for Rebecca and his son and how such heedlessness would affect them. He did not know whether, in his work as constable, such awareness was a curse or a blessing. The trouble was that, when he discovered the answer, it might be too late.

Peter Rawlings, seeing how disconsolately Joshua was drinking his ale and standing apart from the cheerful hubbub around him, walked over to try and lighten his mood.

'I should have thought to see you wildly elated, sir, euphoric even,' he chivvied, good-humouredly, 'since the justice rates you so highly. What was it he called you? Self-sacrificing? A stalwart defender? A credit to the three hamlets and yourself?' He grinned mischievously. 'My life, Joshua, I was so moved that I could scarcely restrain myself from weeping.'

'Then it did not deter you from laughing aloud,' Joshua said dryly.

'It was the unexpectedness of it that unnerved me,' Rawlings admitted, not a whit deterred. 'Our usual lot is to be the justice's whipping boys – to bear the full force of his wrath! I expected to see you canonised on the spot!'

'Martyred more like!'

They laughed companionably, and Joshua glanced towards Robert Knight who was deep in conversation with Emily.

'You had best tell me what you have learned of the smugglers,' he urged Rawlings, 'for I must see the justice before I leave for Porlock. He is sure to catechise me and blame me, whatever occurs, whether I am absent or present!'

'When do you leave?'

'Tomorrow, early, tide and winds permitting.'

'And you will return when?'

'As soon as ever I am able, believe it! The minute my work is done, although I fear it is naught but a wild goose chase!'

'Then it is to be hoped that you will return to join in mine! That venture, too, depends upon the tide. I have set one of my excisemen among the smugglers to gain intelligence of their movements.'

'With success?'

'Some. It is certain that they will move in four days time when the tide is right and the moon full. I have men and guns enough to halt them, and the justice's authority. I would welcome your aid, Joshua, as in the past.'

Joshua nodded. 'I will work with you, if I am able.' He hesitated, glancing about him cautiously before asking quietly, 'Do you know who organises the smuggling? The man who is at the centre of it?' He glanced involuntarily towards where Ezra Evans stood, tankard in hand, listening to one of the vestrymen and smiling unctuously.

'No! Ezra is not involved!' Rawlings exclaimed, grinning, 'And I thank God for it, else we would be deprived of carpenter and undertaker both! No, he has neither the wit nor means to plan on such a scale.'

'Who, then?'

'Hutchings, my informant, cannot yet prove it, but from what he has learnt, a former associate and henchman of Hardee, the wrecker at Sker.'

'Dear God!' Joshua exclaimed, so loudly that the justice, startled, turned to look at him reprovingly and he subsided into shamed silence. 'Hardee?' he persisted less vehemently. 'But surely all his men were taken, captured and hanged after the wrecking of the *San Lorenzo*?'

'It seems not. Hutchings is sure that they were in some way connected either through kinship or past dealings. But how and when he cannot say.'

'But there is no question of wrecking?' Joshua demanded, disturbed.

'None. The full moon would work against it. That is not to say that his hands are free from blood,' he added soberly, 'for Hardee dealt in both. When greed is the lure, it is a small step from smuggling to plundering and murder.'

Memory of those innocents clubbed and drowned in cold blood as they struggled ashore at Sker silenced and set a blight upon them both.

'I had best be returning to the port,' Rawlings said heavily, 'but first I must pay my respects to Rebecca and take leave of her and my other friends.'

'The justice and Ezra will surely appreciate it,' declared Joshua, tongue in cheek. 'If you hurry you might catch them together and double your pleasure.'

Rawlings glanced across to where the unlikely couple stood, apparently deep in earnest conversation. 'I am not sure that I do not find the justice's lavish praise of you, and Ezra's good humour, more sinister than their usual abrasiveness,' Rawlings ventured gloomily. 'It destroys the proper order of things.'

Joshua said, grinning, 'Ezra and the justice are a law unto themselves, that is half their charm and half their aggravation.'

'Then you are lucky,' Rawlings exclaimed feelingly. 'They offer me only the aggravation! They seem to have infiltrated every aspect of my life!'

'No more than mine!' Joshua countered. 'Ezra has carved the very bed I lie on, and now my son's cradle. There is reminder of him everywhere, even in sleep! It seems I can never escape him!'

Rawlings glanced towards where the justice stood, tense and choleric, seemingly laying down the law to a bemused Ezra. 'I should like to be an eavesdropper on that little exchange,' he murmured, amused. 'What do you suppose it is about?'

'I doubt that he is ordering a marriage bed or a cradle.'

'No, unlikely, "Rawlings conceded." A coffin, perhaps?' he suggested, hopefully.

'If it comes to longevity, then my money is on the justice,' Joshua said, 'but if they are haggling a price, then I have to plump for Ezra.'

'I had best be away,' Rawlings declared. 'From the murderous looks the justice is giving me it might well be *my* death they are plotting!' He shook Joshua's hand, murmuring quietly, 'I hope that things go well for you in Porlock.'

'And I return that same hope for your venture.'

'It will need more than hope, or even the justice's prayers,' Rawlings muttered wryly. 'It will need a small miracle!'

'Then I wish you that, too,' Joshua said.

The lone rider taking the Clevis Hill to Dr Mansel's house was well set up a fine chestnut marc and, from his clothing, clearly a man of substance. His coat and breeches were of impeccable cut, his riding boots of softest leather, and his tiered cape elegantly modish. None would have mistaken him for anything but a gentleman and, from the careless arrogance of his bearing, he was not only wellborn, but accustomed to wielding authority over others. As for his colouring and features, it was difficult to say, for his cape collar was deliberately raised high and his hair hidden beneath a beaver hat that shadowed his face. From his figure, he was a man in his prime, for he had not the slenderness of the young nor yet the shrunken brittleness of the old.

The streets, as he had expected, were but lightly peopled, for the affair at the church, and at the Crown Inn, had commanded everyone's attention and relaxed the most vigilant guard. He had rehearsed his role well and knew exactly what he would claim, were he halted and asked to give account of himself. He was a native Londoner, searching for a suitable house in the area where he might first settle then bring his family. His wife, a delicate creature and an invalid from a wasting disease, was in need of bracing air to halt the decline and put new strength into her lungs. Such was the advice of the eminent physician and surgeon who had long attended her. He had written such confirmation and instruction, and asked him to deliver it to whichever local doctor would undertake to accept her as a patient. The letter was genuine, as were the letters of credence he bore, since he was a man of wealth and could buy or command the services of others.

Nothing had been neglected, nothing omitted, his itinerary planned from start to finish, and all tickets and documents scrupulously retained. Even were he to be stopped by someone in authority, he knew that there was little to fear. He had covered his tracks. However expensive and time consuming, such precautions were essential in order to survive. Survival was all. If others must be sacrificed to ensure it, then it was no more than natural law, the law of the jungle – Kill or be killed. Man was a predatory creature. The veneer of civilisation thin. Beneath the skin he was feral, ruthless, bloody in tooth and claw. He took a hand from the reins to pull up the collar of his cape, then rode confidently through the pillared gateway of Dr Mansel's house and along the stones of the carriageway.

Hell and damnation! he thought bitterly, I have been led into a trap. Betrayed! In a moment fury all but unnerved him, and his hand tightened upon the pistol, uncertain whether to protect himself or flee. The groom who came from the stables to take his horse was openly armed, and another, with a rifle, stood guard at the door.

'Your business, sir?' The question was abruptly made.

'I seek the services of a doctor.' He did not dismount.

'Your business, sir?' The question was repeated more abrasively.

'What affair is that of yours, sir?' His outrage was convincing. 'Have I wandered into so lawless a place that an honest man must be challenged if he seeks a doctor? I'll swear that I have never known the like of it! Let me pass, sir, else it will be the justices you are facing!'

'It is upon the justice's instruction that I am armed, and there are more within. Now, sir, if you will slowly dismount,' he ordered curtly.

'Good God, man! Are you deaf? An imbecile? I will not

be subject to such indignity, treated like a common criminal! Call for the doctor. I demand it! I have here introduction from my own physician, proofs of identity and credence. You may inspect them, if you so wish.'

The guard, plainly confused, inspected the documents briefly, looking to the armed groom for support, but finding none. 'Well, sir,' he murmured hesitantly, 'it seems that your papers are in order, your documents and such, but I have no authority to let you pass, merely to detain you, should you arouse suspicion.'

'And do I?' The question was arrogantly posed, his scorn lacerating. 'I come with higher credentials and from higher authority than that which you serve!' He added contemptuously, 'Let the physician decide! This letter will bring him. Believe it!' He thrust the paper angrily at the guard.

'There is no physician here, sir,' he admitted, discomfitted. 'Neither Dr Burrell nor Dr Mansel.'

'Then keep the letter!' he commanded brusquely. 'Show it upon their returning! They will learn what insult I have been forced to bear, what ignorant persecution. Someone will pay for it and pay dearly!' He reined his horse furiously and with a look of disgust was away along the carriageway, stones flying beneath his horse's hooves. He rode, straight-backed and determined, although he felt the raw thudding of his heart and heard its anguished pulsing. Sweat beaded his lip and brow as he first awaited the cry to stop, then the crack of a bullet, searing flesh, splintering bone. There was no cry, no bullet. He had convinced them. He was safe. He had bluffed them, and won. He felt no elation, nothing but an emptiness of relief, an exhaustion that drained him of feeling. Yet he dared not stop. It was but one hurdle overcome, there would be others. Upon an impulse, he wrenched the black hood from the pocket of his coat and hurled it far into the depths of the shrubbery. Now if he were halted none would find evidence upon him, nothing save the innocent credentials of a gentleman.

He hurtled so savagely through the gateway and out on to the highway that he all but collided with John Burrell returning from the Crown Inn in the curricle.

'God Almighty!' Burrell strove to right the delicate carriage, for it was swaying and shaking so violently that he was all but hurled to the roadside. He had barely caught a glimpse of the horseman, and was aware only that he was a stranger, but that did not prevent him from uttering a fierce curse upon all such imbeciles as he strove to soothe the carriage horse, and drove within. Should he return to the inn, and warn Joshua? He swiftly clambered down from the curricle and questioned the guard. The letter he was handed bore the hallmark of authenticity. He could not doubt its legitimacy nor the bearer's honest need. That the man had been so incensed and resentful that he had hurtled so recklessly away seemed proof more of innocence than guilt. Would *he* not have behaved in like fashion, if so provoked? Most certainly, and sworn never to return! No, there was nothing to command Joshua's attention nor the justice's. He would wait upon the stranger's return, then render him full explanation and apology. That there would be messages aplenty within, he did not doubt, and urgent calls for his services. At least Mansel might relax a while longer at the Crown Inn among friends. He was deserving of that. With a sigh Burrell walked within the house and all else was swiftly forgot.

Joshua and Rebecca, undressing by candlelight in their bedroom at Thatched Cottage, knew that pleasurable exhaustion which comes with wining and dining among friends. The hour was late, for they had lingered too long, reluctant to see the day ending.

Stenner, too, in his loft above the stables, stayed wakeful. Yet he felt no exhaustion. Indeed, it seemed to him that he might never relax or sleep again, for every nerve and sinew seemed rawly exposed, his awareness painfully heightened. Oh, it had been a day to remember, he thought. The presentation and reception and all, and he so unsuspecting. He had given the bag of coins to Joshua for safekeeping, but the silver cup he could not part with yet awhile. It was a foolishness, perhaps, to keep so valuable a thing in so impoverished a place and one without protection. Yet its value lay not in what it might fetch, for he would never sell it, not even were he forced to his last crust, and homeless and starving. Its value lay in that he had earned it honestly and in defence of others. It was the first thing of worth that he had owned. It marked his bravery for ever, the justice had said.

Yet it marked more than that; it marked the change from being a pauper and of no account to being like others, one of a community. A community of free men who might come and go at will, not bound for ever in bondage to another. Oh, but he relished such freedom now! The freedom to choose where to work and live, the freedom, if he chose, to build his own 'house-in-a-night', with none to prevent him. He could find some wild forsaken place, a place with a stream nearby perhaps and good fertile soil, unwanted by any other. Then, if he laboured unceasingly by lantern light and roofed it by daybreak, he might rightfully take it for his own. More, by throwing an axe to all points of the compass, he could claim all that land within its fall. One day, perhaps. There was no limit to what he might achieve, what he might own. For the moment he was content to be here at Thatched Cottage, a man respected by others and, more than that, loved by Betty Turner and Thomas. Had not the boy cried out for all to hear that he was to be George Stenner's son, and that he was the best man he knew? Memory of it brought a smile to George Stenner's gaunt face, but a thickness to his throat. A mingling of emotions. The boy had spoken honestly and from love, unashamed to show his feelings. Yet Stenner himself had not yet learned the words or the way. In entrusting herself and Thomas to his future care, Betty Turner had given him the most precious gift she owned. Stenner's hand lingered lovingly upon the cold smoothness of the silver cup, fingers reverently tracing the inscription that he knew by heart, but would never read. He knew what he must do. Tomorrow he would go to Betty and place the cup in her hands, saying that it was a wedding gift to her. He would ask her to be guardian of it until the day when Thomas could properly read the inscription upon it, then, it would be rightfully his. It would give the boy pleasure, he knew, and something to strive for. Yes, that was what he would do. His own words would be poor and halting, but the words upon the cup would be the words of a scholar, and would stand for ever. Thomas would, one day, understand them and be proud; proud as he was today at the church. He hoped that Betty would understand the meaning of what he did, for he could not explain it properly.

291

The cup was the only thing of value that he had ever owned until their coming. Yes, that was the nub of it. Until their coming.

Rebecca snuggled hard against her husband in the big double bed, which Ezra had carved, put her arm about Joshua and sank deeper into the comfort of the goose-down mattress. It had been the most unexpected of days, and the most wonderful and satisfying. The tribute to Stenner had moved her deeply, and the presentation of the cradle from all of the cottagers had made her realise how vital a part of her life and Joshua's the folk of the three hamlets had become. Their affection had been tangible, its warmth as comfortingly protective as a cloak wrapped about her to keep her from the cold harshness of everyday ills.

Ezra had excelled himself in the carving of John Jeremiah's cradle. He had inscribed the child's name upon it, and wreaths of fruit and flowers and plump, mischievous cherubs, not unlike John Jeremiah himself. It had surprised her that the little undertaker had shown such skill and artistry but, more than that, such unrestrained humour and sensitivity of touch. Perhaps we saw in people only the surface flaws and not the kindness and hidden depths beneath. She made silent amends for all the times that she had maligned and vilified the poor man, promising that she would treat him more respectfully in future. Should his cantankerous ways and his parsimony provoke her, she would think of John Jeremiah's cradle, and Ezra's unblemished soul in its beauty! In the morning, as soon as ever she was able, she would drive the gig to Rosa's cottage, and ask if she would accept John Jeremiah's old oak cradle as a gift to Joy.

Rebecca's mind returned to the cheerful excitement of the celebration at the Crown Inn. How light-hearted and pleasant an affair it had been, with the music of the fiddlers and the wining and dining and dancing. Stenner and Betty had enjoyed had as much as any present, relaxed and happy to be among so many admirers and friends. It had pleased her that Illtyd had come to join in the revels and that he had brought with him his lovingly hand-carved gift of a toy for John Jeremiah. He must have spent many a long hour carving and honing it to perfection, she thought affectionately. None could have done it better. It was a perfectly detailed replica of Jeremiah's fish-cart and cob, exquisitely shaped and painted, down to the very lettering upon the side of the cart. It was a gift to cherish as much as Ezra's fine cradle, and she had been lost for words to express her pleasure in it. She would value it as much as John Jeremiah would, she had promised, and it would be loving reminder of Jeremiah and Sophie and Illtyd all the days of her life.

It had pleased her even more that Illtyd had given to Rosa and Joy a gift as thoughtfully chosen and sensitively carved. A perfect copy, in miniature, of Emrys's cart, with the fat Welsh cob between the shafts, and the unmistakable figures of Emrys and Doonan seated, side by side, in cheerful companionship. So alive did it seem, and so droll, that even Emrys and Doonan had been reduced to tears of helpless laughter, and it had been examined and admired as unreservedly as Ezra's cradle.

Yes, Rebecca thought, nuzzling affectionately against Joshua, it had been a marvellous day, all the better for being so unexpected. A day to recall with pleasure and optimism should life ever again grow cruelly harsh. She could not believe that it would ever be so again. The bad days were ended. There would be no more hurt. With Joshua beside her, and John Jeremiah secure in Ezra's fine cradle, naught could disturb the comfortable tranquillity of it, their life and living. Rebecca knew that she was truly happy. There was not a thing in her life that she regretted, yearned for, or would change. Her mind was still aglow with the warmth of her happiness when she drifted into sleep.

Early upon the following morning, Stenner drove Joshua to the port in the gig to sail with the tide. Joshua had earlier booked passage to Porlock upon a small passenger vessel, *The Somerset Maid*, and was grateful that wind and weather were set fair. The journey by road would have proved long and arduous, with time and patience wasted in finding rooms at the inns upon the way. His quest, he knew, was an unlikely one and he held no great hopes of success at his journey's end. The likeness of the dead girl was all he possessed and the word of Mark Gould that he recognised her as a Miss Yeo, a nursery nurse, in the employment of one, Augustus Scurlock. Gould's description of Scurlock had been masterly; aged between thirty and thirty-five years, with dark eyes, pallid complexion and of middle height. He was slight of build, with fair hair, balding at the crown. From all that Gould had inferred the pallidness came from a surfeit of night-time gambling and other less salubrious pursuits. He was, the gentleman from Porlock had insisted, a less than savoury character, one not to be trusted. In short, a cheat and a fraud, and best avoided. Joshua had no wish to avoid him, rather to seek him out, but, as Gould had declared that Scurlock had been forced through his devious financial dealings to flee the county, the prospect of finding him seemed remote. Should Scurlock wish to continue to live by his wits, then he would certainly change his name and remove himself as far as possible from his creditors and the law. Scurlock's wife, Gould had described as 'an exquisite creature. A gentlewoman, certainly, and a perfect English rose.' The only mystery seemed to be why a woman of sensibility and breeding should have stayed loyal to such a man!

When Joshua disembarked from *The Somerset Maid*, he first found a convenient tavern where he might wash and refresh himself, then he enquired of the landlord as to the nearest livery stables. There he hired himself a gig and, armed with Gould's address and the advice of a knowledgeable ostler, he set off for the gentleman's house.

Gould had been flatteringly pleased to see him, bidding him leave the gig to his groom and urging him cheerfully within, plying him with immediate offers of wine and refreshment and a room for the rest of his stay. He would not take refusal, but was insistent that Joshua must stay, claiming that he was sadly in want of company and that the inns were foetid and overcrowded, and that the landlords would fleece him to boot! He seemed altogether more lively and cheerful than when Joshua had first met him at Weare House, his languidness and pallor gone.

When Joshua enquired as to his health, he grimaced, confessing good-humouredly, 'The sea bathing did not kill me, sir, nor did it cure me. The cure lay in my detestation of the place and the primitive ritual! I had to summon the energy to flee.'

'Then I am glad you survived, sir, and accept your offer of hospitality most gladly.'

Gould's bluff face was alive with humour beneath his grizzled eyebrows and hair, as he declared, 'You will wine and dine well, sir, believe it! Self-denial has never been my god. I see no virtue in inflicting misery upon oneself and others. It may purge the body, but it shrivels the soul.'

'You do not consider that it might stand you in good stead in the afterlife, sir?' Joshua asked wickedly.

'That I do not!' Gould said emphatically. 'One must take advantage of the here and now. God would not wish it otherwise.'

'He would not, sir?'

'It is my firm opinion that He has the most exquisite sense of humour, of the ridiculous even, else He would not have created man! The chances are that all who fast and live exemplary lives may be free to do so for eternity, since it gives them pleasure. That is their ideal of heaven.'

'And the rest?'

'Well, we shall see.' He laughed delightedly, 'Yes, sooner or later, we shall see. Meanwhile, I shall continue to celebrate my good fortune as, I trust, will you, sir. I see little virtue in denying oneself all the good things which God so thoughtfully provides, in order to gain sly credit in the hereafter. We are agreed, sir?'

'We are agreed,' Joshua said, smiling broadly. 'As a philosophy, it appeals to me.' Then he declared, more soberly, 'But you have not enquired as to my mission here.'

Gould looked startled, then confused. 'But you have come in answer to my letter, sir. I thought I had made myself clear.'

'I received no letter,' Joshua said, bewildered. 'I have come on my own account to search for the employer of the murdered girl, Augustus Scurlock.'

'Then you might have saved yourself the trouble, Constable.'

'How, sir?'

'It was of Scurlock that I wrote to you. He has been arrested, sir, and awaits trial on charges of fraud and theft. Worse, it seems that he was guilty of making a bigamous marriage.'

'And the woman, sir? The gentlewoman you described as his wife?'

'She was the real reason why I wrote to you, to make explanation.'

'She was not involved in Scurlock's dealings? Did not suspect?'

'Indeed not!' Gould shook his head, saying emphatically, 'She is grieved beyond all endurance, so shocked and distressed that it was feared that she might lose her reason. Her family have closed ranks around her to protect her. There is some further tragedy, it seems, ugly and unspecified, for none will speak of it.'

'You know this family, sir?' Joshua asked incredulously.

'*Of* them, certainly. I had business dealings with the young woman's family in times past. Her father and I were acquaintance, but they removed for a time to London and I lost touch, sir, as people do.'

'Then you have no idea as to where I might find her? Where I might start searching?'

Gould looked at him sharply, then smiled, before admitting ruefully, 'I had forgotten that the letter did not reach you, Constable Stradling. No, the truth is that they have rented a small manor house in the vicinity while awaiting the young woman's recovery. They owned it in earlier days, and felt that its solitude and the country air might restore her.'

'This mystery, sir?' Joshua asked urgently. 'Do you know the root of it? Tell me, I beg you!'

Gould, troubled by Joshua's intensity, shook his head, saying awkwardly, 'You had best ask her yourself, sir, since you have the authority of the law behind you.'

'If you will tell me, sir, where she may be found?'

'I will take you,' Gould said, 'and now, without delay, for it seems there is much at stake. It might serve you best if I make introduction.'

'Yes,' Joshua said. 'It will serve me best.'

Chapter Twenty-Four

It was some fifteen miles and more to the manor house, much
of it along deserted lanes and byways, and Joshua, seated
with Mark Gould within the small coach, had ample time
for reflection. To arrive unheralded upon a family desperate
to retain their privacy was intrusion enough. To force oneself
upon them, when already plagued by sickness and personal
grief, was the cruellest imposition. Despite Gould's offer to
make personal introduction to Andrew Fulmer, Joshua was
awkwardly ill at ease. At best, any explanation he might
make would reopen old wounds. At worst, it would make
the woman with whom Scurlock had lived more tortured in
mind, and sick both in flesh and spirit. Yet, whatever the cost,
he must find solution, if not here then from Augustus Scurlock
in his prison cell.

He fervently hoped that Scurlock's child was safe, here,
with her mother. It was a delicate matter, and one which
he must approach with the greatest discretion. There was
the added complication of the bigamous marriage, and the
child's bastardy. Whatever the outcome, there would be grief
in store, and decisions to be made, which would result in
further heartbreak, whether for the woman at the manor
or for Rosa and Doonan, Joshua could not be sure. There
was only one certainty, and that was that a woman had been
savagely murdered and that a child survived, unnamed and
unknown.

As the coach entered the pillared gateway to the manor
house Joshua felt a churning of sickness within, a cold misery.
He would have given much to return to Porlock, his task
completed. It was, he knew, only beginning, and he dared
not even speculate upon how it might end.

Mark Gould left Joshua seated disconsolately within the

297

coach, declaring that it would serve better were he to see Andrew Fulmer and make brief explanation of Joshua's presence and the reason for his visit. He did not know, he confessed, what his own reception might be, and Joshua had best prepare himself for outright rejection or cold incivility. When he returned, it was with a tall, grave-eyed man beside him, spare but elegant in dress and figure, the lines of tiredness and suffering etched deep upon his face.

Joshua descended from the coach, and the introductions were swiftly and awkwardly made.

'If you will come within, Constable Stradling,' Andrew Fulmer invited with tense civility, 'It will serve us better. My friend, Mr Gould, has told me of the reason for your visit, the death of some servant unknown to me, and in my daughter's employ.'

'If you would have me leave, sir, return to my coach?' Mark Gould offered quickly.

'No. It will not be necessary.' Fulmer's voice was clipped, his discomfort plain. 'I know you to be a man of discretion, sir, from our earlier dealings. There is naught that cannot be discussed openly. Scurlock's trial and imprisonment will soon enough make all common knowledge. I would rather the truth be known to a friend than rumour be spread by others.' He ushered Joshua and Gould within, motioning aside a footman, and emphasising that he had no wish to be disturbed, for his business with the gentlemen was of the greatest urgency. It would bear no interruption.

When they were seated within the spacious well-used library, a familiar masculine stronghold, Fulmer's manner seemed to thaw perceptibly, his anxiety lessened.

'What is it, Mr Stradling, that you would have me do?' he asked quietly. 'I confess that I can be of little help in this matter, but I will hear you out.'

'If you could identify this likeness, sir, put name to the young woman?' He produced the copy of Mansel's drawing.

'No!' With a quick movement Fulmer pushed it away, unseen. 'I have no knowledge of my daughter's servants or their affairs!' he exclaimed abruptly. 'I thought I had made myself clear!'

'Then your daughter, sir? Might she not assist me?'

'No, sir! There is no question of it. My daughter is gravely sick and in constant care of a physician. She is close to breakdown, sir. He would not allow it, and no more will I. Pamela must not be further distressed, I absolutely forbid it!'

'Then I had best seek identification from some other involved.'

'Such "involvements" are no longer my affair! I have neither stomach nor use for him!' Fulmer said savagely. 'He has ruined my daughter's life and all but ended my own. He may rot in hell, sir, for I would not lift a finger to help him!'

His distress was so painful that Joshua said awkwardly, 'I would spare you further hurt, sir, but there are questions I am forced to ask you.'

'Then I would ask you, Constable, to make them brief.'

'Your daughter, sir, has a child, I believe, a child which Scurlock fathered?'

Fulmer rose, chair grating harshly, to exclaim furiously, 'I do not see, sir, that it concerns you in any way! It can be of no relevance to your enquiry or any other.' He was so fiercely agitated that he was spluttering in his anger, and Gould, distressed, put out a hand to steady him. Fulmer shook him away brusquely, to mutter, 'Now, sir, if you will both leave. I have nothing more to say to you, nothing to discuss. You have outstayed your welcome!' He strode unsteadily to the library door, face drained of all colour, so painfully anguished that Joshua feared he would collapse. As his hand settled upon the doorknob, the library door was pushed abruptly open from without and a young woman entered, manner distraught, face ravaged with weeping.

'Tell them, Papa! Tell them the truth of it. I beg you, no more lies!' She stumbled and half fell, but before Joshua or Gould could hurry to help her Fulmer gathered her in his arms and carried her, distressed and all but fainting, to a chair, chafing her cold hands, trying helplessly to revive her. Unbidden, Gould poured some cognac from a decanter on a side table and hurried forward with glass in hand, watching anxiously as she supped it, relieved to see her colour returning.

'If you would have us leave, sir,' he murmured contritely.

'No, sir.' Her voice was strained, scarcely more than a whisper, but her eyes were imploring. 'I beg you will not go.

299

What has been done was to protect me. There is no more need.'
Her anxious glance was turned upon Fulmer. 'Show them the
letter, Papa, the demand for ransom.'

Fulmer walked soberly to a drawer of the library table,
head bowed and with shoulders hunched in defeat. Then he
produced a sealed envelope, handing it to Joshua. 'It is a
demand for one thousand pounds, sir!' his voice was bleak
with pain. 'Against the safe return of my granddaughter,
Pamela's child.'

'And the kidnapper, sir? The blackmailer?'

'Esther Yeo, a nursery maid in my service.' The anguished
admission came from Pamela Fulmer. 'I trusted her, could not
believe she would do her harm.'

'You have a likeness of the child? Can describe her?'

'I have a miniature, sir, painted on ivory. If you will allow
me to bring it. I would have no servant involved.'

Joshua nodded, 'If you feel strong enough, now, to go alone,
ma'am?'

'I have neither strength nor feeling, sir, and have been alone
this long time.' The words were painfully spoken. 'It is not
sickness that plagues me, but loss.'

Joshua, raw with compassion, watched her leave. 'You
believe, sir, that Scurlock is in some way involved? That he
has colluded in this abduction?'

Fulmer shook his head, saying wretchedly, 'I do not know
what to believe! I can offer no proof, no witness. But that he
is capable of it, I cannot deny.'

'Why, then, did not your daughter report the loss of the
child? The kidnapping?'

'She was distraught, Mr Stradling, as one would expect!' The
rebuke was sharp. 'As she said, she trusted the young woman.
Besides . . .' he faltered and broke off confusedly.

'Besides?' Joshua prompted harshly.

'Besides, Scurlock left upon the following day,' he admitted wearily. 'He abandoned her, knowing of her terror and
misery.'

'He left no word?' Joshua asked sharply.

'None. Pamela supposed that he had left to join the woman,
Yeo was it? And had taken her child.'

'Why, sir?'

300

'To cause her grief,' Fulmer said dully. 'Had I but known it, it was the pattern of her life, Constable: whoring, gaming, physical and mental abuse. There was no end to his depravity. He sought to degrade her as he degraded himself and others.'

'You did not suspect, sir?'

'No,' he said regretfully. 'She kept it well hid, from pride or misplaced loyalty, or perhaps she thought that he might harm or abduct the child, for he used it as a threat to silence her. I do not believe that any could know the full measure of her suffering. Had I known, or suspected even,' he faltered into silence, voice thickened with hurt.

'I do not believe, sir, that you have cause to reproach yourself,' Gould ventured quietly, 'for I'll own that I did not recognise your daughter nor associate her with you, meeting her only briefly and in her married name. None could have suspected, for she bore it with such fortitude.'

'And she has paid dearly for it now!' Fulmer exclaimed impassionedly. 'And I hope to God that he suffers as harshly! Scurlock is not even the shadow of a man. He is a monster! Inhuman! Were he not in gaol then I swear that I would seek him out and kill him for his savagery!'

Neither man could doubt that he meant it.

Joshua said urgently, 'The ransom note, sir, I must ask, before your daughter returns. How did it come into your possession? How was she contacted? Was there another? An earlier note?'

'Yes, it came by messenger on the day Scurlock defected, unable to face his creditors, those others whose lives he had ruined. But I cannot show it to you, Constable Stradling.' In answer to Joshua's probing look, he admitted bleakly, 'It so terrified and sickened her that she threw it into the fire, unable to bear sight of it. It was an obscenity, sir, the ramblings of a madman!'

'But the gist, Mr Fulmer? Give me the gist?' Joshua insisted. 'Quickly, sir, before your daughter's return, else I must ask in her presence!'

'The threat, Mr Stradling, was that the child would be hostage, tortured and starved and held in darkness. And should she break her silence, the child would be killed. There, he said bitterly, 'that is the gist of it. I can tell you no more.'

'How, then, were you made aware of it? The kidnapping, I mean?'

'She fled here, to Greycombe Manor, Constable Stradling, all but out of her mind with despair. Thinking, perhaps, to find a refuge, familiar and loved from childhood days. I cannot say why she came here. I can only speak of the terror which drove her.'

'But it would distance her not only from the kidnappers but from news of her child,' Joshua protested.

Andrew Fulmer shook his head, saying with honesty, 'I do not believe she could think rationally, sir. It was my rare good fortune that the manor is in my cousin's keeping – a distant kinsman, who was so concerned at her state of mind and failing health that he called in the local physician who, in turn, alerted me.'

'How does the kidnapper know her whereabouts? How does he contact her?' Joshua demanded.

'It was laid out in detail, in the first blackmail note she received.'

'The one she destroyed, sir?'

Fulmer nodded, blurting distressedly, 'It gave an address in Porlock, the local livery stables. All communications were directed there for safe keeping and all replies sent. It is no more than an accommodation address. A way for the owner to earn a living.'

'You are sure he is not involved?'

'I have defied the kidnappers,' Fulmer confessed, 'and made all known to the justices. It was a risk I was forced to take. I could not rest easy else. My daughter does not know of it, for were the child to be killed she would hold me culpable. She would cut herself off from the only help and affection she knows. I do not think she would survive it, no more would I.'

'I shall not speak of it, sir,' Joshua promised. 'You have my word upon it.'

'As mine, sir,' Gould confirmed.

'I have alerted the authorities, the justices, in all parts of the country where Scurlock lived or where he had business dealings, lest there be someone in his employ as corrupt and reckless as he.' He grimaced, adding despairingly, 'For all the good it may do, for I cannot hope to cover the whole countryside, nor guess the workings of so diseased a mind.'

'And the money, sir? The payment?' Joshua demanded. 'Where is it to be made?'

'I await instruction,' Fulmer confessed. 'But whatever the demand, whatever the amount, I shall pay it for Pamela's sake.'

'Miss Fulmer is an heiress in her own right?' Joshua asked hesitantly.

'Yes. She might have paid, and paid handsomely,' he admitted, 'but Scurlock made short shrift of her money as of all else. He claimed to have "invested" it, but bled her dry. It was provident that her grandfather set up a trust fund which may not be touched for another two years. She will not be in want, sir, not in my lifetime or after, nor the child, if she survives.' He turned apprehensively as Pamela Fulmer thrust open the door, her heightened colour and agitation returning now, some of that exquisite beauty which Gould had discerned and spoken of so admiringly to Joshua.

'Here, Mr Stradling, is the likeness of Alexandra, the miniature of which I spoke.' She placed it carefully into Joshua's hands, saying, voice low,' I cannot believe, sir, that my . . . that her father would do her harm. For all his faults he loved her, I am sure of it.'

Joshua looked at the miniature of the child, features so delicately painted, and so like the anguished face of the woman before him. 'I know where your child is, ma'am. She is safe and well, believe it. None shall harm her.'

Andrew Fulmer, like Gould, stood transfixed for a long moment, then hurried forward to support her as she swayed and then awkwardly fell.

John Burrell was about to set out for Nottage upon an urgent summons to Ben Clatworthy's forge, where his apprentice lad had suffered severe injury from a billhook he had been sharpening for a farmer upon the Downs. The message, delivered by an elderly cottager upon his pony, was garbled and hysterical, and the ancient who brought it had first to be soothed and calmed and treated for shock. Burrell had put the messenger into the gig and tied the pony behind it, declaring

303

good-humouredly that he would sooner sacrifice some of his brandy to revive the old fellow, else he would be treating not one patient, but two!

As the gig rounded the curve of the carriageway, a yard boy leapt out of the shrubbery, all sweat and agitation, forcing Burrell to draw in the reins fiercely and come to an urgent stop. The culprit was white-faced and trembling, and Burrell, who had feared that the boy's recklessness would hurl him under the wheels, was understandably furious. His muttered imprecations only made the boy's distress worse, and a good five minutes were wasted in accusation and tearful explanation before calm was restored.

''tis this, sir, that I was bringing!' the lad mumbled defensively. ''Twas why I bade you to halt!'

'What is it, boy?' Burrell demanded irritably. 'Some useless piece of old rag? A cloth thrown down by one of the gardeners or stable boys? Do not bother me with such trivia. I have an urgent case to attend!' He made to take up the reins again.

'No, sir!' The boy's cry of despair stilled him. ''Tis a hood. A black hood such as the masked man wears, him that set upon Mistress Doonan!'

'Dear God in heaven!' Burrell exclaimed. 'Give it to me, boy. Now! And say nothing to anyone. Keep your silence, else I shall know of it!

'Here,' he delved into his pocket and thrust a shilling into the boy's hand. 'If you keep your counsel there will be more upon my return. You understand?'

'Yes, sir. I understand.'

'But what will you do, sir?' the old man within the gig blurted. 'Clatworthy's young lad is mortally hurt. Scared and bleeding, he is, sir, bleeding like a stuck pig!' He stammered into embarrassed silence, mumbling, 'Begging your pardon, sir, for my forwardness. 'Tis no real business of mine and you would have a right to anger.'

'No,' Burrell said firmly, 'you do well to remind me, and your thought for the lad does you credit. I shall drive to the forge at once to tend him, have no fear. Then I shall drive to the justice's house, for Constable Stradling is away on business in Porlock.' He hesitated before warning, 'I have no need to remind you that the rule of silence also applies to you?'

'None, sir. I shall stay silent as the grave,' he grinned, murmuring sheepishly, 'my rudeness in speaking so hastily to you, Doctor, was from fear for another, for I am too old for fear on my own account! I do not indulge in idle gossip, believe me. It does too much harm.'

'A wise counsel,' Burrell confirmed, smiling, 'as I have cause to know.' He stirred the horse into life and set the gig in motion.

What a fool he had been to take the unknown visitor's claims at face value! It was a stupidity which might cost him and others dear. With Joshua away he could do nothing but take the hood to the justice as evidence, and confess his own regrettable part in the affair. He had been deplorably lax; criminally so. Whatever had possessed him? The celebrations at the church and at the Crown Inn had lulled him into an inertia, a false sense of security. Well, the justice would soon enough disabuse him. Or perhaps abuse him would be nearer the mark! Whatever strictures and contempt Robert Knight heaped upon him, they could be no more virulent than those he heaped upon himself. He could not even describe the man accurately, or give sensible account. The justice would redouble the guard upon Curtis, that much was clear, for it was plainly the stranger's aim to kill Curtis, since the earlier attempt had failed. What was it that the livery owner knew? If he ever regained consciousness there was no certainty that he would be able to speak. His brain might well be affected or his memory gone. Burrell, glimpsing the forge ahead and the anxious, brawny figure of Ben Clatworthy waiting, was sure of his competence to help here. It was for Rosa and the child he feared now. Should danger come to them from his foolish credulity then he could never forgive himself. Past suffering had been forced upon him by others. To be the cause of it to other innocents would be more punishment than he could bear.

When Joshua and Gould prepared to leave Greycombe Manor, all arrangements for the return to Newton had been discussed and agreed. Pamela Fulmer had recovered much of her vitality, but her febrile excitement at news of her child's safety seemed to Joshua as dangerous to her state of mind as her earlier despair. There was a brittleness about her, a fever of agitation, which deeply concerned him; a pressure which might cause her to crack. Fear and uncertainty had held her emotions in check while there was need. Now, with a release of such anguish, he feared that she might break down completely, unable to face the realities ahead. The journey to Newton would prove hardship enough to one in delicate health, and the reunion with her child would take added toll. Yet she was insistent that she must accompany Joshua and her father to fetch the child, and neither the physician's advice nor Fulmer's entreaties would sway her.

At last, consent was reluctantly given and preparations made. They would sail upon the tide, late upon the morrow, for Joshua still had to travel the long distance to the gaol and back to interview Scurlock. The authorities had been warned of the urgent need for passage for all three and the reason for secrecy, and the justices had acted swiftly. The livery stables at Porlock would be constantly watched and, one of the justices' men had been secretly placed among the grooms and ostlers. Any seeking to make demand or hoping to collect his bounty would be immediately apprehended and charged. The wheels were already in motion.

At his own insistence, Gould had given Joshua use of his coach to take him to the prison where Scurlock was held, and offered to accompany him. They had talked long into the night after returning from Greycombe Manor, and Joshua had confided all to his companion, for he was troubled almost as much by Rosa's and Doonan's plight as that of Pamela Fulmer. Whatever had possessed him to plead with the justice to allow them to foster the child? It had been an aberration, a foolish indulgence. How could he have been so crass? So grievously mistaken! Gould tried, in vain, to set things in perspective for him and to offer his reassurance. The child was safe, he insisted. That was what really mattered. Had she been sent to the poorhouse orphanage, there would have been easy access to any who sought to kidnap and hold her to ransom. Such a man would not hesitate to kill a child if it suited his purpose. Was that not usually the case? Once the ransom was collected, the fear of exposure and capture overrode all else. Joshua was forced to agree. Gould was a quiet and attentive listener, saying little, but proffering honest advice when asked. He knew that what Joshua needed most of all was a sounding board for his own theories; someone on whom to test his fears and guilt.

When Joshua retired to his bed the worst of his anguish and self-recrimination was over. Gould had been objective and uncritical, and he was grateful for it, as he would be for his company upon the morrow. Joshua had taken the precaution of sending word by a ship's master to Ayde-Buchan at the port, with an urgent plea to deliver a letter to the justice. He stressed the absolute need for it to be taken, without hindrance, at whatever hour the vessel docked. An identical sealed letter had been written to Peter Rawlings, lest, by some mischance, the harbour master be absent from the port. It would, he reasoned, prepare the justice for the Fulmers' coming, and give him opportunity to prepare Rosa and Doonan for what must be done.

Pamela Fulmer had demanded to know everything that he was able to tell her of Rosa and her affection for the child, and had expressed her determination to visit her and thank her, in person, for her care. Joshua hoped that he had dissuaded her, for he knew that such a meeting would be more than Rosa could bear. It would intensify the anguish of parting from Joy, of sacrificing her to another. Joshua knew that he had no business to advise the justice, and that it might well be construed as unwarranted interference, an impertinence that he might regret. Yet he had boldly advised Robert Knight that it would be kinder were Rosa and Doonan to deliver the child to Tom and Phoebe Butler at the Crown, that such a meeting would be less excoriating for all involved.

He had achieved all that he was reasonably able. There was no more to be done. Yet he felt no release from tension, no satisfaction, only an emptiness within. Tomorrow he would interview Scurlock with the consent of the justices. It was not a prospect he relished, but it had to be done. The man was a villain; a brute and an adulterer. Would he find that he was an abductor and murderer, too?

A little after daybreak, Joshua and Gould were driven by coach to the prison where Scurlock was detained awaiting trial. Joshua had been granted the privacy of a small interviewing room upon the instructions of the justices, and the greatest

307

cooperation was afforded him by the prison authorities and the greatest courtesy shown.

It did not surprise him that, physically, Augustus Scurlock when brought under guard was precisely as Gould had described him. Mark Gould was a singularly observant man, intelligent, cultured and unfailingly good-humoured, and Joshua found him a most rewarding companion. Yet, in one respect, Scurlock was different. His air of arrogance and authority seemed to have deserted him, and the brashness deplored by Gould was absent. He was a man bewildered and broken, and Joshua, who had been prepared to feel antagonism, hatred even, for the cruelties inflicted upon Pamela Fulmer, was grateful that she was not there to witness the change in him. It might well have aroused his victim's pity to see him so helplessly degraded. The mighty, when humbled, have a weapon which power denies them. In a man's eyes, Joshua thought, Scurlock in defeat cut a miserable figure; self-pitying and unprepossessing. In a woman, his little-boy-lost look might well rouse strong maternal feelings. Pity is said to be akin to love, but Joshua did not have to remind himself that Scurlock had shown neither pity nor love for the woman he had degraded and her bastard child.

The interview was stilted, and grudgingly given, with Scurlock unwilling to cooperate. His business affairs were of no concern to Joshua, and about his personal relationships he was not forthcoming. He showed neither interest in Pamela Fulmer's health and present whereabouts nor regret at his treatment of her. His apathy sprang less from hostility, Joshua concluded, than a resolution to be done with the past. All that obsessed him was his own plight; the descent from power to penury. He could cut from his mind all thoughts of those he had ruined and cheated and all blame. He saw himself as victim in a conspiracy hatched by jealous men; men corruptly seeking to destroy him. Joshua was clearly numbered among them, and afforded the cold incivility such treachery deserved.

Mention of Andrew Fulmer aroused the first sign of animation that Joshua had seen; a sudden rage of vituperation and contempt that was lacerating. He was the architect of all Scurlock's misfortunes. He was a scoundrel and liar! Scum! It was Fulmer who had informed against him, inspired by hatred

308

and malice, determined to force him to ruin! Well, he would live to regret it! By God, he would live to regret it! There were ways to get back at such men! Joshua let him ramble on, his fury so utterly consuming him that it robbed him of all sense and discretion.

When he finally left the prison, Joshua was as painfully enervated as Scurlock himself, drained of all energy and emotion. Yet he believed that he had learned all that he wished to know. That he had done it with a stealth and cunning to match Scurlock's own troubled him not at all. Corrupt ills need appropriate remedies. With knowledge of Pamela Fulmer's sufferings in mind, Joshua would not have been averse to beating the truth from her tormentor if need be. He knew that such an attitude did him little credit, although it offered him a modest satisfaction. He would not dwell too deeply upon it. Ethics and morality were the justice's domain.

'You believe that he told you the truth?' Gould demanded, upon their return journey to Porlock. 'He is as adept at lying as at the rest of his treachery.'

'I believe that he told the truth about the child,' Joshua said soberly. 'That he was in no wise involved in the kidnapping and ransom. He swore his oath upon it!'

'As he would swear to anything which might save his own skin,' Gould reminded sceptically.

'No, it had the ring of truth to it,' Joshua persisted. 'The outrage and disgust were genuine, of that I am sure! Whatever else he is guilty of, I am certain that he did not collude in the abduction of his own child.'

Gould was not altogether convinced, 'Who, then? Whom does he accuse?'

'The dead girl, Esther Yeo, certainly. Her murder was a shock to him. He could not have feigned that. It all but unnerved him. Believe it!'

'How was he involved with her? His mistress, perhaps?'

'No, he vehemently denied it. He was contemptuous of her standing as a servant, claiming her to be beneath his notice.'

'From rumours surrounding him,' Gould stated flatly, 'no woman was beneath his notice, from common street whore to ladies of fashion! Yet, perhaps even he would not have been careless enough to indulge in such a liaison in his own household. It would have set his plans at risk, alienated society and those he sought to dupe into investing. No, he would not have openly humiliated his "wife" before others. He had need of Pamela Fulmer, to lend him the respectability his ventures demanded.'

'And she was proud enough, and loyal enough, to give it!' Joshua murmured, shaking his head regretfully, 'whatever the humiliation to be endured.'

'But did he not hint at some possible accomplice, someone who might have aided the girl? She could not have planned and executed it alone. How did she come to be in the Scurlocks' service, since Fulmer denied all knowledge of the girl?'

'It was Scurlock who engaged the girl.'

'The devil it was! Upon what pretext?'

'No pretext, but upon the recommendation of a former business partner of his, Richard Johns, by name. You have heard of him?'

'No, and if he is any partner of Scurlock's,' said Gould dryly, 'then I may thank God that I remain in ignorance. But what has the dead girl to do with Johns?'

'Everything! It seems that they, too, were partners in all – bed and board included. Scurlock employed her as a favour to Johns. That is all he would admit, and that she seemed conscientious and reliable.'

'Until she absconded with the child?'

Joshua nodded. 'Until she absconded with the child.'

'I do not like it!' Gould exclaimed. 'There is something which does not quite fit, does not convince. How does Scurlock explain his own defection, knowing the child to be missing?'

'Pressure from creditors, he claims. The certainty that, if he did not flee at once, all would be revealed about his business dealings. He would face bankruptcy, prison even.'

'And Pamela?' Gould asked sharply. 'What of her?'

'He had no further use for her. Her money was gone. She could serve only as a hindrance, to lead others to him.'

'He is a damnable scoundrel!' Gould exclaimed scathingly. 'A leech and a parasite! It is my opinion that prison is too good for him, Joshua.' Joshua did not disagree. 'But . . . this Johns?' Gould persisted. 'What did you learn of him, Joshua? Could

310

he be involved in Esther Yeo's murder? Did Scurlock give you news of him? Where is he now?'

Joshua answered quietly, 'I learned that he is a Cornishman, with business interests as "varied" as Scurlock's own. Shipping and trade among them.'

He had all of Gould's attention now. 'Smuggling? Wrecking, even?'

'Scurlock hinted as much and let slip that he had been a one-time partner of Hardee of Sker.'

'Hardee?' Gould repeated, perplexed. 'The man you told me of? The one hanged for the wrecking of the *San Lorenzo*? Dear God, Joshua, it is infamous! Past believing! A man involved in such viciousness would not hesitate to abduct a child, even the child of a so-called friend.' He paused, demanding curtly, 'You believe that Johns could be involved in the smuggling you are investigating?'

'That, and murder.'

'It seems possible,' Gould conceded, adding reluctantly, 'but it will be hard to convince others, and harder to prove. You have no solid evidence, only the word of a known liar and cheat, a man discredited. The alleged link between Johns and the dead girl relies on Scurlock's evidence alone. I would not give it much credence.'

'Nor I,' admitted Joshua, 'save that Scurlock's fury lest Johns be guilty of abducting his child led him to speak recklessly and more usefully than he knew.' Gould looked at him enquiringly. 'It seems that the "business" in which Johns is engaged takes him to a small seaport in Wales, a place familiar to him from past dealings with Hardee.'

Gould said soberly, 'Then you had best leave Porlock in all haste! There has been one murder, and another attempted. Johns cannot know what you have learned. The child could still be at risk. It would add tragedy to the Fulmers' grief were you to arrive too late, for he would kill the child without compunction, were his involvement known.'

'Yes. That is what I most fear.'

Gould murmured awkwardly, 'Perhaps, after all, Scurlock is not wholly irredeemable. If he cares for no other then at least he has some affection for his child.'

Joshua shook his head, saying coldly, 'No, he showed no

remorse for what he had done to others, no fear or affection for the child. His anger against Johns was because he had dared to deceive him, to demand money that was rightfully his. He is so immersed in his own misery that for him no other exists.'

'Be damned if there is anything to choose between him and the abductor and murderer!' Gould exclaimed contemptuously. 'They have as little to commend them. They are scarce human! It is to be hoped that they get the punishment they deserve.'

'Amen to that,' said Joshua fervently. 'Amen to that!'

Chapter Twenty-Five

Joshua's immediate need was to return swiftly to Newton in order to ensure that the child was safe. Then, upon the justice's authority, she could be restored to her family, so that they might take up life anew. His most exacting task would be to hunt down the man who had planned the abduction, and bring him to trial. Would he also be held to account for the murder of Esther Yeo and the attempted murder of Curtis? Joshua could not be sure. He could not even be sure that it was Richard Johns he sought, or that he was implicated either in the smuggling from Newton Creek or the child's disappearance. Had Esther Yeo, too, been abducted? Had she gone willingly as accomplice? Had the whole tragic episode been her own idea? How, then, was Curtis involved? The more Joshua tried to reason it, the more his frustration and confusion grew.

He did not relish the awkwardness of the sea crossing with Fulmer and his daughter, for he must keep his fears well hidden. God alone knew what news might await him at their journey's end. He must learn, too, to speak of the infant as Alexandra Fulmer and not as 'the child', or Rosa and Doonan's 'Joy'. He would not dwell upon the grief that the parting must bring them lest it cloud his judgement. Pamela Fulmer had suffered enough and the child Alexander was rightfully hers, her own flesh and blood, as John Jeremiah was his. She must sense no reserve or hidden resentment in him for reclaiming her daughter. She had borne hurt and rejection enough. Oh, but it was a damnable mix-up; a problem to test the wisdom of Solomon. He felt young and inadequate, painfully vulnerable.

His leave taking of Mark Gould had been, of necessity, brief, for they had returned in haste to the port with but ten minutes to spare before the sailing. Preparations were already being made to cast off from the quayside. Fulmer and his daughter were aboard, anxiously awaiting his coming. Gould's handclasp had been firm, his bluff voice warm with sincerity as he bade Joshua send news to him, and to return to Porlock as his guest whenever need or desire for companionship arose. It was, he assured Joshua, for all its brevity and the circumstances surrounding it, an honest friendship and one he would value. Joshua thanked him for his ready welcome and the hospitality shown, begging him stay with him at Thatched Cottage upon the first opportunity, for Rebecca, he knew, would be as delighted as he to further the friendship.

Gould's eyes were alight with mischief as he replied, 'I must extract one promise, sir, before I give agreement.'

'And that, sir?'

'No sea bathing!'

'You have my word upon it . . . more than that, my solemn oath!'

They parted amidst shared laughter, yet with reluctance, as friends do. Each was aware that it was the last carefree moment that Joshua would enjoy until his quest for the murderer was ended. There would be little enough laughter in the days ahead.

Rosa had risen early after a sleepless night. She had wept until she could weep no more and now there was only a dull ache within her, an emptiness beyond pain. In the night Cavan had lain wakeful beside her and she had heard the dry harshness of his sobbing, a man's awkward tears that he had tried, in vain, to muffle. They had clung helplessly together, wordless and bereft, trying to gain comfort from the closeness of flesh and caring. Yet there had been no comfort, no ease. Joy had become a part of their lives, as if formed from their own flesh, and they could not face the bleakness of life without her.

Cavan had wanted to stay beside her, to be there when the justice and Phoebe Butler came to take Joy to the Crown Inn. It was Rosa who had dissuaded him, declaring that he would be better occupied at the quarry face. Work was hard to come by and it would serve no purpose to lose a day's wages. Cavan would have sacrificed a lifetime's wages just to have the child stay, and they both knew it. She had begged Emrys to watch over him and to see that he did not blunder off to the Crown

314

Inn in his misery and demand that Joy be returned to them, for *they* were the only parents she knew. Rosa, too, had thought of defying the justice and fleeing with Joy to wherever she might find shelter and not be discovered. If she had insisted upon it she knew that Cavan would had to go with her. He would have agreed all and willingly. Yet it would have been no more than a futile gesture and he would have sacrificed all, even freedom, for naught. A hue and cry would have been immediately called and they could not hope to escape the vengeance of the law, for she could not think of it as justice.

She had tried, in vain, to think of the other woman as deserving of pity for, as the justice said, she had suffered much and was in no wise to blame. The woman was Joy's mother, her own flesh and blood, Robert Knight had declared compassionately, and Rosa had listened silently. But inside she had screamed; No! I am Joy's mother! She is mine and Cavan's, for we took her in when no other would care for her. How can you know the pain of it? The grief I feel? It was not the coldness of charity we gave her but the warmth of our loving. Has loving no validity in law? No claim? Yet she spoke no word of it to the justice, for what would have been the use? He was a kind man and had done what he thought fitting. His pity and awkwardness were clear. Yet she did not want his pity or any other's; she wanted to hold Joy close and keep her safe for ever; to rock them both into the comfort of sleep and forgetting, even should she awaken no more.

'I will come tomorrow morning, early, to collect her and take her to the Crown,' The justice's voice had been harsher than he had intended, awkwardly brusque.

'Yes. I will see that she is ready.'

He had lingered uselessly. 'You have done well to . . . to care for her so selflessly, my dear.' He had stretched out a hand and clumsily patted her shoulder, saying tentatively, 'I should know how to bring you comfort . . . ease your hurt, but there are not words enough and I am helpless to speak what I feel. Believe, my dear, that the pain will diminish in time . . . in time.' He had stood there helplessly.

Rosa had said, 'Yes, sir. I am sure of it,' but she spoke only to ease his hurt. She was sure of nothing save that naught would ever be the same again. Should the pain diminish and forgetfulness come, it would bring no relief from suffering. It would be the emptiness of death that she knew then. She would but exchange one sorrow for another. That was the truth of it and the burden she must bear.

Now, as she dressed Joy carefully in the fine clothes which Rebecca had given her, Rosa thought that her heart must surely break apart with the hurt of it and the anguish of loss. She wept as her fingers moved clumsily, her tears falling silently and splashing, unhindered, from mouth and chin. She wiped them uselessly from where they dropped upon Joy's robe, and Joy, sensing her grief and not understanding, grew suddenly pale and wide-eyed, anxiety stilling her. Rosa, grieving and ashamed, tried to smile and talk to her reassuringly, but her voice was a harsh croak from the dryness of her throat and the words indistinguishable. She hugged Joy protectively to her, then tied the strings of her daughter's bonnet, waiting for the sound of the justice's carriage without, and the knock upon the door.

She had tied all Joy's clothes into a bundle within a pretty hand-crocheted shawl, all save the christening gown which Emily had so lovingly stitched for her. Joy would have no need of it now, but it would serve always as reminder of her, Rosa thought. It was a pretty and delicate thing as fragile and fine-wrought as she. At the very bottom of the bundle she had placed the little christening cup that Mr Morgan had brought, the gift from a pedlar's tray. It was naught but a trinket, Rosa knew and, like as not, it would be rejected. But if the other woman had love and to spare, might she not keep it for Joy as reminder? Show her that another had once loved her, gave her comfort when she wept, fed, changed, clothed and watched her grow? One who had touched her only in tenderness, believing Joy her own? 'JOY TO THE BABE.' The words engraved were a prayer and a blessing; a tribute from the heart, a kindness from a man who had given of the little he owned with gladness as gladly as she and Cavan had given.

The sharp knocking upon the door startled her and she knew that there was no more time. She wiped the remains of tears from her face and, with Joy held firm, and the bundle beneath

316

her arm, called out that the door was unlocked. It had but to be pushed open.

The justice stood, embarrassed in his awkwardness, with Phoebe Butler beside him, her face, under the coal-scuttle bonnet, sharp-pinched with distress. Rosa spoke no word as she put Joy into Phoebe's arms, but the pain within her was so intense that she felt that Joy had been torn from her flesh in a rawness more violent than physical birth. She would feel the pangs of it for ever. Rosa, dry-eyed, turned to go within. It was Phoebe Butler who wept and Joy, lost and bewildered, who screamed aloud.

Hearing it, Rosa all but rushed after her, but even as she turned the door was quietly reopened and John Burrell walked grave faced within.

'I have come to help you, Rosa, if you will let me. You have but to speak the word and I will go.'

Rosa saw that he relived her despair in memory; the grief of his own child's dying and the endless loss. 'No, I would have you stay. I am alone and bereft.'

The cry was from the heart, and John Burrell stretched out his arms, then enfolded her to him. He did not claim that the hurt of it would diminish or that she would find forgetfulness. He knew that she would not. He could offer her only that warmth of comfort born of his own suffering. He held her firm and unspeaking until she could weep no more, then stayed quietly beside her, willing his strength into her.

The harbour master, Ayde-Buchan, sent word to Robert Knight at the Crown Inn that *The Somerset Maid* was lying off, waiting for the tide, and that it was expected to dock within the hour. The justice immediately ordered the coachman to await Joshua's and the Fulmers' disembarking and to bring them to the inn for a reunion with the lost child. He felt that such an emotionally fraught meeting should be held in private for the sakes of all concerned. Afterwards he would invite them as guests to Tythegston Court to await return passage to Porlock. It was an expedient that he felt necessary. He was not sanguine about the infant's safety, since the hooded man had not been found. He could not rest easy until they were clear of the three hamlets and outside his jurisdiction. Once the

317

child was safely restored, the blackmailer would be impotent to act. There would be nothing to gain by violence and everything to lose.

The justice sighed. It was the Doonans who had lost all. He bitterly regretted it. Memory of Rosa Doonan's ravaged face and her painfully controlled grief came back vividly to haunt him. He glanced towards where Phoebe Butler stood in the small parlour, the infant clasped protectively in her arms. Robert Knight's deep brown eyes, pained and softly unfocused behind the gold-rimmed lenses, burned and grew misted and he blinked irritably, but the blurring remained. He wished to heaven that he could have spoken more passionately to Rosa, convinced her of God's loving protection, given her the comfort she deserved. Yet he was unable. He was a cold man, emotions locked fast within him, distanced from those he served by wealth and circumstance. He regretted it, as he regretted the stilted patronising words he spoke, his set and pedantic ways, his inability to reach out to those in need and grief, even though his heart ached within him.

Richard Turberville, now, he had the gift of being at one with people; a closeness born of love of *them* as well as of God. A real understanding. Perhaps he had best ask Turberville to visit the Doonans to give them the consolation and help that *he* was unable. He had asked Burrell to tend to Rosa after the child was taken. Burrell, too, had that touch of common humanity which he, as rector, lacked. Did it come with suffering, or was it born in the spirit, the soul itself? Robert Knight knew only that he lacked such blessing. He hoped that God knew how desperately he tried to be of help to these people and how his failure grieved him.

Phoebe Butler, seeing the fleeting sadness upon Robert Knight's face, thought compassionately, He is a kind-hearted man, ever ready to help those in need. His very presence is a reassurance, for he is a man to trust. A man of integrity. Yet alone, sadly alone.

She walked over to where Robert Knight stood, and upon an impulse set the child into his arms. Robert Knight blinked, then smiled hesitantly, and the child stared at him solemnly then smiled widely in return, stretching out a curled fist to touch his face. Here was one of his flock who was in accord with him, Robert Knight thought. One who trusted and accepted him without the need for words. A warmth spread within him, joyously comforting, erupting into laughter. He heard it as though it came from some other, so free it was and infectious. It was a beginning, he thought, a small beginning.

Captain Ayde-Buchan was on hand to welcome the Fulmers to the port and to escort them discreetly to the justice's waiting coach. Joshua was hailed and briefly detained by Peter Rawlings with a murmured promise that he would not keep him long, but there was something of import that he must confide in him.

'The smugglers? You have news of the smugglers?' Joshua asked sharply when they could not be overheard.

'Better!' Rawlings declared immodestly. 'Notwithstanding your absence, sir, we have captured them red handed, each and every one!'

'The devil you have!' Joshua was torn between pique and pleasure at such an unexpected turn of events. 'It seems that I am expendable, sir,' he said with mock indignation, adding, smiling, 'You are to be congratulated upon your triumph, Peter, although a little less smugness and a little more modesty would be more becoming.'

Rawlings grinned expansively, declaring, 'Before the justice I am all rectitude and praiseworthy humility, believe it. Before friends, we may show ourselves in our true colours and be damned to the consequences!'

'But the smugglers?' Joshua prompted. 'You have identified them?'

Rawlings sobered immediately, confessing, 'Yes. It was as I suspected. The ringleader was an acquaintance of Hardee of Sker.'

'Richard Johns, a Cornishman?'

Rawlings stared at him, mouth comically agape. 'It seems your visit to Porlock yielded more than you expected,' he said dryly. 'Am I to be privy to the information you gleaned or must I await news from the justice?' He added glumly, 'He will be odiously overbearing if we have both been successful, and will claim all credit without diffidence or shame.'

'As is his wont.'

319

'As is his wont,' agreed Rawlings.

Joshua told him what had transpired at Greycombe Manor and at the prison, and Rawlings listened in disbelieving silence. 'Dear heaven, Joshua!' he exclaimed at length. 'I do not hold out much hope for your chances in securing a confession from Johns! The man is a savage! He is as hardened and vicious as Hardee of Sker! Nothing, and no one, will break him.'

'You have tried? Interviewed him?'

'For the little it was worth.'

'But you caught him red handed. He cannot wriggle out of that. You have proof, surely?'

'Of his smuggling activities, nothing beyond that. He remains obdurately silent, contemptuous even. The man's insolence and conceit are overweening! You will not get far.'

'What of his companions?'

'Driven by fear. They will confess to nothing and do nothing to implicate him further. They will not even admit to his leadership. The hold he keeps over them is greater than their fear of imprisonment or deportation even.'

Joshua said, awkwardly, 'I had best return to the Fulmers, ride with them in the coach.' He hesitated before asking, 'There is no more news of Rosa's attacker?'

'None as far as I am aware, although I am not wholly in the justice's confidence. If he *had* been captured I would surely have heard of it. Well, I have prepared you as best I am able to meet the justice on equal terms.'

Joshua grinned, saying, 'The terms are never equal. The odds are always entirely in his favour. He is omnipotent, omniscient and omnipresent,' he reminded.

'Like God!'

'Like God,' Joshua agreed, straight-faced. 'And with the same powers of vengeance and retribution.'

'And mercy?'

'I have never seen sign of it,' Joshua admitted.

'Nor I,' agreed Rawlings, 'although I live in hope of a miracle.' Grinning, he saluted and turned on his heel as Joshua made his way, more soberly, to the justice's coach.

The journey to the Crown Inn was fraught with uneasy silence, for the three passengers within the coach were occupied with their own thoughts and fears. Yet the reunion between the Fulmers and the child, Alexandra, was so restrained in its quiet simplicity that none present was left unmoved. Phoebe Butler wept quite openly, wiping her nose distractedly upon her apron, face flushed with vicarious pleasure and emotion and the guilt she felt at being happy despite Rosa's loss. Joshua, too, was aware of the painful tightening of his throat, the needle-prick of hurt at his eyelids, for in his mind's eye, Rebecca stood in Pamela Fulmer's stead, reclaiming their son, John Jeremiah. Andrew Fulmer watched all with patient dignity, his gaze centred anxiously upon his daughter, fearful lest she stumble and fall, for she had suffered so grievously that he did not know if she could survive the hurt of such a reconciliation . . . her emotions laid raw.

Dr Mansel, present upon the justice's bidding, watched Pamela with equal concern, for her feverish gaiety seemed unnatural to his trained eye, and he knew that there must follow an equally violent reaction. He murmured to the justice that there should be no delay. She must be put into the coach for Tythegston Court with all urgency, and then put immediately to bed and into a nurse's care. The reaction, when it came, would be disabling, and they had best be prepared, for exhaustion and depression would inevitably follow. She must be afforded complete solitude and rest until she had recovered both spirits and strength. So it was hastily arranged, with Dr Mansel agreeing to travel in the coach beside her, lest his services be required to calm her upon the way.

The justice made gruff apologies to Andrew Fulmer, explaining that he must have word with Joshua, but would follow in a carriage as soon as he was able. A competent nursemaid had been engaged to care for the child and Dr Mansel would procure nursing aid for his daughter. Meanwhile, he trusted that his guest would do him the courtesy of treating Tythegston Court as if it were his own.

Robert Knight, to his intense irritation, was not yet wholly in nervous control of his voice, for he was more disturbed by the scene at the inn than he would admit. It shamed him that Fulmer seemed so fully in control of his feelings, so admirably composed. Yet, when Fulmer made to shake the justice's hand and thank him, the trembling of his hands and the painful rigidity of his face muscles and jaw gave the lie to his equanimity. Their shared handclasp had been long and firm and warm with understanding. They met as gentlemen, equals and friends. There was no need in all the world for dissembling.

After the Fulmers departure, when Joshua and Robert Knight were ensconced, with refreshment, in Tom Butler's private parlour and able to speak freely, Joshua told the justice of all that occurred in Porlock and beyond and of his debt to Mark Gould.

'You really think, Stradling, that Johns might be responsible for the woman's murder and planned the abduction?'

'I have no proof, sir, save what Scurlock confessed.'

'Then you must get it!' the justice declared abrasively. 'It is up to you! You must interview the prisoner at Pyle gaolhouse. Secure his confession. Damnation, sir, that is what you are paid to do! Must I be held responsible for all?' With an effort the justice checked himself, wiping a tired hand across his mouth and admitting shamefacedly, 'I fear that I harangue you unjustly, Stradling. I unload my guilt upon you. I have committed the cardinal sin for a justice. I have become emotionally involved, lost my detachment . . . the Doonans, the Fulmers and all else.'

'It would be hard, sir, to remain aloof,' Joshua said with honesty. 'We are all human.'

'I thank you for reminding me, Stradling!' The justice essayed a dry smile. 'I am under no illusion about my own frailty. I make no claim to divinity. I am sadly aware of my lowliness in the scheme of things.'

'As I, sir,' Joshua agreed, straight-faced.

For the first time Robert Knight smiled freely, then gave an involuntary bellow of laughter, admitting, 'You did well in Porlock. Very well.' In case Joshua grew lax through over-praise, he added, 'As did Rawlings and his men in trapping the smugglers. You carried out your duties as one would expect, but it is only a beginning.'

'A beginning, sir?'

'Smuggling is a grave offence, certainly. The law regards it as such and will give suitable punishment. But there is more at stake, Stradling. It is a murderer we seek, one who callously and deliberately takes human life. Worse, a murderer and an abductor of an innocent child. It is not only the law of the land but the law of God which has been broken. Yes, and lives like the Doonans and the Fulmers . . .' He broke off, awkward at what he had revealed of himself, to say stiffly, 'He must be brought to justice, Stradling. That is all I say.'

Joshua murmured agreement, asking quietly, 'But Curtis, sir? Is there sign of recovery? Has he been able to speak?'

'No, he has not regained consciousness, but Mansel claims that there are encouraging signs, more hope. Yet whether he will be able to speak, or regain full memory . . .' He faltered, only to confess agitatedly, 'Upon my oath, Stradling. It is I who am enfeebled, not Curtis. My wretched memory fails me as badly. I had all but forgotten that another attempt was made upon his life!'

'How, sir?'

The justice told him shamefacedly of the finding of the hood in Mansel's shrubbery and of how Burrell and the guards had been duped, declaring, 'It was a grievous mistake, Stradling. A dereliction of duty upon everyone's part, brought about, in part, by your untimely absence.' At Joshua's expressive lift of the eyebrows, he grinned and said handsomely, 'Not that I hold you in any way to blame. You are in no way culpable. At least, now that Johns is safely behind bars, there will be no further attempts upon Curtis's life. Nor upon Rosa Doonan's, although I fear it will give her scant comfort.' He shook his head regretfully. 'The Fulmers' joy is that poor girl's sorrow. That is the way of life and living. It is not easy, Stradling. No, it is not easy.'

Joshua said quietly. 'I do not think it would be wise to consider taking the guards away from Curtis yet awhile, sir. Nor removing them from the highways.'

'You do not?' The justice was affronted. 'But it is a damnable expense, Stradling. The vestrymen are, quite rightly, complaining. We do not have a bottomless purse.'

'There is no proof that Johns is the murderer, sir, or that he is the hooded man.'

'Then you must find it,' the justice said with acerbity, adding grudgingly, 'meanwhile, I will agree to a temporary retaining of the guard. I will take responsibility for persuading the

323

vestrymen of the need, although I will not be the best advocate, since I remain unconvinced.'

'I hope, as you, sir, that such . . . precautions prove unnecessary,' Joshua said blandly. 'You have always warned me to err on the side of caution, taking no unnecessary risks with the lives of others. I have always respected it as pertinent advice.'

'Indeed,' the justice agreed heavily.

'And that a man must always be adjudged innocent until proven, in law, to be guilty.'

'You have made your point, Stradling. Do not labour it,' he warned.

'No, sir.'

Robert Knight rose to take his leave, saying with a return to humour, 'I am wholly aware, Joshua, that the sea voyage from Porlock has been tiring, and that it is not *my* company that you would willingly have sought at your journey's end.' As Joshua moved to make polite denial he continued imperturbably,' 'No! Do not add evasion to your sins and omissions, the list is already over long.' He continued gruffly, 'You had best take yourself off to see Rebecca and my godson, sir. You have sadly neglected them of late, and I fear that they hold me culpable. I would not put myself into worse odour by delaying you. I am a sensitive man and in need of the few friends I may rely on.'

'I hope that I may be adjudged one, sir.'

'We shall see,' said the justice magnanimously. 'We shall see.'

Joshua's return to Thatched Cottage was swiftly made and his reception exceeded all expectations. His arrival was greeted by delighted acclamation from Stenner and the household staff, and by Rebecca with the most flattering euphoria. Indeed, had he not been a civilised and well-balanced man, Joshua told himself, then he might have become odiously conceited. He hurried to see John Jeremiah, and would have sworn upon oath that his son had grown in his absence, and that he not only recognised his father instantly but gave him the widest, most rapturous, of smiles. In all it was a welcome to gladden the most jaded of hearts and Joshua revelled in it unashamedly. Rebecca refrained from questioning him about his progress at Porlock, ensuring instead that he first had a warm, herb-scented bath to wash away the grime and stress of travel, then victuals and refreshment to fortify himself.

He was in a state of most blissful relaxation when Rebecca said, hesitantly, 'There is but one thing I must confide in you, Joshua, although Ossie has said it will keep . . . he would not have you disturbed.'

'Ossie?' Joshua's voice was sharp. 'What is it that troubles him, Rebecca? He would not seek my help lightly. Did he give you no reason? No clue?'

'No, he said it was a matter for your ears alone, Joshua. He would not confide in me, claiming that it was a matter of small import, scarce worth the bother of the mention.'

'But you thought him troubled, Rebecca?'

'Disturbed rather, as if there were some fear or problem preying upon his mind.'

'I will go at once to see him,' Joshua promised briskly. 'I will not take the carriage, but walk to the Crown.'

Rebecca did not seek to dissuade him. Like Joshua, she held the ostler in affection, and knew that he would not lightly seek his aid.

Ossie treated Joshua to the warmest welcome, seamed face alight with honest surprise and pleasure. Then, at once, he began to make awkward apology for disturbing him, for unfairly bringing him away from Thatched Cottage.

''Tis but a small matter,' he insisted, 'of no great consequence. It was a foolishness of mine and you will think the less of me for it.'

'You had best tell me of it,' Joshua instructed, smiling, 'that I may better judge.'

'Well, as I said, it is the slightest thing, but out of the ordinary. It disturbed me to see the lad so distressed . . .'

'The sweeping lad?'

'Aye, 'twas here, in your absence, when the smugglers were brought to the Crown before being taken to the gaolhouse at Pyle.'

'And?'

'And . . .' Ossie hesitated. 'Well, your friend, the excise officer Mr Rawlings, he took a ruffian by the arm and manhandled him upon the way, but keeping his gun trained upon him. A surly, foul-mouthed fellow the smuggler was, fit to put the fear of God into any man.' Joshua waited, puzzled. ''Twas more than fear of God I saw, 'twas fear of the very devil himself! I tell you, Joshua, the sweeping lad was all but paralysed with terror. He could scarce stand for his trembling, nor utter a sensible word.'

'The sight of the smuggler, you think?'

'I am sure of it. I found the boy later cowering among the horses in the stable. Weeping, and rocking himself in anguish, like one possessed!'

'He could give no reason? Say nothing to help you?'

'Blaze! The one word. He cried it out as he cried it out before, only then it meant nothing to me or any other.'

'And now?'

'It was not terror of the vestryman's horse, you understand? The man, the smuggler, was dark-haired but with a single streak of white – a blaze running through it. Whatever the lad saw here that night when the child was found and the girl was murdered, that man was in some way involved. I would stake my very life upon it.'

Chapter Twenty-Six

Despite his fatigue, Joshua was so disturbed by what Ossie had told him of the sweeping boy's reaction to the smuggler, that he felt it incumbent upon him to ride out to Pyle gaolhouse at once. He knew that it would not please Rebecca, for she had begged him to take rest, declaring severely that he looked, 'Frail as a ghost and as pale and insubstantial.' Yet he could not rest easy with his task uncompleted. He must identify the smuggler whom Ossie had described, not for his own sake alone, but for the Fulmers and the Doonans and the murdered Esther Yeo, and bring whoever was culpable to justice. Seeing his determination and the stress upon his face, Rebecca wisely remained uncritical, upon his return, venturing no opinion. Joshua wrote a hastily penned letter of explanation to Robert Knight to be delivered by Stenner then, with the grey made ready and saddled, he was swiftly away.

When he returned a good two hours later he was not in the best of humour, his anger and disappointment plain. He had learned little, save that Johns *was* the man whom Ossie had described. He knew now that Scurlock had not been lying and that the link with Hardee of Sker gave him just cause for concern. He must move with caution, for without proof that Johns was abductor and murderer he was at a loss to proceed. His patient questioning of Johns and his henchmen had yielded him nothing new. If the rabble who supported Johns knew of his involvement in abduction and murder, then they remained obdurately silent, fearful perhaps of his powers of revenge. As for the Cornishman himself, he was openly contemptuous, as surly and foul-mouthed as Ossie had warned. He did not attempt to hide his hostility, and Joshua's mention of Scurlock was treated with levity and scorn. He was as dismissive of his former partner as of Joshua's attempts to interrogate him, and Joshua had been painfully conscious that Johns openly despised him, and that he had almost as little faith in his own powers cheered him not at all. It was no more than a preliminary skirmish, he told himself. He would return upon the morrow and exact retribution.

Meanwhile there was work to be done within the three hamlets, for crime, like the poor, is ever with us; an immutable fact of life. Joshua was inclined to believe that it had actually proliferated in his absence, like a mushroom field untended. He set about remedying his neglect with little enthusiasm, but was soon wholly absorbed in the day to day trials of a constable's life; the feuds and misdemeanours, the harassment and strife that are the flesh and bones of daily living. When he finally returned to Thatched Cottage he was exhausted, but purged of the irritation which Richard Johns' abrasiveness had wrought.

In bed, that night, with Rebecca lying asleep in his arms, he felt the warm glow of contentment that comes from making love; that fusion of flesh, mind and spirit that is part birth and part death. He was drowsy and at peace, yet strangely wakeful. He had told Rebecca, all that had occurred at Porlock, and she had grieved for Pamela Fulmer's loss, and rejoiced in her good fortune. Yet her tears had been for Rosa and Cavan Doonan whom she knew and loved, and although she had found comfort in Joshua's loving, the tears were still wet upon her cheeks when she fell asleep. He watched her now in the flickering glow of candlelight; the familiar plains and hollows of her face, the heavily lashed eyelids, pale and soft-veined as John Jeremiah's, and her clouding blue-black hair. She was as dear to him as life itself, and he could envisage no future without her. He could not survive her loss. His thoughts turned to the murdered girl, Esther Yeo, so like Rebecca in features and colouring. Was there someone, somewhere, who grieved her death as passionately as he would grieve for Rebecca? Did someone still impatiently await her return, her murder unknown? Had Johns betrayed and then brutally killed her? Was even involved? It would be the devil's own job to prove it, and he did not know how it could be done.

With the candle guttering fitfully and casting light and shade upon the walls, he fell into a troubled sleep. The dappled

328

shadows were as swift changing and elusive as his tortured dreams, and when he awoke to sunlight, his confusion was unresolved. All that had changed was that he was home and with his family; the people he loved. Doonan and Rosa were denied such blessing, and Pamela Fulmer must care for her child alone. He did not know which of them most commanded his pity. It was a new day. A new beginning. Yet old sins cast long shadows, and one cannot wholly escape the past.

While Joshua made ready to ride out again to question Johns and the smugglers at Pyle gaolhouse, Cavan Doonan was banging frenziedly upon the door of Dr Mansel's house. The Irishman's broad, strong-featured face was raw with anxiety as he pounded with clenched fists muttering savagely the while. 'Come, damn you! Come! Are you deaf within?' he shouted furiously, in his agony of frustration all but breaking down the door.

Burrell, hearing the commotion and wild cries, hurried to see what was amiss. Some accident, he feared, or tragedy. Someone deranged by shock or grief. A return of Curtis's attacker even? For a moment he froze, hand upon the bolt that secured the door, then sanity reasserted itself. There had been no warning from the guards, no alarm. It was someone known to them and seeking his services. He drew the bolt cautiously aside.

'Cavan? Cavan Doonan? There has been some accident at the quarry? There is need of my services?' he demanded sharply.

'No, sir,' he was grasping Burrell's arm with such vigour that it jarred the bone. '"Tis Rosa. Come, sir. Come, I beg of you!' He was all but weeping with distress.

'What is amiss? She has not been attacked again? Fallen in some accident? Tell me, man, that I may bring what is needed!'

'I do not know, sir, I do not know. She is deeply unconscious, I cannot rouse her. I am fearful she is dead.'

'The gig,' Burrel said. 'We had best take the gig.'

'No. I have Emrys's cob, and cart, sir. I will take you at once! There is no time to be lost. Oh, come, sir, I beg of you!'

Burrell barely had time to grasp his leather satchel from

329

the table in the hall before Doonan was half pushing, half dragging, him into the battered cart. Then they were away, jolting and shuddering along the stones of the carriageway, then onto the highway without, and all the while Doonan was whimpering uselessly beneath his breath like a whipped dog lost in bewilderment.

When they reached the cottage at the edge of the dunes Burrell had to speak to him harshly, forcing him to sense and reason, commanding him to stay quietly below while he tended to Rosa. Doonan's anguished blundering would be more hindrance than help he knew, and Burrell's immediate concern was for Rosa. She had suffered some emotional collapse, he feared, some trauma of mind from parting with the child, and the grief suffered. Sometimes the body itself rebelled and the mind blotted out those sorrows it could not bear to acknowledge or endure.

Cavan Doonan, sitting in the wheelbacked chair beside the fire, felt only the coldness of grief envelop him. He had lost his daughter, and if Rosa, too, were taken from him, he would be unable to bear it. He rocked himself to and fro in grief, arms clasped around him in anguish, scarce able to see for the tears which blinded him, tears he had tried to hold back before Rosa. He had not shown his grief to those at the quarry face for it was locked deep inside him, and not even Emrys was aware of the fierceness of it. It rose as rawly devouring as flame, searing nerve and will, making of him a charred and useless thing, cold as spent ashes. Yet the very emptiness was pain. Pain of memory. Pain of loss.

He heard the sounds of Burrell's returning, the cold ring of his boots upon the stone stairway, his halting tread, and was afraid. He rose to his feet, stumbling in his awkwardness, trying to wipe away the shaming evidence of his tears. 'Rosa, sir?' His voice was a harshness.

'You had best be seated, Cavan.'

'No!' he brushed aside Burrell's restraining hand, exclaiming, irascibly 'For God's sake, tell me, man! Speak plainly! I am not a fool or imbecile to be humoured. Tell me the truth of it. There have been lies and griefs enough. I can take no more.' He was almost beside himself with rage and fear, massive fists clenched tight, the sinews of his neck stretched taut as whipcord. There was a wildness about him, the feral savagery of an animal cornered and about to strike.

But Burrell felt no fear as he said compassionately, 'Rosa is resting quietly now. There is no need for alarm. She has suffered the loss of . . .' he faltered awkwardly, 'the grievous loss of the child. She could stand no more hurt. It was nature's way of protecting her, deadening all memory, even for so brief a while.'

Doonan wiped a hand wearily across his eyes, saying contritely, 'I have been less than useless to her, so absorbed in my own grief. I will go to her and try to make amends.' He added stiffly, 'As I would wish to make amends to you, Dr Burrell. I am a rough man, sir, I live by my fists and am not easy with words. 'Tis hard to speak openly, for I have never learned how. But I beg you will take no offence at my rudenes. 'Twas not deserved.' His face was as fiery as his mop of unruly red hair.

'There is no apology needed for caring for others,' Burrell said quietly, 'or for grieving their loss. It is to your credit, Cavan.' He stretched out his hand and, sheepishly, Doonan took it in his rough clasp. 'You are to be congratulated, Cavan,' Burrell continued, voice gentle, 'even though you are so in grief, for Rosa is with child.'

Doonan stared at him, face bleak and uncomprehending. 'Rosa?' he demanded foolishly. 'But how can that be? We have tried in vain, sir.'

'That is sometimes the way,' Burrell's smile was warmly reassuring. 'When all tension and fear is removed, there is no further barrier to conception.'

'You are sure, sir? There can be no mistake? No dis-appointment? It would be too hard to bear, losing Joy and all.'

'No. There is no mistake. Rosa will be well, believe it, and the child cannot be harmed by what has occurred. Go to her, Cavan. She is surprised and bewildered, and as much in need of you, whether in sorrow or joy.'

'What shall I say to her, sir? 'Tis hard. I would not make small of Joy's loss in my own happiness. It would not be right. Rosa would think the less of me.'

'You will find the words,' Burrell promised confidently, 'but if you do not, then sometimes there is need for nothing save a presence, the reassurance of touch.'

Long after Burrell had left, Doonan sat uselessly in the wheel-back chair, gazing into the glowing coals, mind working restlessly. Where was the joy he expected? The triumph and fulfilment? He had yearned so long for a child, and in vain, it seemed. He could not rejoice, for memory of Joy was still too raw in his mind. He could not cast her out so easily and for another, unknown. Even his own flesh and blood. It would be a cruelty, A betrayal. As if he had never loved her. It would invalidate all.

He picked up the little wooden cob and cart with the figures of Emrys and himself which Illtyd had so lovingly fashioned, and he felt as if his heart would break with the fearsome anguish of it, the intensity of the pain. One day he would give the precious toy to his own child, and the grief would be shadowed and unreal, and the memory of Joy a gladness, for love was infinite and not diminished by being given to another. But it was too soon! Too soon! His rage cried out within him. He could not accept one child in place of another, as if the past must be sacrificed to the future, unmourned. Cut out of all memory, all feeling.

Wearily he rose and started to climb the stone stairs to Rosa. He would find the words of love he sought; speak them with sincerity, for Rosa was deserving of that. Yes, he would speak them proudly and with conviction. One day, God willing, he would even grow to believe them, forgetting that once, almost too long ago to remember, they were a lie.

Joshua, returning on the grey past the great freshwater pool at Kenfig, saw a skein of wild geese pass overhead. He did not know why the sight so moved him, but the effortless elegance of their flight, its grace and symmetry, stirred in him not pleasure but pain. He had delivered to the gaoler at Pyle gaolhouse those small luxuries which Rebecca had insisted that he take, and asked that they be given to Corinne Blackstock, who had so tragically lost her child. The gaoler was an honest and kind-hearted man with a family of his own, and had promised faithfully that she would receive them.

'For all the good it may do, sir,' he declared pityingly, 'for she is sunk so deep in grief that I fear she will neither know nor understand.'

'Has no one made enquiry about her?' Joshua demanded. 'Has no one visited her or sent word?'

'None, sir, save the justice, Mr Knight. He comes here nigh on every day to give her prayer and solace. He is a fine gentleman. None better.'

Joshua was not inclined to disagree, for he knew that Robert Knight's visits were made not from duty alone, but from a compassion he strove to keep well hid. It would grieve him were his kindness to be made public knowledge. He was a proud and private man and would feel the hurt of it.

But what of Corinne Blackstock's hurt? The murder of her child by the man she loved and trusted? Was there some parallel in the death of Esther Yeo? Had she been as cruelly betrayed? Richard Johns had given him no answers, nothing save a mocking smile, his contempt a studied insolence. Joshua had tried to break him, to trap him into admission, but without success. He felt his failure as keenly as he felt Richard Johns' scorn and his blatant self-satisfaction. As he rode past the justice's house upon Three Step Hill, Joshua felt a sense of anger at his own impotence, his uselessness to secure a confession from Johns. He could see no way of doing so or of proving his suspicions in a court of law. He knew that he should have gone within to apprise the justice of what had occurred and to enquire about the health of Pamela Fulmer and the child, but could not rouse himself to do so. Sight of him might unfairly build up their hopes that the blackmailer and abductor had been brought to justice. No, it was kinder to simply ride on.

He had scarce breasted the final hill when an anguished shout from below halted him. In an instant, Stenner drew up beside him frenziedly in the gig, scarce coherent in his excitement. He was red-faced and sweating profusely, the horse as lathered as he, as he tried to draw breath and explain his mission, blurting, "Tis the justice has sent me, sir, to seek you out! He is at Dr Mansel's house. You had best hurry for he says 'tis urgent! The man, Curtis, is conscious it seems, and has asked for the justice and for you!'

With a curt word of thanks Joshua urged on the grey and

333

was away in a flurry of restless agitation, the grey's hooves clattering upon the stone of the highway as he was lost from Stenner's view.

Mansel came out to greet him the moment he dismounted at the door, hurrying him urgently within and declaring that he did not know if Curtis would survive. He was gravely ill and troubled in mind, and had begged that the justice be brought to him, for there was something he must confess.

'He has a period of brief consciousness, he murmured, 'but he might, at any time, suffer relapse and never fully recover. His heart is painfully weakened.'

'But he is able to speak?'

'Speak and comprehend.'

With Mansel at his elbow, Joshua was forced urgently into the room to see Curtis lying, anguished and pale-faced, against the pillows, with the justice standing rigidly at the bedside, plainly distressed. Robert Knight glanced up as Mansel returned, giving the curtest nod of acknowledgement to Joshua, his dark-grained jowls trembling, eyes shadowed behind the gold-rimmed lenses. Curtis was breathing stertorously, his every word an effort, raked with pain, but despite Mansel's efforts to calm and steady him, he would not take respite nor be gainsaid.

The story was agonisingly pieced together, wandering and often incoherent, but with Robert Knight's gentle prompting all became painfully clear. Joshua was sickened by the callous need to so ruthlessly destroy a dying man, to cause him more anguish than he already bore. He was undeniably relieved when Mansel signalled to him that the questioning must end and that he had best leave the sickroom. Curtis had relapsed into near coma, and Joshua knew that he could not long survive, but Mansel and the justice remained stoically at his bedside to give what physical and spiritual solace they might.

For all that Curtis had confessed, Joshua could find no measure of comfort in the man's dying, save that he would escape the gallows. Death by violence is an obscenity in whatever guise it comes; a reminder of our own vulnerability, our own tenuous hold on life. Curtis' confession was no more than a deathbed repentance, a need to save his immortal soul.

334

The justice could promise in death what life denied us. It was small comfort, yet the only comfort we had.

When the justice, grey-faced and exhausted, left Curtis's deathbed, there was no triumph in him, only a sadness. 'You may send Johns to trial for the murder of Esther Yeo,' he said wearily, 'and for planning the abduction of Alexandra Fulmer, and for attempted blackmail.'

'It will be a relief for the Fulmers, sir, that their ordeal is ended,' Joshua ventured awkwardly.

'I fear that Pamela Fulmer's is only beginning,' the justice said wryly, 'for much that will wound her will be revealed in court. As for Curtis? Well, he must face a higher judge, a higher authority, and one more practised at forgiveness than I.' He hesitated. 'You will write up a full report on Curtis's confession, Stradling. See that all is made plain and I shall sign it as witness.'

'Yes, sir. I will see that it is done.'

'I was wrong about Curtis,' Robert Knight admitted brusquely. 'He *was* involved. You were not blinded by prejudice, 'obsessed' as I accused.' From the justice it was the most handsome apology. It brought Joshua as little comfort as it would bring Curtis.

Joshua returned to Thatched Cottage feeling more dispirited than relieved. With Curtis's death-bed confession, the case was effectively ended. Richard Johns, murderer, abductor and blackmailer, would not escape the gallows. He would get the punishment he deserved. Why, then, did Joshua feel so little elation? Perhaps, he thought wearily, it was because he had played no part in the final act. He had been a passive bystander only; remote and uninvolved. He could claim no credit for either Richard Johns' capture or his conviction for murder. It had been a quirk of fate; a freak accident, nothing more. Had Curtis died from the murderous blows received, or not recovered his speech or senses, Johns might well have been charged only with smuggling. It did nothing for Joshua's self-esteem. It was a hollow victory, although it would give added peace of mind to the Fulmers. They need no longer live in terror of the blackmailer and abductor who had so callously invaded their lives and destroyed that of Esther Yeo.

335

He would ride out to see them and wish them well, Joshua decided, before they set sail for Porlock. He hoped that the future would be kinder than the past for Pamela Fulmer and her child, although the bitter public humiliation of Augustus Scurlock's trial would take harsh toll. Yet, perhaps, it would be less excoriating than the cruelties she had already endured at his hands, and she had the loving support of her family to sustain and protect her. It would take as long to assuage Rosa's and Doonan's hurt.

Johns had much to assuage, much to do penance for beyond the violence of kidnapping and murder. He had destroyed more than flesh and blood, he had destroyed security, peace of mind, the futures of others to slake his own greed. Curtis had come to a death-bed repentance, even if it were to save his own soul. Johns showed no remorse. That was what Joshua found so terrifying. No remorse, and no soul that he might save.

Within the small study of Thatched Cottage, Joshua laboriously penned the report to be signed by Mansel, himself and the justice. Written, it seemed a bleak and sordid little account, as sordid as those who figured in it. Curtis, then, had been in the pay of Johns and his smugglers, his livery stables a convenient cover. He had brought the girl, Esther Yeo, to the disused fisherman's hut in the dunes which Johns had set aside for the purpose, believing it remote and secluded enough to house them in safety. Curtis had, as chief henchman, been privy to the quarrel between them, with the nursemaid, Yeo, foolishly demanding more money and security than Johns had promised. She insisted that she had risked more than he in abducting the child, for her face and name were known to the Fulmers, and should a hue and cry be called, she would be ruthlessly hunted down. In saying so, she signed her own death warrant. Johns had pretended to humour her, ostensibly deferring to her terms, and promising that they would be wed as agreed, as soon as his activities at Newton Creek were ended.

Esther Yeo and the child were set under guard, for Johns was immersed in his smuggling activities, and should they be accidentally discovered it would wreck not only his blackmailing plans, but all else. Yeo, bound by the need to care for the child in so primitive a place, and angered by Johns' neglect, defied the guard, claiming that she would remove herself to an inn and take the child with her. She was in want of food, fresh clothing and civilised company, she argued. None would think it strange that a married woman and child should seek such accommodation when travelling upon the road. She was not a fool; she would invent a suitable story and tell it convincingly. Despite the guard's protests, she had taken a cob and cart belonging to the smugglers and driven it to the edge of the Burrows. Then, fearful of the risks involved and of Johns' fury, she had finally arrived at the inn on foot.

The distraught guard had immediately ridden out to tell Johns of her escape, and Johns had driven to Newton, his sole object to take back the child and to silence her. She had become a liability to him, a danger even, and without her he was clear of suspicion. The blackmailing ransom for the child would be wholly his own and he would have revenge on Scurlock whom he detested.

That much Curtis had known from his own involvement and from conversations with the guard. But what exactly had occurred at the Crown Inn? Curtis was unsure, but from what he had earlier learned and what Joshua had pieced together from his own knowledge and conjecture, it seemed that Johns had intercepted her within the yard of the Crown, and within sight of the sweeping boy had manhandled her roughly, dragging her to the gig waiting without, leaving the child inside the stable against his return. He had glimpsed the terrified sweeping lad but been unable to threaten him to silence. The boy, cruelly lacking in mind and speech, had been powerless to explain the savagery he had seen but, still trembling with terror, had led Ossie to where the infant lay.

Johns planned to disable the girl then hurl her into the sea, making it seem as if she had been accidentally swept from the breakwater, or lost from a passing ship. Yet her frantic struggle for life had defeated him, and he had fatally stabbed her, fearful that her screams would set him at risk. Here, Curtis had been able to take up the sequence again, for he had been an unwilling witness. The livery stables were but a stone's throw away and, recognising the gig as his own and hired by Johns for his smuggling, he had foolishly gone to investigate. He had seen the actual murder and claimed to

337

have been sickened by the bloodiness and savagery of it. He would sooner have fled the scene, keeping his silence, but, to his horror, Johns had seen him and threatened him with the same fate as the girl's should he be tempted to relate what had occurred. His manner had been so abrasive, his threats so belligerent, that Curtis was in fear for his life. The gunshot wound he had later suffered had been Johns' first warning of what he might expect were he to break his silence.

It was then that he had fled, putting as much distance between himself and the murderer as he could. He would hide himself in a shepherd's but upon the windswept shore near Sker, he had decided. None would find him there. Yet Johns, who had secret watchers all along the coast, had learned of his hideaway and followed him, beating him viciously and leaving him for dead. It was the random passing by of Richard Turberville which had protected his life, and Dr Mansel's skills. Yet they had not been enough to save him.

Joshua, who had mistrusted Curtis in life, liked him little better in death, but he could still pity him. His deceit and cupidity had led to his death, but if his confession were the means to send Johns to the gallows, then perhaps he had redeemed himself at the last and made reparation enough. Joshua put his signature to the report, and handed it silently to Rebecca, and she read it carefully and without speaking until she came to the end.

'Johns is a monster, Joshua,' she murmured quietly, 'evil, and past all redemption. The taking of his life will never atone for the savagery of what he has done.'

'No. There is no atoning for that,' Joshua said. 'A life is all we have. Once ended, like Esther Yeo's or Curtis's, there can be no reparation.'

'Save the knowledge that he can murder no more?'

'Yes. That is all we may be sure of in this world and the next.'

Joshua made ready to ride out to the justice's house after claiming Mansel's signature to the confession. He would deliver the report to Robert Knight and take opportunity to bid farewell and Godspeed to the Fulmers. He did not expect ever to see them again, for they would certainly settle elsewhere. They would wish no reminder of Porlock and of

338

Johns' villainy, or of the man who had betrayed Pamela Fulmer's trust and his child's.

First he made his way to the Crown Inn to tell his friend, Ossie the ostler, what had occurred, for he valued Ossie's good common sense, his quick intelligence.

'Well. It is ended,' Joshua admitted, 'but not without grief.'

'Grief mends, like all else,' Ossie ventured.

'I am not certain,' Joshua said despondently.

"Tis the natural way of things. 'Tis like throwing a stone into a pool. The ripples spread ever wider upon the surface until it sinks from sight beneath. Yet, at the very last, the waters close over, and all is forgot. If it were not so it would be past all enduring.'

'Perhaps . . .' Joshua moodily took up the reins of the gig and prepared to ride out, but Ossie halted him, saying slyly, 'I have news of Robert Knight that he might not willingly disclose to you.'

'The devil you have! Where did you come by this information?'

'From the justice himself. He came here earlier, seeking me out.'

'And?' Joshua demanded.

'And it appears that you told him in a letter of the sweeping boy's involvement.'

'With what result?' Joshua asked, mystified.

'It seems that the Fulmers wish to make reward available to whoever is able to identify Johns, and lead to his arrest. The justice will swear that the sweeping boy is the only one eligible; the only one who has seen him, since Curtis is now dead.'

'He will pay reward to the sweeping boy?' Joshua demanded incredulously.

'A fund, he says, lodged here with Tom Butler so that the lad will not be in need of place to lay his head or of victuals. Phoebe Butler will see he is clothed, as needed. They are both sworn to secrecy, as I.'

'But you have just told me,' Joshua protested, laughing.

'Ah, but you are our constable,' Ossie said, 'and must know all for our protection. It is you who have brought Johns to justice. It is you upon whom we depend. Without

339

you, the hamlets would be a poorer, more violent place, and we would not go in safety. Ride safely, Joshua, and have a care for yourself. Good men are hard to find.' With a gap-toothed smile and a brisk slap to the grey's hindquarters, Ossie cheerfully turned away.

'You did not think to commend *me* to the justice for reward?' Joshua called after him.

'You have my advice and friendship,' Ossie called back. 'That is reward enough.'

At Southerndown Court, Sir Matthew de Breos was thinking with regret that already summer was ending. Yet perhaps, he reflected with honesty, it was the best summer he had ever known, made special by John Jeremiah's birth. He had believed, with Rebecca's return to him, that there could never be greater happiness, yet now he had Rebecca and his grandson near to him and in Joshua's safe-keeping. What rare privilege it would be to share the boy's growing days, to watch him explore and learn to know and love the woods and farmlands of the estate; the estate that he would one day inherit. He was grateful that God had seen fit to spare him for so long, and with family and friends like Handel Peate and Robert Knight to soften the way. He was richly blessed. He had made so many new friends with Rebecca's coming, men like Jeremiah Fleet, the old fisherman, whom he had learnt to respect for his wisdom and humour. What was it that Rebecca had called him? 'The salt of the earth'. So he was, for without such people, life would lose much of its savour. Yet, of them all, it was Illtyd to whom he felt closest. The little crippled hayward had made so much of his life, and by his own endeavours; never chafing at the restrictions forced upon him nor harbouring envy or bitterness at his lot. Sir Matthew had grown to think of him as fondly as a son. It pleased him that Illtyd came to make use of the library, a quiet, unobtrusive presence, treating his books with the respect they deserved . . . as if they were living, vital things. And so, perhaps, they were, for they were other men's lives, other men's thoughts, existing long after flesh and bone were returned to dust.

He had set all in order. His affairs were settled, for every day now was a benison; a gift from God. He had seen that all who were in need were provided for, but sensitively and without wounding their pride or giving offence. He had arranged with Handel Peate that, as a celebration of John Jeremiah's birth, there would be gifts for all who had played part in Rebecca's life. Things they would cherish. For Dr Peate and Illtyd, the pleasure and companionship of a Grand Tour, visiting those countries and cities which Illtyd had learnt of only from books, but which were vivid in Handel Peate's life and memory. It was a way to repay them both. Perhaps they would recall him as kindly as those far off places, memories of friendship linked with all that was pleasurable and good, rare and rewarding. Yes, he would like to think that.

Sir Matthew put on his warm, thorn-proof coat and his stoutest walking boots and took his favourite gnarled old walking stick of ashwood to venture into the grounds. He would walk as far as the belvedere, he thought, or the woods and streams beyond. The day was crisp and clear with the first hint of autumn's coolness in the air. Soon enough it would be winter, with all its attendant ills. He had best enjoy the freedom of the estate now, in its muted softness, before the weather turned around. Yet, despite his age and increasing infirmity, the exhaustion that so often bedevilled him, there was not a season of the year which he did not cherish, nor a corner of the estate.

Hughes, the old coachman, watching Sir Matthew covertly from the window of his room above the coach-house, was grieved at how frail his master had grown, how slow and laborious his progress. He walked with the austere bearing of one long trained to uprightness, his spare-fleshed features scarce touched by age. Yet the hand clutching the ashwood stick was as gnarled and worn as the stick itself, hair grown white and fine as in childhood. The old gentleman was failing, as he was, himself. They had come a long road together, with never a harsh word, and naught but respect, one for the other. He had been treated, always, with courtesy, for that was Sir Matthew's way. He knew no other. Gentleness was bred into him. Hughes felt the coldness of age in his flesh, the throbbing pain of his old leg wound, and returned, grateful, to his chair beside the fire. There was an ache inside him, deeper than the ache of his bones, an ache of regret and sadness. When had he

341

grown old? It had come upon him like an affliction, insidious and unnoticed, like the dimming of his vision, the uncertainty of his step. He shuffled now, and his hands trembled and betrayed him, their sensitivity upon the reins lost. He would pour himself a tankard of porter and set a poker in it, hot from the fire. Then, when he was warmed and rested, he would take himself outside to see that the old gentleman was safe. He would do it discreetly, that Sir Matthew would not suspect. Yes, that was what he would do. He would care for the old gentleman as Sir Matthew had a care for him.

Sir Matthew settled himself upon a fallen log beside the stream, its surface crusted with moss and lichen. It was a pretty place, he thought contentedly, with the familiar sounds and sights and smells that were the essence of his childhood and growing. John Jeremiah would like it here. The autumn breeze stirred the leaves in the branches overhead, their rustling as gently soothing as the flowing water beneath. The trees were dappled with sunlight, their leaves pale and translucent, with no promise yet of the fiery brilliance to come. All was restful and quietly subdued. An end to summer.

The fierce crack of a twig underfoot forced Sir Matthew to his feet, shocked and apprehensive. His gamekeeper, Rhys? He called out sharply, but without answer. Awkwardly, he made to follow the sound, dropping his stick in his haste, scrabbling in the undergrowth and fallen leaves to retrieve it.

The poacher who faced him was no one he knew. Sir Matthew saw only the man's anguished face, the terror that possessed him as the gun was levelled. Then he heard the fierce explosion of power, and felt the force of the shot as a blow that took the air from his lungs and sent him awkwardly falling.

'Why?' he said, 'Why?'

There was a redness before his eyes and the salt taste of blood in his mouth, then a lethargy that he knew must be death. A bitterness of exhaustion. He felt no fear. No pain. Only an overwhelming sadness. He did not know if it were blood or tears that clouded his eyes before darkness came.

Sir Matthew's death was a cause for shock and outrage in the

Vale and beyond, and the arrest of the poacher on a charge of murder did little to soften the anger felt. Those in his employ were grieved beyond measure for the useless waste of a good man's life, and none more deeply than Hughes who had found him. It was the end of an era; an end of a friendship which had endured despite the difference in rank and station.

Sir Matthew's funeral had been the grandest and best attended in the Vale of any in living memory, a mark of the genuine respect and affection in which he had been held. Yet, to Rebecca, it had been one more grief to live through, one more burden of sadness to bear. Her grandfather, Sir Matthew, was dead, that was the unalterable truth of it, and none, not even Joshua and John Jeremiah, could salve the hurt of it or know her pain. She had tried to comfort Dr Peate and others, like Illtyd, who so painfully mourned his loss, but the words she spoke were from the numbness of her own desolation, a void that could never be filled.

It saddened her, that they must leave the three hamlets and make their new home at Southerndown Court. It had been welcome refuge to her and she loved it dearly, but without Sir Matthew the joy would have gone out of it. All she could hope for was that she and Joshua could, one day, recreate the tranquillity and order upon the estate that he had so prized and be as loved and respected.

It had been a sad leave-taking of all those in the three hamlets for, although she vowed that the ties of friendship would not be broken, she knew that things could never again be as they were. Jeremiah had said once, long ago, when she had left the three hamlets for Southerndown Court, that it was not only miles that would separate them but a way of life, and she knew the bitter truth of it now. She knew, too, that it was not only she who was forced to make sacrifice, but Joshua. It had been, from childhood, his ambition to become a constable, and it had not been achieved without dissension and grief and alienation from his own family.

She made her farewells in private to those she loved and begged them not to be there at their leaving, else it would be more than she could bear. They would leave quietly and unnoticed, she insisted, for then it would seem no more than a brief parting, and none had argued nor pointed out the foolishness of it.

Yet when the de Breos coach arrived, with Hughes seated beside the young coachman upon the box, Rebecca wept anew for all that was changed and all that was lost to her and for a future unknown, that she did not know if she had the heart and courage to face.

The narrow streets were lined with those wishing to make their farewells. They crowded onto the cobbles, kindly and caring, men called from their labours, ancients, young women with toddlers at their skirts and infants in shawls. Ossie, Tom Butler and Phoebe from the Crown, Ezra Evans and Dic Jenkins, the vestrymen, faces known and unknown. Vivid, blurred, disappearing in a rainbow mist of tears and regret.

Rebecca, with John Jeremiah in her arms, sat rigidly upright, with Joshua's comforting arm about her, willing her to strength. She could not look back at Thatched Cottage. Must not else her resolve would break. John Burrell and Emily would live there as soon as they were wed, and Rebecca was glad of that, as she was glad that Ruth and Richard Turberville were to have a cottage upon the justice's estate. Oh, but she would miss Robert Knight, she thought, more than she could say. It would surprise him to know the affection in which she held him. He would visit them at Southerndown Court, he had promised, for it would please him to see his godson often and his good friend, Dr Peate. And to initiate Joshua into the proper duties of the squirearchy and the responsibilities of a justice. His protuberant brown eyes had been warm with humour behind his gold-rimmed lenses and Joshua had replied, straight-faced, that it would give him the richest pleasure to have such a patient and uncritical mentor in the future as in the past. Their shared laughter had been as spontaneous as of old but, now, it was the laughter of those who met upon equal terms, free from restriction.

They had left the hamlets, now, and Joshua said quietly, 'I would have you change John Jeremiah's name, Rebecca. I would have him called de Breos, for I believe that Sir Matthew would have valued that above all else.'

Rebecca, eyes soft with treacherous tears, hugged John Jeremiah more closely, then reached over and set a kiss upon Joshua's cheek, saying gravely, 'Yes. He would value that above all. You are so like him, Joshua, in thought and feeling.'

'No, Rebecca. I shall never be the man he was.' His voice was low, painfully lacking in confidence, and it wrenched at her heart. 'Sir Matthew was a gentleman. Born and bred to administer his estates. I do not know if I shall be able.'

'Yes, you will be able. You will do it well, as you do all else.' Her voice held absolute conviction and love besides.

'I am a farmer and a constable,' he said.

'No. You are a gentleman, my love. You have always been Joshua Stradling, gentleman, to me.'

Joshua Stradling, gentleman, smiled, and settled his arm protectively about his wife and son. With Rebecca and John Jeremiah beside him, there was nothing in all the world that he could not accomplish, or be.